VASQUEZ

A NOVEL

By Rick Avery

Vasquez
by
Rick Avery

Copyright © 2025

Putnam & Smith Publishing Company

Cover Design by: Rick Avery & Connie Jacobs

Cover photo: Tuba Karabulut

Distributed by:
Putnam & Smith Publishing Company
15915 Ventura Boulevard, Suite 101
Encino, California 91436

www.putnamandsmithpublishing.com

Library of Congress Number: 2024946653

ISBN: 978-1-939986-50-4
Printed in the USA

Author's Note

One day, while driving from Los Angeles to Lancaster, I passed a one-thousand-acre park named Vasquez Rocks. The movement of tectonic plates formed strange formations about twenty-five million years ago. You would have seen it in Star Trek episodes, as well as multiple movies, television shows and commercials.

When I got home, I googled Vasquez Rocks, curious as to how it got its name. I was immediately intrigued to learn that it was named after a Mexican bandit that ravaged California in the late eighteen hundreds and used the rock formations to evade posse's that were continually hunting him.

Vasquez's story is intriguing and complex. I purchased the only comprehensive historical account written to date about him, *Bandido: The Life and Times of Tiburcio Vasquez,* by John Boessenecker.

Tiburcio Vásquez, a notorious Californio bandido, prowled the rugged landscape of California from 1854 to 1874. His name struck fear into the hearts of settlers and travelers alike, as he was known for his bold robberies and daring escapes. One of his many hideouts, the Vasquez Rocks, loom 40 miles north of Los Angeles and still bears his infamous name. This gripping novel delves into the true story of Tiburcio's life, weaving together historical facts with imaginative fiction. It chronicles his carefree childhood days, filled with adventure and mischief, before descending into the darkness of his criminal pursuits. From his multiple escapes from San Quentin prison to his reputation as a ladies' man, readers are left to form their own judgments about this enigmatic outlaw. Dive into the wild world of Tiburcio Vásquez and experience the highs and lows of his tumultuous life.

Ninety percent of the names are accurate, and the story is based on fact. However, as a work of fiction, I have imagined events, actions, additional imagined names and dialog that Vasquez might have taken.

I have based the timeline of Vasquez's life based on the factual one in Mr. Boesseneckers book. The novel is intended to be entertaining as well as a lesson in history, which Mr. Boessenecker reconstructed from the wealth of accounts, newspapers, and photographs available in his non-fiction historical book that I made into a work of fiction. For more refer to page 289.

Prologue

As the sun rose over the horizon on August 11, 1835, the coastal city of Monterey, California, was greeted by a vibrant chorus of birdsongs. The sky, painted a deep shade of red, promised another sweltering day in the Golden State. The sweet melodies of the avian filled the air, creating an enchanting symphony that echoed throughout the city, beckoning residents to start their day. Amidst the harmonious sounds, the sudden screams of a woman shattered the tranquility. María Guadalupe "Doña" Cantúa was in labor, and a Mexican midwife was helping her deliver a precious new life into the world inside a small adobe home. As the midwife worked feverishly helping María, the birds continued to sing their usual breakfast songs, unaware of the miracle happening just a few feet away. Even in the coolness of the morning, sweat poured off María as the screams continued until the inevitable child would leave his home of nine months to the lawless town that would raise him. María would name him Tiburcio. Following Spanish tradition, his birth was celebrated on the day of his namesake, St. Tiburtius.

During the era when Mexico governed California, Monterey, known as Alta, was a hub of joy, but lawlessness and disorder eventually raised their ugly heads. California was home to approximately 300,000 immigrants from Europe, who spoke as many as 90 different languages, making it a melting pot of diverse cultures and backgrounds. In addition, there were 30 native American tribes residing in the state at that time, each with their unique customs and traditions. Despite this rich diversity, the lack of legal protection for children made it a challenging time for families and communities in the region.

The adobe that the Vasquez family occupied had been built when Grandfather Vasquez arrived in the area with the DeAnza expedition of 1776.

While General Washington was leading battles in the East against England, a significant change occurred in the West. Mexican settlers were migrating northwards along the Pacific coast and establishing dozens of ranches in the area. The number had grown in the hundreds by 1782, and the Jesuit Missions actively converted thousands of indigenous people to Christianity. The region was bustling with new settlers, and the transformation was swift.

Tiburcio's father, Juan, was active in raising his nine children, and Tiburcio never knew loneliness owing to his siblings. Unfortunately, when he was six, his sister María died early in her life, and his brother died at the age of nine. It was not uncommon for large families to lose a few children due to nonadvanced medicine in the area. The family did not want and was moderately well-off, owning land that was given to Juan by the Mexican government for his service as a Spanish soldier. The Vasquez family's adobe dwelling held a rich history. It had been constructed during the time of her grandfather's arrival. Despite their comfortable situation, Juan and María were determined to provide Tiburcio with a quality education, including reading and writing in English and Spanish.

Tiburcio's childhood years went by ordinarily, with his days packed with school, play, and daily chores. His teacher considered him a model student who mastered the language and had a flair for penmanship. Outside of school, a robust work ethic was ingrained by the duties the young boy performed on his father's Rancho Felix on the Pajaro as well as his uncle Fernando's ranch a short distance from Pilarcitos Canyon. The long hours spent tending to the animals, fixing equipment, and performing various other tasks kept him busy and taught him valuable life skills that he carried into adulthood. The labor honed his physical strength and endurance, both of which would later define his prowess as a vaquero.

During the early days of Alta California, the populace had ample opportunities to build their success. However, in 1846, war broke out between Mexico and the United States in Texas, a conflict that eventually spread to California. The Monterey area became a significant battleground that led Captain John Fremont, along with sixty men, to survey the region under the pretext of an exploratory mission. It later came to light, however, that the men were soldiers, and their arrival was part of a larger military strategy to form protections for Anglos wanting to develop businesses and farms at the expense of local Californios. Turning a deaf ear to the advice of General José Castro, who warned them to steer clear of the pueblos, Fremont and his men stayed in the area for the winter. They constructed a log fort about twenty-five miles east of Alta, further igniting tensions between the two sides.

Everything changed when Castro found out about the fort. His anger and rage were uncontrollable, and he threatened Fremont, who wisely left for Oregon. The event marked the start of a severe intervention of life-changing events for the people of Alta, including Tiburcio. The Californios (California Mexicans) soon lost their trust in immigrating Americans. The peace and harmony that once prevailed were replaced by fear and uncertainty as war loomed.

In the following year, specifically in 1846, Commodore John Sloat led a fleet of ships to California. Upon arrival, they occupied Alta's Common House and hoisted the American flag. Sloat declared that California was now a part of the United States, a decision that was made under President Polk's directive. General Castro's cousin Manuel entered into battle with Captain Fremont close to Alta. Tiburcio's family lost some of their relatives in this fight, a loss that changed their outlook on Anglos forever and one Tiburcio Vasquez would never forget. He decided to fight his own war in his own way for his people.

~

One

Tiburcio Vasquez was a teenager when the Americans built a new city hall, the most impressive in California at the time, directly across from his family's adobe. It stubbornly blocked their once glorious view of the town and ocean. His mother, Doña, and her daughters were forced to open a small restaurant in their home to earn extra money for their sizable family. Those who frequented it were foreigners and soldiers, the latter of which proved a constant dominating threat every time they entered the adobe. Their crude words and leering gazes lingered in the air like a foul stench. Tiburcio's heart burned with seething hatred as he watched both soldiers and sailors ogle his sisters daily. Being the thin young man he was, he could do little but glare at them with pure disgust. That is, until one late afternoon when Tiburcio caught a soldier forcing himself on his sister Graciela in a dark alcove. It was too much to bear.

With a primal roar, Tiburcio charged forward, the tortillas he had brought for his other sister forgotten on the ground behind him. He screamed in Spanish, demanding that the soldier leave his sister alone. But the soldier, not understanding the language, only sneered as he pinned Graciela against the cold adobe wall and ran his hand up her skirt. Fueled by a fiery rage, Tiburcio kicked at the soldier's shin with all his might, causing him to cry out in pain and loosen his grip on Graciela. She managed to break free and run away while Tiburcio's uncle Fernando confronted the soldiers.

"You gringos have taken advantage of our kindness for too long!" Fernando shouted, brandishing a large knife he had been using to prepare food. "Get out before I slice you like a slab of beef!"

At first, the soldiers drunkenly laughed and moved forward to challenge Fernando, but when they saw the flash of steel in his hand, they pushed him aside and stumbled away from the adobe, not comprehending his words but understanding the intent.

After that incident, Tiburcio's once carefree life gave way to a burning hatred towards Anglos that consumed him completely throughout his adolescence. This force, moreover, urged his growth from prepubescence into manhood.

As the seasons transitioned, once again bringing the arrival of spring, the air became infused with a refreshing scent of blooming flowers. The buzzing of bees could be heard as they fluttered around their preferred plants, spreading their sweet nectar in abundance.

Tiburcio strolled towards his uncle Fernando's ranch after finishing his studies at the local public school. He had been summoned to help with the daily chores, just like his elder siblings, who were raised and trained for the same purpose. The road he walked on was still damp from the morning's rain, and he left a trail of muddy footprints behind him. He made his way towards the barn at the far end of the sprawling ranch when he spotted Enrique, one of the Caballeros, galloping towards him on his stout black quarter horse named Blackjack. Enrique reined into a quick stop, with its hindquarters dropping quickly, kicking up a cloud of muddy clods.

"You're late again, Tibo. Hop the fence and get on with me before your uncle sees you!"

With remarkable agility, Tiburcio vaulted over the white wooden fence. Enrique reached for his forearm, pulling him up to sit behind his saddle. Tiburcio epitomized rugged handsomeness. His muscular frame was evident under his tight-fitting clothing.

Dropping athletically off Blackjack as they approached the barn, Tiburcio sprinted to the door, his heart beating wildly with the fear of being reprimanded by his uncle. He made it just in time to grab his tools and start his chores without being noticed.

The ranch was of good size, about 400 acres, and was built in the early 1800s, starting with a small but clean adobe adorned with red tile. The adobe kept it warm in the winter and cool in the summer.

Tiburcio dropped his bag of books, folded his shirt with them, and walked out the side door to help lay some adobe bricks for an addition his uncle Fernando was building. The warm sun beat down on his muscled back as he worked alongside four other skilled mestizo laborers busily constructing a four-foot wall. The mestizo; meaning mixed person, were mostly European even though their ancestors were indigenous. Tiburcio brought a wheelbarrow filled with clay, which would be used as mortar to bind the wall together. The other artisans added small pebbles from the nearby brooks to create decorative bands across the walls. Tiburcio was well-versed in the traditional tradecraft of building and construction, which he learned from Fernando, who had mentored him in the physical aspects of the craft. At the same time, his parents focused on providing him with a well-rounded education.

As he worked, he turned to the sound of a creaking wagon that caught his attention. It was laden with timber and large stones to be used to complete the barn. The team of four horses pulling the wagon, known as a four-up, was expertly reined in by his stout, well-built uncle. Fernando was a man of great physical strength, with a round face and a large mustache that fell to his chin. As he stepped down from the wagon, he walked over to Tiburcio and greeted him warmly.

"It's good to see you here on time for once, nephew," he said, patting Tiburcio on the back. "Grab a couple of the others and help me unload these supplies."

Tiburcio dutifully nodded his head in agreement and set to work. The heavy timber used for the roof and rafters required the strength of four grown men to lift, and together, they carefully moved the materials into position. The large rocks would be moved later using a boom derrick, a lifting jack, and a pulling jack. The additions construction was an uphill task, but Tiburcio found satisfaction in the work and the knowledge that he was contributing to creating something that would stand the test of time.

Fernando took pride in the horsemen who worked for him. He felt they were the finest in the world. Later, sitting on the porch with a bottle of tequila, he watched the dust-filled corral as a Mustang was being broken. Mustangs could be found running wild, and they were fast and strong. They were also economical because they fed on the abundant grass of the ranch and didn't need grain. Tiburcio was sitting astride the corral fence, watching the vaquero intently. The Mustang lurched and bucked; his rear legs kicked high. He was in awe of how the vaquero held on, as well as the determination of the horse to rid himself of this uninvited guest. Eventually, the horse stopped kicking as it switched to a half-bucking fast gallop circling the enclosure. It then slowly loped and then walked, finally realizing it would not overcome the rider's determination. As the vaquero passed Tiburcio he said,

"We have to get you on one of these soon, Tibo," he said, addressing him by his nickname. "I know you can ride well, but a good horseman should be able to break and control a wild horse."

Standing near the fence, Tiburcio nodded in agreement.

"Sure, Jesus (pronounced Hayzus), I am ready anytime.
I have been riding since I was a kid, and I am confident I can handle any
horse you put me on."

Jesus frowned sternly at the boy's bravado and leaned in challengingly.

"Hmmm, A wild stallion has been giving us quite a bit of trouble lately.
Maybe it's time for you to try your hand at breaking him since you feel so
confident in yourself."

Tiburcio's eyes widened warily as he heard the dare.

"Well, why not Jesus? If you think I'm ready, let's get started."

The boy's enthusiasm took Jesus aback. He didn't expect him to take
the challenge so quickly. He would have to make sure Tiburcio wasn't hurt
by the attempt. He would not want to incur El Jefe's wrath (The Boss), for
he dearly loved his nephew.

Tiburcio jumped off the fence and walked to join his uncle. As he walked,
a sense of pride welled up in him and fueled his anticipation. He knew that
breaking a wild horse would not be easy, but he was determined to prove
himself a skilled horseman. He stepped onto the porch, grateful for the
welcome shade and the gentle breeze it provided respite from the sweltering
heat. Fernando's warm smile greeted him as he approached the rocking chair.

"Come on up here, mijo (son). Have a glass of lemonade. What were
you and Jesus talking about?"

Fernando's voice was inviting and comforting, and Tibo felt at ease as
he settled into the chair.

"Jesus thinks it's time for me to try breaking a horse, Uncle," he said,
sipping the cool lemonade.

Fernando's expression turned serious as he picked up his whiskey and
sipped.

"It's a rough business, Tibo. I'm wondering if you're ready for it.
Breaking a horse is not just about taming the animal; it's about taming
yourself, too. I know you're a good rider, but a wild Mustang is dangerous.
You could lose your confidence, and that's not even considering the risk of
severe injury when you get thrown off, and you will get thrown off a lot.
That is a given mijo."

Tiburcio nodded, acknowledging his uncle's concerns.

"I know it's difficult, Uncle, but I want to try. I want to prove that I'm
capable of handling the ranch's challenges. I'll be careful; I promise."

Fernando looked at his 17-year-old nephew, taking in his determined
expression. Respecting Tiburcio's will to take on a challenge, he nodded
slowly.

"Alright, Tibo. You can try tomorrow after school. But be careful, and don't take any unnecessary risks. I don't want to get in trouble with my brother and your mother."

They both fell silent, admiring the fiery hues of the sunset painting, the sky with shades of red and orange. They signaled the end of another day on the ranch.

The next day was slightly more relaxed with a gentle breeze, and Tiburcio arrived earlier than ever, excited to meet Jesus, the lead wrangler, and try his hand at riding the stallion. He walked directly to the barn and donned his chaps and spurs. The chaps were leather and adorned with buttons down the sides. The spurs were large, as was familiar with the vaquero. When he walked out into the sunlight, he finished tying a bandana around his neck and put on his hat. Jesus was just returning with four other vaqueros as they hazed a dozen mustangs into the South corral. He rode over to Tiburcio and leaned over.

"You're serious about this, eh?"

"Yes, sir!"

"Ok," Jesus answered.

"Follow me to the north corral. The stallion is there."

Tibo walked alongside the still-mounted Jesus to the corral about 100 yards away. As he approached, he saw the magnificent stallion. It was black with a long mane and tail. Its gait around the corral was determined and confident. As they got closer, the horse stopped its proud prance and stared directly at them.

The Mustang had run free in the West for a long time. They descended from horses brought to the Americas by the Spanish. They were considered wild, but their ancestry from domestication made them feral animals That could run long distances and were adaptable in all sorts of circumstances. Mares and Geldings were more easily breakable because stallions could be highly aggressive.

Jesus got off his horse and said, "We have tried numerous times to ride this one. He is strong, and he bucks off riders with ease. I expect it will be the same with you. The dirt in this corral is dug up and soft because I expect you will land on it—a lot."

Tiburcio nodded apprehensively while walking to the gate. Mustangs are smaller horses, but this stallion was larger and more significant than average. His skin shined in the light as he flicked his tail in anticipation, eying the saddle in Tiburcio's hands.

Jesus laughed.

"It has been three months of tries, Tibo, with the longest ride of about 10 seconds!"

The horse pawed at the dirt, daring the teenager to come closer.

"Easy boy, easy," Tiburcio whispered.

The stallion responded by snorting and not turning away. Tibo slowly walked up to him and set the saddle on the fence. He reached out slowly to stroke the horse's neck. The horse turned its neck away.

"OK, you don't want me to touch you? Fine."

Tibo backed off sensing the power and squatted, talking gently and quietly to soothe the horse's nerves. He pulled a carrot out of his pocket. The stallion begrudgingly snorted and backed up a couple of steps. Tiburcio continued his soothing voice and offered the carrot. Eventually, the stallion approached, sniffing toward the squatting person offering the sweet treat and finally suspiciously accepted it. Tiburcio stood and stepped back a few paces, producing another treat. The stallion followed. After a few minutes, the horse allowed Tiburcio to scratch him. The process could have been faster for a teenager, but he remained patient. Eventually, he took the reins and the bridle, placed it over the horse's head and walked the seemingly complacent stallion around the corral. Jesus handed him a small whip.

"Use this to force it to trot around the arena."

Jesus admired the boy's restraint. Tiburcio sensed it was time to put on the blanket. The horse didn't object, so he put on the saddle after several walking rounds and only cinched it tight enough not to spook it. The horse was intelligent and knew of a saddle from previous attempts. Having someone get on it was a different story. They walked together for a while.

"Ok, get on with it!" Jesus yelled.

Tiburcio looked over his shoulder and, sensing it was time, whispered gently to the stallion.

"Easy, easy, my friend. You can trust me. I am not here to hurt you."

The horse's eyes gave clues to its demeanor. If they were wide, and its ears were standing straight up. Neither was a good sign. With a steady hand, Tiburcio tightened the cinch a little more. He then grabbed the horn on the saddle, feeling the worn leather beneath his palm. He put his left foot in the stirrup and waited as the horse took two slow steps forward, sensing the rider's presence. Tiburcio patiently let him settle and stop, feeling the horse's muscles rippling in anticipation beneath the saddle. He then swiftly swung his right leg over the saddle.

No sooner than his leg reached the right stirrup, the horse lunged and bucked, catching its unwelcome rider off guard. Tiburcio grabbed the horn with all his might but to no avail. He was sent eight feet into the air, hat flying, before landing abruptly on his ass as the horse loped away triumphantly, leaving a cloud of dust that settled on the vanquished rider. Tiburcio groaned and looked up at the sky, feeling the wind knocked out of him. He heard the stallion moving away, snorting with success. Its mane flitted in the wind as it threw its head up and down in triumph.

Slowly, the vanquished rider rolled over and saw Jesus standing nearby, shaking his head back and forth, laughing.

"You, OK?"

Tiburcio groaned, rubbing his sore backside.

"Yeah, I'm OK," he replied with a rueful smile.

He knew he had a long way to go before he could ride this wild stallion, but he was determined to succeed. He slowly rose to dust himself off and put his hat back on. He repeated the process, waiting for the horse to come to him. The horse approached with a sense of assurance, knowing the ride would end the same way. Tiburcio tried four more times, each attempt slower than the last, always brushing dirt from his clothes and face.

Meanwhile, Jesus had been observing from a distance.

"Are you finished yet?"

Tiburcio looked back, disappointed in himself, and limped sorely around the arena, trying to loosen his tightening muscles. The late after-noon shadows cast across the corral marked the passage of time. Eventually, Tiburcio gave up and walked over to the horse, who willingly allowed him to remove the bridle and saddle. For the horse, this was just another day of throwing off unwanted riders. Jesus shook his head knowingly as he walked by, giving Tiburcio a conciliatory smile.

Breaking wild horses was challenging, even for the most experienced horsemen, but Tiburcio's determination was unwavering. He thought he might just have a process that could tame the wild animal. At first, he led a roan mare around the stallion's corral to show the stallion what it could be used for. The mare moved gracefully, and the stallion seemed to be paying attention as any male would. Tiburcio repeated this routine, leading the mare near and far to the corral. He wanted the stallion to understand that he was there to help it and even used treats to entice it.

He could barely lift his leg as he mounted the beast of an opponent on the third day. The stallion bucked and whinnied, trying to shake Tiburcio off its back, but this time he held tight. He urged the stallion to a wild, half-bucking, unrhythmic gallop, forcing him to circle the corral until it was exhausted. The stallion's ears lay back in submission. The hardest part was over.

That weekend, they raced from the corral across the adjacent open field, the wind rushing through the hair below his hat and the stallion's mane. Tiburcio felt the power and grace of the horse beneath him, and it was a feeling he would never forget.

After a while, the stallion began to tire, and Tiburcio knew he had won. He slowed their gallop to a trot, leaned over, and stroked the robust and muscular neck. They had become one, a bond that would last forever. The next day, he rode the stallion out of the corral. They galloped fast and far; the stallion was finally experiencing the freedom it had longed for.

As the sun set, Fernando made his way to the arena where he found his nephew brushing the magnificent horse with great care and attention. Fernando was deeply impressed by Tiburcio's patience and determination and couldn't help but feel proud of the young man he had become.

"Tibo, I have been watching your hard work and tenacity, and I must say, you have truly become a man in my eyes. As a reward for your dedication, I want to give you this beautiful horse as a token of my admiration. Why don't you ride it home this weekend and enjoy the fruits of your labor?"

Tiburcio was overwhelmed with gratitude and humbly accepted the gift from his uncle. He thanked him profusely and promised to take good care of the horse and always remember the opportunity he had been given. The next day, Tiburcio arrived at his house in the late afternoon with a beaming smile and immense pride in his heart. His parents and siblings were delighted to see him riding a horse of such grandeur. They welcomed him inside their comfortable abode, where a lavish feast of meats, enchiladas, beans, and tamales awaited him. The aroma of the delicious food filled the room, and everyone sat down to enjoy the meal together. Juan, Tiburcio's father, washed down the flavorsome food with a popular liquor called aguardiente, which complemented the meal perfectly. It was a moment of contentment shared by all.

Two

As the days were growing shorter, Tiburcio often found himself at Fernando's ranch to earn some extra money and train the stallion he had named "Viento," which translated to "Wind." The Alta community was always festive, especially at the week's end. The locals entertained themselves with gambling, horse racing, and bull baiting, an immense joy to all who participated. One could also witness vaqueros showcasing their horse-riding skills, while others enjoyed dancing to release stress and socialize with members of the opposite sex.

Tiburcio, soon to celebrate his eighteenth birthday, attended the famous dance hall in town to join the festivities hoping to meet someone special. He made sure to dress the part of a vaquero, which translated to "cowboy" or "someone in charge of cows." He wore a white silk shirt, tan striped pants tucked into his high boots, and a three-inch wide leather belt to look his best. He also donned a short, vested-type jacket. The jacket, which protected him from the night air, had a shirt-style collar with an open front look and long fitted sleeves with classic open cuffs typical of Mexican Vaquero Jackets. The lace detail on the front and sleeves gave it an eye-catching look, which, along with the fine stitching, made its innovative style desirable. A red bandana tied neatly around his neck finished the look. Although many of his friends preferred to wear sombreros, Tiburcio opted for a hat with an almond-shaped crown, ribbon hatband, and flat brim. It looked like the modern Stetson Star Gazer hat.

As Tiburcio approached the Fandango House, he could hear the lively sounds of guitars and fiddles being played, mixed with boisterous laughter. The music grew louder as he walked through the front door, revealing a large, dimly lit room filled with tables and dancers. The hall was crowded and raucous, with all dressed in their finest. As he scanned the room, he pulled the brim of his hat lower on his face to look older and serious.

The packed bar smelled of stale booze and sweat. Everyone inside smoked cigars and pipes. The scent of chili peppers, chorizo, and spicy cumin hit like a wall. The barkeep, a fat woman in her late fifties, poured drinks like a fire hose for the crowd. He quickly spotted some older friends from school at the bar and approached to join them. They watched the merriment before them from their vantage point as couples danced exuberantly. The atmosphere was electric, with the crowd's energy filling the air. A famous bright melody was being played called "Spanish Fandango" by British composer and guitarist Henry Worrall.

The wild cowboys and miners twirled and kicked up their heels with their partners, hooting and hollering only to pause for another drink. Trampled toes were commonplace and sometimes caused a minor fight.

Tiburcio ordered a whiskey and watched the choreographed pandemonium. As much as he loved his daily life, he loved his social life even more. He finally made eye contact with a woman who appeared to be a couple of years older than he. She smiled invitingly, so he conjured up the courage to ask for a dance. She readily accepted with her hand out for payment as she was employed to do so. They had a couple of dances, and after one more whiskey, Tiburcio found himself exhausted from the week with Viento and left early. When he got home, he found his mother praying at the home chapel. She was a short, powerful woman whose life of raising nine children and losing two was etched on every wrinkle of her face. Her gray hair fell in strands across her shoulders. A devout Catholic, she always attended daily prayers and mass. She turned, seeing Tiburcio stagger slightly as he walked by. She made the sign of the cross and called for him.

"Tibo."

"What, Mama."

"Where have you been?"

"Dancing."

"And drinking, too, I see."

Tiburcio nodded, slightly embarrassed.

"Drinking and staying up late only leads to trouble, Tibo, and we do not need it to happen in this family…understand? We have enough trouble with the gringos as it is. I don't need you to get in trouble with our kind as well."

Tiburcio sauntered to her and pulled her body to him in a loving hug.

He looked down at her raised face.

"I love you, Mama. All is well; get some sleep."

She kissed his cheek in exchange.

"I love you too, mijo. "Mind me."

The following weeks found Tiburcio herding cows and sheep on the ranch; he roped and branded cattle and sheared and tied wool. He also became enamored with guns and became an expert with the rifle and pistol while spending endless hours with Viento. The stallion proved a great cutting horse. Working as one, they cut out cattle to get them culled for branding.

With a mix of curiosity and confidence, Tiburcio entered his steed on a weekend race to measure it up against the other locals. He found that Viento was the fastest horse in the Alta area, winning every horse race they entered.

Tiburcio was growing into a gallant and handsome young man. He had a natural charm with women and gradually refined his flirtation skills. He learned to play the guitar, which he used to serenade and woo the ladies. He also had a passion for poetry that he had developed since school, and he occasionally wrote short poems for his chosen beauties.

Near the waterholes were stone washing tubs where he would often find women and banter with them, exchange playful touches, and share furtive glances. His neat, form-fitting clothes and beautiful hair that fell from under his favorite hat captivated the women. As he walked along the stream, he admired the way the sunlight danced across the pretty girls' faces. He smiled back at them, his deep brown eyes sparkling with mischief and charm. He was aware of his good looks but didn't like to admit it. He simply enjoyed the attention he received from the girls who walked alongside him. Walking around the stone tubs, he would flash his pearly whites at them, making them giggle and blush.

One girl had particularly caught his eye. She had long, curly black hair that cascaded down her back in soft waves and a smile that lit up the world around her. Her name was María García, and she was the most stunning girl Tiburcio had ever seen. She was a vision of youth and beauty. Her green eyes sparkled with mischief and curiosity reflecting her Mexican heritage. Her tight breasts and slim figure were accentuated by the form-fitting dress she wore, which hugged her curves in all the right places.

Her hips swayed with a natural grace as she moved, drawing the eyes of all fortunate enough to witness her beauty. Her skin was smooth as silk, with a golden glow that spoke of days spent basking in the sun. She was a young woman who knew her allure, and she delighted in the attention she received.

Tiburcio slowly approached her, his heart beating faster with every step.

"Need any help with that?" he asked, gesturing to the pile of clothes in the tub beside her.

María blushed and nodded shyly.

"Thank you, Tibo."

Tiburcio couldn't resist stealing glances at María as they worked together. He longed to touch her soft skin, to kiss her rosy lips. He suddenly noticed her eyes darting to someone else. He turned to see a tall, handsome man walking towards them. His heart sank as he recognized the man as his rival, Pedro. Pedro was just as good-looking as Tiburcio but had a dangerous air that made the girls swoon.

He tried to ignore Pedro and focus on the girl he was flirting with, but her attention had shifted to his rival. It wasn't long before she excused herself and ran to talk to him. Tiburcio felt a twinge of rage and jealousy, emotions he had never felt before but would feel many times more over the coming years.

To his mother's disappointment, Tiburcio was not religious and rarely spent time in church. His innocence gradually gave way to a deep-seated hatred for gringos. He watched as they walked the streets of Monterey with self-centered authority over the locals. Monterey had become one of the most violent towns in the country, with a high murder rate. As a result, many began to carry guns for their protection.

Salomon Pico, who was married to Tiburcio's cousin, Juana Vasquez, hated Americans. He had been cheated out of his property and wanted to kill everyone he came across. Rumor had it that he had killed over thirty-nine Americans on El Camino Real (now the 101 Freeway) between Los Angeles and Monterey. He cut off his victims' ears, tied them together, and hung them from his saddle. This was a tradition in the area that started when Native Indians who had stolen horses were killed and their ears kept for proof. Everyone, even the Mexicans, feared Pico.

Domingo Hernández was yet another dangerous bandit. He had a younger brother, Augustín, with whom Tiburcio was destined to become friends. Domingo had no ethics and shot his victims in the back. He also had an ear collection.

He was a towering figure of a man, easily six and a half feet tall, with broad shoulders and a barrel-like chest. He had a rugged, slovenly appearance, with a wild mane of jet-black hair and a thick, bushy beard that covered most of his face. His eyes were dark and piercing; their glint of madness hinted at the violence within him.

His clothing, stolen garments he had collected over the years, was as unkempt as his appearance. His shirt was torn and stained with blood, his pants threadbare and patched in several places. Over it all, he wore a long leather duster, the sleeves cut off to allow him greater freedom of movement. The coat was stained with dirt and sweat, and the smell of unwashed leather hung heavy wherever he went. Characteristically he had strapped to his back a large, razor-sharp curved machete and a pistol that the sheriff had confiscated at the time of his recent arrest. Despite his slovenly appearance, there was no mistaking the raw strength and power beneath Domingo's rough exterior. His muscles rippled with every movement, and the sheer force of his presence was enough to strike fear into all. His boots were heavy and scuffed, the soles thick.

Domingo had lived his entire life as a criminal. Irrespective of all the murders and other crimes he committed. However, he had recently been sentenced to hang for stealing a horse. Although Tiburcio had never met him, only hearing the stories and references to him when hanging out with Agustín, he decided to attend the hanging and watch from a distance.

On the day of the execution, a large crowd formed, and many in it were desperados like Domingo. They yelled obscenities when the rope was put around his neck. The executioner adjusted it, ensuring it was tight, and stepped back, ready to pull the lever that would send the bandit to die. Domingo closed his eyes, praying for a quick death; his mind raced with regret and fear. He knew he was paying the price for all his sins.

The crowd's shouting reached a fever pitch. Domingo took a deep breath and opened his eyes. He looked at the sea of faces, all twisted with anger and hatred and wondered if they had ever felt what it was like to be so desperate for money that they would do anything to get it—whether they had ever been pushed to the brink of madness by circumstances beyond their control. Members of his gang amongst the locals watched the unbelievable horror of their leader meeting his destiny. They knew as well as he did it was too late for regrets. Domingo closed his eyes again and waited for the end to come. A black hood was placed over his head. His breathing quickened in anticipation of the inevitable when he felt the sudden jerk of the executioner.

The trapdoor opened, and the rope stretched, snapped, and swiftly broke, sending Domingo to the dirt like a sack of potatoes, hurt but unscathed.

The attending priest screamed, "Mother Mary, God has saved him!"

"It is a miracle!"

Even the desperados made the sign of the cross. The sheriff attempted to re-arrest Domingo, but the crowd overwhelmed him, denying him the ability to exert any authority. Heightening the fiasco and securing the failure, the priest's status and decree carried weight within the community. His exclaiming the botched hanging as a miracle prevented any further prosecution of the notorious bandit.

Domingo and his gang made their way to the Fandango House to celebrate the triumph and ultimately to get drunk. Tiburcio, curious, followed them out of deference to the moment as well as in unintended defiance of his mother. The floor was sticky, worsened by the stagnant hot air. The crowd, most of them drunk and many of the men armed, reveled in dirty work clothes. It was a rough atmosphere fitting for the bandit's celebration. Seeing Tiburcio, Domingo motioned for him to come over. Tiburcio approached with apprehension. The giant of a man grabbed Tiburcio around the neck, pulling him so close that he could smell the hot breath and alcohol emanating from his oversized mouth of rotting teeth.

"You know Tibo, my brother loves you. I don't know why you don't hang around us. He tells me you are good on a horse and just as good with a pistol. Let me buy you a drink."

Tiburcio nodded hesitantly. He didn't like Domingo and feared him.

"Good!" Domingo yelled.

He ordered two tequilas, and they clinked glasses.

The floor was overfilled with the raucousness of the drunken crowd, and just as Domingo lifted his glass, a cowboy bumped into him, spilling the drink all over the bandit's vest.

"Pinche Cabron!" Domingo yelled.

He pushed the innocent man back to the ground, his temper set off quickly and aggression building by the second. No one was paying attention except for Tiburcio, who watched intently as Domingo pulled a knife from the belt of his friend sitting nearby and plunged it into the man's chest as he tried to get up. The cowboy stumbled back, clutching his chest where the blade had entered. Domingo stood over him; his face contorted with anger, his fellow gang members forming a tight circle around he killer and his victim to ensure no one could interfere or see.

"You gringo fool!" he shouted.

"You thought you could come in here uninvited and disrespect us?

The cowboy spat blood onto the floor.

"I ain't disrespecting' nobody," he gasped.

"I just wanted a drink."

Domingo kicked him in the side, making him choke with pain, and continued with a nonsensical rant to justify his maniacal actions.

"You wanted more than that! You wanted to show us all that you were better than us. Well, look at you now. Bleeding on the floor like a stuck pig." He laughed nonsensically, his rant making no sense but to excuse is violent act.

The cowboy tried to stand, but his legs gave way. Domingo caught him, grabbing his shirt and hoisting him to standing level.

"You're going to pay for what you did to our people and our land," he hissed. Indifferent to the blood gushing from the cowboy's chest, Domingo leaned in close.

"You take our women, our land, and our pride? Think again."

The cowboy was heaving for breath as his panicked eyes darted around the room, looking for any possible means of escape. Domingo pressed the blade deeper into his chest, relishing the feeling of power it gave him.

"You're going to die here, gringo."

The cowboy gritted his teeth, trying to summon the strength to fight back, but the pain was too much. He could feel himself slipping away. With his vision fading, he whispered, "God help me."

Domingo's face was gnarled with rage.

The cowboy glared up at him, his eyes defiant as they surrendered to a death stare. Domingo's friend, who had been standing beside him, grabbed the bandit.

"Domingo, what have you done? Let's get out of here!"

Domingo pushed him away, but two others from his gang stepped in. They knew their leader would be hanged again if anyone found out. Domingo called to Tiburcio.

"Come with us, amigo! We have great things in mind!"

Their best efforts failed to drag the young man out of the bar. As the gang mounted their horses and galloped away Tiburcio stood in disbelief of what he had just witnessed. He looked around, bowed, pulled his hat over his eyes, and immediately left the Fandango House.

Three

Monterey continued to change, as did its citizens. Tiburcio's father and uncle made every effort to defend their ranches from land grabbers and rustlers. Their waning control of the young man was being replaced by the influence of his peers, as happens with all teenagers. He sought the company of more exciting people, like his new friend Alejandro Ramos, whom he saw as a rebel, and he was no longer interested in the ranching life. Growing lazier by the day, he wanted only to experience the thrill of living dangerously. He saw how people like Anastacio García didn't work as lowly laborers and vaqueros yet still had money. Tiburcio spent most of his night gambling and drinking at the local saloon, surrounded by gun-toting ruffians. He discovered a taste for aguardiente and American whiskey. He wasn't a heavy drinker but sometimes carried a bottle in his pocket for social reasons while enjoying an occasional cigar. More than anyone, Sheriff Andrew Watson took notice of Tiburcio's change in values and made a promise to himself to keep an eye on him.

After racing, gambling, and winning another horse race with Viento, Tiburcio found himself in the company of José Garcia, Ramos, and a few other ruffians, all of whom were in their thirties. Not knowing how it started, Tiburcio happened to see Ramos pushing another man. A crowd formed around them as a fight ensued. A blood-curdling scream was heard, sending the bystanders to scatter, all shouting in fear. Tiburcio walked over to where Ramos was standing. The body of a Texan, his eyes cold and unfeeling, lay at his feet.

"What did you do?" Tiburcio asked, his voice barely above a whisper.

"He insulted me. You know I can't tolerate that," Ramos said defensively; his voice was devoid of emotion.

Tiburcio knelt over the body. The man had been stabbed to death and profusely bled out.

"You killed a man over a few words?" Tiburcio asked, his voice rising in anger.

"He insulted me," Ramos repeated, his gaze fixed on the dead man.

Tiburcio shook his head in disgust.

This is crazy, Ramos!"

Ramos turned to face him, his eyes blazing with fury.

"How dare you judge me?" He waved his knife hand low around his waist erratically.

"You're no better than I am."

Tiburcio stepped back, his hand instinctively reaching for his gun.

"I'm not like you, Ramos. I don't kill over words."

The crowd continued to disperse as Ramos stood there, his breathing labored, staring at the lifeless body. Sensing the older man's heightened tension, Tiburcio spoke to him cautiously. He nearly panicked and ran away.

He tried to pull him away and said, "Ramos, we have to go. The sheriff will be here soon."

Ramos looked up with his eyes feral with adrenaline.

"I had to do it," his voice shook imploringly.

Tiburcio shook his head.

"Whatever. It wasn't worth it, Ramos."

Ramos shrugged him off, looking away as he whispered, "I don't care. Fuck it!"

Tiburcio sighed, realizing there was no reason for him to be in this state not to mention a reason to stay and help.

"Come, let's go!"

He dragged Ramos to his horse. He was about to help him mount when he heard a voice yell out from over his shoulder.

"Hold it right there!"

Tiburcio and Ramos exchanged glances before slowly raising their hands in surrender. They both understood the gravity of the situation. Sheriff Watson marched towards them, his eyes narrowing with suspicion, and trained his gun on them.

"What the hell happened here?"

Tiburcio looked down at the large muzzle of the 44-caliber revolver and hesitated for a moment before responding.

"We were just uh... we were just passing through," he said, his voice shaking slightly.

The sheriff's gaze shifted to the body on the ground.

"And this poor bastard just happened to get in your way?" he asked sarcastically.

Ramos stepped forward, his hands still in the air.

"We didn't kill him, sheriff. We found him like this. We were going to get help."

The sheriff lowered his gun slightly with keen skepticism.

"Why should I believe you?"

"Please, Sheriff," Tiburcio said, holding up his hands in surrender.

"We didn't do anything wrong."

Watson, wholly unconvinced, inched closer and immediately saw a glint of metal in Ramos's belt still covered in blood.

"Get away from the horse," the sheriff ordered.

"And drop that knife."

Ramos glanced down at his knife and realized he was found out. He quickly dropped it and stepped away from the horse. The sheriff motioned for Ramos and Tiburcio to walk toward Monterey's overcrowded jail.

Two days later, Ramos was charged with manslaughter.

Tiburcio was released but was now on the radar of law enforcement due to his perceived antisocial activities. Neither the murder nor his short stint in jail inspired Tiburcio to return to the lifestyle he was born into. He spent less and less time at home but also found the unpredictability of gambling and horse racing less than lucrative. He obtained employment as a vaquero, working on different ranches to secure his freedom from reliance on his family.

The bright sun shone down upon the dusty track, and six horses took their positions at the starting line. The air offered a potpourri of hay, horse sweat, and the chatter of gamblers. The grandstands were packed with people eager to bet on the upcoming Saturday race. Mexican men in sombreros, American cowboys in wide-brim hats, and ladies with para-sols were all vying for the best view of the racetrack. The fine clothes of the spectators seemed to validate their palpable excitement as they waited for the race to begin. Some had brought fruit baskets and sweet biscuits to picnic with their friends and family in the sunshine. The clamor of gamblers placing bets, many of whom were rough-and-tumble vaqueros and cowboys, intensified the enthusiasm, as did the sleek and muscular horses restless in wait for the starting gun. The riders gripped the reins of their steeds tightly to dissuade their eagerness to bolt forward.

William Pyburn was an overweight man with a round belly. He wore thick wool trousers that hugged his ample hips and leather boots that gleamed in the sunlight. He sported a neatly trimmed mustache, curled up at the ends. It complemented a full head of salt-and-pepper, slicked back hair that he kept meticulously combed. His clean-shaven jawline, along with the finely tailored suits that hugged his large frame boosted his status in the community. His wealth couldn't be denied. Pyburn was a man of many talents. He was a merchant, selling all types of goods from his shop on the corner of High Street. Shelves stacked high with bottles of wine, whiskey, and brandy from worldwide distributors identified him as a purveyor of fine spirits. When not involved with his business, Pyburn could be found at the gambling tables, throwing down his hard-earned coins with the confidence of a man who knew he couldn't lose. His over-whelming gambling passion was for horse racing. He admired the riders, and Tiburcio was the one he favored most.

Despite his love of risk-taking, Pyburn was always a man of his word; his dealings were likewise fair. His unmistakable presence could be felt throughout Monterey, and his influence extended far beyond the walls of his shop. He had been watching Tiburcio for some time. He had won money every time Tiburcio raced aboard Viento and admired how he carried himself with a confident flair. He had frequented the fandango hall, watching Tiburcio and his unsated hunger for women, romancing them around the dance floor.

Today, both men were gambling on the horses. Pyburn walked over to Tiburcio, who was placing a bet on a friend's horse, greeting him with an extended hand.

"Tiburcio, my name is William Pyburn, and I've watched you race here many times. Why aren't you racing today?"

Tiburcio extended his hand in return and shook Pyburn's.

"There isn't any horse that Viento and I haven't beat that's here. No one will give me good odds, so I must bet on friends' horses."

"Well, let me use your expertise," Pyburn engaged.

"Which horse are you betting to win?"

"The white Arabian that my friend Miguel Hernández is riding,"

Pyburn called to one of the bookmakers. In lieu of paper money, which did not exist and was prohibited by California's constitution in 1849, Pyburn handed over foreign coins and gold slugs while stating his bet.

Pyburn chuckled as he sipped his whiskey from a flask that he had pulled from his coat pocket. He offered some to Tiburcio, who took one sip.

"Thanks."

"I like to take risks, Tiburcio. It keeps life interesting."

Tiburcio nodded, eyeing his hand.

"I can understand that. But what brings you here to Monterey? You could make a pretty gold piece elsewhere."

Pyburn leaned back on his seat and gestured to the crowd around them.

"This is where the money is, my friend. And speaking of money, I've got a proposition for you."

Tiburcio raised an eyebrow.

"Oh?"

Pyburn nodded and leaned in closer.

"I'm opening a new dance hall in town and need someone to run it."

Tiburcio nodded slowly, unsure of where this was going.

"I would like you to run it for me," Pyburn said.

"Why me?"

"You're a winner, Tibo. May I call you Tibo? I see you and how you relate to the people around you. Your horsemanship is unsurpassed, and I am told you know how to handle a gun. What more do I need to have confidence in someone looking for an honest way to make a living? Aren't you tired of sweating out on the range hazing cattle and sheep?"

It was true that Tiburcio had grown lazy without his father and uncle pressing him. The influence of his peers had moreover taken root, further diminishing any incentive to make the uphill living the life of a vaquero guaranteed.

Tiburcio couldn't believe his luck. He had just turned nineteen and was being offered a job as a manager of a new dance hall.

"This is amazing, Mr. Pyburn," Tiburcio said, his eyes wide with excitement.

"I've always loved music and dance, and now I get to be a part of it all!"

Pyburn chuckled.

"Glad to see you're excited, Tiburcio. But remember, this is a business. We need to make money and keep the customers coming back."

"I understand, sir." Tiburcio nodded eagerly.

"I'll work hard and make sure everything runs smoothly."

Pyburn leaned forward, his eyes intense.

"Good. Because if you mess up, there will be no second chances. You hear me?"

Tiburcio swallowed nervously but nodded again.

"Yes, sir. I won't let you down."

Pyburn sat back with a satisfied smile.

"Good."

Above the din, the starting sound of a pistol clapped in the air, and the six galloping horses thundered past the grandstand, the air overwhelmed with dust kicked up by the force of their hooves. Tiburcio stared into the distance and wondered how and if this good fortune would fare for him in the future. It was as though no time had passed when the reverberation of their galloping signaled their approach toward the finish line. The crowd, on the edge of their seats, were cheering and hollering.

The Arabian horse with Miguel on its back was in the lead, kicking up a trail of dust behind it. The other horses struggled to keep up. Their nostrils flared as they were pushed to their limits, feeling the whip of the reins from the riders on their flanks.

Miguel urged the Arabian horse forward, his eyes locked on the finish line. They pulled further ahead with every stride, the wind whipping past their faces.

The crowd erupted into a frenzy as the Arabian horse crossed the finish line, leaving its competitors behind. Miguel let out a triumphant whoop, his heart pounding with adrenaline and excitement as he stood in his stirrups with raised arms. Pyburn raised his arms as well. Such is the addiction one has as a gambler—the orgasm of victory.

The bookmaker confidently strode over to where Pyburn and Tiburcio were waiting with bated breath. They had placed their bets, hoping for a big win. He handed Pyburn a pouch full of gold coins that filled his hands. Tiburcio, who had bet a smaller amount, received a modest handful. Both men were pleased with their winnings and thanked him. Pyburn turned to Tiburcio and shook his hand, a gesture of camaraderie and gratitude. Tiburcio was surprised when Pyburn slipped a handful of gold into his hand, a generosity that spoke volumes about their newfound business relationship. He looked at Tiburcio.

"This is the start of a good business relationship, I hope, Tibo."

He walked away, leaving Tiburcio excited about what the future might hold.

~

The newly built dance hall attracted both Anglos and Mexicans alike owing to the addition of a large dance room with a bar imported from the East Coast. The walls were a forest of tapestries and light that filled what was once a darkened room. Pyburn had expanded the hall's initial medium-sized adobe structure to accommodate the growing number of patrons.

Tiburcio, who had known María from their days of washing clothes by the stream, noticed that she had become a regular dancer at the hall. Her sensual beauty was undeniable, but unfortunately, it also became the cause of several violent episodes involving some of the Anglo visitors and Tiburcio. His increasing disgust and hatred of them cultivated a level of resentment that would eventually lead to more misbehavior on his part.

Four

As days turned into weeks and weeks into months, Tiburcio's humble hall gradually became a hub of activity, attracting diverse individuals from all walks of life. Among the regulars were some of the most brutal and notorious men in Monterey, hailing from Anglo as well as Mexican backgrounds. Despite their rough exterior, they found solace in Tiburcio's warm hospitality and soon became his closest confidants. Over time, the hall became a melting pot of cultures and personalities united by friendship and camaraderie. However, this could be disturbed by jealousy over women by the visiting gold rush miners and sailors who would frequent the hall on leave from their ships and mines.

As usual, on Saturday night, the dance hall was packed with people, the air thick with the smoke of cigarettes, the scent of cheap liquor, and the sound of laughter and chatter. The band, playing a hit song from the east, "Saint Louis Rondo," enlivened the sea of swaying and twirling on the dance floor. A group of sailors stumbled into the hall, changing the atmosphere immediately. Their voices were loud and boisterous as they made their way to the bar, forcing the dancers to move out of their way. They began to drink heavily and harass some of the women in the room. Tiburcio stepped in to dissuade one of the more prominent sailors whose face was in a young woman's neck, while his hand slid under her dress. She was trying to push away when Tiburcio intervened.

"Hey, why don't you leave her alone and act like a gentleman?" he said firmly.

The sailor turned to him, his face bent with aggression.

"Who the fuck are you?" he spat, shoving Tiburcio away roughly.

The laughter and cheer of the other sailors emboldened their friend to continue.

"We're just here to have a good time," one of them said, slurring his words.

Tiburcio stood his ground, determined to protect the women in the room from the sailors' unwanted advances. The intensity of the confrontation made it unclear how it would end.

We don't put up with that kind of shit pal. It's time for you to leave," he said.

Tiburcio was never one to back down, and he didn't see another sailor off to his left who sucker punched him in the side of his head. He went down, falling hard to the floor, but quickly got up, only to be promptly knocked on his ass by a shove from another sailor.

"Fucking Mexican!"

Tiburcio didn't miss a beat as he briskly jumped up and physically tackled the sailor, lifting his drunken opponent and sending him over the bar, creating an explosion of breaking glass and bottles.

Seeing this, Tiburcio's friends dropped their drinks and set in for the melee. They started throwing punches, and soon, the dance floor was a chaotic mess of flying fists and profanity. The Mexican men fought back with equal ferocity, their insults and curses a match for the sailors' rough language. Bottles were broken over heads, chairs were smashed, and blood was spilled on the dance floor. The sound of fists striking flesh and shattered furniture silenced the music as the brawl continued. A drunk miner sitting in the corner leaned his chair back to the wall just in time to rescue his whiskey from two brawlers falling onto his table.

Tiburcio struggled to get his wits back, his head throbbing from being blindsided. He could see his friends fighting fiercely against the sailors as he dodged a punch from a rather tall sailor and, grabbing a broken glass, shoved the sharp end into the sailor's eye. He pushed the sailor to the ground. The sailor's friends rushed to his aid, but Tiburcio's friends pulled out their pistols to hold them back. The two men struggled on the ground, rolling and punching until Tiburcio gained the upper hand and pinned the sailor's arms to the sticky liquor-stained floor.

He looked up, breathless, and saw the other sailors backing away from a couple of armed vaqueros who, having had enough, had pulled their guns out, too. The sailors' faces contorted with fear and anger. Tiburcio dropped an elbow onto the sailor's face, breaking his nose. The crack of it could be heard above the commotion, blood gushing from open wounds and his nostrils. Tiburcio unmercifully punched him again into unconsciousness.

There was silence in the room for a moment, broken only by heavy breathing, moaning, and glass crunching underfoot. Then, one of the sailors shouted something in a language Tiburcio couldn't make out due to his ringing ears. One of his friends put his hands under Tiburcio's shoulders and lifted him while another pointed his gun and ordered the sailors to leave.

"Cabrónes, get the fuck out of here!"

María walked over to Tiburcio, pulled up a part of her long skirt, and dabbed blood from his face. It was the first time she had touched him intimately. His heart raced as her gentleness wiped away sweat from his face, astonished by her tenderness and caring. He had been admiring her from afar for years, never once thinking he would be this close, let alone feel her touch. While María continued cleaning his face, he let out a small moan of pleasure. She looked up at him with a curious expression. Tiburcio couldn't help but lean in and kiss her. Her lips were soft and sweet, and he felt like he was in heaven. Their kiss lasted for what felt like an eternity, their tongues tasting each other's, but eventually, they pulled away from the embrace.

Tiburcio looked into her eyes and saw a fire burning inside. He knew he had to have her and would do whatever it took to make it happen. The crowd began picking up the overturned furniture and attending to the broken glass. Some teeth had been knocked out and found on the floor, and faces were swollen, but that was put right by Tiburcio's generosity.

"A round on the house!"

The crowd cheered, and the band played its favorite upbeat dance song, "Mexican Airs."

Over time, daily life for the locals continued to deteriorate. The bigotry of the Anglos ensured the Californios immeasurable suffering, economic and otherwise. While Tiburcio had the privilege of comparing his early years of joy and labor in Alta with the circumstances unfolding before him, others could only guess why its young people were experiencing such drastic life changes. Some blamed hormones. For that matter, with Tiburcio, it may have played a part. Still, no one could deny how effective peer pressure had become in the backslide of values on which the town once prided itself. The once peaceful society so loved and respected as Alta was disappearing under the weight of Monterey's corruption.

It was in response that Tiburcio announced his intention to his parents that he would exact a price for the insults leveled at his people daily.

"I am going to be a bandit."

The shocking declaration took them aback. They had always hoped for Tiburcio to seek a better life where he wouldn't commit crimes, but as they looked into their son's eyes, they saw a fire burning within him that couldn't be contained. They had always taught him to be hardworking and find a righteous path, but they could also see his growing frustration.

"Tiburcio, my son, you can't become a bandit. It will only lead to your downfall," his mother pleaded.

"Mother, I understand your concern, but these Anglos are taking everything away from us. We worked hard to build this land, and now they come and claim it as their own. They insult us, they take our jobs, and they treat us like we are nothing. I cannot sit by idly while they continue to oppress us."

Tiburcio's reply was firm.

His father, silent up until now, spoke up.

"We understand your anger, Tibo, but becoming a bandit is not the answer. It will only bring shame to you and our family."

Their spoken wisdom fell on deaf ears, and Tiburcio spent little time in the coming weeks at home. He instead gathered a group of like-minded individuals who all shared the same goal: to regain from the Anglos what was rightfully theirs. At first, their operations were small, like stealing from Anglo merchants who were known to cheat the Mexicans, but they soon grew bolder and began to plan larger heists. The biggest one of late was to rob a stagecoach.

~

The setting sun cast long shadows across the dusty plains. Tiburcio and his novice banditos crouched behind a band of rocks, watching for the coach to approach. They had tracked it for days and were committed to this perfect opportunity to strike. The coach drew nearer, and Tiburcio signaled his men to move into position. They emerged from their hiding spots, brandishing their weapons and firing shots into the air while shouting demands through their bandana-covered faces. The passengers inside the coach screamed in terror, but Tiburcio and his men paid them no heed. They were after one thing only: the valuable cargo inside the coach.

Tiburcio approached the coach with his gun drawn.

"Open the door!"

He then lowered his voice, addressing the passengers and the sole stagecoach driver.

"We mean you no harm, but we will take what we want by force if we have to."

The door creaked open, revealing a huddle of frightened passengers.

Tiburcio moved forward, his eyes scanning the interior for anything of value. His men followed suit, removing jewelry from the two well-dressed women, a watch, and cash from two men traveling with them. One of the men in a top hat tried to pull a gun when Tiburcio slammed his own down on the man's forearm, causing it to fall to the floor.

"Ah, ah, ah," Tiburcio warned with a waving finger.

He picked up the passenger's gun and tucked it into his waistband. Fear filled the man's eyes. Reaching into the man's breast pocket and taking out a cigar, Tiburcio's white teeth filled a wide, calming, pleasant smile.

"Hmmmm. Thank you, Señor," he said with glee.

He then walked forward to the six-up that pulled the wagon and slapped the left rear horse's rump. The team pulled the wagon away at a gallop, leaving him in a cloud of descending dust. His fellow bandits gathered their horses and brought him Viento. They hooted in victory as they galloped away, Viento leading the way.

The following week, Tiburcio and María met at the local cantina, where she helped her mother. Their sultry glances at each other sent shivers down their spines. He approached her with a sly grin, his eyes locked onto hers. María was a vision of beauty, with her long, sleek black hair tied back in a ponytail. Her vibrant green eyes held a mischievousness hinting at the adventurous spirit that lay within her. Her complexion was a mix of Mexican and other ethnicities, giving her an exotic allure that was impossible to ignore. Her tight breasts added to her already stunning petite frame. Every curve of her body was lean and toned, a testament to her dedication to maintaining her appeal. It was impossible not to be captivated by her charm and beauty.

"May I buy you a drink?" he asked, his voice thick with desire.

María nodded, biting her lip as she followed him to the bar. While he ordered two glasses of their finest tequila, their eyes met again, and Tiburcio leaned in close to whisper in her ear. It had been a while since the fight and the kiss they shared at the dance hall.

"I've been thinking about you all day," he whispered, his breath hot against her face.

María felt her heart racing as she gazed into Tiburcio's deep brown eyes. A sudden rush of heat spread through her body as he leaned closer, their faces now an inch apart. The warm tequila coursing through their veins only heightened the sensation. Without a word, Tiburcio took her hand and led her outside into the sweet, warm night air. The music and laughter from the bar faded away as they walked silently, their fingers intertwined under the starry sky. The streetlights cast a warm glow on their faces. As they turned into a secluded alleyway behind some homes, the smell of jasmine flowers filled the air.

María's heart was pounding as Tiburcio pulled her close, his lips meeting hers in a passionate embrace. Light reflecting off a nearby window illuminated a silhouette of them on the nearby building. Reaching into María's blouse, Tiburcio found her dainty breasts and kissed them, feeling them rise and harden. They continued to kiss profoundly, and then Tiburcio turned her to lift her dress. He could smell the desire emanating from between her legs. Overcome with lust, he gently entered her from behind. She leaned on the alley wall to welcome his slow, probing thrusts. As they became one with their rhythmic dance, she reached down and pleasured herself. Tiburcio's arousal heightened until he erupted with an orgasm that filled her swollen vulva. The passion and love were over-whelming. The pleasure that glowed on her face left little question that the climax she enjoyed with him was equally gratifying. A sound alerted her to immediately pull her dress down, and Tiburcio pulled her into shadow. It turned out to be only a bird that fluttered in a nearby tree. They both giggled, slightly embarrassed. They kissed again slowly as the intensity of the sex subsided.

"I love you, Tiburcio."

"I love you too, mi amor. Let's get you back before your mother sends out a search party for you."

Five

During the fourth to eighth decades of the nineteenth century, the U.S. Government, with the help of private citizens, killed thousands of indigenous people. Estimates were that between 9,000 and 16,000 Californians had been killed by non-natives. If not killed, they had been worked or starved to death. Countless crimes of rape and kidnapping had exacerbated the displacement of families and children resulting from this conflict. Local and state authorities had largely ignored—tolerated, even—these heinous acts.

The U.S. Congress voted to admit California as the thirty-first state of the union on September 9, 1850. Still, it did little to redress these injustices, and it did nothing to solve the ever-growing crime in the region. The new state of California, Monterey, certainly suffered under unprecedented lawlessness, and it boasted the highest murder rate in the country.

The citizens of San Francisco, deeply angered by their local officials, created a "Vigilance Committee" to take matters into their own hands, and it wasn't long before those individuals had executed four people, and handed fifteen more over to police. Not to mention they whipped or deported twenty-nine other individuals. The success of these vigilantes led to similar committees in other towns and mining camps, but all efforts were provisional at best. When two marshals and one newspaper editor were killed in 1856, a second Vigilance Committee was formed, going so far as to seize weapons from the local militia. In the time it took for sheriffs and marshals to regain control, the bandits along Camino Real had filled their pockets while stealing horses and murdering those who got in their way. Fights broke out among rival crime lords or their soldiers, with almost always one left dead.

It was under these conditions that Anastacio García entered Pyburn's bar seeking Tiburcio. Pyburn and Tiburcio were reviewing the week's receipts, and Pyburn had just complimented his manager on his work. Anastacio approached them, and since Pyburn had finished his business with Tiburcio, he tipped his hat and exited the building.

Anastacio was a man of short stature with a stocky build and a thick goatee covering most of his chin. His skin was a deep shade of burnt caramel, and his dark eyes were sharp, darting around the room with suspicion. He wore a black leather vest over a crisp white cotton shirt, opened at the neck, and a large cross hanging on a leather necklace. A silver pistol strapped to his right hip glinted in the bar's dim light, matched only by the large menacing knife also attached to his belt. He was a master of both weapons if one believed his reputation. His sour demeanor darkened as he sat at the counter to order a drink.

Drumming his thick fingers impatiently on the counter, Anastacio's eyes narrowed under his giant sombrero to survey the other patrons. It wasn't that he was always spoiling for a fight. In fact, anything could set him off. However, tonight, he wasn't there for that.

Tiburcio walked to him, extending his hand for a shake. Meeting Anastacio's, he felt his calloused fingers rough against his own.

"Thanks for seeing me," Anastacio grunted, pulling his hand away as Tiburcio sat on the stool beside him.

Tiburcio motioned to the bartender to bring a bottle of tequila. The overweight bartender did so with Tiburcio politely waving him away. He poured Anastacio a drink and eyed him warily in silence. He knew the man was trouble but was intrigued by his reputation. Anastacio's eyes gleamed fiercely, and his muscles bulged beneath his shirt, both suggesting a man not to be trifled with.

He downed his drink in one gulp, then slammed the glass back onto the counter.

"Another," he growled, his voice low and menacing.

Tiburcio obliged, filling his glass once again. He wanted to throw some ideas past the seasoned bandit for his upcoming plans and how they might work together. Anastacio drank as he listened, all the while studying the other patrons in the bar. As his eyes scanned the room for any signs of trouble, Tiburcio noticed them stop abruptly on José Higuera, who had just walked in.

José was also a shorter man with a fiery temper. His curly, unkempt black hair hung wildly from under his sombrero. A large pink scar above his left eyebrow gave him an intimidating look. He wore a brown jacket over a blue shirt, and his large hands were calloused from years of working in the fields. He, too, wore a pistol on his belt turned backward for quick draw with his opposite hand. He overlooked Anastacio and walked to the opposite end of the bar.

"Tibo, what is that piece of shit doing here?" Anastacio asked.

"Who?"

"Higuera," Anastacio replied with an air of disgust. "He's a cowardly killer and thief who has shot men in the back. One knows not to turn their back to him in order not to fall to his fateful reputation."

Anastacio hated Higuera because he had stolen his wife and left him heartbroken. Higuera was a notorious womanizer in their village, and Anastacio's wife was but one of many he had seduced. Anastacio had loved his wife dearly but was no match for Higuera's charm and rough looks. Now, he couldn't stand the sight of him. Every time he looked at him, it brought back painful memories of his lost love. He swore he would make Higuera pay one day for what he had done, even if it meant risking his own life.

Tiburcio didn't know Higuera or the misgivings they shared.

"I don't know him, amigo. Have another drink on me, and let's talk business. I have some ideas on how we can work together."

Anastacio ignored his gesture and, with his eyes still locked on Higuera, pushed himself away from the bar and shouted to Higuera.

"What are you doing here, cabrón? I don't want to look at your ugly face while I drink!"

Tiburcio sensed the tension and weighed the possible outcomes of this challenge. He attempted to calm Anastacio by putting his hand on his shoulder, but the bandit brushed it aside and walked toward Higuera, itching for a fight.

"I don't need any trouble," Higuera countered.

Tiburcio nodded to the bartender as a signal to have the shotgun below the bar handy. The older man didn't need to nod back as he slowly glided to a better position.

Anastacio walked toward Higuera and, once within distance, threw a punch that missed him by a mile. Higuera ducked and delivered a sharp jab to Anastacio's gut, causing him to grunt in pain. The two men circled each other, looking for an opening. Tiburcio tried to intervene but was quickly pushed aside as Anastacio and Higuera were exchanging blows. Higuera landed a solid uppercut to Anastacio's jaw, causing him to stumble back. Anastacio shook his head and charged again, catching Higuera off guard and slamming him against the nearest wall. Higuera groaned as Anastacio rained down a flurry of punches, each landing with a sickening thud.

Tiburcio tried to pull Anastacio off Higuera, but he was met with a sharp elbow to the face that sent him reeling. Anastacio continued to pummel and kick Higuera, his rage taking over with unleashed fury. Taking the advantage of being on top, he pulled his revolver. Anastacio immediately grabbed it, and they both grappled for purchase.

Constable William Hardmount was walking by on his regular rounds when he heard the commotion. Poking his head in the door, he rushed to break up the fight. A sudden gunshot rang out, and the constable fell before reaching the two struggling on the floor almost instantly. He had been inadvertently shot through the heart by Higuera as he was wrestling with Anastacio for the gun.

One of the vaqueros ran from the bar to get help. Tiburcio surprised Higuera and grabbed the gun from his hand. Anastacio became enraged by the interference, but Tiburcio had enough of the violence, and this time, he would be on the right side of it. It had proven to be a big mistake to meet with the wild and unpredictable Anastacio. He turned the gun on Higuera just at that moment a group of vigilantes entered the bar. He could hear their boots hitting the wooden floorboards of the dance hall some distance away. He knew his situation was precarious, but he was determined to protect himself and ensure justice was served. The vigilantes had a reputation for being ruthless, and he didn't want to end up as a target of their wrath. They approached him, their faces shrouded in darkness, eyes glinting with malice, their tone menacing.

"Hand over the gun, boy, or we'll make you wish you had."

Their leader, a tall, imposing figure, strode forward, his large spurs jingling loudly in the quiet room. Tiburcio, Higuera, and Anastacio waited anxiously, with Tiburcio standing his ground, holding the gun out before him. The vigilante leader assessed the scene, his eyes sweeping over the dead constable, the bloodied man on the floor, and the weapon in Tiburcio's hand.

"What's going on here?"

Tiburcio hesitated for a moment before speaking.

"This man," gesturing to Higuera, "shot the Constable. I took the gun from him."

The vigilante leader nodded, his expression demanding and unreadable.

"And you," he said, turning to Higuera, "what have you got to say for yourself?"

Higuera still breathing heavily said, "My gun went off by accident during out fist fight. I don't know how."

"You killed a lawman," the vigilante said, his tone flat.

"We don't tolerate that here."

Higuera replied, "I didn't know he was a lawman. I didn't even see him. It was an accident! I didn't start the fight!"

"Doesn't matter, mister, out constable is dead, and you will have to pay for it."

The head man turned to four others and continued.

"Take him away, boys, to the barn."

The leader turned back to Tiburcio and Anastacio, who had already disappeared out the back door, never to be seen by them again.

The vigilantes took their prisoner to the barn, where the local blacksmith boarded and owned horses. They grabbed a cord and roughly tied his arms behind his back. Then they made a noose with a long rope and put Higuera on one of the horses. His face was filled with fear and sweat. He begged for mercy, but the vigilantes were unrelenting. They tightened the noose around his neck and then tied the other end of the rope to a beam above. Higuera's feet dangled off the horse's flanks as he struggled to breathe. The vigilantes stood around him, seething with anger and hatred, their faces unwilling to hide the pride felt in the justice they believed they were serving. Higuera knew that he was going to die. As he gasped for air, he looked around at the faces of the vigilantes. He saw the hatred in their eyes, fear of the unknown, fear of all matter of things, all mixed with morbid curiosity. He knew that he was being punished for being different, for being a Mexican in a town that didn't want him. His thoughts turned to his past crimes and, with that, an expected realization that his demise was inevitable, though he didn't expect it to happen on this day. The vigilantes pulled on the rope, lifting Higuera off the ground and suspending him in mid-air. He struggled and gasped for air, his eyes bulging with terror. Kicking his feet for nonexistent purchase to save himself, he knew this experience of death would soon be over.

The leader looked up at Higuera.

"Your friends will hear of this, and maybe they will know that from now on in this town, scum like yours won't be tolerated."

Higuera kicked his last. His head turned red as it swelled, and his tongue hung from his mouth as his body went limp.

"Take him down and bury him without a marker outside of town in Potters Field." the leader said.

One man lowered the rope as the others carried the lifeless body from the barn. For now, in Monterey, street justice would have to do.

Pyburn had had enough. Tiburcio's reputation for being around trouble grew, and he decided he was bad for business and the spirit of the dance hall. The vigilantes also were not enamored with his involvement in recent events and had Pyburn's ear, guilty or not. It seemed to many that Tiburcio attracted trouble wherever he went, and he felt their cold stares and whispers as he walked the streets of his once beloved town.

Walking along Monterey's busy main road, he took in a chaotic scene of miners, carriages, horses, men, and women bustling about their day. The sun blazed down on the dirt, sending shimmering heat waves into the air. Miners trudged along, their pickaxes and shovels slung over their shoulders, their faces dirty and worn from long hours in the mines. Some of the men carried guns, a reminder of the lawlessness that still haunted the remote town. The cacophony of horses and carriages as they clattered over the parched earth left a wake of dust clouds that stuck to everything, haphazardly coating the buildings and passersby.

The buildings that lined the side street were a mix of styles, from the simple wooden shacks of the miners to the more ornate structures of the wealthy merchants who called Monterey home. Saloons and gambling halls stood alongside shops and boarding houses; the buildings on either side of the street were diverse in their architecture and purpose. A general store with "Supplies" painted in bold letters on the front stood beside a saloon with "Whiskey" written above the door. Further down the street, a brothel with red velvet curtains and dimly lit windows contrasted with the whitewashed adobe walls.

Tiburcio was lost in thought yet no less aware of how much the streets had changed in ten years. He walked over to the cantina where María worked, but she wasn't there. He swung his leg up onto the saddle of Viento and loped out of town to his father's house. Juan was sitting in the shade of the porch in his rocking chair. Tiburcio dismounted, tied Viento to the hitching post, and started to walk past his father. His father stopped him.

"Tibo, some men came by earlier looking for you."

"Who?" he replied.

"They didn't say, but I recognized one of them as the local marshal. Strangely, they only asked if I had seen you but didn't identify themselves or say why. They just asked and left after I told them I hadn't seen you in days."

"Thanks, Papa," Tiburcio muttered.

It had taken little time for local authorities to catch wind of Tiburcio and his gang's activities, and they had put out a warrant for his arrest with a small bounty placed on his head. Although only on suspicion, it was enough to get his attention and was the reason for their visit to the family home. Tiburcio, however, far too clever for them, was always one step ahead.

He continued into the house for his belongings to pack. He filled his saddlebags with hardtacks, a dense bread made with few ingredients that resemble modern-day biscuits, edible for years and hard as a rock. They had to be soaked in water or milk to soften them. He also grabbed a bag of dehydrated beans and some apples. He walked past his father without saying anything and threw the saddlebags on Viento. He then tied his blanket and poncho behind the saddle using some latigo. He finished by dallying his lasso around the horn of his saddle. His father watched curiously as the son he knew only as a stranger now mounted the muscular black stallion and galloped away without looking back.

The crime in Monterey was so rampant that for the small number of bandits caught, as many or more got away. They committed horse thievery and murder with reckless abandon.

Since they had the best horses, most of which they stole from rich Anglos, they could, and were always able to escape utilizing their expert horsemanship.

Tiburcio decided to meet up with Anastacio and ride to Mendocino County to visit Tiburcio's cousin, Elisa, in Rancho De Sanel, which was 250 miles away and in a sparsely populated area of California. Only a few hundred settlers lived there, and they were under the constant hostile threat of attack by Indians. There was no communication with the outside world and no roads. It also had no sheriff or government officials; for that matter, it was the Wild West. The ride took almost a month through the Pomo Indian territory.

To restock their dwindling supplies over the following weeks, Tiburcio and Anastacio made easy prey of lone travelers camped out or in transit on horses or wagons. It was one such heist that gifted Tiburcio a new Colt 44 six-shooter second-model dragoon pistol to replace his single shot. He relieved it from an Anglo who had been napping under a tree and startlingly awakened by two disheveled Mexicans leering down at him. Tiburcio had his revolver's barrel inches from the man's chin.

"You like your chin gringo?"

The wide-eyed man nodded in the affirmative.

"Do you want to keep it?"

Anastacio smiled as he looked on at Tiburcio's bravado. The word

Machismo had not been invented yet, but had it been, it would have characterized the bandit perfectly.

Tiburcio pushed his revolver's barrel into the man's face, unstrapping the man's gun belt with his free hand. Meanwhile, Anastacio grabbed the man's saddlebags and placed them over his horse's saddle. They mounted their horses and slapped the hindquarter of the Anglo's horse, which galloped away. The man probably found his horse later that day, but the bandit duo was long gone by then.

The following night, Tiburcio and Anastacio sat by a modest campfire, their faces illuminated by its dancing flames. The night was quiet save for the crickets chirping in the distance. Tiburcio took a swig from his bottle of tequila and passed it to Anastacio, who did the same before speaking.

"You ever think about how we got here, Tibo?"

Anastacio raised the bottle to his lips, taking another long swig. After a moment, he lowered it and looked at his companion.

"You ask if I ever think about how we got here," he said, his voice low and gritty.

"All the damn time, brother," Tiburcio responded, leaning back against a small boulder, his eyes distant.

"I didn't start this way. I was a happy kid, living a good life at home. But then the gringos and Europeans came. They kicked us all aside and treated us like their underlings. And so, we were born into this life, like our fathers before us."

Tiburcio paused, taking a bite of hardtack.

"I say that because they had to adapt to changing times just like we have to now. It's in our blood, you know? That need to survive, to do whatever it takes to make it through another day and fight back against those who oppress us. They have killed thousands"

Anastacio nodded in agreement.

"It isn't on us, Tibo. They're the ones who pushed us to this life. They stole our land, killed our people, and left us with nothing."

Tiburcio spat into the fire.

"Always taking, never giving. They think they own the world, but they don't have a hold on you and me, amigo."

Tiburcio poked the fire with a stick and sighed.

"I never thought this would be my life, you know? Being a bandito." Anastacio took another swig of his tequila and nodded.

"Same here. But what choice did we have? Well, you had one Tibo. I was not educated, but you were."

Tiburcio contiued tending the fire with a stick.

"True, my friend, but unfortunately, I never got the opportunity to use it. So here I am with your ugly mug."

Anastacio leaned back again and looked up at the stars.

"I used to think we could make a difference. You know, fight back against it all. But now? I don't know. It seems like our destiny is set in stone. Here we are, just the two of us in the middle of nowhere, trying to survive. Right now, I don't see an end to it or a pathway out of it."

Tiburcio shook his head.

"That's the thing, amigo. We don't have a destiny yet. The Anglos made sure of that. But I will damn sure not let them control mine. For now, we'll be banditos on the run."

Anastacio agreed.

"Our lives depend on keeping on the move right now, Tibo. If I have to survive, I'll do it as I please."

Tiburcio carefully laid out his blanket by his saddle and used his poncho as a makeshift pillow. He gazed up at the stars twinkling above as he lay down and heaved a weighted sigh.

"Don't misunderstand me amigo."

"I don't take pleasure in stealing. It goes against everything I believe in, but these are desperate times. California is in chaos. Unfortunately, we are part of that chaos. I see that, and I hope to remedy it if we survive."

Anastacio had just settled down a few feet away and let out a loud and hearty burp as he made himself comfortable for the night.

"You're right." he said, patting his full stomach.

"We'll need all the rest we can get to make our destination. We've got a long ride ahead of us tomorrow."

He lowered his sombrero over his face and, within two minutes, was snoring like a bear.

Tiburcio's cousin's name was Elisa, a plain woman with tough skin from the hours she worked daily in the sun. Her husband Felix, a slight man balding with no chest muscle and a gut for a belly, put the two men to work as herders, not knowing of their criminal past. The hacienda was of good size and well-kept, and he was happy to have these two experienced horsemen to help.

Anastacio grew tired of the boredom after a mere two weeks and returned home, where he was ultimately prosecuted for suspicion of murder and robbery while riding with the Belcher gang. Rumor had it that the gang promised to break him out while he was in jail. They eventually did, but since he was a witness to their crimes, they strung him up to a beam, tied a heavy log to his feet, and left him dangling till he expired.

Tiburcio, however, stayed for a couple more weeks before moving on to his sister's house at the base of the Sierra Nevada Mountain range in Sonora. He visited and worked there for a short time before moving on.

During his solo journey south, he stole two cows from a ranch fifty miles away. He sold them one hundred miles later and made fifty-two dollars to buy supplies for the rest of his trip. Although he could easily steal supplies on the way to Ventura, his new destination, he preferred to pay with gold to avoid unnecessary risks. Whenever he passed a pecan plantation, he would stock up on the sweet nuts and fill his saddlebag. The same was true for wild apples. He sometimes bought dried apples when available, though fresh ones were invariably better. He always left some space in his supply bag for coffee and the occasional wild peach, apricot, or cherry. He spent the next six months living off the land and even admitted to himself while lying on the grass one night, looking at the star-filled sky with his head on his saddle, that he was indeed a thief without a home or a plan. Depression set in, and he drank himself to sleep every night.

Meanwhile, Tiburcio's father was having problems keeping his home and land. At the age of 72, he was becoming infirm, but he was determined to prove his claim to the property. Land sharks were ever on the rise in the area and spent every day trying to scalp land from someone. Juan had been their latest target. He was told to bring in witnesses who could testify to prove his land ownership. He attempted to raise funds to do so, but without help, he was left to his own. He tried to enlist the help of his brother Fernando, but he also was under attack in an endless fight to keep part of his ranch. When the case finally came to court, no witnesses appeared, leaving the faithful soldier with no recourse but to vacate his land. Before he could do so, however, he died, skeletal and heartbroken, his family with no source of income and his wife's health deteriorating; she moved in with Tiburcio's uncle, who, in the end, did manage to keep a small part of his ranch.

Six

Tiburcio had finally finished his long journey and now resided in Ventura with his older brother, Chico. He had no money and was living day to day by the grace of Chico's kindness. There was not much to do there, so Tiburcio had begun hanging around with a new friend, a horse thief named Raul, whom he had met at the local bar. Unbeknownst to Tiburcio, his compadre had stolen some horses and pawned them a week earlier.

The rain was pouring down the day the two decided to ride into Ventura for drinks at Raul's favorite cantina. Tiburcio was on Viento as they trotted down the muddy street toward the bar, their hats pulled low, and their collars pulled up under their full-length ponchos.

Tiburcio and Raul heard horses approaching fast from their rear. They exchanged wary glances as two sheriffs' horses galloped and pulled up beside them, splattering mud all over their boots. The rain hammered down, making it difficult to see or hear much, but the urgency in the sheriff's voice riding alongside them was unmistakable.

"Hey, you two! Hold up!"

Tiburcio and Raul pulled the reins of their horses and turned to face the law enforcement officers. Tiburcio knew the encounter wasn't going to end well.

"What's the problem, Sheriff?" he asked, his voice calm despite his racing heart.

"We received a report that two horses were stolen from a nearby farm last week. We have reason to believe that you and Raul are the ones that pawned them. We're going to need you both to come with us."

"What?" Raul protested, his voice rising.

"I didn't steal any horses, and these are ours!"

The sheriff's eyes locked onto Raul's, his hand resting on his weapon as he spoke slowly and deliberately in a commanding tone.

"Take your gun out, slow, by the handle, and hand it over to me, son."

His partner, a stern-faced deputy, mirrored his instructions to Tiburcio.

Raul's hand twitched, instinctively moving towards his holster before he managed to steady himself and pull out his gun. Tiburcio followed suit, his eyes nervously moving between the sheriff and Raul. He noticed that the officials had the new Colt 44 six-shot revolvers, and their demeanor showed an immediate desire to use them as their hands were already on the pistol grips. For a tense moment, the two law enforcement officers faced off against the two suspected criminals. Raul's eyes pierced his opponents with anger, but he knew better than to make a move in this situation. Tiburcio, on the other hand, seemed ready to bolt at any moment.

Finally, sighing with resignation, Tiburcio spoke up.

"You're making a big mistake, Sheriff. We haven't done anything wrong."

The sheriff stared at Tiburcio but didn't respond. Raul and Tiburcio exchanged worried glances.

"Is there anything we can do to prove these horses are ours?"

Raul spat on the ground; the spit joined the spattering raindrops; his voice was laced with disdain.

"Fucking bullshit!"

The sheriff's face remained stoic, betraying no hint of apprehension.

"Sorry, boys, but we'll have to take you in and sort this out at the jail-house," the first sheriff said, reaching for his handcuffs.

The sheriffs leaned over from their mounted positions and cuffed both suspects in front so they could still ride to the jail. No one wanted to walk in the pouring rain and mud.

Tiburcio happened to be in the wrong place at the wrong time. He had found himself in an untenable situation due to his affiliation with Raul and the illicit activities involving them. He was found guilty merely by association, but he knew fate had caught up with him and would ensure justice for his past and the previous transgressions which had gotten away with. It was a harsh reality that Tiburcio would have to live with for the rest of his life.

When they got to the jail, the sheriff asked for proof of ownership of their horses.

Tiburcio pleaded with the officer.

"Please, sir, I beg you to let me keep my horse. He has been my loyal companion since I was a boy. My uncle gave him to me, and I cannot stand to lose him."

The officer eyed Tiburcio with suspicion.

"Son, do you have proof of that?"

"No," Tiburcio answered.

"If you cannot provide proof of ownership, then the horse rightfully belongs to the State. We can't make exceptions."

Tiburcio hung his head in defeat.

"I understand, sir, but may I at least say goodbye to him?"

The officer nodded.

"You have five minutes."

Tiburcio rushed over to Viento, tears streaming down his face. He hugged the horse's neck, whispering in his ear.

"I'm sorry, boy, I'm so sorry. I couldn't save you." Viento nuzzled Tiburcio's cheek as if to comfort him.

Tiburcio reluctantly let go, handing the reins over to the officer. He watched regretfully with sadness as Viento was led away. He knew he would never see Viento again.

The sheriff gave a cold, hard stare at Tiburcio as if trying to identify any ounce of weakness that could be exploited.

"I'm sorry, son, but the law is the law. Your horse is now evidence in a criminal investigation, and we can't afford to take any chances."

Tiburcio's heart was breaking at the thought of losing his beloved horse. He had ridden Viento since the beast was broken, winning every race he had entered. They had traveled together through the roughest terrains, and Viento had never let him down. He wondered what would become of his horse now in the hands of the law. No one would be able to ride him. Would he be sold to the highest bidder or a slaughterhouse?

Raul and Tiburcio exchanged glances, both feeling helpless, trapped and at a loss as to what awaited them in the immediate future

The jail was a decrepit old building with cold, stone walls that reeked of mildew and despair. The only light source was a small, barred window that barely let in sunlight. The rain outside continued to pour, making the atmosphere inside the jail sorrowful.

Tiburcio felt overwhelming sadness. If only he had made better choices in life, he wouldn't be in this predicament. He kept thinking about Viento, wondering how he would fare in the stable without him. The thought of losing his loyal friend brought with it devastating grief.

Raul, on the other hand, seemed resigned to his fate. He had been in and out of jail before and knew the drill. He sat on the unforgiving bench and lit a cigarette.

"Well, Tibo, I guess this is where we part ways. Try not to get too comfortable in here. The food is shit."

One of the jail's deputies awakened Tiburcio the following day.

"Wake up!"

Tiburcio had not slept much and groggily looked over to the cell door where the deputy was standing with the wanted poster of Tiburcio facing outward.

"Yep, I think this looks a lot like you, cabrón. Get your stuff. Time for you to see the magistrate."

In 1849, California elected judges to serve in their courtrooms. Unfortunately, the ongoing crime epidemic had caused a significant increase in workload for these judges, leading to heightened stress and impatience. In one county, only two judges were available to preside over cases, both overburdened with a seemingly never-ending stream of legal proceedings. As a result, they were often short with defendants, making it difficult for them to receive a fair trial.

When he met his appointed lawyer, Tiburcio immediately detected the lingering scent of alcohol on his breath and stale tobacco smoke reeking from his pasty white complexion and skinny frame. This disheveled appearance did little to instill Tiburcio with the confidence needed to overcome the complex legal battle he faced. He looked for Raul but didn't see him. Within a few minutes, it would become apparent why.

Previously accused of theft, Raul cooperated with the authorities by turning in state evidence and implicating Tiburcio as the thief they sought. Tiburcio was already a wanted man, which made the prosecutor's case even more vital. Despite being overworked, the prosecutor offered Raul immunity for his cooperation. Although arguably unfair, the arrangement allowed the authorities to bring a criminal to justice and potentially forestall future crimes. The case was quickly settled without opposition. Tiburcio, a wanted man, had no alibi, and his inept, hungover lawyer wasn't up for sparring with the prosecutor.

The judge was a very thin man with a hooked nose and greased down hair. He displayed an air of dispassionate disassociation and glared at Tiburcio with a severe expression.

"The evidence is conclusive, young man. You have been convicted of stealing horses. I sentence you to five years in San Quentin Prison. The bailiff will escort you to the prison wagon, and you will be taken immediately to the ship *Euphemia*, by which you'll be transported to your destination to serve your sentence."

"But I didn't steal those horses." Tiburcio protested.

"Raul did."

The prosecutor scoffed.

"That's a likely story. The defendant is a known criminal with a history of theft and violence. Whether it was these horses or others, he must be locked up to be taught a lesson to protect society."

Tiburcio gritted his teeth in frustration.

"I may have made mistakes in the past, but I'm telling you the truth. I didn't steal any horses."

"I have heard enough, Mr. Vasquez!" the Judge bellowed, his gavel pounding against the wooden block.

Losing interest and patience quickly and wanting to feed his skinny frame to a hardy lunch across the street he waived the defendant off.

"Bailiff, please escort the prisoner out of the courtroom."

Tiburcio slumped in his seat, knowing what would follow. The bailiff, a burly man with a stern expression, approached him, had him stand and firmly handcuffed his wrists. Tiburcio's head hung low as he was led out of the courtroom, his feet shuffling against the cold tile floor.

The bailiff marched him outside, where a prison wagon awaited. His stomach churned as he saw the cramped space he would be confined in for transport to the ship. The buggy would take him to Ventura Harbor, where he would board the ship bound for San Francisco Harbor to begin his new life behind bars.

As he climbed into the wagon, he took one last look at the outside world, trying to fathom that he may never know and live in it again as he formerly had.

The ride aboard the prison ship *Euphemia* was unbearable. The inhospitable cells were built in the belly of the boat. The seventeen others traveling with Tiburcio were a motley crew of hardened criminals, all with unique stories and reasons for being there. Some had tattoos covering their entire bodies; others had scars and bruises, testaments to their lives of violence. There were murderers, thieves, drug dealers, and even a few corrupt politicians thrown in for good measure. Tiburcio surveyed the rabble, of which he was now a member. Two particularly stood out.

Big Tony, a towering man with a shaved head and tattoos covering his face, had been convicted of multiple counts of armed robbery and assault and had a reputation for being one of the most dangerous men in the prison system. Beside him sat an Italian named Rico, a wiry man with a thin mustache and a constant sneer on his face, who had been caught stealing horses. He had a history of opium abuse and was one of the most cunning prisoners on board.

The prisoners were tossed around like rag dolls as the ship rocked back and forth across the choppy waters. The smell of sweat, vomit, and feces oppressed any hope for fresh air, and the constant sounds of men getting sick made it nearly impossible to sleep. The only respite from the monotony was the occasional meal, which was invariably bland and tasteless. In the corner, a group of men were playing poker, their faces identifiable only by the dim light of a large candle. One had a thick scar running down the side of his face, and another sported a missing finger. They appeared indifferent to their cramped quarters so long as they had a deck of cards between them and the bottle of whiskey they had smuggled to pass around.

Overlooking San Francisco Bay, San Quentin opened in 1854. Prior to that, prisoners were incarcerated on prison ships in the harbor. Indeed, the *Euphemia* transporting Tiburcio was now to be permanently parked. The prison's construction began two years earlier and was built on the backs of prisoner labor. Its private management corrupted its promise, as its officials were allowed to hire out the inmates for profit. The facility, only a few years old, housed crowded and inhumane living conditions beset with brutality, including floggings and shower baths where inmates were stripped and sprayed with high-power hoses by the guards. The security at the prison left much to be desired, and in its first year, more than 80 inmates escaped.

Tiburcio had heard countless stories of the infamous San Quentin prison and the horrors that took place within its walls. The heavy iron gates loomed ahead as he stepped onto the rough wooden wharf. The tower had been built from stones from a nearby quarry and stood two stories high. Referred to by the prisoners who made it as 'The Stones,' it housed over five hundred prisoners, one-quarter of whom were Spanish, sentenced there for livestock theft like Tiburcio. Escorted through a second gate that surrounded the prison yard, he eyed five watch towers operated by guards with colt dragoons or model 1844 percussion rifles nicknamed the Mississippi Yager.

His spirit dwindled under the deafening clanging metal and echoes of heavy footsteps. The correctional officers, if they could be called that, lacked any sense of order or discipline, and they had no uniforms. Worse, many showed up for duty inebriated. Since there were only twenty guards to manage a prison teeming with dangerous criminals, certain trusted inmates were tasked with supplementing the guards' numbers, some of whom were even allowed to carry guns. It was tricky to distinguish guards from inmates.

Reaching the innermost areas of the prison, Tiburcio sickened from the stench of sweat and despair. The walls were a dull gray, and the dim lighting cast eerie shadows over everything, imparting darkness and austerity opposite the vibrant world outside. The life full of vitality and color that Tiburcio once knew was gone, replaced by one bereft of aspiration. Feeling small and insignificant within its drab and lifeless walls and sizeable prison yard, he couldn't help but be overtaken by hopelessness. This would be his new home, his new life for the foreseeable future. The prisoners around him were a rough and intimidating bunch, their eyes perversely scanning the new arrivals. Tiburcio did his best to keep his head up and eyes averted, but he couldn't shake off the physical weight of their curiosity. He'd need to be tough to survive.

He entered a large room, where he was strip-searched and sprayed down with a hose. Notes were made in a register with his height of 5'8", black hair, and brown eyes. Without photography for mug shots, all the convict's identifying features were noted. Tiburcio had a scar on his left breast, left forefinger, and left thumb. He was given the convict number 1217 and handed his clothing back. There was no prison uniform.

"Hey, you there!" shouted one of the guards, a burly man with a thick mustache.

"Go over and grab a mattress and blanket."

Tiburcio walked over to an inmate who stacked a straw-stuffed mattress and blanket onto his arms. The items appeared clean, but he later discovered they were infected with lice. He trudged along the dank corridor, his path obstructed by the crisscrossing of shadows cast by the bars in the sunlight emanating from the tiny windows above. As he walked down the grimy hallway, he heard the coarse voices of the guards yelling at the prisoners.

"Get in line, you scum!"

"You ain't nothin' but a bunch of fuckin' lowlifes!"

They continued shuffling past cells, heads bowed, finally entering their claustrophobic compartments. Some of them were covered in bruises and cuts, evidence of the brutal beatings they had endured at the hands of their keepers. As he passed one of the cells, Tiburcio heard a man sobbing.

"Please, God, help me."

He finally reached his cell and was physically pushed into it by the stone-faced guard escorting him. Tiburcio looked back at him as he slammed the sheet iron door closed. Its small opening for ventilation and the critical turn of the lock reinforced the finality of it all. The stench of the cell hit him before turning to see two bunk beds to house four prisoners. The three in there just lifted their heads and turned away. The four of them would share one slop bucket to relieve themselves.

Night fell upon his new home, and he lit the small candle provided. Eventually, the noises of the prison's interiors settled into silence, with an occasional voice yelling out profanities and challenges. Finally turning in, he could hear rats scurrying across the floor and the echoes of cockroaches climbing walls of corridors. Tiburcio was lucky compared to the three hundred other inmates housed in the main dormitory. They slept in bunks stacked three high. More than one hundred of the convicts didn't have shoes.

Waking the next day, Tiburcio was marched to breakfast behind a skinny, sickly-looking inmate in tattered clothes. The meal consisted of meat, beans, and bread. The unbearable smell was one his nose, over time, would get used to. They marched through the inner prison's west gate and then to the outer gate, where bricks were made. It had been years since he had made the adobe clay bricks for his uncle's barn. Now, he was put to hard labor digging clay for the brick molds. Those not used in prison were sold to the outer civilian population.

As he began digging, a voice called out from behind.

"Hey, new guy. What are you in for?"

He turned to see a burly man with a shaved head and rough features. One of his eyes was blind and milky white.

"Uh, I don't want to talk about it," he replied, trying to keep his head down and focus on his work.

"Suit yourself," the man shrugged, "but if you need anything, you come to me. My name's Tito."

"Thanks, Tito," he muttered, feeling a glimmer of hope in this bleak place.

They worked in silence for a while, the only sounds being the scraping of shovels and the clinking of chains. Eventually, Tito spoke up again.

"You know, I've been in this place for five years. And it doesn't get easier. You have to find ways to survive, you know? Like finding a friend or a connection to the guys in charge here."

Tito chuckled and moved closer to Tiburcio, leaning in so that his lips were almost touching Tiburcio's ear.

"I can offer you more than just a job, Tiburcio. I can offer you protection. You do know what happens to men in prison who don't have protection, don't you?"

He made the sign of humping with his hips.

"I don't need your protection, Tito," Tiburcio said, shaking slightly.

"I can handle myself."

Tito's expression darkened, and he grabbed Tiburcio's arm, pulling him closer.

"Don't be foolish. You don't want to end up like those other men, do you? I can make sure you're safe. All you have to do is agree to work for me."

Tiburcio's heart was racing, and he felt a bead of sweat trickle down his forehead. He knew he was in a precarious position but wouldn't accept Tito's offer.

"I can't do it," he said, his voice barely above a whisper.

Tito's grip on his arm tightened, and Tiburcio winced in pain.

"You'll regret this, "Tito growled.

"Watch your back, cabrón."

Tiburcio swallowed hard and backed away from Tito, his eyes wide. A guard yelled over to them.

"Quit fucking off and get back to work!"

For some unknown reason, Tito wasn't present the next day. Tiburcio felt happy for such small favors—as he did his weekly bath in an open pool of cold, often foul water nicknamed 'The Rose Bowl.' Any free time he had was spent out of the cell reading a book or, mostly, gambling. Winning most games brought him notoriety for his card skills. He had a knack for reading people and playing his cards in a way that he always came out on top. This night was no exception. He sat at the table with four other inmates, each wearing a playful smirk as they exchanged witty insults.

"Hey, Tiny, you going to bet or just stare at me all night?" one of the guys said, poking fun at the petite man at the table.

"At least I don't need a booster seat to see over the table,"

Tiny shot back, causing everyone to laugh.

Another inmate joined.

"Hey, Tibo, have you ever played poker with a deck of Tarot cards?"

Tiburcio raised an eyebrow.

"Can't say I have. Why do the cards predict my winnings?"

Tiburcio took the opportunity to give a lighthearted warning to his cellmate, Hector.

"You shouldn't smile so much, amigo, with all those gold teeth. Someone might be tempted to knock them out."

An uneasiness washed over Hector as the game continued. He knew that Tiburcio's caution wasn't mere idle chatter. After all, he had seen his fair share of violence in prison and knew that showing any signs of vulnerability would only make matters worse. He did his best to keep a straight face and couldn't help but feel joy as he laid down his next card. The thrill of the game was irresistible.

Tiburcio watched his cellmate as he laughed and smiled, the sparkle of his gold teeth catching the candlelight. He knew that his earlier warning had fallen on deaf ears, but, he could only do so much to protect his fellow inmate.

"I'm tougher than I look," Hector boasted.

"Besides, nobody's stupid enough to mess with me."

Tiburcio wasn't so sure. He'd seen plenty of guys get hurt over the years for much less than a flashy set of gold teeth. He watched Hector to ensure that he didn't get in over his head. As the game continued, Tiburcio sat with a sense of resignation. He knew violence was an unyielding fact of life in prison.

"It's only gambling if you lose, right hombre?" Hector quipped.

The table erupted in laughter, causing the guard on duty to peer over his shoulder, wondering what all the commotion was about. Later, Tiburcio watched Hector strut around the cell.

"You think you're invincible, don't you?" he said, eyeing Hector skeptically.

Hector chuckled confidently.

"I know I'm not invincible, but I can handle myself. You worry too much, Tiburcio. Loosen up a little."

Tiburcio shook his head.

"You're drawing too much attention to yourself, and that can be dangerous, Hector. I share this fucking cell with you, and I don't need the added attention or headaches."

Hector shrugged.

"I'll be fine; we'll be fine, my friend."

Hector always talked tough, a front necessary in prison. In reality, he was frail and couldn't fight his way out of a paper bag, which, depending on the situation, made him Tiburcio's responsibility.

Suddenly, as if on cue, footsteps echoed down the hall, drawing closer and closer until they stopped in front of their cell.

"Hector, you in there?" a voice called out.

Hector stood up, a cocky gold tooth grin spreading across his face.

"Yeah, who's asking?"

The cell door creaked open, revealing a burly man with a scowl.

"You owe me some money, Hector, and I'm not leaving until I get it."

It was Tito, whom Tiburcio had not seen since his first day when he turned down protection. Hector's bravado faltered for a moment before he regained his composure.

"I told you; I don't have it right now. But I'll get it to you, I swear."

Tito shook his head.

"Sorry, Hector. That's not good enough. If I have to, I'll take your teeth as payment."

Tiburcio watched as the situation escalated. Tito moved swiftly, slamming Hector against the wall. Tiburcio stepped forward, his eyes fixed on Tito's towering figure. The muscles in Tito's arms bulged as he pinned Hector against it, but Hector refused to back down.

"Hey, leave him alone," Tiburcio defended, his voice firm.

Tito turned to face Tiburcio, his one good eye flashing with anger as sweat poured down his filthy, beard-filled face.

"Mind your own business, puto," he growled.

Tiburcio stood his ground. He knew he couldn't let Tito hurt Hector anymore, and if he did, he knew he would be next, so he took a deep breath and stepped into the fight. Tito punched Hector again, knocking him to the floor, then turned toward the lunging Tiburcio, their fists flying in the confined area. Tiburcio dodged and weaved economically, his heart pounding. For a moment, it seemed as though Tito had the upper hand, but with one unhesitating move, Tiburcio landed a quick left jab followed by a powerful right punch on Tito's jaw, sending him reeling backward. Tito stumbled but stayed upright against the wall, blood gushing from his nose. Tiburcio was too far in now to stop, so he kicked Tito in the balls. Tito dropped to his knees puking all over the floor. Without slipping in the vomit, Tiburcio drove his thumb into Tito's good eye, blinding him. He screamed in pain, grabbing his face. Tiburcio helped Hector up, and they both dragged the defeated Tito out of the cell, leaving him moaning in the hall.

"I told you, Hector! I fucking told you!"

Hector replied, gasping for breath.

"Yes, you did, Tibo, and you were right. But so was I."

Hector wiped some blood from his lip.

"We beat his sorry ass. Thanks for jumping in but I would have had him."

"Bullshit!" Tiburcio yelled.

"I had no choice, moron! You were going to get your ass kicked! I'm done with you and your false bravado! Get out of my sight!"

Hector reached in and wiggled his gold tooth while spitting some blood to the floor.

"See! Loose but still in there!"

Hector left the cell, calling for a guard to attend to Tito. The next day, Hector was reassigned to another cell.

Seven

Tiburcio, a multilingual speaker, had now served two months of his sentence at San Quentin. He spent time socializing with two different groups: Anglos and Mexicans. He would join a clique of eight to ten people and listen to their stories of past adventures. The Mexicans often reminisced about their homeland, sharing tales of their culture and traditions, while the Anglos talked about their hometowns and families. Tiburcio found solace in these conversations as they provided a temporary escape from the rigors of prison life. He was liked and respected for his intellect and education. Being the interpreter caused both Anglos and Mexicans to see him in a positive and friendly light.

The word was out that Tito wanted revenge and was looking for his closest friends to help take down Tiburcio and Hector. Tiburcio thought back to his first day when Tito offered him protection, which he had refused. Now, he was on his own, a death sentence for many inmates. For the first time, he thought of escape.

Successful escapes from San Quentin were not out of the ordinary, and half of the prisoners who got away were never caught. Those captured were flogged at 'The Ladder,' a leaning wood post shaped like a cross where the prisoner would be tied to receive sometimes up to fifty lashes. Minor infractions in prison started with five. The offender was then put in a dark, solitary cell with only bread and water for the remaining duration of the punishment.

The pier for deliveries and transport was connected to the outside gate of the prison. While helping to load a yacht with brick and walking back toward the yard, Tiburcio heard a guard shouting toward the boat. About twenty prisoners were hopping on and pushing off. The guard continued yelling for them to come back. Still not responding, the guard shot a load of grapeshot with his six-pounder, killing five of them and maiming half a dozen others. Tiburcio had never seen such mutilation, and his confidence in an escape shriveled but didn't disappear.

Over the next couple of weeks, Tiburcio and a large group of his everyday social club devised an escape plan, studying every inch of the prison, memorizing every detail, every guard shift, and routine. They were determined to break free from the oppressive walls that had held them captive for so long, not to mention the threat of Tito and his gang.

The morning of their escape was dark and gloomy. The San Francisco Bay fog blanketing the prison obscured their view of the world outside. The group moved silently through the prison, their senses vigilant from adrenaline and fear. Tiburcio led the way, his eyes darting from one guard to the next, searching for signs of trouble. His mind raced as he considered the many ways in which their plan could go wrong, but he pushed the thoughts aside to focus on the task at hand.

The morning routine started with fifty inmates lining up to cut wood in the forest. The procession would be led by the prison's head carpenter and five heavily armed guards. The gate opened, and one-half of the prisoners led by Tiburcio got through; the lagging twenty-five caused a commotion to divert attention. As the interior guards immediately responded with drawn pistols, Tiburcio and his lot pulled shivs on their two front guards, taking them by surprise and promptly relieving them of their weapons and keys. They shoved the gate closed and locked it, throwing the keys on the ground out of reach. They kept the carpenter and guards tight to them so they would not be shot by the other guards looking down from the towers. They ran for the heavily wooded hills of Mount Tamalpais. Marin County was sparsely populated, so it was not hard for the inmates to split up and scatter themselves.

The news got back to San Francisco, where it was over-reported that hundreds had escaped, and some guards killed. This disinformation helped the prison to form large local armed possies to capture the fugitives. Ten convicts were arrested, a few were killed, and some were wounded. However, with his former travel knowledge, Tiburcio successfully evaded his pursuers. He knew that separating himself from the larger pack was necessary, so he and a fellow inmate, Jaime Mendosa, traveled together. Since striped prison uniforms had not yet become standard at San Quentin, the civilian clothes the two escapees wore allowed them to move inconspicuously. They made a 150-mile hike through Napa and Sacramento counties, ending up in Amador County, followed by a two-week leg to Jackson, where they rested for a few days, completely exhausted. They had made it.

They returned to the trade they knew best and stole two of the local minister's horses riding bareback through Stockton and into the High Sierras. It felt good to be on a horse running free again. Tiburcio felt the wind rushing past his face and through his hair as he leaned forward on the horse's neck. He clung tightly to its mane with his hands as there were no reins or a saddle. He could feel the muscles of the palomino rippling beneath his thighs and their powerful surge of energy as the animal galloped through the pine trees and across the open fields.

As the horse picked up speed, so, too, did Tiburcio's heart. He felt a rush of adrenaline coursing through his veins and let out a whoop of excitement as the world around him became a blur of green and brown. The rhythm of the horse's gallop and its hooves' steady beat against the ground was a primal, exhilarating sensation, and Tiburcio felt like he was flying. The horse's mane whipped across his face, and he could taste the dust and sweat on its skin. His mind went back to being on Viento. The sound of the wind and the horse's breathing filled his ears, drowning out all other noise. Every muscle in his body tensed and relaxed with each stride of the magnificent animal as its raw power effortlessly carried him up a small hill. He urged the horse to go faster. The palomino responded, stretching out its powerful legs. They crested the top of the mountain in a burst of speed. There, he saw a beautiful valley open to him in concert with a large grinning smile on his face.

They had a 100-mile start on their pursuers, and before long, they found themselves in Tiburcio's old neighborhood of Monterey County. After days of surviving on wild berries and nuts and occasionally stealing food from nearby ranches, the two Mexicans were desperate for a decent meal. Their prayers were seemingly answered when they stumbled upon the tavern at Chamberlain's Ferry. Their stomachs grumbled with anticipation as they pulled up to the establishment. However, their hopes were dashed when they noticed two local cattlemen sitting on the porch, Dow and Land. Whispering to each other suspiciously, they eyed the two disheveled Mexicans with mistrust. The weight of unease in the air was palpable as Tiburcio and Jaime cautiously dismounted their horses and approached the tavern.

Tiburcio asked the two men about getting dinner. Land spoke first.

"Where are you men coming from?"

"My uncle drove these horses with a carriage, and we are bringing them back to him. That's why we are bareback," Tiburcio responded.

Dow looked at Tiburcio warily suspicious of his torn old clothing..

"Those are two fine American horses you Mexicans are on."

The cattlemen's suspicions were growing.

"They stopped serving here an hour ago. There's no food for you here."

Jaime felt the rising suspicion and tension.

"Let's go, Tibo; we'll find food elsewhere."

They slowly mounted by grabbing the horse's manes and throwing over their right legs. Dow, now emboldened, instigated Land.

"Let's follow them and see where they're going."

Land nodded in agreement.

"Those horses are damn well stolen. Too good for Mexicans, especially with no saddles."

They mounted their horses and followed at a distance at first and then, about a mile out, closed in on the duo of escaped convicts.

"Hold up!" Dow called out.

Tiburcio and Jamie stopped their horses. Dow and Land approached on each side, sandwiching them between their own. The tall cattlemen had seasoned faces and beards that projected personas not to be messed with.

"The two of you will ride back with us to Stockton," Land ordered.

"Why? We mean no harm. Please let us be on our way," Tiburcio asked.

Dow and Land ignored the plea and put their hands to their pistols. Tiburcio acquiesced while judging the men's intent to use their guns.

"Since you are armed, we have no choice Señor, as you wish. Just remain calm."

"We'll let the sheriff sort this out," Land continued.

"You know damn well you lied to us and that the horses aren't yours or your uncle's. I knew you Mexicans were up to no good, as usual."

Stockton was fifteen miles away.

"I can't go back to jail. Don't take us there, please," Jaime pleaded as he confessed.

"So, you admit to it," Dow persisted, ordering the bandits sarcastically in their native language.

"Vamos, amigos!"

Nearing Stockton, the four stopped, and Dow tied the necks of the convicts' horses together. He then secured the prisoners' feet under the horses bellies so they couldn't escape. They arrived at the hitching post outside the jail. While Dow waited outside, Land went in to get the sheriff. After untying them from their horses, the sheriff immediately led the prisoners into the building. The wooden floors creaked beneath their boots as they made their way inside. A few moments later, another sheriff from

Amador County barged in, breathing heavily. He looked around frantically, his eyes glaring through the open door to where the horses were tied.

"I've been searching all over for those horses!" he exclaimed, his voice filled with urgency.

"Are these the men you found on them? If so, I would like them turned over to me, Sheriff."

"They're all yours," the local sheriff said.

"I'll just put them behind bars for the night. Let me help you find a room and some grub sheriff."

The two sheriffs left a deputy in charge and left.

The following day, Tiburcio and Jaime found themselves in front of a judge, facing the consequences of their actions. They admitted to escaping and stealing the horses, explaining that they had attempted to make the journey on foot but had been unable to. The judge reasoned that was the worst excuse for stealing horses he had ever heard, convicted them both of Grand Larceny and wasted no time ordering them to be transported back to San Quentin that same day. The judge knew there would be sufficient punishment waiting fior them at the prison.

Even though Dow and Land were entitled to a fifty-dollar reward for each of the prisoners they had brought in, neither cattleman claimed it. Perhaps feeling the satisfaction of seeing justice served was reward enough given the extent to which horse thieves were despised. Whatever their reason, they instead took time out of their day to make sure the horses were returned to the minister.

The habitual morning fog crept along the San Francisco Bay into San Quentin, bringing with it an ominous feeling. It had been two weeks since Tiburcio and Jaime had escaped. They knew what would come next. A guard came to Tiburcio's cell to collect him for his punishment. The two entered the main yard and were marched past a yard full of prisoners to an expectant Lt. Moon. In his hand, he held a four-foot strand of rawhide. Tiburcio's heartbeat quickened as he approached Moon. He knew what was coming: a public flogging in front of all the other prisoners. He tried to steel himself and his mind against the pain he would have to endure.

Lt. Moon held the rawhide loosely in his hand, seeming almost bored by the whole affair.

"Tiburcio Vasquez," he said, his voice devoid of emotion.

"You know why you're here."

Tiburcio nodded, unable to speak.

"You escaped from the prison for which you will receive fifty lashes."

Tiburcio nodded again, his eyes cast downward. He leaned forward, and a guard tied him to 'The Ladder.' Then he pulled
Tiburcio's shirt up over his head, exposing a naked back that would never look the same again after the day's punishment.

The first lash ripped his skin ten inches in length; those subsequent were shorter and longer by comparison. By the time the tenth had struck his bleeding back, tears had welled up in Tiburcio's eyes. He grunted with every lash but did not scream, although his mind was bellowing his ears to do so. The lashes were so deep they had ripped a hole in his back. Blood swelled from it profusely. His body was drenched in sweat from the fear of death burning in his heart. As the lash marks reached his trousers, the pain had grown so unbearable that Tiburcio wished he could die. He prayed to God to grant him death, for he could not endure the torture. The mercy of God seemed to hear his cries, for the whipping ceased for a few moments. He took them for granted as a respite and prayed fervently to the Almighty for deliverance. However, not a mere moment later, the punishment resumed. His body tensed from the tormenting pain of every unrelenting whip. In desperation, his mind went to his mother, who had pleaded with him to attend church. Having then dismissed her wishes, Tiburcio now believed it was the reason why God was ignoring his prayers.

It was hard to know how much time had passed since the last blow, but Tiburcio felt certain it had been only seconds. Lt. Moon seemed to derive more than a warranted satisfaction from thrashing a Mexican. Indeed, one could, at times, confuse his grimace while administering lashes with a smile. No one counted to fifty; some who watched were astonished and said it was more than that. Moon's face was twisted into a malicious grin, his eyes brimming with sadistic pleasure. Tiburcio could feel his body trembling with anger and fear, but he refused to let Moon see his weakness.

When Moon had exhausted himself, his uniform soaked in sweat even in the cool air, he motioned to trustees to take Tiburcio to the prison hospital for treatment. Four prisoners lifted him by his hands and feet and carried him. Since antiseptics were not yet invented, the doctor, who was more than familiar with such torturous wounds, applied salt water to keep the shredded flesh from rotting. Tiburcio groaned with pain, his eyes welling up with tears every time the physician touched his back. It was far from the touch he had once felt from María caring for his wounds.

He had known he would be punished and accepted that, but a bitter grudge festered toward Moon for enjoying the whipping and demeaning slights he whispered between lashes.

"Dirty little Mexican thief, I will make you bleed like a stuck pig. Yeah, for that is what you are. A pig. A stinking, groveling pig."

Tiburcio felt his blood boil as he relived the cruel words and the pleasure his tormentor took in punishing him. Looking back at Moon with hatred, he vowed to get revenge someday, even if only wishful thinking.

After seeing the doctor, Tiburcio was put in a dark, confined cell in the dungeon below the hospital with only bread and water. Thoughtless rats, mosquitos, and cockroaches climbed on and across him at will. He had no way of knowing how long he would be there or how much time had passed. The doctor attended a couple of times to change bandages and check for infection. He couldn't sleep or get comfortable owing to the unbearable pain. There were no tears left to shed, only intolerable agony to endure.

Eight

Tiburcio found the extended solitary confinement to a dark cell the hardest. He would lie there alone with only the sound of an occasional water drip from a leaky pipe and the movements of rats and giant insects. His mind drifted back to his carefree days with Viento, his family, María, and the ranch. He remembered waking up to the smell of the fresh hay and the usual morning sounds of the horses whinnying mixed with roosters honking as they chased clucking hens. He recalled the sun's warmth on his face as he rode Viento through the fields, feeling free and alive. He thought of the time he spent with the pretty young women, their laughter and teasing filling him with excitement and possibility. He remembered the songs he had played, the poems he had written and the dances they shared, moving together in synchronized steps to the rhythm of the music. Memories of the vaqueros, the skilled horse riders who worked alongside him, filled him with a deep sense of camaraderie and belonging. How had he come to this?

It was not unusual for those in prison, as in regular life, to review their circumstances as the last thing before sleep. For Tiburcio, regret always crept in. Criminals and the prison replaced the vaqueros and the ranch. Deep in his soul he searched nightly for the innocence he enjoyed as a young man. There was the good, the hope of love and success. He knew it was still there, but his environment forced him to deny it. In prison, goodness made one weak. And, although the memories were sweet, he refused to dwell on them until he was once again free. Only then would he strive for a better life. This night in the dungeon, though, inspired him. The spark of determination to make things right, and succeed in life, would not be smothered by the darkness. He would not let his past mistakes or incarceration at San Quentin define him.

Time passed slowly, and with it, the physical healing of Moon's torture.

Once he was well enough, he was returned to brick duty. He wrote to his mother, Doña Guadalupe, explaining what had happened and that he had been caught on his way to visit her. Tiburcio had always been her favorite child until his turn to a life of crime. He was the only one in the family who had so much potential, throwing it away to become a bandit, and at this point, not even a successful one. Ashamed and embarrassed by his behavior, she refused to respond.

He resumed his plans to escape once released from the dungeon. This time, his fellow conspirators were mostly Anglos and only a few Mexicans. As a consequence of the last breakout, the entire prison was locked down. All weapons found were confiscated, and the guilty parties were each given twenty lashes. That didn't stop Tiburcio's new friends from making new shanks and shivs as is common in all prisons.

Two months after his last escape, Tiburcio and his crew loaded bricks onto a schooner named the *Bolinas*. Lt. Moon was in charge of the work crew. He barked orders and cursed at inmates for being too slow.

"You useless fucking Mexicans take forever every time we load. Move it, or my club will feel your ass!"

He held a short club with which he would strike the workers if they didn't respond to his disparaging threats. He was about to deliver a blow to Tiburcio when another prisoner grabbed Moon's arm, twisting it. Moon screamed in pain. Twenty of Tiburcio's Anglo conspirators restrained him and boarded the *Bolinas*. Tiburcio was set to exact revenge on the Lieutenant and pulled out his homemade dagger. He rushed toward Moon.

"You son of a bitch, I am going to stick you to your spine!"

The other inmates edged him on.

"Kill him, Tibo! Cut his throat!"

He was about to sink his dagger into Moon when another inmate named Charles Ryan intercepted and took the knife away. Moon had treated Ryan well in the past, and they had what seemed a strange, if uncomfortable, friendship. Ryan threatened the crowd to move away from Moon. All complied except Tiburcio, who stood his ground.

"Fuck you, Ryan! Get out of my way!"

He moved toward Ryan, who took a slice at him. His reflexive step back evaded the knife. Just then, an explosion thundered from the prison and distracted Ryan's second attempt to do it again. Guard Post Five had fired their six-pound cannon into the mob of potential escapees, releasing a barrage of alternating grape shots (small caliber rounds packed tightly in a canister bag) and canister shots (iron balls). The convicts instinctively grabbed Moon and held him in front to shield themselves, but this time, the guards had orders to disregard the safety of the hostages. The cannon boomed relentlessly in concert with the guards' Mississippi Yager rifles. The momentum of the lead shots hitting the schooner sent timber and splinters raining down on the escapees. One bullet shattered Moon's whipping arm. Ryan grabbed him and retreated below deck, covering him with bags of grain to protect him. On deck, the prisoners faced an unabating incoming assault. Burke, "Long John Dixon," and Winchell were killed. More grapeshot sheared off the limbs of six others and ravaged the *Bolinas's* sails and rigging with equal ferocity. It collapsed on the escapees who couldn't find an inch to hide. They screamed above the blasts of cannon and rifle fire.

"We surrender! Stop killing us!... Please!"

As firing ceased, twelve guards approached in whaling boats to secure the inmates. They climbed onto the blood-splattered deck and stepped around the moaning wounded and dead to retrieve the prisoners. Searching the boat, they noticed the shocked faces of the convicts, their eyes glazed over, and some nearly catatonic. Tiburcio Vasquez had survived without so much of a nick. To his good fortune, Moon's whipping arm was so severely injured it would be long before he would again revel at 'The Ladder,' and, since Tiburcio himself was still healing from Moon's previous lashing, he was again confined to his solitary dank cell - a boon, it seemed, for any further punishment would have killed him.

A month later, Tiburcio gave S.T. Berreyesa a letter to deliver to his mother, Doña Guadalupe. S.T. had visited a family member, Damaso Berreyesa, an inmate at San Quentin. After the visit the fellow bandit and two friends rode to Alameda County, where they stole several horses, moving on to Lafayette County, where they stole three saddles. The posse, formed as soon as the owner discovered the saddles missing, followed in pursuit, catching up with the three bandits at the base of Mount Diablo. The thieves were unwilling to turn over the saddles. The posse fired on them, and Berreyesa took a bullet in the head. His companions raised their arms in surrender. The bleeding and disoriented leader was still breathing as the posse members approached. They hoisted him onto one of the stolen horses without hesitation and rode towards the nearest doctor's office. Berreyesa's friends followed on foot, their hands bound together in a tight knot.

The doctor was known to be a bit of a miracle worker, and he managed to stabilize Berreyesa's condition. However, it was clear that he would never fully regain consciousness. The authorities found Tiburcio's letter in

Berreyesa's pocket. In it, he spoke to his mother about his writing earlier, not hearing back from her. He lied and noted that he was now trying to live a life of virtue, was looking to the future, and sending his best to the family. He wished her happiness. These words were not faithful to form and were overtly manipulative. The letter was forwarded to her, and his mother took it to heart. She bought tickets for a steamer to Los Angeles to meet with a family friend, Juan Sepulveda. Sepulveda had been a judge from a highly respected family and had ties to Governor John Downey, who was originally a California pioneer.

After hearing the pleadings for help from Doña Guadalupe, Sepulveda went to Ezra Drown, the prosecutor in Tiburcio's first case, where he was convicted of horse thievery. Drown read Tiburcio's letter to his mother, which deeply moved him, particularly the bandit's change of heart at such a young age. He felt that he might be redeemed to a more virtuous life, so he petitioned Governor Downey to release Tiburcio, citing that the length of imprisonment was too much for the young lad. He set out to acquire petition signatures of prominent Anglos. The nearly fifty who signed did so unaware of the other offenses Tiburcio was involved in since his first arrest; however, the otherwise good plan to get him out of prison legally failed when the other details of his offenses saw the light of day.

Tiburcio was frustrated and again began plotting another escape. He befriended Damaso Berreyesa, the twenty-three-year-old family member S.T. had visited. Damaso was a large and powerful man and a notorious outlaw. Damaso tried to be a model prisoner and was incarcerated on flimsy evidence that charged him with horse theft. A petition for his release had also been denied, and they discussed at length what to do next. Sitting on their cell's dusty, concrete floor late one night with only the dim light of a candle casting shadows across their faces, Tiburcio ran a hand through his unkempt hair, his eyes fixed on the ceiling.

"We can't stay here forever," he said soberly.

"They'll work us to death, or worse."

Damaso nodded, his own eyes dark and brooding.

"I know. I'm tired of being treated like an animal. Even as prisoners, we deserve better than this."

Tiburcio leaned forward, his voice dropping even lower.

"We need to escape. Get out of here and start fresh. Somewhere they can't find us."

Damaso's eyes widened.

"Are you crazy? You tried twice and failed. What makes you think the next break out will end better?"

Tiburcio shook his head.

"I learned from my mistakes and all hope is now lost. Listen, a lot of cons have escaped successfully and not returned. This time, I will review every detail and refrain from being reckless. We have to plan the way out. I have been talking to others about many of us going simultaneously. A rainstorm next week will help cover our escape, especially our tracks."

And so it was, only three short months after the last attempt, thirty prisoners again planned their test for freedom. It was mid-afternoon in the middle of January, and the clouds had just let loose a torrent of rain. Deputy Warden Pennie, Lt. Moon, turnkey John Davis, and Sheriff Kennard were huddled, smoking with their collars up under the porch roof outside the prison offices. Kennard had just dropped off a convict and wasn't armed since it wasn't allowed in the prison itself.

The thirty inmates were out of sight, just around the corner from the office. Because of the storm and fog, the visibility was so low that the guard tower assigned to that area could not see them.

The main gate had just opened to let in a supply cart when part of the group of convicts burst into the turnkey's office, as planned, to get weapons. Though they frantically looked, they found none. The rest of the group pulled out their homemade knives and grabbed the four officers on the porch. The crowd moved through the downpour, roughly pushing them forward. Kennard slipped, falling into the mud, but was immediately lifted by Damaso's strong hand, half dragging him along as they approached the open gate. The riotous mob rushed the gate guard and stabbed him in the stomach. Tiburcio pushed past a guard as the prisoners behind Tiburcio knocked him over and took turns stomping him until the blood gushed from his head into the brown mud. It was a frenzy moving quickly.

Pushing and shoving the hostages forward, they shouted, "Out the door, out the door!"

Guards screamed from the other towers, finally witnessing the escape, and the gate was quickly reinforced and closed. Only half of the prisoners, including Damaso and Tiburcio, made it through.

Damaso's wet grip slipped, and Sheriff Kennard pulled away, ripped off his rain-soaked coat, and threw it over Damaso's head. While Damaso was fighting his way out of the coat, the sheriff ran back to the gate to retrieve his pistol. He shouted to the guards, quickly assembling,

"Get your Yagers, men, and follow me!"

Visibility was still bad—only about 20 yards.

"Hurry, we must catch them before the creek!"

Damaso looked back and saw his pursuers. He grabbed the deputy warden and put his knife to his throat.

"Tell them to stop, or I will stick this deep in your neck!"

The warden did the opposite and shouted to his men.

"Shoot the bastards. Shoot them!"

Damaso repeated his threat.

"I'm not fucking around here! Tell them to back off!"

He pushed the knife slightly forward, drawing blood that started mixing with the descending rain. Tiburcio watched in horror. Escape was one thing; he didn't want to be part of the warden dying. The warden was unfazed and yelled again.

"Shoot now! Kill them! Anyone who doesn't will be fired immediately! Shoot! Shoot!"

Damaso hit him across the side of his head, stunning him, to shut him up.

The first to fire was the sheriff, who made an accurate shot with his colt, hitting Damaso in the head. His legs faltered immediately, and he dropped like a rag doll face-first into the mud. He was dead before he landed. The guards continued, firing their Mississippi Yager rifles and Colt pistols into the mob. Two more of the dozen left fell dead to the ground, and the hostages were freed from their grasps. The volley of repetitive onslaught took the multitude of escapees to the mud. All received wounds, including Tiburcio. The guards approached the sodden heap of moaning and wounded bodies writhing on the ground and kicked them.

"Get up, you piece of shit. You will all see the ladder for this!"

Carts were wheeled out from the prison to move the severely wounded back to the hospital, where all were eventually treated. Those who had received only minor wounds due to the weakness of gunpowder, not unusual in the early days of firearms, got their comeuppance at the hands of Moon, who was now ready and meaner than ever. Most got fifty lashes for their sins, an effort that exhausted Moon. He handed the rawhide to his associate to finish the punishment. By the end, those whipped only wished they had been shot, like Tiburcio, who was spared 'The Ladder' thanks to his severe gunshot wound.

Repeated attempts at escaping the hell of San Quentin continued, inspired as they were by the successes of the many who had. In that year alone, eighty-three prisoners had escaped, and upwards of 460 found freedom in the nine years following. The stories became lore in the prison and incited continual attempts. There was always a chance of getting out, and most would rather die trying than endure the brutality behind its walls. This, at least, is how Tiburcio saw it. The punishments he endured had their effect, and for the time being, he put the thought of escape far from his mind.

Nine

Over the next eight years, Tiburcio grew into his late twenties and became highly respected by his peers in the prison. He had friends of both races, Anglo and Mexican. He was admired for his sense of humor, quick-wittedness, and ability to think under pressure. Outwardly, he projected confidence and strength. Inwardly, he loathed every minute spent in the hell hole, so much so that with only one year left of his already extended sentence, he committed his brilliance to one of United States history's most significant and most prominent prison breaks.

He had always been a mastermind when it came to planning. It was the execution of the plan that had failed in the past. He had worked out every detail of this next break, from how they would acquire the necessary tools to the exact moment they would escape. This time, the plan involved seizing weapons and hostages and putting the cannons out of commission. But Tiburcio knew he couldn't do it alone. He called upon his closest friends inside and outside the prison to help. They all agreed, even knowing that if the plan failed, they would face the most severe consequences yet.

As the escape day approached, Tiburcio's nerves were getting the best of him. Previous failures at escape were analyzed over and over. Previous mistakes were reviewed, and plans were made to correct them. Of course, 'The Ladder' was always in his mind as a punishment if caught. Nonetheless, he projected confidence. Many of the failed attempts previously were due to the mistakes of his fellow inmates. He couldn't let his fear show, not in front of his team.

The inmates planning to escape had just left the mess hall at noon that hot July day to return to work in the brickyard. On Tiburcio's cue, seventeen of the 134 total broke into a sprint. The seasoned guards immediately opened fire. This time, Tiburcio didn't lead them to the creek. They had learned from experience not to run for the hills unarmed. Instead, they headed for the main outer wall and ducked behind it for cover. The air quickly filled with the smell of gunpowder and the cacophony of rifle fire. Men were screaming orders from guard positions.

Tiburcio quickly signaled for his men to stop and take cover. They crouched behind the wall, catching their breath and listening to the chaos that ensued. One of his men turned to him.

"What now, boss?"

"We wait for the guards to reload. Then we make our move."

Tiburcio's voice was steady, unaffected by the chaos around them.

As they waited, Tiburcio thought back to the weeks of planning that led up to this moment. He had studied the guards' routines, memorized the prison's layout, and even bribed a few guards to look the other way. All for this moment.

"OK, let's go!" he shouted.

They ran to the warden's office where the pasty white, obese warden, John Chellis, hid cowardly behind his desk chair. Chellis had no qualifications for the office he held. It paid well, and his family influenced him to get into office in the hopes of taking care of them in return and using the position to springboard into higher office.

Tiburcio grabbed him by the back of his collar.

"Come with me, warden; you're our ticket out of here. If you do what I say, you can feed your fat belly tonight. If not, you had your last meal at lunchtime."

Chellis immediately broke out sweating profusely, his eyes wide and searching for divine intervention to save him. The gate guard, Murphy, who had every key to the prison on a large, heavy chain, used them to fight off the escapees. He was a brave and dedicated soul and continued his losing fight as Chellis ordered him to give them up. Still refusing, he was beaten to the ground and only gave them up when prisoners pried his hand open by breaking his fingers.

While protected by the wall, Tiburcio led his men around the wall to the opposite side of the prison, where a second main gate was. They used the keys and broke back into the main yard, allowing more men to escape.

"Run, men, Run! Freedom! Freedom for all!" they yelled.

The sound of clanging metal and shouting filled the air as more prisoners emerged from their cells, finally joining the growing swarm of over two hundred and fifty men. They grabbed hammers and axes from the tool sheds. The sounds were jarring. Tiburcio's heart swelled with pride at the sight of his fellow inmates finally tasting the sweetness of freedom. They had been denied it for so long.

Their moment of triumph was short-lived. As they made their way toward the outer walls of the prison, they were met with a barrage of gunfire from the guards stationed on the watchtowers. Tiburcio's men scattered, seeking cover behind whatever they could find, but the hail of bullets was relentless. Even still, hundreds stormed through the gate to feel free, overwhelming the outside guards and taking their weapons.

Tiburcio gritted his teeth and pressed on, determined to lead his men to safety. He could feel the heat of the bullets whizzing past his face, the acrid smell of gunpowder filling his nostrils. Smoke enveloped the prison. He had never been so alive and so scared. He shouted over the noise, his voice barely audible.

"Keep moving, boys! Don't stop until we reach the tower!"

The men nodded; their faces promised determination. They knew the risks they were taking but had no other choice. They had to get to the tower and remove the guards to aid in the escape. They continued nearing the tower with bullets whizzing, grazing their clothes, or hitting the wall behind them. One of the men next to Tiburcio fell to the ground. He screamed in agony as he clutched his leg. His artery had been shot, and with every heartbeat, crimson red pulsed from his body. He was dead a minute later.

"Keep moving!" Tiburcio yelled, trying to keep his voice steady after watching him bleed out. He couldn't let himself be distracted by that or the surrounding chaos.

When they finally reached the tower, Tiburcio signaled for the men to split up and remove the guards from different angles. He climbed the stairs, adrenaline coursing and his heart pounding, and upon reaching the top, he found two guards waiting for him, their rifles aimed directly at him. He had yet to arm himself. As both guards prepared to fire on him, he realized he was about to die when he heard the loud crack of two Mississippi Yager rifles that came to rest from behind on each of his shoulders fired by his comrades. The guards fell, one hit in the face and the other in the chest. Tiburcio welcomed the ringing in his ears as a reminder of an angel who saved him.

At another tower, two guards were firing cannon shots into the large crowds. Each volley wounded and killed at least two or three men below. The lead grape shot blasts tore flesh and limbs from bodies in horrifying concert with screams of pain. The overweight warden, one among the mob, was not nearly as brave as the one in the last escape attempt.

"Stop firing! Stop! I order you to stop!" he repeatedly yelled.

After a time, he whimpered.

"Please, for the love of God."

The guard firing the cannon into the prisoners saw Chellis and swung his gun away and toward the ocean. He drove a spike into the touchhole after firing it, which rendered the cannon useless. Several of the prisoners arrived in the tower. Infuriated to find that the guard had spiked the touchhole, they lifted and threw him from the tower. He landed hard with the sound of breaking twigs that turned out to be his two legs. He would survive the fractures but writhed in pain for hours.

Tiburcio and his men moved past the brickyard workers. About fifty of them refused to join the escape as they were short timers. One of his men held Chellis as a shield as they moved toward the harbor. Just then, the nearest guard tower opened fire despite the warden's pleas not to. The grapeshot tore into bodies. Bits of blood-stained flesh mixed with screams as half a dozen mortally wounded men fell to the ground. The cannoneer reloaded and fired again, repeating the hellish devastation. Through the smoke, fire, and screams, Tiburcio watched some inmates board the prison sloop a distance away from him. They managed to get aboard since many of the original hundreds of prisoners were returning to the yard to surrender. The firepower and death were simply too much for them.

Tiburcio watched as the crew hoisted sail into the breeze, but the sloop foundered in the mud because it was low tide. The cannoneers and riflemen were wresting back control of the situation and now turned their attention to the sloop. They fired grapeshot into the rigging, killing three escapees. Having been through this before, Tiburcio knew how it would end. So, rather than join the prisoners who boarded the ship, he ducked away in the confusion with a small group and Chellis, who was now exhausted and had to be dragged. After thirty minutes of evading the eyes of the guards, who were busy with hundreds of others, they ran away across several pastures and came to a farm. They tried to lift Chellis on a bareback horse, but he only slid off. They half-carried him, finally making it to Ross Landing, the upper part of the creek. Possies of freemen with guards were fast in pursuit.

Tiburcio crossed the creek, thinking the posse on horseback could not travel across. They dragged Chellis into the chilling water, which was chest high. They ran the next 200 yards to Mount Tamalpais. When they tried to hoist the warden over some rocks, the dead weight of his exhaustion and obesity compelled them to leave him face down, panting in the dirt. It appeared that they were nearly finished as they raced to higher ground. Even though the posse was a hundred yards away, their sharpshooters had opened fire when Chellis was released. Immediately, ten of the prisoners fell. Some returned fire but quickly ran out of ammunition.

Possies continued to be formed from the surrounding county as word got out, and they tracked and covered a large extent of the area. Eventually, as evening was approaching, forty-seven more escapees were rounded up, many starving and wounded. In the coming days, scores more were found and returned to the prison, where for the next two weeks, the moans and screams of suffering and death were heard day and night. Two days after the initial break, Tiburcio and two compadres were forced to surrender. In the end, the fiasco left fifteen convicts killed and thirty wounded.

Tiburcio became a hero despite the failure and the pain and death that had ensued. The prison was on lockdown for a month while government officials had multiple closed-door meetings on how to prevent further escape attempts. Meanwhile, Tiburcio and the others were permanently secured in their cells and were fortunate not to undergo whippings because of the government meetings.

New rules, such as time off for good behavior, better food, medical care, and sanitary living conditions were implemented. A dozen guards, including the Warden and Moon, were fired. These changes promised to reduce future prison breaks.

Tiburcio finally relented to completing the final year of his sentence and, with much self-reflection, deemed his efforts a failure. His only comfort was that they forced changes in the prison.

He had entered prison as a boy and, after six years of living with the worst criminals in society, had learned a trade. Because criminals have nothing more to do than share stories and trade secrets all day, Tiburcio became a master at breaking into locks, the ins and outs of highway robbery, and burglary. And, even though he had made many Anglo friends during his incarceration, albeit not society's best, they were not enough to change his hatred for gringos. Moon's sadistic lashes wouldn't let it be.

The previous prison breaks attested to the horrors of bloodshed and how badly a man can treat another man. They groomed Tiburcio for any battle, his maturity built on surviving massive gunfire and barbaric torture at 'The Ladder.' He still had a soft-spoken voice from his youth, however, and his early education elevated him above his criminal peers. As a bandit chief, he was now respected by some of the nation's most brutal men. They appreciated his will to persevere and his sense of empathy toward his friends and fellow Mexicans.

The night before his release, Tiburcio welcomed into his imagination the glorious memories and happiness of his youth. While at San Quentin, his introspection every night before falling asleep led him to understand his decisions, especially those that brought him trouble. His parents and uncle had attempted to protect his innocence, but as with all young teenagers, Tiburcio's peers had gained the upper hand, influencing what ultimately proved life-altering decisions for him. He thought that was the reason why he had begun hanging out with ruffians and brutes in the first place. Spending less time at home where people truly loved him and instead rebelling into a life of crime with those who had not shown him an easier path to money through stealing. He had admired those who lived brazenly, though the price paid for that had been immeasurable pain.

Ten

It was a warm August day in 1863 when Tiburcio walked out of San Quentin's main gate as a free man. Life within the grim prison walls changed into one effused with joy and light. He took a deep breath, savoring the fresh air he had not felt for years. The sun was high, illuminating the world around him. He felt its warmth on his skin; it was a comforting embrace in contrast to the cold, damp prison. Looking around, he again heard birds singing in distant trees. He took in everything he had been denied in those years. He stepped onto the prison launch that transported him across the bay. The sweet smell of clean seawater filled his nostrils.

The guards on the boat were chatting about the civil war that had started back in the East. He listened with half an ear, for it was a world away. Besides, he was intent on returning to Monterey. While in prison, he learned that María, his first love, had married and was now the mother of three children. His mother, Doña, had moved southeast of San José with her daughter to San Juan Bautista and shared an adobe with her son-in-law. Her net worth was a mere one hundred dollars. Now that he was free, he would try to help. Hopefully, she would forgive him.

The morning air was crisp and cool as it brushed past the red-tiled Mexican adobes and shingled roofs of the Anglo homes that made up the fast-growing, vibrant town of San Juan Bautista. The sun had just risen over the horizon, casting a warm glow on the dusty streets and quiet buildings. The birds sang sweet melodies, and dogs barked in the background, a soothing symphony that filled the air and made one feel at ease. Emanating from the quaint cafes and bakeries that lined the streets, the smell of fresh coffee and sweet pastries wafted through the air. The town was alive with people going about their daily routines, chatting and laughing as they made their way to work or school. The colors of the buildings and bright-colored bougainvillea introduced to California in 1860 adorned a multitude of walls. Flowers that adorned the streets were spirited and eye-catching, as were those of the distant mountains bathed in golden light, their majestic peaks standing tall against the clear blue sky.

Doña Guadalupe stood at the door of her adobe in the early morning sun. She wore a faded, floral-print dress, which hung loosely from her thin frame, and a shawl wrapped around her shoulders. Her grey hair pulled back into a messy bun exposed the deep wrinkles on her face. Her eyes were dark and heavy, and they reflected a hint of sadness and tiredness. She held a large clay jug filled with dirty, soapy water in her hand. Determined, she slowly lifted the jug high above her head, her thin, bony arms trembling slightly with the effort. With a deep breath, she heaved the contents of the jug out into the yard, the murky water splashing against the dirt with a dull thud.

She stood momentarily, wiping her hands on her dress, while she gazed out at the dusty street beyond her doorway. Her dark brown eyes seemed to drink in the morning rays. She watched as the water disappeared into the ground with an awareness of having aged a lifetime in the years that she lost Tibo to prison and her husband to bad health. She turned her head toward the rising sun to hear approaching hooves and raised her hand to her eyes to shade them from the glare behind the silhouette of a lone rider. Doña repeatedly squinted at what appeared to be a vaquero wearing a flat sombrero pulled low on his brow. He pulled his horse up to her and dismounted. The horse grunted with relief. The rider's leather chaps and vest creaked, as did his gun belt, and complemented the sound of his large spurs tinkling when his feet hit the ground. She looked up and gasped in surprise when her gaze met with her youngest son's.

Tibo was standing within arm's reach. Instantly, all the anger and resentment she had held onto for years melted away, replaced by an over-whelming sense of love and joy. The two closed their remaining distance and embraced each other tightly as though holding on for dear life. Time seemed to stand still, and tears streamed down their faces as they repeat-edly kissed each other's cheeks. Every detail of the moment was etched into their memories, creating a cherished moment they would carry forever.

Tiburcio eagerly sat down for dinner with his family that evening. The aroma of his mother's cooking wafted through the house, making his mouth water and his stomach grumble in anticipation. Before him was an array of dishes: enchiladas, tamales, rice, beans, and various salsas. Doña spent hours in the kitchen perfecting each dish carefully and precisely. The enchiladas were made with tender chunks of slow-cooked pork smothered in a rich red sauce and topped with melted cheese. The tamales were wrapped in soft corn husks and filled with a flavorful mixture of chicken, vegetables, and spices.

As he took his first bite, he closed his eyes and savored the explosion of flavors in his mouth. They brought back memories of the meals of his youth. The savory pork, tangy salsa, and creamy cheese were delightful. The beans had a satisfying smoky flavor with fluffy and perfectly seasoned rice. He couldn't help but go back for seconds and then thirds. By the end of the meal, he was utterly stuffed, surrounded by the familiar faces of his family. The room was filled with laughter and chatter, and a warm contentment settled over him. He felt grateful for this moment, for the delicious meal they had shared, and for the love and support of his family. It was a memorable evening, even more so because Tiburcio's sister, Graciela, was there to share it with him. Even though her husband, Manuel Lara, disapproved of Tiburcio and his past, he had put aside his differences for the sake of the family dinner. Other cousins and relatives had also joined in to welcome Tiburcio home.

In the coming months, Tiburcio worked odd jobs and helped his mother with his pay to open a family-run restaurant, *La Fonda Mexicana*. It was the talk of the town. His mother and his sisters, Graciela and Manuela, worked tirelessly to ensure that the patrons were served delicious food and had an exceptional dining experience. The restaurant quickly gained popularity and a loyal customer base within the community. However, a devastating fire destroyed the restaurant after four years of operation, leaving the family and the community heartbroken.

The cause of the fire turned out to be a candle, which left lit, fell over onto the floor and into a small pool of grease. The candles were always snuffed out at closing, which made the event even more shocking. The fire had smoldered on the floor for a while, but a Santa Ana wind blowing hard below one of the doors at 60 mph had pushed the flame throughout the building in minutes. By the time the town's fire crew got to the scene, the restaurant was fully engulfed. Their only recourse was to protect the surrounding buildings, which meant abandoning all hope for Doña Guadalupe's enterprise.

A sunny day greeted the town's residents the following month with warmth and cheer. The townsfolk were moved by compassion and generosity as they gathered at the grand church in the city's heart.

The Church of San Miguel stood tall and proud amidst the dusty streets of Monterey. Its adobe walls, weathered by the harsh sun and winds, displayed faint traces of faded frescoes depicting biblical scenes that attested to the passage of time. At one time polished to a gleaming luster, the wooden doors were now worn and chipped, bearing the marks of countless hands seeking solace within its hallowed embrace.

The purpose of their assembly was to donate funds for a noble cause to support Doña. Tiburcio attended Sunday Mass for the first time in years to support his devout mother. As he knelt before the cross next to her, he felt a sense of gratitude and humility and offered his thanks. He then received communion with reverence and devotion, which pleased his mother considerably.

During the service, the priest spoke about giving back to the community and the church. Doña, moved by the priest's words, contributed some of the donated funds back to the church's collection. Tiburcio took note of his mother's generosity and felt inspired by her selfless act. The charitable act gave his mother a warm feeling of satisfaction and contentment. It also reminded Tiburcio of helping others and being part of a larger community. He promised himself to follow his mother's example and give back to his people in the future.

The townspeople, too, were known for their collective acts of kindness and selflessness. Their willingness to help one another in need was a testament to the power of community and generosity. This sense of togetherness and goodwill made their small town a unique and welcoming place.

When he wasn't working, Tiburcio enjoyed spending time in the rougher part of town, where he felt most at ease. This area was called the "Waterfront" by the Anglos and "El Bronco" by the Mexicans. It was a bustling area filled with bordellos, saloons, and dance halls. While a rather ruthless and careless area, Tiburcio felt a sense of belonging there as old habits die hard. San Juan Bautista was still predominantly Mexican, and life there was much like in the Monterey of his youth. He had a few favorite spots along the Waterfront, but none compared to The Plaza Hotel. He would go to this elegant establishment to engage in his favorite pastimes whenever he had free time. The Hotel was known for its lively atmosphere, with music and dancing filling the air and the sound of shuffling cards and clinking glasses adding to the nightly carousing. From the balcony, several beautiful women would watch the revelers below, hoping to catch the eye of a potential dance partner. Tiburcio was a regular and came to life in this vibrant setting. He spent his time dancing to the lively beats, strumming his guitar, and enchanting the women with his romantic poetry.

Horse racing, cock fighting, and other forms of gambling were present all over town, especially on weekends. However, when he heard of a race, he would not attend. It reminded him too much of Viento and how they would race and outshine all the other equines in the county.

Although Tiburcio had been raised with strong values and had been experiencing moments of joy in his new life, the allure of excitement and danger was irresistible. The more he surrounded himself with fellow criminals, the stronger the pull became, and he soon found himself addicted to the thrill of wanting to break the law again. He longed for the rush of adrenaline that came with each successful heist and the sense of power and control it gave him. Consumed by the demons of attraction to a life of crime, Tiburcio increasingly became a shell of the innocent child he once was and how his mother so recently had hoped he would become.

Tiburcio sat nervously at the hotel's bar, his eyes reading the dimly lit room. He had been waiting for his cousin Faustino for hours and regretted agreeing to meet him in this seedy part of town. As soon as he saw Faustino's scarred face and muscular build walk through the door, however, all his fears melted away.

Faustino Lorenzana, a career criminal whose body was covered in scars from gun and knife fights that exemplified a life of violence.

"Hey, Tibo!" Faustino boomed, slapping him on the back with a force that made him stumble.

"Long time no see, cousin!"

Tiburcio felt a surge of excitement as he hugged Faustino tightly. It had been years since they had seen each other, and he had always been fascinated by Faustino's dangerous lifestyle. He couldn't help but admire how his cousin carried himself, as a wolf among sheep.

"I've missed you, Faustino," Tiburcio said nonchalantly.

"What have you been doing lately?"

Faustino leaned in closer to Tiburcio, his voice low and conspiratorial.

"Listen, primo," he began.

"I'm going to let you in on a little secret. Do you know how I've been making all that money lately? I've been stealing horses and taking them down south to sell."

Tiburcio's eyes widened in surprise as he listened intently to Faustino's words, processing the implications of what was being said. Confirming what he already knew, he maintained his composure and responded calmly, his voice tinged with a hint of curiosity.

"I see."

Faustino rummaged in his pocket and produced a handful of gold coins he carelessly threw on the bar. The bartender, who had been polishing glasses at the other end of the room, heard the clatter of money and turned to see what was happening. As he approached, Faustino spoke confidently.

"The best whiskey you have for me and my friend and leave the bottle. We have much to discuss."

His words were laced with authority, and the bartender quickly nodded his head in agreement, eager to please his wealthy patrons.

Faustino held up his hand.

"Yeah, I've been stealing them from gringo farms and ranches around here. It's easy money, primo. And down south, they pay top dollar for them. I can make more money in one sale than working on the farm for a year or more. You have experience at this as well as being an expert horseman."

Tiburcio's expression suggested a mix of concern and apprehension as he contemplated Faustino's proposal.

"Sounds risky, cousin," he said hesitantly.

"Especially for an ex-convict like me. The last place I want to see is San Quentin again."

Faustino was undeterred.

"It's only as risky as you make it. I've been doing it for over a year without hinting at a problem. We take the horses from here and Santa Cruz to southern California, where we sell them at a tidy sum. We only take one from each farm, and none are close to each other. The buyers always need fresh stock for their farms and ranches, and we provide them with quality horses. Then we steal more for the trip back. It's a win-win!"

Faustino's face lit up with a broad smile as he spoke, and his eyes sparkled with enthusiasm for the scheme. He was convinced that the plan's rewards were well worth the risk and that the two of them could execute it without being caught.

"We'll make the trip down there and back. I know the safest routes primo," he said confidently.

"And our fortunes will improve once we have the gold in our pockets. Tiburcio, you want to take advantage of this opportunity. It's a chance to be part of something big that could change our lives forever."

Tiburcio was barely making ends meet as a vaquero, earning just enough to cover his expenses. He spent most of his money on women, gambling, and his mother's bills. He knew this scheme could be his chance to turn his fortunes around. He was only making thirty dollars a month as a vaquero. If he could make one or two successful trips, he would have enough money to pay off his debts and start a new life. Despite his reservations, he couldn't resist the lure of the potential rewards and agreed to join Faustino in the daring plan.

"OK, cousin. I will trust your judgment. But, if for a second it looks like it's going to fail and I am to go back to that shithole up north, I will leave you." Tiburcio said with all seriousness.

"Understood Tibo. I wouldn't want you to go back either."

Faustino poured two more shots and clinked glasses with his new partner.

As a skilled vaquero, Tiburcio had an eye for a good saddle horse that could fetch a handsome sum of two hundred dollars. He knew precisely which horses to steal from the farms they raided, having spent years working with these majestic animals. The horses were often left to graze in vast fields long distances from the ranch's hub, making them easy targets for Tiburcio and his accomplices to snatch and make a quick getaway. His one rule was to never steal from a Californio's ranch.

~

The enormous Almaden quicksilver mines stood about ten miles south of San José, where more than 500 Mexicans were employed. The miners lived in cabins in the forested hills nearby, which provided a perfect hideout for many outlaws.

The area was dotted with small gambling dens and bars where people could spend their stolen money. It was a place where tempers ran high, and the threat of violence lingered over disputes about money, women, or cheating at cards. The atmosphere was invariably tense, and anyone who dared to enter knew they were taking a risk.

After a successful trip to Southern California, Faustino and Tiburcio returned to their Almaden encampment with numerous heads of horses they had stolen, eager to sell in the Monterey area. They knew they had to be cautious with the horses, so they paid the corral owner to keep a watchful eye on them and headed to a nearby cantina to unwind.

At the cantina, they sat back and watched the locals play cards while they sipped their drinks. They noticed a group of three miners drinking heavily and playing cards with a local Italian butcher named Joseph Pellegrini, who was still wearing his blood-stained apron. To their surprise, Joseph was flashing a lot of cash, which made him a prime target for the intoxicated miners. Clearly, he was oblivious to the danger, drunker than the miners.

Cash was novel, still. His was some of the first paper money, or greenbacks, in the United States. The start of the Civil War gave cause and validated the printing, and while not backed in gold, they were nonetheless legal tender that carried various payment promises. The paper cash activity caught Faustino's attention, and when Pellegrini decided to leave, Faustino leaned in close to Tiburcio, his breath reeking of tequila.

"Hey, I got an idea, primo," he slurred.

"What's that?" Tiburcio asked, feeling a little tipsy while eyeing him warily.

"That Italian butcher over there," Faustino nodded toward Pellegrini.

"He's got all that cash. What do you say we relieve him of some of it?"

Tiburcio shook his head.

"I don't know, Faustino. That sounds like a bad idea. We have a lot of greenbacks too, and he is local. We would have to leave immediately, and if someone chased us, we would be slow with all the horses. Let's not be greedy."

"Come on, man. We just stole fifteen horses. What's a little pickpocketing going to hurt?"

Tiburcio hesitated, but the lure of easy money and having drank too much was too strong.

"Alright, I'm in. But we have to be quick about it. If it turns into a fuss, I will walk away, Faustino."

Faustino grinned, his teeth yellowed and painfully crooked.

"That's my boy," he said, clapping Tiburcio on the back.

They both stood up and proceeded to follow the Italian about a quarter of a mile to his home. Pellegrino entered his front door and closed it behind him but failed to lock it in his drunken state. Faustino grabbed Tiburcio, hurrying him along.

"Come on, Tibo, Andale!"

They pulled their bandanas over their faces as Tibo caught up to Faustino, who angrily kicked open the cabin door. The front room was empty, but a lantern was lit in the adjoining bedroom. Pellegrini was drunk but not that far gone and grabbed his pistol. It was an old single shot. He aimed it wildly, fired, and missed them both. Faustino lunged forward and punched Pellegrini, who took it in stride as he felt no pain. He struck Faustino's back in turn. Tiburcio reached down for the gun as he had not noted whether it was a six-shooter.

Faustino and Pellegrini started to wrestle and fell to the other side of the bed, away from Tiburcio's line of sight. Since he was a butcher at trade, Pellegrini always carried a knife. He pulled it on Faustino. With continued struggle, Faustino overwhelmed Pellegrini and put the knife into his grip. Lying on top of the butcher, he slowly pushed it toward Pellegrini's chest. Pellegrini was strong, but the weight of Faustino pushing the knife down with both hands was too much. Their faces were almost touching as Pellegrini's eyes widened in fear, their hot foul breaths intermigled.

"No, no, please don't," he whispered, pleading.

Faustino continued to push the knife slowly and silently through his chest. The life in Pellegrini's eyes left as his body slowly went limp. Faustino caught his breath and stood up into Tiburcio's view.

"Let's vamos Tibo! Someone may have heard the shot."

Tiburcio grabbed the greenbacks that Pellegrino put on the nightstand, and they fled.

Running, and as if out of nowhere, Faustino yelled, "I left my hat back there!"

He turned to go back, but Tiburcio overpowered him.

"Too late, amigo, we can't go back now. I'll buy you a new one on the way to Monterey."

They returned to the corral and slept the few hours left of the night. They woke up early and walked back to the cantina for breakfast.

The gunshot had attracted a few local miners to Pellegrini's cabin. They found his stabbed body near the bed in his bedroom in a pool of blood. They found his watch and forty dollars in his pocket, so they were initially bewildered about what had happened.

Word quickly spread throughout the town, and soon enough, the local sheriff from San José arrived to investigate. He walked by some miners leaning against the porch.

"Good day, I'm Sheriff Adams. Is anyone here a witness?"

They all shook their heads negatively.

"Alright then, move aside so I can have a look."

He entered the crime scene, but the only evidence he found that day was Faustino's hat.

Before the sheriff could form a posse, another killing occurred the same day. Julio Almanca, who had lost an arm back east in the Civil War, shot and killed an unruly guest, Juan Rodriguez when an argument broke out in Julio's cantina.

The sheriff mounted his horse and rode to the cantina from Pellegrini's. He dismounted with a loud groan, pushed through the crowd, and went to the bar, where he found Julio pouring himself a drink.

"Julio, we need to talk," Adams said, his voice stern but calm.

Julio turned to face the sheriff, his one good arm braced against the bar, with a motionless scowl and his eyes blazing with exhaustion and anger.

"What do you want from me, Sheriff? I am a one-armed veteran trying to run a business and keep these drunk assholes from killing each other."

"I want you to come with me," Adams said.

"For now, you're under arrest. We'll sort this out at the jail."

Julio's face twisted into a sneer.

"You can't do that, Sheriff! Who is going to watch this place? That man was about to shoot another! I only stepped in to save a life!"

One of Julio's customers told him he would lock up for him as the sheriff took him away.

Meanwhile, Tiburcio was unaware that Pellegrini was dead. The two bandits planned to keep a low profile and leave at ease without arousing suspicion since it would be slow going with the horses in tow.

Sheriff Adams didn't speak Spanish. He found out that the only person fluent in both languages was a man named Tiburcio Vasquez. He needed an interpreter to help interview witnesses, so he sent a deputy to find the man named Tiburcio.

Faustino and Tiburcio had finished breakfast in a small outside café with only four tables. Faustino took a long sip from his coffee and sighed contentedly.

"Last night was wild, huh?" he said, grinning at Tiburcio.

Tiburcio nodded with slight reservation in his eyes.

"Yeah, it was something else, all right. But I don't know, Faustino. That guy we robbed...he seemed like a decent sort. I wouldn't say I like taking advantage of someone like that, even a gringo and especially if it's unnecessary. You've become too greedy."

Faustino rolled his eyes.

"Come on, Tibo. We got what we came for, didn't we? And we didn't hurt him too badly. Just a little stab wound to scare him. He'll think twice before flashing money around again, and he was too drunk to identify us."

Faustino chuckled.

"Well, it helps when the mark's drunk. I don't think he even realized what happened until it was too late. Another drunk fucking gringo."

Tiburcio leaned into Faustino with a look that he had never seen before. It made him ill at ease.

"I'm going to make this clear for you, Faustino. I'm not for robbing Californios. Gringos are open season, but I never want to see a Mexican harmed. Got it?"

Faustino was a tough man, one of the most indurate bandits on the coast. Still, he had watched Tiburcio for months now, and even though Tiburcio had never killed anyone, he could see that he was deftly profound in his warning to him. He looked back eye to eye to Tiburcio. The stare lasted a long moment when Faustino unexpectedly broke into laughter, slapping Tiburcio's leg.

"Don't worry, Hermano; all will be fine."

Just then, a deputy approached the cantina owner, asking if he knew who Tiburcio was. He pointed directly at him. The deputy moved toward the two bandits. They slowly inched their fingers toward their pistols. The deputy didn't notice their hands under the table, but they noticed the badge on his vest.

"Are one of you Tiburcio Vasquez?"

"I am," Tiburcio said.

"Sheriff Adams would like to see you. Come with me, please."

"What about?"

"Not sure, but you're not in trouble."

He got up, looking at his cousin.

"OK. Faustino, I'll meet you back at camp."

Faustino glared back suspiciously and went back to finishing his coffee.

Tiburcio warily walked into the sheriff's office with the deputy.

"Tiburcio?" Adams inquired.

"Yes, I am," he replied.

"Call me Tibo. How can I help you?"

"I don't speak Spanish, and I need to interview some witnesses about a robbery and murder of a local butcher and a shooting in a bar last night. Can you do that for me?"

Tiburcio replied, hiding his surprise at the news of the butcher's death.

"Sure. I'm happy to help, Sheriff."

"I found this hat at the robbery scene."

It was Faustino's.

"Have you ever seen this on anyone's head around here?"

"Can't say I have, Sheriff," Tiburcio lied as innocently as he could.

For the next three hours, the sheriff, with the help of his newfound interpreter, was able to interview a dozen witnesses. Unbeknownst to him, his interpreter was a master manipulator who was ensuring that no suspicion or evidence led to him or Faustino.

When the interviews were done, Sheriff Adams thanked Tiburcio repeatedly. He left leisurely, but when he got to camp, he told Faustino the butcher was dead and that they needed to leave at first light. Faustino feigned no knowledge and the following day they gathered their horses and drove them north.

After the murder of Pellegrini, the sheriff launched a thorough investigation into the case but couldn't find any concrete evidence to solve the mystery. He eventually had to close the case and let the murderer go free. A few weeks after that, he received a tip that the guilty party might have been Faustino.

With Adams unable to prove his involvement in the crime, he was allowed to remain free. Continuing his investigation, however, some witnesses came forward and identified Faustino's hat as the one found at the crime scene. The sheriff now knew that Faustino might indeed be the killer, yet the hat was not solid enough evidence. Adding to his disappointment, he was later shocked to learn that Tiburcio was seen riding with Faustino. He felt like a fool for trusting Tiburcio in the translations.

In the meantime, the case against Julio, the barkeep, was dismissed thanks to the difficulty of protecting patrons in his bar. Even with a lack of evidence, the sheriff knew the real killer was still out there, and he was determined to bring him to justice.

Eleven

Tiburcio had been a horse thief for most of his adult life, but he now endeavored to master highway robbery. He returned to Monterey County to finish his last trip with Faustino and then to his new home in Salinas with a pocket full of money, which he spent buying new clothes. He gave a substantial amount to his family. He had not forgotten his mother's generosity at San Miguel's and went there to meet with the priest.

Father Ignatius Martinez, a revered figure in Monterey, had a tall, imposing frame that, enveloped in the traditional black cassock, demanded respect and admiration from the close-knit community. With his salt-and-pepper hair and deep-set eyes that appeared to hold ancient knowledge, he emanated an air of wisdom and compassion that drew people to seek solace and guidance in his presence.

Tiburcio's reputation as a notorious bandit continued spreading throughout the region. Despite his infamous notoriety, he longed to be loved by his people and ensured they knew that the only ones who should fear him were the Anglos. He approached Father Martinez outside the adobe church wearing a sleek black suit complete with a matching vest and tie, unlike any other bandit. His large, black, flat-top hat rested confidently atop his head, adding to the mystery and danger surrounding him. And yet, even with a Colt revolver strapped to his hip, there was something disarming about Tiburcio as he extended his hand and smiled.

Tiburcio's dark eyes met Father Martinez's gaze as he shook the priest's hand. Curiosity melded with apprehension in the bandit's expression, for he had heard tales of Father Martinez's charitable works and unwavering dedication to helping the poor and oppressed. In his free hand Tiburcio held a sack filled with unknown contents, a small offering perhaps for the respected priest before him.

"Thank you for seeing me, Father. May we go inside for a moment?"

"It's my pleasure, Tibo. Your mother told me you were coming and to expect you. Please, follow me."

Stepping into the church, Tiburcio felt an involuntary sense of awe and unease. He was uncomfortable, just as he was the last time he was in a church with his mother, but it was vital for him to make this connection.

The church's grand interior was imposing, with a soaring ceiling that seemed to reach the heavens. Intricately carved wooden beams supported the roof, their detailed designs evincing the skill and craftsmanship involved in their creation. The sunlight streaming through the stained-glass windows cast a shower of vibrant hues onto the pews arranged in neat rows beneath them. The hazy air inside smelled of incense mingled with the musty aroma of old books and the whispered prayers of the faithful.

Making his way further into the church, Tiburcio couldn't help but notice the shadows dancing along the stone walls. The hundreds of lit candles scattered throughout the space illuminated the statues of various saints, creating a warm and comforting glow that contrasted with the extraordinary stone surroundings. Every detail of the church had been designed to inspire a sense of reverence and awe, from the soaring arches to the intricate carvings and flickering candlelight.

"I wanted to give you this gift for the church and your congregation, Father."

Father Martinez glanced suspiciously at the sack.

"I know of your reputation, my son. I am guessing that the fruits of your labors are in there. If so, it would be hard for me to accept something unlawfully taken."

Tiburcio looked down, glancing at his polished black boots before responding in a low, modest tone. He could sense the disapproval in Father Martinez's eyes but stood his ground.

"No, Father." he said firmly.

"This is money I earned legitimately. I wouldn't give you stolen goods."

He knew he was lying but had to maintain his cover.

"I have watched my community suffer since I was young, and I want to help however I can. And I feel you know better than anyone where to put this money to good use, sir."

Tiburcio could feel the intensity of the Priests' gaze at him, but he refused to back down. He had to keep up the charade, no matter how difficult. He hoped Father Martinez would believe the lie and not ask any more questions.

Father Martinez stared into Tiburcio's soul for a full minute.

"Sit with me for a minute, Tibo."

They sat in the frontmost pew facing a large cross bearing a crucified, life-size Jesus.

The priest turned toward Tiburcio, his eyes locking with those of his town's most notorious bandit. The air in the small church hovered calmingly as the priest extended a hand to accept Tiburcio's generous donation.

"My son," Father Martinez began, his voice steady and filled with warmth and authority yet compassionate.

"I appreciate your generosity towards our church, but I must also speak from my heart concerning your life choices."

Although his face had weathered hardships and dark deeds, Tiburcio still had kind eyes that looked at Father Martinez with skepticism and curiosity. A lecture from the priest was unexpected; he merely wanted to make amends.

"What can you tell me that I haven't heard already?"

Tiburcio replied respectfully.

Father Martinez's calm demeanor did not waver as he responded.

"I understand that you have committed crimes in your past, Tibo. We are all sinners in our way."

Tiburcio smirked, his eyes betraying underlying mischief.

"Ah, Father," he said gravely, "even bandits have their moments of repentance, you know."

Hearing Tiburcio's words, Father Martinez raised an eyebrow, perhaps surprised by the emphasis on repentance, which, of course, involved more than giving back to the church. He seemed to have detected Tiburcio's skepticism and nodded thoughtfully before responding.

"Yes, my son, it's not just about giving back to the church. It's also about finding a path to redemption in how we live our lives."

Tiburcio understood the priest's message.

"Ok, Father, I will believe you because you are telling me this in the house of God. Thank you for your words. Please see that the donation helps the neediest."

After the long conversation with the priest, Tiburcio shook his hand and left, feeling a renewed sense of purpose and direction. He walked away with a sense of clarity he had lacked for many years. He knew what he had to do. He decided that day to change his ways and make certain that whatever he took in his robberies would be shared as tithing to his fellow Californios in need. He felt a deep sense of responsibility towards his community and was determined to make a positive impact. Mounting his horse riding away, he felt something he had not for a long time: the weight of his past misdeeds lifted off his shoulders. If only for that moment it was the start of a new beginning, one where he could live a life with integrity and meaning. Having lost what little money he had left to gambling, Tiburcio intended to make more—easily and quickly. Robbery was simply the best way he knew how.

The following day, the late afternoon sun was scorching under a cloudless sky. Tiburcio set out to hone his new skills and hid in some tall sagebrush ten miles out of town. He patiently awaited the first traveler, who happened to be a Jewish merchant sitting atop his wagon pulled by two horses. When the merchant got close, Tiburcio came out slowly, edging his horse forward. No less startling for the traveler, he pulled out his pistol and pointed it directly at Tiburcio.

"Easy there, friend," Tiburcio said, smiling.

"I don't mean you any harm. Just looking to see what wares you have for sale."

The older merchant narrowed his heavy-browed eyes, keeping his pistol casually trained on the stranger. After sizing him up, he decided that business is always an opportunity one should not miss, especially with a man who appeared to be unarmed.

"Okay, no problem. Let me show you the back of my wagon. Maybe I can sell you something."

As the merchant tucked away his gun and turned his back, Tiburcio cautioned him.

"You're a trusting merchant, my friend, which one should never be in this area. Never turn your back on a stranger to make a sale."

The merchant turned, his eyes wide and mouth agape with surprise, both immediately giving way to a look of overwhelming despair.

Tiburcio had pulled his pistol from behind his back where it had been tucked into his waistband out of sight.

"You've got the coin to spare, I am sure. And I've got a need for it. It's a fair trade. Your life for that. I will let you keep the rest of it."

Trying to show some bravado, the merchant hesitated for a moment, glancing around nervously.

"I won't give you a penny. But I'll make you a deal. Let me go, and I won't tell anyone about this little encounter. Deal?"

Tiburcio considered the offer momentarily before nodding slowly with a wide smile.

"That's pretty funny, my friend. I must say you have a set of balls on you."

He walked closer. The glare of the sun behind him hurt the merchant's eyes and reinforced his vulnerable position. Tiburcio put his 44 Colt revolver barrel close enough to touch and swirl around the man's greying beard.

"This bitch of a .44 has no conscience, my friend. Do you want to lose your head to it for a few bits of gold?"

Tiburcio had no intention of shooting the merchant, but the threat needed to be compelling. The wealthy merchant stepped back from the gun barrel and fumbled through his pockets, searching for something to appease the menacing Mexican who was towering over him. Finally, he produced a small, worn leather pouch heavy with gold coins. His hands trembled as he offered it to the bandit.

"Take it." the merchant pleaded, his voice quivering with fear.

"But please, leave me be."

Tiburcio snatched the pouch from the merchant's hands. A satisfied grin spread across his face as he opened it. Inside was a mix of coinage amounting to about one hundred dollars. Tiburcio's grin widened, and his eyes gleamed with satisfaction.

"Let this be a lesson, my friend. Don't expect me to be so lenient if we meet again."

Tiburcio grabbed the tip of his hat to salute the merchant.

"Thanks for your cooperation. If you'll excuse me, I've other matters to attend to."

As the bandit turned and disappeared into the brush, back over the knoll he had come from, the merchant sat on the back of his wagon and breathed a sigh of relief.

Twelve

Whereas Tiburcio navigated a life of crime, his older brother Antonio carved for himself a different path. Through hard work and determination, he achieved a level of success that allowed him to purchase a 320-acre ranch in the Carmel Valley. Always mindful of his finances, Antonio dedicated himself to a simple life of cultivating crops and raising cattle. Tiburcio managed to visit his brother on the ranch in spite of his previous legal issues and troubled past. The visits offered respite from the constant stress and fear of being caught by law enforcement. During them, he found solace with his family, and he gave some money to his brother to help him through tough times. He cherished these moments with his family and was grateful for their support and love.

The high sun and dry air accompanied Tiburcio on his way back to Antonio's ranch. He had made a brief visit to town and now found himself in a narrow gully between connecting roads. Suddenly, without warning, a rattlesnake appeared out of nowhere and spooked his horse. The frightened animal reared up on its hind legs, throwing Tiburcio off balance. Under all other circumstances, he would have been able to compose himself to control the horse, but the suddenness of the attack caught him completely off guard. Thrown from his saddle, he landed with a thud and hit his arm on a rock. The snap was followed by excruciating pain. He lay there, unable to move or think clearly for what seemed like an eternity. Eventually managing to gather his wits, he slowly stood up and stumbled around, dazed, looking for his hat. A ranchero was approaching him, looking down from the parallel road above the gully.

"Are you alright?" he asked with sincere concern.

Tiburcio could barely speak from the pain coursing through his body, but he managed to nod his head in agreement while holding his limp arm at his side.

"I think I broke my arm," he groaned.

"I'm sorry, Señor, you seem to be in quite bad shape," the ranchero said.

"Let me help you to my home. I can give you some water and a place to fix that arm."

Tiburcio gritted his teeth and nodded his head in agreement.

"Thank you," he managed to say as he grabbed his hat with his good arm, dusted it off, and put it back on.

"I don't know what I would have done without your help."

The ranchero smiled kindly.

"It's no problem. My home is close to here. I can take you there to tend to your wounds."

The ranchero slowly helped him up, guided him to his horse, which surprisingly had not run off, and hoisted him onto the saddle with difficulty. As the ranchero's hands touched his broken arm, it sent waves of agony through his body.

The ranchero responded to the wince of pain, "Oh, sorry!"

Tiburcio tried to focus on anything other than the throbbing, searing discomfort during the ride to the ranchero's home. He looked around at the rugged landscape, which turned to towering pines and green fields. He felt a sense of awe at the beauty of the expansive property surrounding the hacienda they approached. Horses grazed in the corrals and pastures, and multi-colored bougainvillea adorned the ranch building walls and white fencing that separated the fields.

"What is your name, Señor?" Tiburcio politely asked riding alongside the ranchero.

The ranchero, dressed in a brown leather jacket and wearing a wide-brimmed hat, replied in a calm, collected manner.

"Esteban Morello, my friend, at your service. And yours?"

Tiburcio needed to be more cautious about his true identity. His name had been circulated among law enforcement agencies for his alleged involvement in a series of crimes. For this reason, he had no intention of revealing his real name to the man and risk being caught.

"Raphael Moreno."

He used a distant cousin's name, hoping it would sound familiar and garner some recognition from the ranchero. Concealing his fears, Tiburcio maintained his composure and friendly demeanor throughout the conversation.

Tiburcio marveled at the size and beauty of the hacienda as they approached it. The courtyard was filled with the sound of horses and the smell of fresh hay, and the main house towered over everything else. Its balconies and windows offered a commanding view of the surrounding countryside.

The horses' shoes echoed on the cobblestones, bringing to attention a heavy-set vaquero who wore a giant sombrero and wooly chaps. He trotted up on a palomino and glanced at Tiburcio holding his broken arm.

"Patrón, are you ok?" he asked the ranchero.

"I am fine, Pablo. Help this man get off his horse and into the house so we can tend to his arm."

"Yes, sir."

He got off his horse quickly, his large spurs jingling as he hit the ground, and helped Tiburcio off his horse.

The remarkable hacienda in the heart of California was a true testament to the luxury and wealth that the ranchero possessed. Tiburcio, even in his discomfort, admired the exterior of the building. Walking through its intricately carved wooden doors into a spacious foyer, at the same time politely brushing aside help from the owner, he marveled at the grand staircase leading up to the second floor. Flanked by large oil paintings of the ranchero's ancestors, it could not have been more majestic. The rich mahogany furniture in the main living area was upholstered in luxurious fabrics, and the sitting room boasted plush armchairs and sofas, ornate coffee tables, and a stately built-in fireplace with a marble mantle. The dining room was equally stunning, with a long table made from solid oak surrounded by high-backed chairs. Oil paintings depicting the rolling hills and landscapes surrounding the hacienda hung on the walls in ornate gold frames.

A female voice suddenly came behind the men.

"Papa, who do you have there? What's going on?"

Tiburcio's eyes were drawn to a magnificent sight as he turned around. A striking young woman descended the staircase. Her curves were elegantly accentuated by a form-fitting red dress that hugged her body in all the right places and emphasized her figure's natural beauty. The dress flowed delicately as she descended each step, and her every movement seemed calculated, almost as though she had practiced this impressive entrance. Tiburcio couldn't help but admire her confidence and poise. Her dark hair cascaded down her back in loose curls, bouncing gently with each step taken toward her father and him. Though innocent in her youth, there was a subtle yet undeniable sexiness about her, a sultry confidence in her movements that left both men entranced by her presence.

As she reached the bottom of the stairs, she offered a shy smile to the bandit, her eyes offering a coy invitation. It was clear she had caught his attention, and she seemed to revel in her power over him. For all her playful demeanor, however, there was an air of mystery about her, a hint of danger that made Tiburcio's heart race with arousal.

"Ah, my love. This is Raphael Moreno. Raphael, this is the love of my life, my daughter Anita. He fell from his horse, and his arm needs tending. Would you send someone for the doctor, please?"

"Yes, Papa, right away."

Tiburcio watched her stride briskly away, estimating her to be in her late teens.

"Let me show you to a guest room where you can rest until the doctor arrives, amigo," Esteban said, offering a glass of quickly poured whiskey to ease the pain.

While Tiburcio was shown around the magnificent house, he couldn't help but admire the bedrooms he passed, each with a luxurious four-poster bed. Arriving at the room he would occupy, Esteban proudly showed him the bathroom with the latest toilets, invented in 1850, which captured his attention even more. The plumbing was still imperfect, but Esteban had taken the initiative to install double doors to prevent any unpleasant odors from escaping. Tiburcio found the innovation amazing and felt an immense sense of gratitude toward his host.

As Esteban continued the tour, he proudly displayed his latest product, medicated toilet paper, which he purchased for fifty cents for a pack of five hundred sheets. He explained that this paper was designed explicitly for wiping oneself after using the toilet. Tiburcio was used to sleeping in various environments, including the outdoors, using dried corn cobs, leaves, or straw. He couldn't help but feel a sense of wonder at the advancements of modern civilization. He let out a shy giggle at the thought of using such a luxurious product while still trying to shrug off the pain in his arm.

"The doctor does not live far away. I will send him to your room directly, Raphael," Esteban politely offered.

"Please make yourself comfortable until he arrives. There is a water pitcher on the nightstand, and I will arrange to send some food up to you."

Tiburcio promptly expressed his gratitude for the kind gestures.

"Thank you, sir."

That evening, Tiburcio was feeling much better. The doctor had realigned his radial bone to its original position. He was gentle as he maneuvered the bone, but it hurt like hell. He then put a plaster cast made of gutta percha around the arm to protect it. He was lucky that it was a simple fracture, the doctor told him, because forty to fifty percent of compound fractures resulted in death. He prescribed some opium and alcohol for the initial treatment of pain, so when Tiburcio joined Esteban and Anita for dinner, he was exceptionally comfortable.

Esteban sat at the head of the table, his proud, discerning gaze surveying the spread of food before him. Tiburcio was seated to his right, a respectful distance between them. Anita sat across from Tiburcio, her eyes shifting between her father's and those of the handsome man before her.

The meal was simple: roasted rabbit, spicy chicken enchiladas, and potatoes, but it was well-prepared and plentiful. Esteban took the first bite and savored the flavor with a nod of approval. Tiburcio followed suit, complimenting the cook, which pleased Esteban greatly.

The conversation was light and easy as they ate, filled with talk of the weather, the recent gold rush, and the state of the land. However, Anita was largely silent, content to listen to Tiburcio's soft-spoken words as she watched how he used his experience and obvious education to convey entertaining conversation.

Tiburcio, a man of great awareness and acute perception, was help-lessly drawn to Anita's presence. However, out of respect for Esteban, he maintained a certain distance. Dessert was served, a magnificent white mountain cake covered in fresh raspberries. Tiburcio's eyes were fixed on Anita's lips as she savored each bite. Her manner of eating the dessert was nothing short of mesmerizing to him.

After dinner Tiburcio and Esteban sat on the porch with some fine whiskey and cigars. Tiburcio was feeling no pain between the medications and alcohol. He was happy and content for the first time in a while, prob-ably because he was somewhere safe and protected by a powerful ranch owner who didn't know Tiburcio's true identity.

"The doctor tells me that I will have to wear this cast for eight long weeks, but he expects a full recovery. Esteban, I cannot thank you enough for what you have done for me. I will forever be indebted to you, sir."

Esteban smiled.

"It was my pleasure, Raphael. I'm glad you will be okay. It's been a long day; we should both retire and get some rest. I will see you at breakfast in the morning."

"Thank you," Tiburcio replied.

Tiburcio passed out when his head hit the pillow and slept late the following day, missing breakfast. When he finally came downstairs, he was greeted by Anita, who was standing in a stunning white linen dress that revealed her sensual figure. The dress hugged her curves perfectly, creating an alluring flow as she moved. He was captivated.

He greeted her with a warm smile.

"Good morning, Raphael," she said.

"Are you hungry?"

He chuckled at the question and rubbed his stomach.

"Famished."

"The cook has gone to town for necessities," she said, knowing the news would be disappointing for him.

"But don't worry, I can fix you some chorizo and eggs."

Tiburcio's mood immediately brightened at the thought of a delicious breakfast.

"That sounds fantastic. Thank you," he said gratefully.

As she moved around the kitchen, he watched her with admiration. She was so skilled and confident in the way she handled the ingredients. Soon enough, the aroma of a freshly cooked breakfast filled the air.

He sat at the small kitchen table and smiled at her as she brought him a steaming cup of coffee, some orange juice, and a plate of food. It was a simple breakfast, but one that he enjoyed thoroughly. Seated beside him, she closely observed his mannerisms. How he moved his hands, the expressions on his face, how he carried himself. She was impressed by his eloquence. His refined language and carefully chosen words showcased his education and intelligence. When he finished, Anita spoke up.

"If you're interested in exploring the ranch, we can have one of our skilled vaqueros saddle up horses for us."

He looked at her with interest as he dabbed his mouth with a napkin.

"Sounds like a great idea! I'd love to see more of this beautiful place."

Tiburcio and Anita mounted their horses and took a breathtaking ride through the sprawling California horse ranch. The sun beat down on them, warming their skin and filling the air with the sweet scent of wildflowers. As they rode, Tiburcio took in the scenery around them. The fields were alive with the sound of horses whinnying and the soft rustle of the breeze through the trees. The grass swayed under the wind, and birds circled overhead. The sky was painted stunning blue, and the occasional fluffy white cloud drifted lazily by.

Anita smiled at Tiburcio, happy to be with him, and the ranch's beauty added to the experience. Tiburcio met her gaze and smiled back, feeling his heart swell with affection. As they reached a bend in the trail, Tiburcio spotted a grand oak tree in the distance.

"Look, Anita," he called out, pointing to the tree.

"Let's stop there and rest for a bit."

She nodded in agreement, and they spurred their horses forward. The tree was massive, with sprawling branches that provided shade and shelter from the sun. They dismounted and sat on one of the blankets that had been tied to their saddles. As they rested, they talked about their dreams and what they wanted from life. Tiburcio had a way of charming women since his youth, and he would make no exception with Anita. He recalled a poem by Rosalía de Castro that he gently recited to her.

> *"I know not what I seek eternally*
> *on earth, in the air, and the sky;*
> *I know not what I seek; but it is something*
> *That I have lost, I know not when,*
> *and cannot find, although in dreams invisibly*
> *It dwells in all I touch and see.*
> *Ah, bliss! Never can I recapture you*
> *either on earth, in air, or sky,*
> *Although I know you have reality*
> *And are no futile dream."*

Anita sat on the edge of the blanket watching Tiburcio intently. His words flowed like honey, each syllable a note that lingered in the air. She could feel the heat rising in her cheeks as she listened, her heart beating faster and faster with each passing moment. She leaned forward as he finished the last line and touched his cheek, looking deeply into his eyes.

Moving even closer her lips brushed against his, and he eagerly wrapped his arms around her and pulled her in. Her lips were soft and warm, and she could taste the sweetness of the words he had just spoken on his tongue. Anita deepened the kiss, her tongue exploring his mouth as she pressed her body against him. She could feel the heat between them growing more robust, the passion igniting, the intensity as though a spark in dry tinder. She ran her hands through Tiburcio's hair, pulling him closer and deeper into the kiss. She could feel his heart beating fast against her. She never wanted this moment to end. Suddenly, she broke away, gasping for breath.

"I don't know what overcame me. Oh my! My father will be wondering where we are. We need to go back now."

Tiburcio was stunned but understood. He believed her to be a virgin and figured she must be overwhelmed. He lowered his head and smiled while nodding in agreement.

As the weeks passed, Esteban invited Tiburcio to stay and work as a vaquero on the ranch. Anita took it upon herself to tend to his needs when two arms were necessary. Tiburcio found himself growing increasingly attracted to her. Knowing her father would be furious if he found out about their feelings, they kept their attraction a secret and refrained from showing any affection in front of him and the other workers on the ranch.

While there were various challenges, they found solace in each other's company and cherished the moments they could steal away from prying eyes. The passing of time also allowed Tiburcio to assist the vaqueros. With his one good arm, he herded cattle and performed other necessary chores. Esteban was often gone on short business trips and was grateful for his help.

After eight weeks, the doctor returned to remove the cast. Tiburcio noticed that his arm had lost some muscle mass, and he began to work diligently to regain strength. With determination and hard work, he gradually repaired the atrophy and could perform all the duties required of a healthy vaquero. Notwithstanding the setback, he was eager to get back on the road, only this time an insatiable hunger had grown inside him. There was no other way; he was taking Anita with him.

Whenever they got the chance, they would steal away to find a spot on the ranch to explore each other's bodies. She was still a virgin, but through their touches and kisses, she felt like she knew every inch of him. It was more complex and more challenging for him not to just take her forcefully. A man could only take so much temptation. Lying in a hay loft in a secluded barn, he leaned in close.

"I want you to come with me when I leave tomorrow."

She shivered at the thought at how livid her father would be if he found out. She hurriedly put her clothing back on, struggling to remove pieces of hay stuck to her hair and skin.

"Why so sudden? Raphael, why would I go with you?" she asked disappointedly.

He took a deep breath before responding.

"I have been here too long, and I have pressing business...Listen, my name is not Raphael. It is Tiburcio Vasquez. I was hoping you would go with me to start a life together and eventually be married."

She immediately felt betrayed by his lies; the revelation took her aback.

"Tiburcio? Why did you lie about your name?" she asked, trying to make sense of the situation. Before he could answer, she realized something else.

"Wait! I've heard that name before. Are you Tiburcio, the bandit people talk about?"

Raphael, or rather Tiburcio, hesitated. At last, he was admitting the truth.

"Yes, and that is why I couldn't tell your father my name," he answered regretfully.

In her innocence and love for him, Anita was oddly now more attracted to him because of his bandit reputation. She couldn't fathom being with someone with a criminal record but also couldn't deny feeling drawn to him.

"Your father will never let me marry you, so we cannot stay if you want to bear my children," he said urgently, his voice low but persuasive.

"Tiburcio," she interrupted.

"Call me Tibo."

She hesitated for a moment before continuing.

"Tibo, I love you. I want to marry you, but my father will hunt us down."

"Many have tried, my love, but no one has succeeded. We can leave the state to raise our family," Tiburcio said reassuringly.

Anita knew leaving everything behind to be with this man would be a considerable risk, but she was willing to take that chance for love. She looked into his eyes and knew he was the one she wanted to spend the rest of her life with.

The next night, in the early morning, they packed their saddle bags with provisions and bedrolls and silently walked the horses from one of the corrals.

Esteban had been gone on a trip to Monterey. He wasn't expected back for a couple of days but arrived home early. Ordinarily he would have been greeted warmly by Anita. She was nowhere to be found. He raced through the house and found her personal things gone. It didn't take long for him to realize she had left. Raphael, also gone, was likely responsible. He got on a fresh horse and galloped away in pursuit. It was early evening when he caught up to them resting under a large oak tree.

Tiburcio jumped to his feet, adrenaline coursing as Esteban stealthily approached from behind. Esteban's hand moved faster than his eye could track, and he was suddenly aiming a pistol at Tiburcio's head.

Anita shrieked. "Don't shoot him, Father! If you do it, then shoot me too!"

Esteban roared with rage at Raphael.

"What were you thinking? Did you lure my daughter away from her home with false promises of love? After I cared for you, you dared to disobey me? I should kill you both!"

Tiburcio remained calm.

"I love her."

Anita mirrored his words or tried to.

"And I love Tibo...er..."

"Tibo? Tibo, who?" her father asked.

"Tiburcio...Vasquez," She replied.

Esteban paused reviewing the name.

"The bandit?" Esteban spat in disgust.

Without warning, Esteban fired his gun at Tiburcio and struck his arm, the same one he had previously broken. Tiburcio screamed in pain, and as Esteban reached for another bullet in his old single-shot pistol, Tiburcio bolted for his horse and galloped away like a man possessed. None of them would ever see each other again.

The wound to Tiburcio's arm turned out to be only a deep abrasion, fortunately, and it did not inflame the earlier injury. The .44-caliber bullet had still torn away muscle and skin, however. Once he was about five miles away, he tended to the bleeding using his bandana as a pressure bandage. The following day, the bleeding had subsided and along with it the throbbing. His arm was sore and stiff, but he could still move it. He fixed himself some breakfast of coffee and hard tack.

Reflecting on the loss of his love, he admitted to himself that lust had overcome his better judgment.

"What was I thinking?" he said to himself.

"I was in love, but it would never have worked out. I am a bandit at heart. That ranch life was wonderful, but I am a wanted man and will remain so for some time."

With that thought, he set out toward the Barbary Coast in San Francisco.

Thirteen

The air grew cold and moist as Tiburcio rode his horse into the fog enveloping San Francisco's Barbary Coast. Now 1865, he was about to celebrate his thirtieth birthday. The 1848 gold rush in California drew men to this area who were overtaken by greed and blinded by the promise of gold. It brought out the worst in men wanting to make a name for themselves. As with any growing city, the area needed a place for them to blow off steam. Lawlessness was rampant. Murderers and thieves rubbed shoulders at saloons, bordellos, and opium dens. The vilest forms of debauchery occurred. Naturally, Tiburcio found it easy to hide, away from legal prying eyes.

The houses of disrepute were a crossroads for the wealthy and poor. An American senator from Illinois could be found bare-chested with a woman whose beauty was half-shadowed by desperation. The rich had their rooms, but those men who made their livings cleaning stalls in the stables or running errands for politicians often paid more than they could afford to ease their loneliness at the brothels, lured as they were by prostitutes exposing themselves on the street and from balconies. Disease ran rampant from the constant influx of immigrants from Asia and other European countries bringing new blood to San Francisco daily.

There were also lovely concert saloons and hotels outside the nine-block area of the Barbary Coast. With only a hundred police officers for the whole city, however, law enforcement was overwhelmed with every crime imaginable. The unbridled prostitution led many to refer to the Coast as the Paris of America.

Tiburcio found a clean and quiet hotel just a few blocks from the action. He went into town to celebrate his birthday. He walked down a crowded Pacific Street and was thrilled to find a watering hole, Barbary Coast Cocktails. Everyone was dressed in suits, ties, and hats. The establishment had fifty women on payroll, most making about twenty monthly dollars plus room and board. Their clientele were miners, wayward husbands, and sailors. The hall was filled with music and dancing, bringing Tiburcio back to his Fandango days. After a few drinks, he felt at home again.

A beautiful woman who appeared to be his age caught his eye from across the smoke-filled room. She was a stunning thirty-something prostitute with fiery red hair in loose curls. Her alluring eyes were a piercing green, sparkling with mischief and seduction. Her skin was pale, almost alabaster, and her lips were stained an inviting deep red. Her outfit, equally seductive, comprised a low-cut corset that enhanced her already ample bosom and accentuated her curves in a way captivating to all who saw her. Her dress was short and flirty, revealing shapely legs that seemed to go on for miles, and was adorned with intricate lace and ribbons that contrasted starkly with her bold and confident demeanor. Every aspect of her attire exuded elegance and sophistication. Indeed, she was the main attraction in any room she entered.

Tiburcio paid for a dance, and a few minutes into it she asked if he wanted to go upstairs. He was weary from the long ride, and the romantic in him decided that sleeping in a warm bed with a beautiful woman, albeit a hooker, was a perfect birthday present. He had been paid well by Esteban and, for the last three months, had had nowhere to spend it.

He followed her up the creaky staircase, her perfume filling his senses. The room was small, barely accommodating the bed and dresser. She lit a candle and turned to him, her eyes scanning his face. Tiburcio's heart raced as she slowly walked to him, her hips swaying sensuously. She reached up and gently ran her fingers through his hair.

"My name is Elisa. I can make you happy in many ways. What is your name?" Tiburcio closed his eyes, feeling the warmth of her touch.

He lied yet again. "Fernando."

He leaned forward to kiss her, but she pulled away with a coy smile.

"Not yet," she whispered.

"Let me dance for you."

She moved to the rhythm of the distant music from downstairs, her body undulating before him. He watched in awe, mesmerized by her fluid movements and irresistible sensualness. His desire and arousal heightened with each moment. Sensing his eagerness, she undressed him, moving her hands over his muscular chest. He couldn't believe he was spending his birthday with such a beautiful woman. He started to kiss her passionately, and she moaned softly, encouraging him to continue.

They made love for hours, and her skill and passion utterly took Tiburcio by surprise. She taught him things he had not experienced before, and he liked it. As they lay together in bed he wondered about her story.

"How did you end up here and in this line of work?" he asked.

Her voice was soft and hospitable.

"I was an orphan, grew up on the streets of San Francisco doing whatever I could to survive. Facing challenges every day, some extraordinary, I learned never to let anyone push me around. I tried other jobs, but they never paid enough to keep me off the streets. So, I turned to the oldest profession in the world. It gave me a sense of power. It's not glamorous, but it has been a living."

Elisa had her regulars who treated her well and paid top dollar for her services. There were others, though, who tried to treat her like garbage, believing they could do whatever they wanted because they were paying for it. They never got very far, as she would call in the bouncer to take them away. She no longer had the patience to be muscled around by stinking, abusive men. She otherwise kept her head down, never let them see her vulnerabilities, and always made sure to get the money upfront. She knew how to protect and defend herself before things got out of hand.

"Fernando, I sense an intriguing combination of strength and tenderness emanating from you. However, I also sense a hint of recklessness lurking beneath the surface. Is this an accurate assessment of your character?" Elisa whispered.

Tiburcio nodded in agreement.

"Yes, your observation is quite insightful. I've always been aware of these contrasting qualities within myself."

"What are your interests, Fernando? Nothing personal; I don't need to know what you do or if you are married. What do you love that makes you happy?"

He thought momentarily.

"Well, I love horses, especially one I lost named Viento; I also love music and poetry. I sense that you are educated, Elisa."

"Yes, I went to school, and I love books. She pointed toward her bookcase in the dim light. I have only read one poem my whole life and liked it. Do you know any Fernando?"

He reached over and kissed her cheek and whispered slowly into her ear.

"Between the earth and sky that keep
eternal watch,
like a rushing, headlong torrent
Life passes on
Restore fragrance to the flower.

"Did you write that?"

"No, it's a poem by Rosalía de Castro. She is my favorite poet. I am still struggling to write my own."

"You are an interesting puzzle, Fernando. I like it. You may come back to me anytime. Don't wait for another birthday."

She rolled over, and they both fell asleep.

Tiburcio awoke feeling at ease and ready to start his day. He planned to have breakfast at a cantina two blocks away. As he strolled down Washington Street, he passed a photography studio and thought, I'm looking my best today; why not take a portrait photograph?

He walked into the studio without further ado, causing the bell above the door to ring. A thin man with a mustache and pasted down, rigorously parted hair came out from a back room and greeted him with a warm smile.

"Good morning, Sir; my name is Wilbur Bayley, the proprietor. May I help you?" the man asked.

"Yes," Tiburcio responded with a grin.

"Can you take a portrait photograph of me this morning?"

"Of course, it would be my pleasure, sir. Please stand against this blanket-covered pedestal." the man replied, leading Tiburcio to the staging area.

Tiburcio was always a man of impeccable taste, obliged with grace as he adjusted his attire. He looked striking in his hip-length wool coat. Its beaver collar added an air of sophistication to the ensemble. Underneath the coat, he wore a fancy velvet vest perfectly complemented by a crisp white shirt and a matching short-hanging bow tie. With a watch on his wrist, he leaned slightly to his right, his left hand holding his jacket lapel and his right one casually holding against the blanket a flat hat that he cherished dearly. His neatly parted hair enhanced his handsome features, as did his luxuriant mustache and small beard, the latter adding ruggedness to his overall refined look. He crossed his right leg in front of his left, a gesture of confidence that displayed his shiny black boots.

Wilbur Bayley, a skilled photographer, instructed Tiburcio to remain motionless in order that his likeness be captured in crisp focus. To achieve this, Tiburcio leaned on the pedestal for support. The wet collodion glass negative Bayley used took around 30 seconds of exposure time. The wet-plate process, as it was called, was far less time consuming and expensive than the earlier daguerreotype process and allowed the photographer to make a chemically processed negative ending with a printed photograph, and negative from which multiple prints could be made.

Bayley, unaware of Tiburcio's history, had no clue that the portrait negative of his sitter would be valuable in the coming years. Tiburcio was delighted with the outcome and showed his gratitude by paying Wilbur twenty dollars and a warm "thank you" as he departed.

Two weeks of indulging in a carefree lifestyle along the Coast was beginning to wear on Tiburcio. He felt depleted. The constant partying and excessive rest periods had taken their toll, not to mention that his funds were dwindling rapidly. It was time for a change of scenery.

He decided to venture to the Marin County region just north of San Francisco. There, he invited himself to stay at the Rancho Laguna de San Antonio, which was owned by the Bojorques family, distant relatives of his. Tiburcio quickly became the center of attention. He captivated the Bojorques family with his talents, including guitar playing, singing, dancing, and poetry. To them, he was a true Renaissance man. Pedro and Angel, two of the family's sons and reputed gamblers who frequented Spanish Town near Petaluma, found themselves especially drawn to Tiburcio's charm and charisma.

Working on the ranch as a sheep herder, Tiburcio took the name José Mauricio and soon became well-known in the area by Californios and Anglos alike. Petaluma was a small town of 1,500 people, so anonymity was rather impossible. It didn't take long for him to befriend Manuel Rojas, Jesus Hilario, and Juan Soto at the gambling tables. Juan was tall, skinny, and had a noticeably pockmarked face. Tiburcio nicknamed him "Pimples." Within no time, the gang was wreaking havoc in the area committing burglaries, robberies and stealing horses. A few of the townspeople took notice of how the increase in crime coincided with Jose Mauricio's arrival. While they didn't know his true name, ongoing descriptions were leading the local marshal to suspect the connection among the four bandits.

~

It was late afternoon when Tiburcio stopped by the local bordello to have a drink and chat with one of the girls. It was located right on the bank of the Petaluma River. A small commotion started when some girls noted that a large fancy boat had pulled up to the adjoining dock. Tiburcio walked over to the window and peeked over one of the girl's shoulders.

"Holy shit, it's Charlie Dade!" he said, nibbling on her neck.

He walked briskly to the dock and addressed Charlie, who was tying up the boat.

"Charlie, what the hell are you doing here? It's been a long time since San Quentin."

Charles Dade was a man of impressive stature. He had long hair that flowed down to his shoulders and accentuated his barrel chest. The finely kept long beard surrounding his round face framed his naturally big smile. He welcomed Tiburcio with a big hug.

"Tibo! How are you, amigo?"

"Not too loud, my friend. My name here is José."

"Ha, yes, I understand," Dade whispered while laughing.

"Come inside, Charles. There are beautiful women, and the drinks are on me. Let's catch up."

"That's why I am here, Tib,...err, José. I'm horny as a stallion, and I need to find some fine mares to ride."

Dade was wanted for burglary and the murder of a Chinese man near the town of Folsom. He was an exception to the rule of Tiburcio's hatred of Anglos, for their friendship had been forged in the brickyards of San Quentin.

The arrival of Dade in the small town caused quite a stir. He was a wanted felon, after all, and his face had been seen on several posters. People were curious about his sudden appearance and wondered what had brought him there. Even the town's newspaper, The Petaluma Journal, reported on his arrival. It was hard not to notice the large boat behind the bordello and Dade in his oversized hat. To them, he looked like a wealthy industrialist.

Marshal Knowles was enjoying his morning coffee with his feet resting on his desk when he stumbled upon the article. His facial expression changed from calmness to disgust as he read.

"The audacity of this asshole," he whispered to himself in disbelief.

After finishing his coffee, he went straight to the judge to present his case. His determination brought him a warrant for Dade's arrest for a burglary that had taken place in Lakeview, a small town located a few miles downriver. Knowles wasn't going to let Dade get away, especially when he knew where he was and how easy it would be to catch him at the bordello with his pants down.

The marshal arrived late that evening and peeked in a window. He saw Dade drinking with a man he recognized as José (Tiburcio's alias). He staked out the brothel for the rest of the night and, at daybreak, with the help of two interested citizens as backup, entered the building. No one had awakened aside from a man working in the kitchen.

"I'm here for Charles Dade. What room is he in?" he said quietly.

Sweat trickled down the forehead of the thin, balding man who had all he could do to answer. Knowles had a reputation for being ruthless, and without hesitation, he reached out and grabbed the man. He could feel the marshal's iron grip tighten on his shirt as Knowles yanked him forward and pushed him against the wall. The man's back hit its rough surface with a thud, making him wince in pain.

"I'm not going to ask again," Marshal Knowles whispered menacingly, his eyes fixed on the man's face.

The man's eyes bulged with fear as he stammered.

"R...Room 218."

Knowles released his grip and straightened the man up brushing imaginary dust from his shirt with his hand.

"Thanks for your cooperation. Give me the key."

Hands trembling, the man fumbled in his pocket for a key he handed to the marshal. Knowles snatched it from him and strode purposefully toward Room 218, leaving the man leaning against the wall, gasping for breath.

The three men walked upstairs and quietly unlocked the door to the room. They found Dade passed out in between the nude bodies of two women, one of whom was snoring. Knowles was a towering man. He approached Dade and tapped him on the forehead twice. Dade struggled to open one eye slowly, and when he did saw the badge on a large chest.

"Well, good morning, Marshall. Can I help you? I see you caught me in a compromised position," he grumbled, hungover.

"Get up and get dressed Charles; you are under arrest. Be quick about it."

There was nothing quick about it. Dade was still drunk and required the help of the two men backing the marshal to put on his clothes.

Knowles reached over and took a revolver from beneath the pillow, which sat next to a set of brass knuckles and put the gun into his coat pocket. One of the citizens, Isaac, who was dressed in merchant clothes, couldn't take his eyes off the nude women. The other, Jeremy, watched silently, his eyes taking it all in, an adventure not to be wasted. Helping Marshal Knowles would be a great story in his favorite bar that night.

Marshal Knowles didn't bother to handcuff Dade and instead held him as he stumbled down the stairs of the bordello out to the jail.

Two days later, the witnesses failed to show up at Dade's trial, so the judge had no choice but to dismiss the charges. As he left the courtroom, he gave Knowles a wink and a large smirk. He didn't respond but looked right through the ex-convict. Assholes like you never learn, he thought; our paths will cross again, for which I have infinite patience.

Dade invited Tiburcio to join him on his boat for the July 4th fireworks. After the crowds dispersed, they drank a large bottle of tequila and, with drill and crowbar in hand, broke into the two-story Sargent and Barnes General Store and walked away with a double-barreled shotgun worth sixty dollars, a couple of watches and an ample amount of clothing.

Marshal Knowles had been keeping a close watch on Dade and was aware of his friendship with José (Tiburcio). He had long suspected the two responsible for a string of recent thefts but had no evidence to prove it.

Although it did nothing to help him build his case, his suspicions were confirmed when he bumped into them on the street. Dade tipped his hat, smiling as he passed by, but the expressions of guilt on both bandits' faces, seeing his badge, were all Knowles needed to seek a future arrest. It sadly never came to pass, for Dade left for Napa a little over two weeks later.

Napa was not unlike the Barbary Coast, a place of refuge for prostitutes, murderers, thieves, and escaped convicts. Joining forces with another bandit, Dade robbed a teamster at gunpoint taking his watch and a pouch of gold coins. The following day, a sheriff's deputy arrested Dade on suspicion of armed robbery and, finding his black bandana with cut-out eye holes on his person, arrested him and sent him back to San Quentin.

Tiburcio continued his gregarious pursuit of women and criminal activities around the Barbary Coast in Dade's absence and was riding with Pedro Sais, the son of a prominent local ranch owner, Domingo Sais. Pedro was known for his extravagant clothing choices, always wearing gaudy, wooly chaps, fine-knitted vests, high calf-style boots, and a traditional sombrero. The two met in a bar, striking up a conversation. Pedro had always been something of a restless soul, so it didn't take long for it to turn to their shared desire for adventure and excitement. Tiburcio's charismatic personality and the stories told of his exploits drew Sais like a moth to a flame, and the friendship soon supported a variety of illicit and criminal activities. As the person responsible for hiring vaqueros for the ranch, Pedro was drawn to a criminal element, for many of the vaqueros he hired were horse thieves and ex-cons released from prison.

A successful Anglo owner of many cattle, John Walker was a prime target for theft, and he knew it. He routinely had his men keep night watch on the herds.

Pedro and Tiburcio often patrolled the fence line of Walker's ranch on their horses to look for breaks where cattle might wander off. Pedro rode up beside Tiburcio and leaned over, speaking in a hushed voice.

"I've got a plan," he said, grinning mischievously.

Tiburcio raised an eyebrow.

"A plan for what?"

"To steal some of John Walker's cattle. Think about it, Tibo. We could make a fortune selling them in town."

Tiburcio shook his head.

"I see. Yes, there is a lot of money to be made that way. I have a lot of experience with it. First, you must ensure they are not branded."

Pedro scoffed.

"You're always too cautious, Tibo, but I will ensure that we do it when he gets a new shipment of unbranded cows. I know someone who works there and can bribe him for the information. Think about all the money we could make."

Tiburcio remained firm.

"Yes, I'm cautious. I have spent years behind bars, deprived and tortured. You want me to go along with your inexperience and jump right in without the proper precautions, Pedro?"

Pedro's enthusiasm deflated as he realized the seriousness of the situation.

"I apologize, Tibo. I respect you and your experience. Will you consider it?"

Tiburcio remained firm.

"I will, but only if they are truly unbranded. Otherwise, count me out."

Pedro's expression turned into a giant smile.

"You made my day. I know where we can go out of town to sell them after we steal them."

Walker's ranch was seventeen miles north of Petaluma, a small city in California's Sonoma County. The moonlight that night helped Tiburcio and his four accomplices steal sixty heads of cattle from the ranch. They silently caught the two guards sleeping by a fire, gagged and tied them both to a tree and took their horses. The rustlers quietly drove the cattle south-wards doing all they could to avoid alerting anyone. When they reached San Rafael, a city in Marin County, they sold a portion of the herd. They proceeded further south to San Pablo, a city in Contra Costa County to sell the rest.

Discovering that a good deal of his cattle had been stolen, Walker quickly organized a team of fellow ranchers and set off in hot pursuit of the rustlers. They scoured the countryside for any signs of the thieves, eventually coming across a group of men believed to be involved in the theft as purchasers. Even with that evidence, they could not apprehend Tiburcio and his gang, who fled deep into the hills, successfully evading capture. The authorities ultimately succeeded in recovering forty of the stolen cattle, although Walker was frustrated and disappointed that the culprits had escaped justice.

He brought the case to Marshal Knowles, who like Walker was determined to uncover the truth. He conducted a thorough investigation, gathering witness statements from the buyers of the stolen cattle. Pedro was quickly recognized by the flair in his clothing choices, so with this evidence, Knowles arrested Pedro on charges of grand theft. Even though Pedro was released from jail on a $3,000 bond, Knowles relentlessly pursued justice. He interrogated Pedro extensively, hoping to extract information about his accomplices, but Pedro remained tight-lipped and refused to implicate anyone else. Nevertheless, the marshal had his suspicions.

Through his investigations, he established that the description of one of the other thieves matched that of Tiburcio Vasquez, the gang's ringleader responsible for most crimes in the area. He noted that it all started when the Mexican, who always dressed in black, arrived in the area.

The criminal activities that plagued the county included a string of burglaries, theft of horses and hundreds of cattle and seemingly countess armed robberies. The witnesses' accounts provided crucial details, including the clothing stolen from the general store Tiburcio and Dade had burglarized. They proved incredibly valuable in confirming Tiburcio's identity. They described his mannerisms, the way he walked, talked, and gestured, and that he presented as well-educated. They also noted his height, weight, and voice intonation, all of which were crucial in identifying him as the culprit. Another important detail that emerged from the witnesses' accounts was that Tiburcio only targeted Anglos as his victims. This was a particularly noteworthy aspect of his crimes, as it revealed the deep-seated hatred he felt toward this group of people.

Tiburcio regularly performed acts of kindness by handing out money to the needy he encountered daily on the streets. He had made this promise to himself after the visit with Father Martinez, and he remained committed to it even as he carried out his illegal activities. His generosity was noticed. Those who had received his help often spotted him in public and would approach him to thank him, usually repeatedly. During these encounters, the bandit would always reach in his pocket for more coins, a further act of giving that was reciprocated with their loyalty. These tips and warnings about law enforcement inquiries helped him stay ahead of the authorities and evade capture, for which the bandit was deeply grateful.

Fourteen

Charles Dade woke up shivering to the sound of cockroaches running along the floor of the damp, dark, solitary cell he had occupied for the previous two weeks. The smell was overpowering to the senses, compelling him to make a vital decision. He slapped his hand on his thigh and yelled.

"Guard, Guard!"

He repeated his call a dozen times until a half-awake guard finally appeared at his cell door.

"What do you want, Charles?" he asked impatiently.

"Tell someone to get in touch with Marshal Knowles. I have some essential information that he will want to hear."

After three long days of travel, Marshal Knowles arrived at the imposing walls of San Quentin. He identified himself, surrendered his pistol, and went to Dade's cell in 'The Stones.' Dade's heartbeat quickened, for he knew this was the chance he had been waiting for.

"What is it you want to tell me, Dade?" Knowles asked as he entered.

"I traveled a long way, and it better have been worth my damn while."

Dade wasted no time getting straight to the point. He pleaded with Knowles to get him out of his confinement so they could talk privately. A guard was called and escorted them to a room upstairs equipped with a table and chairs.

As they sat down, Knowles nearly gagged at Dade's smell.

"Jesus, Dade, you smell like shit."

"That's one of the reasons I called for you, Marshal. I'm suffering here while my ex-partner in crime is living the high life outside. I can't take it anymore. If you can get me out of here, I will give you the name of my accomplice, who is also responsible for a large amount of the crimes in your area. I have overheard conversations between fellow convicts about his recent robberies and have all the information you need to putthe asshole behind bars."

Dade not only reeked, but he had also lost a significant amount of weight, and his skin had turned ashen in color. His hair was greasy and unkempt, and he had open sores all over his body. As much as Knowles wanted to take pleasure in the famous criminal's suffering, he did not indulge himself in the satisfaction.

With this offer, Dade knew there was no turning back. He had put everything on the line with the ultimate hope that Knowles would come through for him.

"You have to get me out of here, Marshal."

"Give me the name."

"Guarantee my release first."

"I can't guarantee shit, Dade, but I will do my darndest. I'm not going to the warden's office without the name."

He let out a long sigh and sized up Knowles, measuring his sincerity.

"His name is Tiburcio Vasquez," he said begrudgingly.

After a short pause to assess the plausibility of the statement, Knowles responded.

"I am not surprised, Charles, but the confirmation will allow me to get a warrant to arrest him. Let me talk to Warden Holohan."

He headed for the warden's office, telling the guard to bring Dade some hot food.

James Holohan was an aspiring politician who planned to run for the California Senate seat in a few years. They greeted and shook hands warmly.

"Have a seat, Marshal. Can I get you some coffee or water?"

"Coffee would be fine. Thanks, James."

"What can I do for you?" the warden inquired.

"As you know, James, crime is rampant in California, especially in my neck of the woods, and I believe one man is responsible for most of it. Charles Dade was another of them, and he is already rotting in here. Due to his deteriorating condition, he gave me the name of his co-conspirator in exchange for a release from here."

Holohan looked through some files in his desk drawer.

"Dade, hmm. He has been a repeat offender here, serving in solitary as we speak."

After shuffling through the documents, he placed them neatly on his desk.

"He still has a year to go, Marshal. Is this important enough to put one ex-con back on the street?"

"I believe so, James. Plus, we know Dade and how he works, and I believe this time you broke him. My inclination is that he won't want to come back."

The warden groaned.

"Ok, who is the grandiose criminal you want to catch?"

He leaned back in his chair and waited for the answer.

"Tiburcio Vasquez."

The warden stroked his graying beard.

"Ah, yes, Vasquez. He has a reputation here. He led four prison breaks and is still looked up to by all the convicts."

Holohan walked around the office while Knowles sipped his coffee. He reasoned that it would be a political feather in his cap for a future campaign to put Vasquez back in prison, not to mention his cooperation in solving many outstanding crimes.

He slowly turned toward Knowles.

"OK, Marshal. Tell Dade he has a deal. I will release him in two weeks. Knowing him and his ways, he will be back soon enough, and then we will have them both incarcerated."

Word spread about the Dade deal, and Pedro Sais became an informant on Tiburcio's crimes. He wasn't released immediately but received a better cell and a shortened sentence.

The marshal's persistence paid off. He brought Tiburcio Vasquez to justice a week before that 1866 Christmas and put an end to the crime spree that had terrorized the region. The arrest went without a hitch since Tiburcio had just been seen by a street transient walking into the gambling hall. Knowles and two deputies simply walked up behind him.

"Tiburcio Vasquez, I have a warrant for your arrest."

A few of the patrons who knew Tiburcio started to protest, but the deputies drew their colts and kept them at bay while Knowles walked out with the handcuffed bandit.

Tiburcio was convicted only for the break-in of the Sargent and Barnes store with Dade and theft of the rifle. In a plea deal, Tiburcio pleaded guilty to that charge and a second for grand larceny. He was sentenced to two years on each count to be served consecutively, and another year for being a repeat offender.

Walking out of the courtroom, Tiburcio said under his breath, "I will kill Marshal Knowles as soon as I'm released. I hate that fucking Anglo."

Four days later, the bandit was again surrounded by the callous walls of San Quentin. Dread overwhelmed him as he walked through the prison gates. However, it was soon apparent that changes had been made since his last stint and for the better. He was relieved of his civilian clothes and, after a demeaning and thorough strip search, given prisoner clothing: striped pants and a shirt. He was escorted to his cell and discovered that he would have only one cellmate. New prison policies and added buildings minimized overcrowding.

He had only been in the cell for a minute when a guard approached him.

"Tiburcio, Warden Holohan wants to see you."

"Ok."

He entered the warden's office and found him sitting in an oversized leather chair behind an enormous mahogany desk smoking a cigar. The room was immaculate, with books fighting for space on three of the four walls. The fourth presented photographs of the prison. Indeed, a lot had changed since his break-in years ago to kidnap Chellis.

The warden didn't acknowledge him for five or so minutes, his intent clearly to make Tiburcio stand before him uncomfortably as though he didn't exist.

Finally, looking up, he examined Tiburcio with the same curiosity one might look at a wild animal in a zoo.

"My name is James Holohan. I am letting you know how things have changed since your last stay with us, Mr. Vasquez. As you can see, you will wear clothing that identifies you as a prisoner. You will be responsible for keeping it and your cell immaculately clean. The food here has improved dramatically, and we reward good behavior. For every year you serve without causing problems, two months will be deducted from your sentence. You will note that the number of guards has doubled, and we have not had an escape since your last visit."

The warden stood up with a groan and walked around his desk. He was a large man and towered over Tiburcio.

"I know your history here, and the multiple riots and prison breaks you organized. Men died, and as far as I am concerned, you should have been hanged by now. We now reward time off for good behavior because the state legislature mandated it owing to the Goodman Act two years ago. You understand this, correct?"

"I do," Tiburcio nodded.

"Then let me make this abundantly clear, asshole. As much as we reward good behavior, I have no God damn patience for bad. If you try to organize any disruption in my prison, I will come down on you, and you will be put in the dank and wet solitary cell we reserve for criminals such as you. You will regret the day you were born as you scream out loud to empty ears. I will make it my personal goal to see that it is enforced until I break you like the wild animal you have been. You will plead with God to save you from crying like a child. Do I make myself clear?"

"Yes," Tiburcio responded, looking forward.

Holohan smiled and slapped Tiburcio on his back as if they were old friends.

"Good; with that said, enjoy your stay, Mr. Vasquez. Guard! Take him away."

Doña Guadalupe was sixty-three years old when she arrived outside the walls of the prison. She was a frail woman, and the weight of Tiburcio's incarceration had taken its toll, but she felt it necessary to see him, for she didn't know how long it would be until God again brought her into his arms.

Her frailty posed no threat. She was nevertheless subjected to a thorough search for weapons and contraband before being allowed to proceed. She was even made to remove her shawl, which seemed unnecessary given her meek demeanor. Once the guard was satisfied that she was not a danger, he apologized for the inconvenience and directed her to the proper visiting room. The woman's patience and composure in the face of such indignity were admirable.

Both thrilled and embarrassed to see his mother, Tiburcio entered the visitor's room and saw how much she had changed. She appeared much weaker than he had imagined and was no longer the strong woman who had raised many children and had defied all that life threw at her.
He sat down and took her hand, feeling her skin's roughness and her grip's infirmity. Tears welled in his eyes.

"Mama, I'm sorry. I'm so sorry. I never meant to cause you any pain. Thank you so much for coming to see me. I know it was hard."

She looked at him with tears of sadness and compassion filling her own.

"Tibo, my son," she said softly, gently.

"I forgive you. I know you didn't want to do the things that you did. You were trying to survive. I remember when you told us you would live the life of a bandit. On that day, God showed me a picture in my head of you sitting where you are right now. I have been sad ever since. I hope you change your ways before it's too late. Your road will only lead to misery and death, my son."

Tiburcio felt a visceral pang of guilt. His past mistakes had always haunted him, and his mother's forgiveness, expressed as a warning, only made him feel more unworthy. He knew he had to say the right thing at this moment. He shook his head.

"No, Mama. That's no excuse. I should have done better . . . have been better."

She squeezed his hand reassuringly.

"You're a good boy, Tibo," she said, her voice filled with love.

"You made mistakes, but that doesn't make your soul bad. I know there is still hope for you. Pray to God every day, Tibo. Ask for forgiveness in His grace and for Him to lead you to live a better life. You're still my son, and I love you."

Tiburcio felt a wave of relief wash over him. His mother's words were a balm to his wounded soul. He knew he could face anything with her forgiveness.

She handed him some homemade food wrapped in cloth as she slowly rose to leave. He got up, moved toward her, and as he did in younger and happier days, hugged her tightly. He felt grateful for her unwavering love and support and kissed her cheeks repeatedly.

Two years later, one dark May afternoon, Doña Guadalupe passed away in her sleep at a friend's house in Monterey, clutching a rosary over her heart.

During his tenure in 'The Stones,' Tiburcio became reacquainted with old friends from Monterey. Francisco "Pancho" Galindo and Abelardo Salazar stood out as notorious thieves. Both men were serving multiple sentences for their crimes; their once youthful faces were now hardened from years behind bars. Whenever they found themselves in each other's company, the stories flowed from one to the next, each more embellished than the last. Their presence created an atmosphere of sweat, stale tobacco, and desperation. For them, it was just another day in their world of violence and survival. They traded tips and tricks on evading capture and staying ahead of the law.

Tiburcio, meanwhile, chose his friends carefully, seeking those who would be released around the same time as he. This new gang held the promise of a continued life of crime outside the walls of the prison, and he decided that Pancho would be one of them.

Tiburcio's incarceration went by relatively quickly and without significant incident. He stepped out of his prison stripes and into his own comfortable clothing that early June day of his release, with bright, sweet sunlight welcoming him once again as a free man.

He immediately headed north twenty-five miles to Spanish Town in Marin County, where his distant Bojorques cousins welcomed him again with open arms.

He stayed for the next two months, making various trips to Petaluma. Marshal Knowles was still serving his community. He was aware of Tiburcio's threats and hatred and, of course, that the bandit had been released. Neither was surprised to bump into each other at the door of the general store Tiburcio had robbed years earlier.

Knowles stopped and eyed him.

"Tiburcio Vasquez. I see you're out again. Things have changed around here, and we keep a tight rein on your kind. I'll be keeping my eye on you. The first thing you need to do is turn around and not come into this store again."

Tiburcio silently glared back.

"You're known by all now in these parts, and I have eyes everywhere. To me, you are just another common, piece-of-shit ex-con, and as far as your threats to me go, hombre, I am easy to find and happy to serve at your pleasure. Just give me a reason to finish this permanently. Nothing would make me happier."

Tiburcio took a moment to make direct eye contact.

"Nor I, Marshal. Be careful out there. You have a dangerous job."

Knowles, a head taller, would not be intimidated and poked Tiburcio's chest hard.

"Step aside, little man, you're in my way."

Smart enough not to be goaded, Tiburcio stepped aside and walked in the opposite direction.

Fifteen

Tiburcio traveled to his mother's last-lived town, San Juan, in pictur-esque Monterey County. It had grown considerably in his years away, now with a population of around 1,200 inhabitants. The city boasted several amenities, such as schools, four churches, ten stores, and three hotels. It was particularly noteworthy that seventeen saloons and several brothels dotted Fourth Street, making the town's nightlife vibrant and colorful. The residents had also moved beyond pedestrian horse racing events on the streets and had established a proper racetrack just outside the city, a place given to any number of exciting events. He was thrilled to reunite with his siblings and explore the various offerings of this bustling town.

Riding slowly down the main street, he saw an old friend, Frank Soto, walking up to a hitching post to untie his horse. Tiburcio spurred his and trotted over to Soto.

"Frank! You cross-eyed son of a bitch."

Frank indeed had cross eyes but was a hell of a shot with his pistol. He stood over six feet and weighed more than two hundred pounds, and at twenty-eight years of age, he had the reputation fit for a ruthless highway robber. He turned to the insult and immediately recognized his old bandit friend.

"Tibo! I thought you were in prison. When did you get out?"

"About two months ago or so," he said as he dismounted.

"Just looking for work," he added.

Conventional thought was that gangs of bandits lived in the mountains together. The truth was that many had regular jobs and teamed up in small groups to commit crimes, only to disband and meld back into society.

"Things are changing fast here, amigo. The railroad is being finished bringing all sorts of people here from the east. The Anglos are taking over, forming new towns in Hollister and Gilroy, replacing the Californio towns we grew up in, like San Juan. Did you hear that our old friend from San Quentin, Abelardo, opened a cantina here?"

Tiburcio's face lit up with recognition as he responded.

"Abelardo Salazar?"

The name brought back memories from their past adventures as bandits. His curiosity was piqued as he wondered what had become of his old friend.

"The one and only amigo. He has gone straight and runs a legitimate business, but don't worry, he hasn't forgotten his friends."

With a friendly smile and a pat on the back, Tiburcio suggested they go over to Abelardo's for some grub. Frank mounted his, and the two bandits trotted towards the cantina, eager to catch up and reminisce about old times.

Abelardo was a pleasant man. He had a soft face with heavy eyebrows and a trimmed mustache. He wore a salsa-stained apron over his wrinkled shirt and never stopped moving as he cooked and served the crowded room. For the next two hours, every time Abelardo could catch a break, the trio caught up telling stories and lies, all the while gorging themselves on chorizo and eggs topped with Abelardo's famous salsa, of which he was proud.

Frank and Tiburcio finally rose, stuffed from eating, and bid Abelardo a warm farewell, promising to catch up with him soon. Tiburcio decided to use the cantina as his temporary headquarters but had yet to try to enlist their friend's help. Abelardo had met a beautiful woman, whom Tiburcio had also set his eyes on, but to no avail. His natural charms failed, and he quickly found himself uninterested in the woman. She had already given her heart to Abelardo and had ignored Tiburcio's flirtations. In due course, Abelardo and she fell in love and married.

Tiburcio spent a good amount of time catching up with his family, yet well aware that a brand-new Wells Fargo stagecoach made regular late-night trips from the San Joaquín Valley to the coastal towns. The coach was primarily used for carrying passengers, but rumors were circulating that it also transported an iron-bound box filled with valuable coinage for banks. A plan was made to rob it.

It was around one o'clock in the morning, and Tiburcio and Frank were waiting for the stagecoach to approach the Pacheco Pass from Bells Station. They had picked a strategic location to intercept the coach as the road narrowed and began to climb in elevation, which would force the six-horse team to slow down. The two men were well-prepared for the heist.

Frank was on the left side as the stage approached and Tiburcio on the right. They mounted their horses, and both pulled their bandanas over their faces and immediately bolted into the path of the stagecoach. Its climb was slow as the grade was steep. It would eventually force it to stop. The six-up driver appeared caught off guard.

"Whoa! Whoa!"

The young armed guard beside him tried to pull up his shotgun, but Tiburcio's rifle was already out and ready.

"Don't move another inch, hombre. I swear even an inch will guarantee not another second on this earth for you. Throw it out to the dirt."

The guard complied, immediately sensing the seriousness in Tiburcio's voice. He had a newborn at home and was not about to risk his life against these odds.

Frank remained atop his horse and approached the carriage with three passengers inside, two women and one man, none were able or equipped to defend themselves. Frank had no intention of robbing them personally because he had a more significant target in mind—the box atop the stage.

Frank addressed the passengers politely to keep them calm, his words slightly muffled through his mask.

"Good evening, friends. I hope you are having a nice evening. Don't be alarmed; we are not here to hurt you unless you do something stupid. We don't want your valuables. Just be good boys and girls and sit on your hands while we finish our business outside. Alright?"

The passengers looked shocked and confused.

"Yes, I meant to put your hands under your asses and sit on them," Frank repeated.

The passengers, understanding the gravity of the situation, promptly placed their hands under their butts and nodded their heads in agreement. Frank then proceeded to carry out his plan, confident they would remain cooperative throughout the ordeal.

On top of the stage sat the young guard, who was barely out of his teens. He had but a few strands of hair on his lip, a futile effort to look older.

"Turn around, pick up that box, and throw it down," Tiburcio ordered.

The young man struggled to lift the heavy box but eventually complied with the request. He threw the box to the ground. Since it was strapped with metal, it didn't break apart. The sound of the heavy box hitting the road echoed through the area. The guard looked a little embarrassed that he had struggled with such a simple task. As soon as the box hit, Frank fired two shots from his 44-caliber pistol, causing the six coach horses to gallop off with the driver frantically trying to maintain control.

The sound of the retreating horses faded in the distance, and Frank dismounted, using a crowbar to break open the box. He approached Tiburcio and looked up with a seemingly boundless smile.

"Look what I found, amigo."

In his outstretched hand was a bag of five hundred dollars in gold coins.

The next morning, Tiburcio slowly opened his eyes. As he lay in bed, he felt the warmth of the morning sun on his face as it shone through the open window. He stretched and felt a tingling sensation in his left arm, which had fallen asleep under his bed partner. He looked to his side and saw the stunning figure of a beautiful Eastern European gypsy woman lying next to him. Her petite frame was crowned with jet-black hair that fell in soft waves around her face. Her eyes were a mesmerizing shade of greenish hazel, inviting him in with their sultry gaze. He was undeniably drawn to her and knew the passion they had shared the night before had taken him to new heights of excitement never before experienced. She was expensive but worth every penny. Besides, with the gold from the previous night's heist, money was of no object.

Tiburcio lay there, once again reflecting on his life. His youthful innocence and the work ethic instilled in him at his uncle's ranch had been taken from him by the foreigners who had overtaken his community, who had taken his and his loved ones' assets for their own. That deep hole in his identity was now filled with an unadulterated hatred of Anglos, who looked down on the Californios as second-class citizens. He thought back to the days when he was incarcerated and how the prison walls had seemed to close in on him daily.

He pushed the thoughts way in favor of his present reality.
He was resting in a warm, comfortable bed with a beautiful woman by his side, and he was grateful for his newfound freedom. Moments like these reminded him of how far he had come since the countless nights he had spent shivering on a straw mattress.

Tiburcio's philosophy of life was changing. Gradually but surely, his purpose had evolved into a pattern of criminal activities necessary to sustain his fondness for nice clothing and expensive women. Convincing himself that he could steal enough without getting caught, he dreamed that someday he would buy a ranch and return to the life he had once led while working for his Uncle Fernando. He missed dearly the feeling of satisfaction that came after a long day of hard work. The difference now, however, was that he wanted to work for himself, not for someone else, no matter what it took. To meet this goal, Tiburcio needed more extensive and lucrative robberies. He needed more significant rewards.

First things first, he thought, as he rolled over and pulled down the sheet, exposing the beautiful petite body of his lover lying on her stomach. He put his lips to the small of her back and kissed her up to her neck. She moaned and rolled over, pulling him to her. He was immediately ready and entered her slowly for a morning of lovemaking and room service.

The bandits had let things settle for a month before trying the same heist in the same location. Of course, Wells Fargo had been on its toes since the last one for its nightly transports, but after four weeks of no other attempts, monotony once again replaced vigilance.

Tiburcio planned for a distraction for the approaching stagecoach. He filled up a bottle with flammable lantern fluid and put a soaked rag into the neck, to throw to the opposite side of the road, a device not unlike a Molotov cocktail, which would not be invented for another sixty years or so.

As the coach approached the same area climbing the hill as before, Tiburcio lit the soaked rag and threw it across the road to the base of a tree where he had rounded up a pile of dry leaves and tinder. It exploded into flame on impact, starting an immediate fire that spooked the approaching horses. The driver had his hands filled with panic, and the guard was distracted by the fire. They didn't notice Frank step out from behind a boulder to haze the horses to a halt. Tiburcio fired three shots into the air, galloping toward the guard, who fired two shots from his shotgun, grazing Tiburcio's left neck. The guard's shotgun was now out of ammunition, and as he drew his pistol, Tiburcio fired, blowing the guard's large hat off his head. His reaction, besides astonishment and panicked eyes, was to immediately drop his gun.

"Don't shoot! I am now unarmed!"

Tiburcio was pissed for having been shot.

"Drop your pants to your knees and tie the belt tight around them, and you too," he told the coach driver.

"Huh?" the guard replied.

"You heard me. There are five more bullets in this pistol and only two targets."

Both men quickly pulled their pants to their knees and tied their legs tight together with their belts. Frank started laughing behind his bandana as he grabbed the metal-strapped box from the coach's top. He pulled it off and dropped it.

Tiburcio's gun was fixed on the two men. It started to rain. Frank shot the lock off the box and emptied it of papers he let fly away. He then counted another seven hundred dollars in gold coins and some paper money in a sack. As the rain began to pour, the bandits donned their ponchos to stay dry and turned their horses to leave. The guard went for his gun but failed because his haltered pants tripped him onto the dickey seat behind him. Frank and Tiburcio laughed as they rode away into the lightning-lit sky.

Dawn approached, and the duo found themselves crossing paths with a man, Eugene Sawyer, who it turns out was a writer and author. He was driving half a dozen head of cattle alongside the road in the opposite direction. Eugene was soaked to the bone when Tiburcio and Frank approached him. They looked severe; their large hats tipped down over their eyes and in drenched ponchos that flowed down to their boots.

"Hola, amigo. Where are you heading?" Tiburcio asked.

"I'm going from Gilroy to Hollister to sell this beef."

"You look freezing, my friend."

Tiburcio pulled out a black flask partially filled with whiskey and offered it to Eugene, who graciously took two swigs.

"Thank you very much, friend. That warms my innards, indeed my soul."

"Keep the flask, and good luck," Tiburcio encouraged.

The following day, Eugene recounted the events of the rainy night meeting to a friend over coffee at the local newspaper office in Hollister. Going into more detail about the mystery men, his friend quickly interrupted.

"That was none other than Tiburcio Vasquez. He left town just this morning and caused quite a commotion when the marshal attempted to find and arrest him. In his usual, notoriously cunning way, he managed to evade capture by donning a skirt and mantilla borrowed from one of the Mexican women who worked at the bordello he was celebrating in."

Eugene's eyes widened in surprise.

"Goodness gracious, that was Tiburcio Vasquez! He could have easily robbed me but instead shared his whiskey bottle, warming me from the storm. This is a story that must be told."

The excitement in his voice was palpable as he eagerly began planning how to incorporate this encounter into his upcoming piece for the paper.

In the following months, Eugene met with Tiburcio in secret through friendly contacts to conduct numerous interviews and gather material for Tiburcio's biography. Their bond grew, and the writer and bandit became good friends. Not only did Eugene go on to successfully write the biography, but he also wrote several articles for the local paper detailing the bandits' incredible adventures.

Whispers of Tiburcio's fearless exploits and unwavering devotion to his people echoed through every dusty street and crowded marketplace in California and Mexico. He was becoming a legend, a folk hero whose name struck fear in the hearts of Anglos and admiration in the eyes of Californios. The women, especially, were enamored by his charm and bravery, typically flocking to catch a glimpse of the man who had become an icon of courage and defiance. This regularly drew the attention of law enforcement, whose attempts to find charges to arrest the bandit continually failed.

Tiburcio's attire was, in a word, distinctive. He preferred to stand out in a crowd. In his younger years, which were more spirited, he often donned a short-waisted vest, a wide-brimmed hat, and fancy pants with intricate buttons down the legs. The wisdom of his more mature years welcomed the clothes of a gentleman. In both periods of his life, his style set him apart from other Californios, who typically wore more practical attire such as canvas trousers, vests, and army coats.

His love for glitz extended to great care and effort put into posing for photographs, as he did for the early portrait by Wilbur Bayley. He typically wore all black—trousers, coat, and velvet vest with a striking silver watch and chain shining against the dark fabric. Little did Tiburcio consider, though, that wearing this characteristic outfit made it easier for the authorities and witnesses to identify him.

In fact, the flashy exterior hid scars from past battles, which, for him were constant reminders of his dangerous life. Bullet holes marred his left chest, neck, and arm and added a rugged edge to his otherwise polished appearance. The scars on his back from Lt. Moon's madness were a map adding mysteriousness. The women he bedded took pleasure in running their fingers over the scars, further seduced by the stories behind them.

Sixteen

People around Tiburcio treated him with cautious admiration. Women found him utterly irresistible, and the bandit typically had one in his company. His prized sixteen-shot Henry lever action rifle, a revolutionary weapon that fired metal cartridges, and a sleek Colt dragoon pistol were his constant companions. Both hung at his side ready for use at a moment's notice. A sharp bowie knife secured to his belt further symbolized his formidable reputation. His presence alone demanded respect and instilled fear in those who dared to cross his path, and his reputation preceded him, whether by word of mouth or telegraphed communications. The latter committed to ink what rather passed in everyday communication, but it also ensured that Tiburcio's reputation and past were continually made known to various counties, marshals, and sheriffs. Since all forms of communication called attention to the bandit's appearance, law enforcement and the public were regularly on the lookout for the man dressed in black.

He noticed the increased glances and attention of people walking by, as well as those in the bar who he thought were whispering about him. His wonder of what words were hushed led him, again, to ponder his position in life.

"What was this inclination I have towards a life of crime?" he thought.

"Why do I have it? Is it evil or a result of my early life experiences and surroundings?"

It didn't help that the new railroads brought in an increasing number of white people, like locusts, he thought, capable of only voraciously consuming the land. The situation made him feel helpless and frustrated. With his cultural heritage continuously under threat, the world unfolding around him often felt like an assault on his identity and, thus, his choices.

"Are these excuses for my behavior?" he whispered to himself.

"Or am I just a common criminal looking to legitimize myself?"

In truth, it was hard to say. Crime mattered little to his people; he had earned their admiration and love, and they revered him as a champion of the oppressed rather than the common thief perceived by the Anglo majority. Tiburcio decided that he was a hero fighting for the rights of those persecuted. He believed in his cause that it was just, and not out of desire to commit crimes for the sake of it. At the very least, he thought, it was a living. His conviction drove his continued life of thievery, and he knew it was the reason why he had spent the lion's share of his life constantly looking over his shoulder and why he would continue to for the foreseeable future. He also was honest enough with himself that much of his introspection led to the self denial of his actions.

Monterey County Sheriff Thomas Watson had grown up with Tiburcio and knew him well, as had his deputy Jacob Leese. Watson was about five foot eleven and 180 pounds. He always sported a trimmed mustache, kept his hair short, and wore a shallow brimmed hat. Leese was about the same size, with medium-long, combed-back hair and a long beard. There were countless times that Tiburcio had the upper hand on the sheriff but always spared him due to their shared history.

Sheriff Watson and tax collector Alonzo Allen needed to cross the Salinas River in their buggy. Allen was transporting a large amount of tax money with Watson's protection. The impenetrable foliage of towering willow trees provided cover for members of Tiburcio's gang, who lay in wait to ambush and kill them without their leader's presence or knowl-edge. As soon as this imminent danger reached Tiburcio through one of the crew who had refused to participate in the robbery, he raced to the site on horseback, arriving in a cloud of dust. His jaw was set with steely determination, and his hand gripped tightly around his revolver as he confronted the armed criminals hiding behind the trees, their rifles aimed at the unsuspecting men in the buggy.

"If you dare fire on that buggy, you must go through me first," Tiburcio barked.

One of the bandits, Refugio, responded.

"Tibo, there are hundreds of dollars on that buggy. It is filled with the monies from our people."

"I'm not fucking around here, Refugio! Put your goddamned guns down."

Refugio lowered his rifle reluctantly.

"OK, we won't kill them. Just let us go get the loot."

Tiburcio remained adamant, wholly convinced of their stupidity.

"Don't be an idiot, Refugio. They are armed; do you think they will comply with your threats? Get on your horses. Go back to camp! Now! Don't make me ask twice."

Tiburcio was resolute in his allegiance to his old friends and refused to back down. The fearlessness and loyalty he embodied struck fear into the hearts of his gang while at the same time inspiring their admiration. They mounted their horses and trotted off to camp. Watson and Allen had no idea how close they had come to death as they continued their trip.

The following week, Sheriff Watson received a warrant for the arrest of Tiburcio Vasquez for suspicion that he had recently robbed a stagecoach. When he summoned Deputy Leese into his office, he instructed him to go to the Union Saloon, where Vasquez was reportedly hanging out, and arrest him immediately.

"You're coming with me, right?" Leese asked.

"I have to attend to some urgent business in Hollister and can't assist you. You think you can handle it, Jacob?"

"Do I have a choice?"

He grabbed a rifle from the gun rack.

"I'll do it. I'm not going to like it, but it's my job, so what the hell?" he said as he walked out into the dry summer day, slamming the door.

Leese knew the situation could turn dangerous. He suspected the sheriff's decision to leave was partly motivated by his fear of the notorious outlaw. Leese shared the same unease but knew he had to accept the task. Bracing himself for the challenge, he headed towards the Union Saloon, hoping to catch Vasquez before he could slip away.

Tiburcio was having a drink with two friends at the dimly lit bar. He was wearing his usual all black clothing. He saw the deputy walk in the front door and, immediately recognizing him, called over.

"Jacob! What is going on, amigo? You look like you're on some kind of business carrying that rifle. Come over and have a drink with us."

Leese hadn't expected a warm reception, especially with his assigned mission.

"Sure, Tibo, I can do that."

"What will you have?" Tiburcio asked.

"Whiskey is fine, thank you," the deputy answered as he hesitantly placed himself between Tiburcio and the other two men, leaning his rifle against the bar wall.

He quickly downed his drink for courage. Tiburcio ordered a second round.

"Let me pay for this one, Tibo."

"I won't have it, amigo. I make my money much easier than you do, Jacob. Being a deputy is dangerous, and you risk your life for every dime, right?"

The two bandits with Tiburcio smiled in mocking agreement. Tiburcio continued.

"You never know, Jacob; a man in your position might get all shot up someday and have to use whatever money you have to get yourself patched up. No?"

Tiburcio's stare at the deputy was intimidating and unyielding, forcing Leese to look away. The look on Tiburcio's face and that of the other two bandits accompanying him made the message clear. The deputy chose not to arrest him. After a moment of silence, Tiburcio broke in with a laugh.

"Finish your drink, Jacob. Let's go to Simona's restaurant and get some steaks for lunch. You're hungry, no?"

Leese nodded affirmatively with relief, grateful for the distraction.

They went to the restaurant, ordered lunch, and reminisced about the good old days. They talked about their youth, their dreams, and the experiences they had shared. As the memories unfolded, Tiburcio saw beyond those deeper feelings in Jacob's face. The deputy had been through a great deal of late. His burdened expression and unease were palpable.

They savored the juicy steaks and crispy potatoes and sipped on some cognac. The restaurant's warm ambiance and good food lifted their spirits. After lunch, Tiburcio paid the bill, and they shook hands before parting ways. Leese returned to the jail, relieved both from the camaraderie shared with Tiburcio as well as the sheriff's departure. He put the rifle away and sat at his desk. Staring out the window, he couldn't have felt more ashamed for backing down from his assignment if he had wanted to.

Sheriff Watson walked into the jail from the rain the next day and found Leese reading the paper with his feet on the desk. He knocked the rain off his hat, removed his slicker, and hung it up.

"Where did you finally put Vasquez? What cell?" he said, looking around.

"I didn't arrest him."

"Why? Wasn't he in the saloon?"

"He was in the saloon, alright, with some friends. I wasn't about to do it alone. It would've been better if you had come with me. But, even so,

Sheriff, I don't want to be killed by that man. If you want him arrested, you can do it yourself. Here is the warrant; he'll be returning in a few days."

Sheriff Watson did not arrest Tiburcio. Either he knew he was inept, or he was flat-out scared, but, in any case, the bandit was never detained on his home turf of Monterey County.

Tiburcio was now a renowned bandit and had been operating with impunity in Monterey for quite some time. Realizing it was time to relocate his headquarters to a more secure location, he chose the rugged and rocky Calera Canyon Gorge, situated approximately twenty-five miles east of town, which was the home of Pedro Regalado's ranch. The move showed a total lack of respect for Watson, who owned a farm named Corral de Tierra in the neighboring canyon.

Tiburcio was no lone ranger, as he had a group of hardened bandits fiercely loyal to him. Francisco Bardenas, Manuel López, Pancho Galindo, Fernando and his brother Chavo Arceo, the brothers Narciso and Gracia Rodriguez, Pepito Salazar, and Rita Miranda were some of the most prominent members of Tiburcio's gang. They were all skilled and ruthless criminals willing to do whatever it took to help Their leader achieve his objectives and, so, enrich their own.

Seventeen

Sheriff Harry Morse had been on Tiburcio's trail for quite some time, but the notorious outlaw was always one step ahead. Morse was determined to catch Tiburcio and end his reign of terror. Although aware that Morse was hot in pursuit, Tiburcio continued to plan and execute daring, increasingly audacious raids with each passing day. The tension between them grew. Tiburcio remained unfazed and continued to operate with bold impunity; Morse's setbacks fueled his mounting frustration.

In his efforts to take down Tiburcio's gang, Morse had dispatched several spies to infiltrate their ranks. Unfortunately, even these attempts proved futile, and the sheriff grew increasingly desperate. In a last-ditch effort, he reached out to Tom McMahon, a prominent merchant who conducted business with the local Creole population and was believed to know Tiburcio's whereabouts. In a letter to McMahon, Morse implored him to contact him immediately if he found any information about the bandit's activities.

Tiburcio was a man of honor and integrity, always standing up for his beliefs, albeit illegally. He was outraged when he heard of McMahon's willingness to help Morse. He had always been on good terms with McMahon. He saw the behavior as a betrayal, one that would not be tolerated. McMahon needed to be taught a lesson he would never forget.

He learned that the merchant was traveling to Salinas to pay some taxes and planned to intercept him. Accompanied by the Rodriguez brothers, he approached McMahon's two-up merchant wagon on horseback appearing casual and non-threatening. They had carefully positioned themselves on the opposite side of the road from McMahon's direction of travel, waiting for the right moment. As he and the brothers calmly closed the distance, McMahon waved and smiled. Tiburcio started the conversation by looking down from his lofty position.

"Hi, Tom. How are you?"

"I'm fine, Tibo. How are you?"

"I'm perplexed, Tom. I have always treated you with respect. Have I done something otherwise to piss you off?"

"Err, no, not at all," McMahon replied more cautiously.

"My informants have told me that you have been in contact with Sheriff Morse, the Anglo prick who has been hunting me. Don't deny it, Tom, because the Rodriguez brothers here would feel no remorse in stripping you naked while unharnessing your horses and running them off. He leaned down toward McMahon from his horse and stared glaringly in his eyes.

"So, is it true?"

McMahon looked down, embarrassed, and whispered, "Yes, I suppose so."

"Was that a yes I heard? I think it was Tom, so to teach you a lesson, I will need to relieve you of some of your belongings, my friend. Damnit Tom, I thought you were my friend."

McMahon's head, dripping with sweat, hung in shame at being caught.

"Give me your brand-new-looking Colt revolver and that handsome ring on your finger."

The merchant relented, handing over his pistol and ring.

"Men like you are cowards, Tom. I should have the Rodriguez boys do what they will with you, but not today. Today, you can go back to Morse and tell him that I have ears everywhere and that I will see him well before he ever sees me. That might be his last day on this lovely earth. Understand?"

"Yes."

With that, Tiburcio slapped the hindquarters of the McMahon's horses, sending them trotting. His head jerked, and his hat blew off, but he didn't once look back after gaining control of his horses. He was thankful to have gotten off so lightly.

Tiburcio spent a week resting and laying low in his secluded Calera Canyon hideaway before planning his next heist. Tiburcio partnered with Pancho Galindo, a fellow inmate from San Quentin. Pancho was a diminutive, yet fierce Mexican man dressed in traditional vaquero attire. Despite his small stature, Pancho was known for his quick temper and love for wearing a massive sombrero that made him look somewhat comical. His skill with his fists and as a marksman was not to be underestimated, however. His right eye had a scar across it from a knife fight in his youth. He was fiercely loyal to Tiburcio and would do anything to protect him. They made for a formidable duo riding out into the day's sweltering heat.

They went down the Old Stage Road to the Deep Wells Stagecoach Station with the intent to rob it.

They arrived at the small wayside station exhausted from their journey. Tiburcio knocked on the locked door after tying their horses to the hitching post. A moment later, a sleepy-looking Jimmy Nance opened the door in his long John blue pajamas, with unkempt long hair and a beard. He appeared completely disinterested.

"What do you guys want?" he said, yawning.

Tiburcio cut straight to the point.

"We need a bottle of whiskey."

Jimmy nodded and stepped aside, inviting them in. The bandits entered the dark main room, which was stocked with essential goods for travelers. The cool air was refreshing. They were grateful for the respite from the heat outside. It took mere minutes for Jimmy to fill a bottle of whiskey for them, and Tiburcio handed him a twenty-dollar gold piece.

"I'll need some change," Tiburcio said.

Jimmy frowned.

"I can't change that much. Let me check."

"I'll make it easy for you; just add this two-dollar can of beans to the bill," Tiburcio smiled.

Jimmy unlocked the cash box to get the change when Tiburcio and Pancho slowly pulled out their Colt pistols, pointing them at his face.

"No need for the change, Jimmy. I was just kidding. Empty the box of bills and coins; for that, you get to keep your face."

Tiburcio's voice was low and menacing. Jimmy's hands started to shake as he emptied the cash register and surrendered its contents to the bandits. Pancho smiled a wide, yellow-toothed grin.

"Thank you, amigo. Now put your hands up and walk to the front door with us. Don't let your hands down until you see our horses disappear. Comprende?"

Jimmy obeyed the short Mexican and watched them ride away. He then dressed, locked the station, and rode into town to report the theft to Sheriff Morse, hoping the bandits would soon be caught.

Over the past few years, California had become increasingly known for its frequent stagecoach robberies. These heists were usually carried out similarly to the ones that Tiburcio had committed on high-incline roads, where the Wells Fargo cargo boxes were thrown off the stagecoach. While the passengers were usually not hurt, they were relieved of their valuables, which often included gold, jewelry, and other precious items.

These commonplace robberies created a constant fear for travelers and merchants alike. The authorities had been trying to crack down on these crimes, but the robbers were often quick and elusive, making it difficult to catch them.

Two days after Tiburcio had robbed Jimmy Nance, he decided to act again. This time, he planned to rob a different stagecoach line and execute one of California's most daring heists. With no railway travel yet available, the stagecoach business was booming. Passengers who wanted to travel to Southern California had no choice but to rely on stagecoaches. As a result, it wasn't unusual to see up to twenty individuals crammed inside and on top of it for their commutes. Extra horses were added for longer trips that went up inclines. Male passengers were asked to disembark and walk up the hill if the grade was too steep.

Dennis Conroy, a former Pony Express rider who later became a stagecoach driver, took pride in his appearance. Like many of his fellow drivers, his style was fashionable for the time. Men who dressed that way were often called dandies. On this particular day, driving a stagecoach traveling south from Gilroy, he wore a "sack suit," a precursor to the modern business suit. The suit consisted of a jacket, vest, tie, and hat and was made of high-quality material reflecting his prestigious driver position.

Drivers like Conroy were among the highest-paid workers of their time and were afforded certain luxuries that other workers could only dream of. For example, they could have free drinks, food, and lodging at any station nearby. As the stagecoach approached within ten miles of the Deep Wells station, Conroy's thoughts turned to the cool, refreshing drink that awaited him after a quick shot of whiskey.

Narciso Rodriguez, Pancho, and Francisco Barcenas joined Tiburcio and waited nine miles north of the Deep Wells Station on the Old Stage Road to intercept it.

The bandits were dressed in equally exquisite clothing, previously stolen. Tiburcio and his gang were now well known, and having a reputation to uphold, they did not conceal their faces. They took pride in their notoriety as the protectors of their people—or, at least, that's how they saw themselves.

Before the stage passed by, the gang stopped Shelby Moore, who was driving his one-horse buggy to a political meeting. They blindfolded him, tied his hands behind his back, and robbed him of the fifty dollars he had in his vest pocket. Narciso then hopped onto the buggy and drove it through a broken fence into a thick grove of oak trees in the adjoining pasture.

Barcenas next stopped a sixteen-year-old boy on horseback, tying and blindfolding him as well. He took the fifty cents from the boy's pocket, but Tiburcio, shaking his head, made him give it back. The boy was placed under the same oak trees with his horse tied next to the buggy and Shelby Moore.

The stagecoach finally came into view and made its way towards the steep incline. Tiburcio noticed there was no guard aboard due to the number of passengers. The horses were slowing, showing signs of fatigue, when he called out to the driver.

"Hey, why don't you stop and let those horses rest?"

Conroy, a seasoned veteran, refused to comply with the suspicious request. Having been robbed before, he was anxious to reach their destination and used his long-handled whip to urge the horses to gallop the hill. Tiburcio would not be ignored after the polite approach. He quickly spurred his horse into a full gallop, blowing past the stagecoach and through the dust cloud it created. He positioned himself in front of the team of eight horses, at the same time firing his pistol in the air.

"Halt! Stop now or I'll blow a hole in you!!" he shouted.

Conroy was frightened by Tiburcio's unexpected move.

The abrupt, loud noise and the sight of the bandit startled the horses causing them to come to a complete stop. They huffed and snorted, fighting back at Conroy and pulling hard on the reins.

Tiburcio approached the shocked driver, who knew better than to draw his gun, and explained the importance of treating the horses with care and respect.

"You know better than that, amigo. Really? Do you think that you can drive this monstrosity of a wagon filled with people up a hill to get away from us? Only to hurt these beautiful equine specimens. Take out your pistol and throw it down."

Conroy acknowledged the bandit and threw his revolver to the ground.

Narciso, Francisco, and Pancho approaching from behind and on each side, surrounded the stagecoach. Pancho was the only one not dressed for the occasion, still in his sombrero and vaquero gear.

Tiburcio leaned over to Conroy.

"Drive your team through the fence into that grove of oaks."

Conroy pulled on his reins, turned the stage around, and went into the pasture, where he saw the previous victims tied up in the shade. Narciso gave orders to the passengers.

"Everyone, get out and give up your valuables. Don't make me waste my time searching for each one of you. If you value your life more than your belongings, be smart and give them up now."

Conroy and one of the men in the Dickey seat stepped down, and the rest of the passengers exited the coach. There was only one woman onboard. She stayed in the Dickey seat atop and refused to leave it. Ever the charmer, Tiburcio guided his horse next to her.

"What is your name, Ma'am?"

Her face was shaded beneath a wide-brimmed bonnet. Her full dress buttoned tightly and conservatively to her neck. She was stunningly attractive and had a strong will about her for being so young.

"My name is Mrs. Murphy to you, sir."

"Are you traveling alone, Mrs. Murphy?"

"No, I am with my husband, who is stepping down with the driver."

"Alright, Mrs. Murphy, you can stay here. Mr. Murphy, you can join the others, please."

Tiburcio was puzzled as to the whereabouts of the express box. However, Mrs. Murphy, a wise and crafty woman, was well aware of its location. It was partially under her seat. Thinking quickly, she slyly concealed it by pushing it further under her dress, under the dickey seat.

Meanwhile, Pancho and the other bandits continued tying up, blindfolding, and searching the passengers. Mr. Murphy had one hundred and fifty dollars and a gold watch. Pancho loved the clock and put it in his vest pocket for himself. Mrs. Murphy, feisty in attitude, pressed them to let the passengers keep some money for food for the remainder of the trip.

"You're barbarians. Would you have us all starve?"

Pancho laughed loudly, showing his yellow teeth. He brought out five dollars and tucked it back into Mr. Murphy's jacket pocket.

"See, Señora, I am not a barbarian. Now you can eat."

He took off his giant sombrero and bowed to her as he continued searching the others. Narciso and Francisco pushed the passengers into a close circle when they finished their searches. Francisco strode confidently towards Tiburcio, a sly grin on his face as he counted the spoils of their robbery.

"Eight hundred sixty-five dollars and a haul of watches and necklaces, Tibo."

Tiburcio's expression was anxious, his eyes scrutinizing the situation nervously.

"I couldn't find the express box. We need to leave now before they catch onto us. Wells Station will be alarmed that the stage is late and send out a posse."

The gang hastily mounted their horses and prepared to ride off. Tiburcio turned to address the hostages, his tone polite but intense in its warning.

"Thank you for your cooperation. But don't think this is the end. We'll be back, and if we don't find you right where we left you...well, let's just say your worst nightmares will pale in comparison to what we'll do to you."

Tibo rode past Mrs. Murphy, who was still perched at the stagecoach. As he passed her, he tipped his hat in a gesture of respect, acknowledging her presence.

"Ma'am."

He had been fooled by the clever woman, never knowing that she concealed the valuable express box beneath her dress.

As the gang was leaving the pasture through the broken fence, a teamster with a two-up pulling a wagon full of fence posts and wire approached. They pulled their guns and forced him off the road and under the trees with all the other victims. They tied him up, blindfolded him, and took his twenty dollars.

"OK, men, we can do this all day and tie up the whole population under that tree, but let's get going while we can."

Tiburcio led his cohorts back to the road to hightail it south. Galloping at breakneck speed, they saw Sheriff Watson and a passenger in a wagon come quickly into view. The former lawman, now running for mayor, recognized the ruthless bandits, but he dared not make eye contact or get involved in any trouble. He gripped the reins tightly, trying to keep his composure as the gang passed, their laughter echoing in his ears and a taunting reminder of his powerlessness.

The passengers of the stagecoach entreated Mrs. Murphy to untie them. She was hesitant to act, fearing the bandits would be back for the express box and would harm them if they found she had been hiding it. Mr. Murphy was growing increasingly impatient, reminding his wife that they had been waiting for over an hour and needed to act if they wanted to escape unharmed. Letting out a sigh of resignation, she clambered down from the carriage. She worked feverishly to undo the others' restraints.

Being an experienced stagecoach driver, Conroy was quick to load everyone. The other prisoners were now also released. None wasted time getting back on the road. Conroy whipped his team of horses, urging them to get to the nearest station at Wells. Once there, they reported the harrowing robbery and sought immediate assistance. They were relieved and grateful when the stagecoach company offered accessible hotels and meals for the night. Having survived the memorably dangerous encounter, the victims hastened to give their statements to the local sheriff, Nick Harris.

Meanwhile, the bandits continued riding south. They chuckled as they rode past the Wells Fargo Station. A posse of five agents was heading quickly in the direction of the stagecoach. Tiburcio watched them intently as they disappeared into the horizon.

The bandits Tiburcio rode with were never satisfied and took every opportunity they had to rob and steal. Abram Grewell's farm had come into view, and their gazes settled upon the aging man who was busy mending a broken fence. Grewell was about sixty years old and a former Confederate soldier who hated anyone of color, especially Mexicans. His dirty bib overalls, worn over a stained red shirt, did nothing to hide his grossly large gut. Grewell's face was etched with bitterness and preju-dice, as were his weathered hands. He looked up from his diligent work with the fencing tools, eyeing the approaching strangers with suspicion. He then paused his repairs completely to greet Pancho, who had broken away from the group. The kicked-up wake of dust made it clear that the rider was there for him. The old man turned to face him, his brows furrowing as he assessed the newcomer. He spat chewing tobacco from his stained lips.

"Can I help you?" he asked curtly.

Pancho immediately pulled out his pistol.

"Yes, you can, amigo. Empty your pockets."

Grewell glanced toward his Henry repeater rifle, leaning on a fence post ten feet away and spit another glob to the ground at the feet of the bandit's horse.

"Ah, ah, ah, my friend, that would be a stupid thing to try and get to that rifle. I am really good with this pistol. I won't kill you, but I will shoot you in your kneecap. That would hurt badly. No? Now empty your pockets."

Grewell paused.

"God damnit," he said under his breath.

He reached into his pocket and pulled out eight dollars. Pancho leaned over from his horse and grabbed the greenbacks.

"Muchas Gracias, my friend."

Pancho's spurs dug deeply into his horse's flanks, sending the animal into a frenzied gallop toward his comrades, who had anxiously watched the robbery. Unlike them Tiburcio was feeling bored and impatient. He noticed Grewell running for his rifle and swiftly dropping to his knees, pointing it at them. The former soldier was a crack shot, firing a quick round and levering the second.

With a fierce cry, Tiburcio yelled, "Let's go!"

But, before they could mount their defense, Grewell unleashed the second shot from the rifle, again shattering the tense stillness. The second shot caught Pancho in the side.

"I'm hit!"

Realizing Grewell's marksmanship abilities, the gang decided not to return fire and instead retreat as fast as possible. The old man was levering in more rounds and firing them quickly.

"You fucking Mexicans! I'll see you hang someday!"

Sheriff Nick Harris hastily organized a posse, their eagerness for justice fueled by the testimonies of the frightened stagecoach passengers. The descriptions of the bandits—Tiburcio Vasquez, Francisco Barcenas, and Pancho Galindo were consistent and irrefutable. Having encountered them i previous, now infamous, exploits, their faces and clothing styles were indelibly etched in his mind.

As if on cue, Grewell trotted into town on his ragged old roan, his filthy clothing covered in sweat from his encounter with the bandits. He corroborated the descriptions given to the sheriff by the witnesses, which added to growing evidence against Tiburcio and his gang. According to Grewell, the outlaws had vanished into the rugged mountains east of Hollister.

Luck was on Tiburcio's side as he and his cohorts evaded capture yet again in their persistent game of cat and mouse with the law. Harris was not a man easily daunted; he guided his posse west through Hollister into the San Galindo mountains, where he ran into another victim, a sheepherder named Patterson, who was robbed by the same gang of three dollars and fifty cents. The descriptions were always the same, and "the short man with an overly giant sombrero" (Pancho) and the leader, who was "dressed all in black" (Tiburcio), consistently stood out.

Tiburcio and the gang continued their trek through the arid streets of a small Mexican populated village. Their horses clopped along with determined strides. As they passed an old, weathered building with a faded sign reading "Orfanato de La Esperanza," Tiburcio's eyes wandered towards the orphanage. He nudged Barcenas, who was riding beside him, his gaze now gleaming with compassion and mischief.

"Francisco, pull out one hundred dollars from the saddlebag."

"What for, Jeffe?"

"We should donate it to this orphanage. These are our people. I do this for my mother; God rest her soul. Don't give me any shit about it, get it."

"No problem, Tibo. We have plenty, and why not? I was an orphan myself once."

Barcenas reached behind, his rough fingers fumbling with the worn leather bag strapped to his saddle. He carefully retrieved the money and handed it to Tiburcio, who held it tightly in his calloused palm. He dismounted and approached the front door. Clutching the bundle of crisp one-hundred-dollar bills, he breathed deeply and rang the bell. A nun dressed in the traditional black and white habit greeted him at the entrance with a warm smile. She did not speak.

Tiburcio removed his hat respectfully.

"May I come in? I'd like to speak with the Mother Superior."

The nun motioned him to follow her. Her veiled face held an air of mystery as she led Tiburcio down the polished hallways. They were adorned with religious paintings and crucifixes, and the soft sound of their footsteps echoing in the vast space created an aura of reverence.

They passed through a room filled with sunlight. Two nuns surrounded Tiburcio, their graceful presence filling it. Young children were running in and out of the doorway to the play area. Their laughter filled the air with innocent joy, almost tripping Tiburcio, who laughed, rubbing their heads as they passed by. The décor was humble yet elegant, simply a few vases filled with fragrant wildflowers. He passed several nuns clad in modest black habits. They welcomed him warmly, and their serene smiles lit up the dimly lit corridor. The scent of incense wafted through the air and added to the atmosphere of tranquility within the orphanage's walls. He was led through another door, his stride as purposeful as it was entering the building.

Mother Superior Graciela, the gentlest of the nuns, approached him, curious about what he wanted. She recognized him for who he was and knew his name, which had been passed around by priests and the needy on the street. Her eyes radiated kindness. She wore a simple white veil that gracefully framed her face. Her soft voice resonated with reverence as she spoke.

"How can I help you, Mr. Vasquez?"

"Reverend Mother, please, I wish to donate this to your orphanage. Please accept it if for nothing else but to help the children."

He handed over the money, and the nun graciously received it.

"Bless your heart, Tiburcio. Your generosity knows no bounds. May

God reward you abundantly for your selflessness."

"Reverend Mother, it is an honor to help those in need. These children deserve a chance at a brighter future."

He bowed slightly to her as he left the room and the orphanage to once again join his gang.

Eighteen

Sheriff Harris and his posse had been hot on the notorious gang's trail for a grueling week. They had traversed treacherous terrain, battled dense forestry, and scaled towering cliffs. Harris, a seasoned lawman known for his relentless pursuit of justice, had faced countless outlaws, but none had proven as elusive as Vasquez and his entourage. These men acted brazenly, he judged, with a will to strike fear into the hearts of townsfolk and dare anyone to challenge their reign of terror.

Aside from an Italian sheepherder he happened upon, whom he tried to question, Harris found himself hitting a wall in his efforts to get information from the Mexican population. They adored Vasquez, after all, and even the sheepherder claimed ignorance and simply pointed in a general direction. Harris's frustration intensified with repeated empty holes and dead ends. The days blurred together as he tirelessly tried to gather clues and interrogate informants, hoping to gain an edge. He failed to complete his mission, and, worse, the bandit's revelry had mocked him at every turn.

Tiburcio was now a seasoned thief. His many heists and certainly his most recent adventure, which the public and law enforcement knew as the Soap Lake stage robbery, had gained widespread attention in every newspaper across the state. The scale of his criminal activities had been unprecedented in recent memory, and his notoriety among law enforcement agencies was growing as well. His reputation, already established in Northern California, now preceded him throughout the state.

After days of searching and inquiries, Sheriff Watson finally received a tip-off that the Vasquez gang was hiding in a canyon just a stone's throw away from his ranch. The revelation shocked the public, who were outraged that their appointed law enforcement officer had been ignorant of Vasquez's presence in the area. The community's faith in Sheriff Watson's ability to perform his duties was shaken, and many expressed their disappointment and disgust at his negligence in apprehending the dangerous criminal.

Determined and humiliated, Watson formed a posse of fifteen brave Anglo men armed with repeating rifles and pistols, ready for any eventuality. They were all eager to bring justice to the area and end Vasquez's criminal activities. The posse set out on horseback, following the bandits' tracks to the suspected location. They dismounted about one hundred yards away from the site to avoid detection since they knew that surprise was critical to catching the bandits off-guard. They carefully made their way toward their target, taking cover behind rocks and trees as they went.

The tension felt unbearable as they closed in on the hideout. The armed deputies approached from every direction, quietly and with precision, prepared to catch their prey. It was deathly quiet until one of the men tripped on a log. The posse expected to receive gunfire but could only hear a dog barking. Getting closer, they spied a young man shoveling hay near the barn. Watson grabbed him by his shirt.

"Where is Vasquez?"

"I don't know, sir," the boy answered, stunned by the sheriff's unprovoked aggression.

"They all left before you arrived,"

"Fuck, which way, boy?"

"Up the canyon. I think they were leaving permanently sir. They had all their bedrolls, rifles, and full saddlebags."

Watson yelled to his men.

"Spread out and search all the buildings! It seems we're too late but be safe as you check!"

"What is your name, boy, and what are you doing here?"

"My name is Rigo, sir. I am paid to do chores. They let me sleep here, feed me, and give me money."

To the deputies' surprise, they found only three horses with saddles and bridles, which they later discovered were stolen. The bandits had fled the area, leaving no other clues as to their whereabouts. As the sheriff and his deputies investigated the area, they came to realize that they had narrowly missed their prey. Warm pots over smoldering fires still warm to the touch attested to that.

The posse re-mounted in pursuit but gave up after two days. Watson returned to town to face an angry populace that blamed him for the escape. His previous successes in arresting other criminals did not matter. His perceived ineptness in handling Vasquez was too much for them to overlook. The agreement was widespread, and as a result, they called for him to be removed from his position.

The gang journeyed together to Santa Cruz save for Pancho, who had stayed behind in Natividad, California, to receive treatment for the gunshot wound Grewell gave him. He was fortunate to have found a doctor willing to treat him and keep quiet about it, and the bandits paid him generously for his services and that secrecy.

The town now had a population of over 2,500, with modern brick buildings dotted between equally modern wood homes and businesses. The only persons who recognized Vasquez were his old friends who had grown up there. The rest of the population was new, sparing him the risk of immediate identification.

It was afternoon when the bandits traveled the main road toward a new hideout at Tiburcio's cousin's ranch. The sun was in its late stages of the day, painting brilliant colors in the sky, preparing for an enormous sunset of sun rays and clouds. Approaching the crest of a hill, Tiburcio noticed the silhouette of a solitary horse frolicking in front of the sunset in a field off the road. There was something familiar about how it moved with such strength and grace, and it didn't take but a moment for him to realize why.

"Can this be true?" He thought. "How is this possible?" Tears welled up in his eyes, and with a lump in his throat, he whispered, "Viento."

He screamed to his fellow bandits.

"I cannot believe it! It's Viento! Oh my God!"

The gang was confused by what was happening as Tiburcio galloped his horse to the fence yelling, "Viento, Viento!"

His voice echoed through the meadow, causing the frolicking horse to halt. The horse's mane glimmered in the sunlight and swayed as it turned to pinpoint the source of the sound. Its front legs pounded the grass as it forcefully stamped its hooves. The horse soon recognized Tiburcio's voice and trotted towards him. Already off his horse, Tiburcio approached the stallion with open arms and wrapped them around the horse's neck. The stallion, in return, leaned its head over the fence and snorted affectionately, happy for the reunion. Tiburcio rubbed its snout and neck.

"Viento, I have missed you, old friend," he whispered.

Tiburcio looked in the distance, seeing a farmhouse attached to the pasture. He told his men to wait as he rode to the house. Viento followed along the fence line, unwilling to leave Tiburcio's side. The bandit cautiously approached an aged farmer tending to his crops. The gold afternoon sun added to the nostalgia in his eyes as he silently observed Viento grazing peacefully nearby. His sleek black coat shimmered. He seemed to be waiting.

Clearing his throat, Tiburcio spoke up.

"Buenos tardes, Señor. I couldn't help but notice that you have a magnificent stallion over there. Goes by the name Viento, if I'm not mistaken."

The farmer turned around, his weathered face creasing into a smile.

"Ah, you've got a good eye, Señor. That there is a fine horse indeed. How do you know of him?"

Tiburcio nodded approvingly and bit his lip in thought before posing his request.

"You see, Señor, Viento once belonged to me before life had different plans for us. I was hoping you might sell him back to me."

"I don't know, sir." the farmer replied.

"This is a good horse, and I had never considered selling him."

"I don't blame you, Señor; finding a horse as stunning as this one is hard. I will pay whatever price you feel he is worth. I see you toiling here in the field and would happily pay you enough to help relieve some of that burden."

"I see," the old man replied, removing his hat and wiping his balding head with his bandana.

"Hmmm, I don't know what that price would be, do you?"

Tiburcio didn't want to haggle. He could have just stolen Viento, but his relationship with his horse was sacred, and he wanted to make an honest agreement with the older man. He also wanted a bill of sale. That had been the nail in the coffin, sending him to prison the first time.

"I'll give you five hundred dollars and the horse I am on."

The older man was taken aback. He thought to ask only two or three hundred. He looked back toward Viento, who was watching intently and recognized the attachment between him and his old master.

"You are very generous, sir. I will accept your offer. Let me go inside, and I will write up a bill of sale. I need your name."

"My name is Tiburcio Vasquez."

The older man's jaw dropped, and he began to shake.

"I have heard of you, Tiburcio. I have also heard that you are a famous bandit but are kind to the Mexican community. I am surprised that you want to make an honest purchase, and it is my honor to do business with you."

He went into his house to write a bill of sale. Meanwhile, Tiburcio trotted back to his friends.

"All of you empty your pockets. I need five hundred dollars to repurchase my old horse. I have three hundred in my pocket, so cough up two hundred."

They all moved to protest, but Tiburcio cut them off.

"I'll pay you all back. Just give me the money, and I'll explain later."

They all could hear the emotion in Tiburcio's voice. They dared not challenge him and gave him what he asked for. He turned his horse and rode back to the farmhouse, getting there just as the farmer came out.

"Gracias, Señor. You have helped make my heart full again. If you ever need anything, don't hesitate to find me."

He took the saddle off the horse he was riding and whistled for Viento, who came trotting up to him. He hugged the huge stallion, kissing its cheek and rubbing his nose. He put the reins on and saddled him.

He bid farewell to the old farmer with a simple "Adios" and spurred Viento to rear up before returning to the ground. They galloped back to the road. Everyone admired Viento's beauty and strength. As they continued their journey, Tiburcio shared with his friends the history of his relationship with the magnificent animal and recounted tales of their shared adventures and experiences.

Vasquez, Barcenas, and Jorge Rodriguez parted and made their new temporary residence at Tiburcio's cousin Lorenzana's ranch in Blackburn Gulch, a remote area outside of town. Blackburn Gulch was a forgotten corner of civilization, untouched by the rapid progress of the outside world. It was a place where the men sought refuge from prying eyes. It only took two days for boredom to overwhelm them. The novelty of the recent influx of stolen wealth had worn off, and two days of stagnant isolation had pushed them to madness. Desperate for release, they set their sights on the town, ready to unleash their pent-up energy in a violent frenzy.

Nineteen

The sun dipped low over the horizon and painted the vast countryside warm shades of amber. The air smelled of freshly turned earth. Tiburcio and his gang were eager to reach the town. Each thudding, rhythmic beat of their horses' hooves on the winding trail echoed through the quiet wilderness. It added to the excitement of finally having a night out and the women they looked forward to spending intimate time with once they reached their destination. They had brought a bottle of tequila and were taking turns sipping it. The warmth and camaraderie as they rode towards Water Street on the outskirts of town were of life's simple pleasures.

The group reached their destination later in the evening. The moonlight softly illuminated the dilapidated building and its surroundings. Tiburcio squinted through the dimly lit street, his gaze fixed on the gaudy sign of Tom Cramer's bordello. The bandits had ridden hard. They were dust-covered, weary, and in need of a reprieve from their troubles. By this point, they were also happily inebriated.

Tiburcio dismounted, adjusting his hat as he approached, half stumbling to the entrance. His companions lingered behind him on their horses, hungry for a taste of pleasure. He banged on the door repeatedly. The urgency in his voice carried through the stillness of the night as he demanded entry. It also signaled desperation.

"Madame Pauline…Madame Pauline! We've come a long way. Our money is good, and we seek nothing more than your services."

Madame Pauline's tired face appeared at the small, barred window. Her sleepy eyes framed by a weary face that even heavy makeup could not disguise.

Barcenas echoed the request.

"Madame Pauline! Open up, woman! We've come a long way, and we're itching for some fun!"

The wooden door creaked open partly, revealing the Madame's silhouette framed by a flickering lantern. Her response was one of defiance and authority.

"It's too late, Tiburcio! Go away! It's been a busy night; the girls need their rest."

Her voice betrayed a hint of sympathy as the madame shook her head firmly, her gray curls swaying with the motion. Tiburcio exchanged glances with his gang members.

"What do you think, amigos?"

Without a cue, they all pulled out their guns and started firing into the air and the building with reckless abandon. Tiburcio had to duck away from the door himself to prevent being hit by the drunken crew. Madame Pauline, in a panic, slammed the door shut, further provoking the gang's fury. They blasted a dozen rounds into the bordello. The women inside scattered desperately to escape the hail of bullets. The noise was deafening between the guns and their screams. The barrage shattered windows and sent shards of glass raining down on the terrified occupants. One of the wild rounds hit Madame Pauline in the chest. The force and impact of the .44 caliber round knocked the wind out of her and put her on her back. It took her a few minutes to realize she had been spared. Not so for a couple of male customers who had grabbed their clothing and were running down the stairs. They were wounded but not mortally.

Gasping for air from the sharp pain radiating through her body, the madame clutched her chest. The bone busks had taken the brunt of it, leaving a deep dent and splintered bone in its wake. She lay on the floor, overwhelmed by relief and shock. With shaking hands, she reached for her corset. It was a prized possession, not just for its exquisite design but for its concealed layers of protection. She was grateful it had done its job. Had it not been for that sturdy piece of whalebone, her life might have been cut tragically short.

A wave of panic flooded the room as chaos continued. The smell of gunpowder was nauseating. Madame Pauline looked around the bordello. The sight of the blood-stained bodies of those who had fled for safety, which now trailed down the stairs, only added to the mayhem. Slowly regaining her composure, she pushed herself up, grimacing at the lingering pain in her chest. She noticed a familiar face in the chaos. A man known as Francisco, one of her loyal employees and confidants. He grabbed a rifle and raced to one of the shattered windows. She watched as he bravely returned fire, quickly levering numerous rounds toward the bandits outside.

Tiburcio's gang did not mean to hurt anyone in their drunken state. Men, when they are drunk and horny, will be stupid and undeterred. Francisco's gunfire sent the bandits running. Tiburcio vaulted himself over Viento's hindquarters and, with his crew behind him, skedaddled to another area in the city to find a more welcoming bordello.

Deputy Robert Liddell was patrolling a nearby neighborhood when he heard the loud sound of gunshots. Blood pounded in his ears as he urged his horse forward. Arriving at Madame Pauline's, he quickly dismounted and inspected the damage. The door and windows were riddled with bullet holes. When he entered the brothel, his jaw clenched angrily as Madame Pauline immediately described the bandits responsible for this chaos. He viewed the two wounded men on the stairs. She did not mention Tiburcio's name, knowing she would see him again. She was damn well determined, though, to make him pay for the damage. Francisco approached her.

"I'll go fetch the doctor, Ma'am."

Liddell was back on his horse in a flash, galloping to where the bandits were last seen. As another bordello across the river came into view, he spotted three men matching the descriptions tying their horses to a hitching post. Liddell dismounted and in a booming voice commanded.

"All of you stand as you are! Put your hands up!"

The three bandits wasted no time opening fire on Liddell, their bullets whizzing past him like deadly hornets. He remained unfazed. His resolve to bring these ruthless animals to justice sharpened his focus and steadied his aim. Each pull of his gun's trigger unleashed hot lead upon them. As he reloaded with practiced efficiency, a bullet found its mark and sent searing pain through his thigh. He gritted his teeth and retook aim at one of the closest men. He fired, his bullet hitting Tiburcio with brutal accuracy and knocking him off his feet. It pierced his side and lodged itself deep in his back. Barcenas rushed to his side and helped him up onto Viento. The three bandits galloped down Front Street, continuing their escape. Tiburcio could barely hold on. Liddell lay in the street writhing in pain. One of the citizens, an accountant, ran out to help him into the nearby Pacific Ocean House.

Liddell's wound would heal as it was in the muscle. The two patrons shot in the bordello happened to be prominent persons. Their wounds were only minot grazings. While not surprising to the locals, the men's illicit activities were, up to that point, unknown to their wives. The sheer embarrassment of getting caught with their pants down in a house of ill repute forced the men to leave town, a disgrace worse than a flesh wound from a bullet.

Deputy Charlie Lincoln had an unwavering strength of will and boyish charm. He admired Sheriff Liddell and made it his sole mission to track down the men responsible. The randomness of the incident had left the once-peaceful town in fear and uncertainty, and Lincoln knew that bringing the perpetrators to justice was the only way he could hope to restore order. He prepared for another day on the treacherous path ahead with three others in his posse: Charles Haynes, Bill Dickerson, and Bob Majors. They had learned that the bandits might be held up at the Lorenzana ranch. The posse reached the cabin and surrounded it. When no one answered, they entered. Not a soul was there.

They continued scouring the property and found three saddled horses hidden in a thicket of heavy bushes. They led the horses back to the barn, where they saw Lorenzana's son Jesus talking to other ones stabled. At least, he seemed to be. Lincoln was not fooled, and they all surrounded the barn. The deputy approached the barn on high alert, knowing whoever was inside would not go down without a fight. With his gun drawn and ready, he cautiously entered, keen to any signs of movement. No one was on the ground floor. He noticed a ladder leading up to the second level. He climbed determinedly and not without dread, his heart quickening with each step.

Reaching the hayloft, he saw nothing, but thick, loose hay scattered everywhere. The low roof forced him to tuck his gun into his belt and crawl on all fours, sifting through the hay methodically in search of hiding spots.

Suddenly, he touched a hand. The man attached to it leaped out of the hay to his knees, startling Lincoln, who sprang back and instantly reached for his gun, only to find it missing from his belt. Panic set in as he realized it must have fallen out while he was crawling. Before he could react, Francisco Barcenas was kneeling before him, with a gun in hand. The young deputy's mind raced as he assessed the situation and in one swift move, rolled towards the loft's edge and dropped down onto some hay bales, using them as cover. Barcenas wasted no time in following. He was now standing only a few feet away from Lincoln.

"One of them is here! He's armed! Shoot to kill!" Lincoln shouted to the posse outside.

Majors was first to the door but couldn't shoot at Barcenas since Lincoln was racing toward him. Barcenas fired two rounds, which narrowly missed the posse men and struck the barn door inches from their heads. With guns blazing and shouts echoing through the barn, Lincoln and Barcenas engaged in a fierce battle for survival. Lincoln was determined to win.

Haynes then leaned into the doorway opening.

"Get out of the way!"

His fellow posse members ducked as he aimed his two-barreled shotgun at Barcenas, pulling both triggers together. Unfortunately, it was an old firearm, and all he heard was two clicks. It had failed to fire. Barcenas stuck his head out again to fire from the hay bale.

"Shit Haynes, get the fuck out of my way!" Majors shouted.

Haynes ducked back, and Majors fired one accurate bullet that struck Barcenas in his jaw. Barcenas shot back as he staggered backward, narrowly missing Majors, who immediately fired again, this time striking Barcenas in his right eye. The bandit fell to the ground, mortally wounded but was still trying to cock his gun.

Lincoln could hear his own heart beating as he entered the barn. The smoke was clearing. He knew the gruesome death and the smell of gunpowder mixed with hay would etch an unforgettable picture of the battle in his mind, a memory of triumph mixed with sorrow. The barn was now quiet, save for the agonized gasps from the outlaw trying to breathe from his soon-to-be fatal wounds.

Lincoln cautiously approached Barcenas, his boots softly walking on the hay-strewn floor. His eyes locked onto the bandit's bloodied face. His jaw was hanging by a thread, with most of his teeth missing, and his right eye was a bleeding black socket—chilling signs of the violence that had transpired. Barcenas seemed to inch closer and closer to the abyss with each labored, hollow breath.

"Was it worth it?" Lincoln whispered, his tone a mix of anger and anguish.

He had sought revenge and justice for those who had suffered at Barcenas's merciless hands. But, as he stood there surrounded by carnage, he knew the price of such vengeance was steep. Majors approached from behind him and finished him with a shot to the heart.

Interestingly, Deputy Lincoln did not know the identity of the man whom Majors shot. They took the three horses they found, tied Barcenas's body face down over the saddle of one, and headed back to town. Jesus could not, or would not identify the man's name, so they left him at the ranch.

The town was buzzing with speculation as news of the unidentified man spread like wildfire. The townsfolk anxiously gathered around the sheriff's office with their gaze transfixed on the sight of the open coffin leaning against the wall. The attached note fluttering in the wind invited the community to help solve the mystery.

The local undertaker, Bartholomew, was standing nearby. He was dressed in black with a top hat and sunglasses, his wrinkled hands clasped behind his back. He observed the crowd feeling both fascinated and morbidly curious. He had encountered such situations before when photographers would want to record the dead bodies of bandits, a peculiar position in his line of work. He also wanted to know who this mysterious man was and what led him to such a tragic end. He knew the identification would be challenging due to his missing jaw and the blasted eye socket, which had forced the corpse's head to swell unnaturally. He thought the clothing could be helpful, too. He leaned against a nearby post, taking it all in.

Mary Whitman, a young woman amongst the crowd who had an insatiable thirst for adventure, was inexplicably drawn to the scene. Her hazel eyes sparkled with excitement as she pushed her way closer to the body. It was hard at first to bear witness to the dreadful sight, but she knew who it was. She knew the face from the recent stagecoach robbery; she'd never forget it. Barcenas was one of the men who leaned in to blindfold her. She immediately informed Sheriff Liddell. The evidence helped link the dead bandit to the Vasquez gang. Soon after, one of the girls from a local brothel walked by, and they got a name to put to the face.

A warrant was sent the next day by telegraph from Monterey. It named Tiburcio Vasquez and Narciso Rodriguez as wanted men and linked them to the Soap Lake stagecoach robbery.

~

During the shootout at the Lorenzana ranch, Gracia and Narciso had crouched behind some thick brush as soon as the gunfire erupted between the posse and Barcenas. Their saddled horses were nearby, ready for a swift escape. The posse was dangerously close, unaware of Gracia and Narciso's presence and the hidden wounded Tiburcio. They mounted their horses and set off on a slow, tense journey to Juan Perez's hideout, praying they would make it there alive.

The trio rode silently in the night. The very rustle of leaves and every snap of a twig sent chills down their spines. They knew they had to remain vigilant, with danger lurking around every corner. They wanted to gallop away, but Tiburcio's wounds would not allow it. Even though they moved slowly, he was still in significant discomfort.

Relief washed over them as they arrived at Juan Perez's secluded cabin. The familiar sight brought a glimmer of hope. They dismounted their horses and led them to a small stable nearby. Tiburcio was in great pain by that point but took time to pat his loyal horse's flank before tying it securely, whispering words of comfort in its ear.

As the cabin door slowly opened, Tiburcio's breath hitched as he bent over with the pain and glanced up at a menacing figure before him. Juan Perez's weathered face betrayed a lifetime of hardship and survival. His body had been weakened from his recent escape. Tiburcio concealed his uncertainty as to how the next few minutes would pan out.

Perez was infamous for his skill with knives, having been in numerous fights with Anglos and harboring a deep-seated hatred toward them. Though he had never taken a life, he had left many maimed or disfigured in his wake.

"Juan," Tiburcio stammered, his voice barely audible.

"I... I need your help." He hesitated, trying to find the right words to convey the urgency of his situation.

"The sheriffs'.. they're after me."

Perez was shirtless and had two large knives hanging from his belt. His beady eyes narrowed below a protruding forehead upon seeing Tiburcio's disheveled appearance.

"Why should I help you?" he growled suspiciously.

Perez leaned against the doorframe. His dark, predatory eyes curiously sized up the wounded man before him and his two friends. Tiburcio could sense the sharp blades shining intermittently in the dim candlelight. A chill ran down his spine. He felt crushed by desperation. He swallowed hard.

"We've known each other for years, Juan. You hate gringos just as much as I do. I can offer you gold coins if you let me stay here until I heal and can safely leave."

Perez's distrustful gaze shifted to the two bandits huddled behind Tiburcio. His voice suggested his familiarity with danger.

"Fine, Tibo. You can stay until your wounds heal. But you will pay me in gold and leave as soon as possible."

A sense of duty to his fellow Californios had won out.

The next day, Narciso Rodriguez went into town for medical supplies, stopping at a cantina before picking them up. Sheriff Liddell was still nursing his shot-up leg and knew who Narciso was. He had just received a tip that he could find him in a downtrodden bar just outside of town. Knowing he had to act quickly to apprehend the bandit, he gathered some deputies and headed for the cantina.

Liddell limped into the dimly lit bar. Even with a crutch, his authoritative presence commanded the attention of everyone within. His piercing gaze scanned the room, searching for the notorious outlaw, Narciso, and, of course, hoping to find Vasquez. The mood grew tense as the chatter dwindled into silence. All were aware that trouble had arrived. The wiry and rugged looking Narciso was eyeing the sheriff warily from his spot at the far end of the bar while nursing a shot of whiskey. His weathered hat was pulled low, almost hiding his identity. He slowly looked up, his dark eyes meeting Sheriff Liddell's steely stare. He knew that his time had finally run out. The stagecoach robbery had been his boldest yet, and justice was now closing in.

As Sheriff Liddell approached Narciso, his deputies fanned across the room like wolves encircling their prey. The patrons backed away with bated breath, both worried and curious about how this confrontation would unfold. Liddell's voice cut through the murmurs.

"Narciso, I hope you're ready to come along peacefully."

Narciso's lips curled into a wry smile as he casually reached for his drink.

"Sheriff, I'm afraid you've got me all wrong. I have done nothin'. I think you have the wrong man."

Liddell wasn't fooled.

"Keep your hands on the bar. If I see one finger even flinch, I will have these deputies open fire on you. They're crack shots, Narciso."

"Ok, Sheriff, I'm not moving. Be careful about your triggers. I won't put up a fight."

Liddell motioned for the deputies to take Narciso into custody and directly to the Monterey jail.

Narciso's back ached as he awakened on a shoddy straw mattress. Opening his eyes to a dilapidated ceiling above, he wrinkled his nose. The place reeked of urine and sweat. But he refused to let himself be consumed by the desolation surrounding him. He would rise above his circumstances and find a way out of this nightmare. He pushed himself up from the mattress and made his way to the rusted iron bars. Peering through the narrow opening, he saw a world beyond the cell's walls. The salty breeze from the nearby ocean teased his senses and ignited a spark of single-mindedness within him. His gaze fixed on the distant horizon. Waves were crashing against jagged rocks with resounding strength.

The despair otherwise surrounding him was palpable, and each criminal in adjoining cells was lost in their private torment. The crumbling walls and rusty bars served as a stark reminder of their captivity, trapping hope within their suffocating grasp. His mind drifted back to the events that had led him to this wretched place. It seemed like a lifetime ago when he had embarked on his journey, chasing dreams of a better life. But fate had a cruel sense of humor. It had led him down treacherous paths into a web of deceit and betrayal. Closing his eyes briefly, he summoned the strength to push aside the memories now threatening to consume him. He knew dwelling on the past would only serve to weaken his resolve. Instead, he focused on the present, searching for a glimmer of opportunity within the bleakness. For the rest of the day, his mind wandered back to half a dozen years ago when his brother Pedro was taken by vigilantes and hung in a barn. He started to sweat with the realization that he might be the next Rodriguez to die in such a demeaning manner.

That night, he heard shouting coming from the front of the jail. The deputy on duty named Jackson, was being hailed from outside by another law enforcement officer. The sound pierced the otherwise quiet night. Curious, he went to the bars of his cell and saw Jackson frantically trying to make sense of a situation down the hall. A forceful knocking could be heard from outside.

"Jackson, unlock the front door; we have a prisoner!" another deputy yelled.

The urgency in the man's voice made it clear that this was not a routine occurrence and that something serious was happening. After a moment, the deputy opened the door, only to be confronted by a dozen men with bandanas hiding their faces. One of the men was Sheriff Lincoln. A couple of the mob members grabbed Jackson, tied his hands behind him, and put a sack over his head, leading him back into the jail, where they retrieved the cell keys.

The vigilante mob descended upon Narciso's cell, unlocking it with a loud crash. They grabbed him by the scruff of his neck and brutally tied his hands behind his back, dragging him down the steps and onto a waiting horse. With grunts and curses, they rode out to the Lorenzana ranch. They looped a rope tightly around his neck before throwing the other end over a stout tree limb and hoisting him, the rope digging into his skin. Sheriff Lincoln loomed over him. The vengeful grin on his face behind his bandana couldn't be seen, but Narciso could feel it as Lincoln threatened to hang him—that is, if he did not disclose Tiburcio Vasquez's whereabouts.

He sneered sadistically.

"Tell us where that vermin's hiding, or not only will you swing from this tree, we'll hobble your horse, so it takes you a long time to die."

Narciso refused to break and spat at them through gritted teeth.

"Fuck you, you coward. Please do it! Just like you did to my brother. Burn in the depths of hell!"

With those defiant words, he was ready to face his fate with unwavering strength and courage. Sheriff Lincoln, however, was not about to hang Narciso. It was a bluff. Bent for another tact, he had one of the mob members cut him down.

"Strip off his shirt," Lincoln ordered.

One of the smaller men walked over and cut the shirt off Narciso's back.

Right out of the book of the San Quentin correctional office and mauler Moon, Lincoln had another man lash the bandit's back. Once every time he refused to answer the same question of where Vasquez was located. He received forty lashes and still refused to give up his friend. The vigilante bluff failed, and he was returned to jail. The deputy was released and threatened not to reveal what had happened and to fetch a doctor to tend the wounds.

Narciso remained in jail for one month. When he finally went on trial, his family lied about him being with them when the Soap Lake robbery was committed, but the driver, Dennis Conroy, testified as a witness. Narciso was found guilty and sent to San Quentin for eight years. Vasquez was also named in the case, and another warrant was issued adding to the many prior for his arrest.

Twenty

It took seven weeks for Tiburcio to heal from his wounds. He thanked Pedro and gave him five hundred dollars in gold for helping him heal and hide out. He'd had a lot of time to think and plan. He could no longer seek help from most of his immediate family, who had been pressured by authorities constantly questioning them as to Tiburcio's whereabouts. They repeatedly refused, but the embarrassment and shame they felt was too much for them. He needed to let things cool down, he thought, in northern California, where he had resided most of his life. He left Viento with Pedro and borrowed a horse to ride to San Francisco. His hair and beard, untended while he was healing, were long and rugged looking. He decided to keep that look and wear farmers' clothing as a disguise to catch a steamship to Mexico. He needed to lie low for the time being.

The city streets of San Francisco pulsed with life as Tiburcio weaved through the bustling crowd, his horse's hooves clattering against the cobblestones. He kept his gaze low, avoiding eye contact with anyone who might recognize him. The decision weighed on his mind, but he knew he had no other choice. As he made his way to the harbor, he caught glimpses of the familiar sights and sounds that once filled him with joy. The scent of saltwater and the aroma of exotic spices from distant lands beckoned him toward a world beyond his troubled past. The ship's foghorn echoed in the distance, a siren's call tempting him towards a new beginning.

Each step brought a deepening feeling of liberation. Responsibilities and expectations had always bound him, but he was now shedding those layers. They were old skin. The disheveled appearance became his armor, shielding him from prying eyes and unmasking. He carried an old suitcase packed with his revolver and regular clothing and made his way to the gangplank of the *Rosario*.

The steamship swayed gently as it cut through the rolling waves of the

Pacific Ocean. His disguise as a weathered farmer brought with it feelings of relief and trepidation as he looked out onto the water's expanse. The last time he was on a boat was to San Quentin. The journey to Mexico was not simply an escape but a chance for him to embark on a new chapter of his life.

His mind wandered back to Monterey, the small town in the heart of lush green valleys and towering redwoods. It brought memories that warmed his heart but also haunted his present endeavor. The pressure he had left behind was an invisible burden only he knew how to carry. Lost in his thoughts, he rubbed his hand along his unkempt beard, feeling the roughness against his palm. He had chosen this disguise deliberately—an outward reflection of his turmoil. It helped him blend in with the common folk aboard the crowded vessel, their faces as nondescript and weary as his.

During his journey, Tiburcio formed connections with some unscrupulous individuals. He thought it funny how experience with these types made it easy to spot and approach each other in commonality. They shared stories in secrecy, all withholding their true identities. Through these conversations, Tiburcio learned about Tess Malverde, originally named Jesus Juárez Mazo, born near the capital city of Culiacán in Sinaloa. The story resonated with Tiburcio.

As it happened for Malverde, the introduction to Sinaloa brought newfound wealth through agriculture, widening the gap between prosperous landowners and its already struggling peasant population. His parents died of starvation from poverty, a loss that left a foul taste in his mouth moreover because he felt their untimely deaths could have been averted. That is if the landowners they worked for had lent assistance and intervened on their behalf. He left his hometown and went to work for the railroads. He learned valuable skills in carpentry, but his intense hatred for the wealthy continued to grow. With every day that passed he had become more and more determined to fight against them. Eventually, Malverde crossed paths with others like him known for their viciousness but also generosity toward the underprivileged. Seeing an opportunity to make a difference, he joined forces with them and stole from wealthy ranch owners. He gave back to the poor, earning a reputation for his kindness and selflessness. Word of Malverde's deeds soon spread throughout the region, and he became a legendary figure among the people. He was likened to a modern-day Robin Hood. Upon hearing the stories, Tiburcio became curious and decided to seek out Malverde himself. The man ultimately was known as "The Generous Bandit" (El Generoso Bandido) and "The Angel of the Poor."

When he arrived at his destination, Culiacán, Tiburcio immediately booked a hotel room. He paid for a hot bath and changed into his usual black clothing, deciding to keep his hair and beard long for the return trip home but refined their look. He shared a drink downstairs at the bar with one of the bandits he had met on the steamship. His name was Rugerio

"Gordito" Alvarez. Now aware of who Tiburcio was, Alvarez held a lot of respect for him.

"Rugerio, do you know this man, Tess Malverde?" Tiburcio asked as he paid for his drink.

"I do."

"Is there some way that I can meet him?"

"Tibo, you are famous in the exact way in California as he is here. I think he would like to meet you as well. Let me look into it, and if it pleases him, I will arrange it and contact you. Meanwhile, let's drink, have some food, and find some women to have fun with. Sinaloa women are the hottest in Mexico."

Two days later, the meeting was arranged, and Tiburcio rode out to a small country cabin with Rugerio to meet Malverde. The rugged Sinaloa countryside and hot, humid air heightened the anticipation. Tiburcio felt nervous and excited in equal measure. This meeting with Tess Malverde was something he had been hoping for since he set foot on Mexican soil. The man was a legend in these parts, revered by some as a folk hero and feared by others as a bandit lord.

The unpretentious cabin they arrived at was situated amidst a grove of ancient mesquite trees, whose gnarled branches reached toward the heavens. The weathered wooden structure evidenced a life lived in a constant struggle against the forces of law and order. Dismounting their horses, Tiburcio noticed the faint smell of lingering gunpowder. It seemed fitting, given the violence that accompanied Malverde's name. Four men armed with rifles stood at relaxed guard, knowing Rugerio but eyeing Tiburcio suspiciously. Both men were asked to leave their pistols outside. Rugerio complied immediately, and Tiburcio as well, though more reluctantly.

Inside the cabin, shadows from flickering candlelight danced on rough-hewn walls. In the corner sat Malverde. His face had a relaxed look of disinterest and unapproachability. His hair was black, slicked back, and he sported a well-trimmed mustache. He exuded authority and strength. There were two other armed guards in the opposite corners. Rugerio started the conversation.

"Tess, this is Tiburcio Vasquez, whom I told you about."

Malverde had that unfriendly resting face that kept people away, but when he saw Tiburcio, it broke into a wide, bright smile. His voice was inviting as well as friendly.

"Tiburcio, I had heard of you before you came to Mexico. It is my pleasure to meet you, amigo, and welcome."

"Please call me Tibo. I too, have heard of you, and it is an honor to meet a man of such great integrity toward his people," Tiburcio replied.

Malverde got up, walked to Tiburcio, and hugged him.

"You will be my guest tonight, Tibo. We will drink, enjoy women, and tell lies. I will not take no for an answer."

"Your generosity precedes you, sir, and it would be my pleasure."

That night, Malverde and his gang brought in local cooks; a guitar ensemble played, (Mariachi bands weren't formed until the 1890's), and some local women for a frolicking fiesta. The cooks carried trays of mouth-watering dishes, and the band made the event festive. A group of local women added to the vibrant atmosphere. Their colorful, low-cut dresses invited companionship with every swaying step. The night was filled with laughter and indulgence as the men feasted on the rich flavors of the region's cuisine and downed countless tequila bottles. With each passing hour, the stories became wilder and more unbelievable, earning the admiration and respect of all who listened. As the clock struck three in the morning, each man took two women to their beds, their voices still ringing with laughter and merriment.

They didn't emerge until one the next day. Their spirits remained high, notwithstanding their aching heads.

Malverde escorted Tiburcio to a small cantina and ordered a breakfast of chorizo, eggs, and fresh fruit. A large, overweight woman kept the coffee coming to their table. Malverde started the conversation in almost a whisper to avoid aggravating the pain in his head.

"Tibo, can you remember anything about last night?"

"Barely, amigo, my head hurts as a horse stomped on it, but there are bits of last night that bring a smile to my face. Those two women you sent to bed with me were insatiable. When they weren't busy with me, they kept themselves alive with each other."

"Ha! I knew they would. It was a good time, my friend. Eat up and take the rest of the day to go back to bed and recover. If you like, I plan to raid a rich hacienda late tonight. You're welcome to accompany me and see how we work down here."

"The rest of the day off would be well advised for me, Tess. I think the ladies you left me with will have to leave, however, for me to get the rest you are talking about. And, yes, I would like very much to see how you do things down here."

"Ha, I will see that they leave you alone, Tibo. We will have dinner tonight and go over the plans."

The dinner meeting covered various angles of the raid. A bag of green camouflage clothing was brought into the room, which raised Tiburcio's curiosity.

"What is this for?"

"The hacienda we're robbing is in a thick, tropical, broad-leaf forest with multiple armed guards patrolling it. The green clothing will help us blend in with the surrounding foliage to avoid detection and disarm or eliminate the guards."

Tiburcio nodded supportively.

Around two A.M., Tiburcio, Tess, and six others left their horses a quarter mile from the hacienda. It belonged to Don Hernández, who owned a part of the railroad and several warehouses in the area. They walked stealthily, gathering behind some foliage to locate the guards still on patrol. There were only three. Malverde motioned to his six men, three pairs each, to take the guards out. Tiburcio had never seen men move with such stealth. They all attacked the guards simultaneously and knocked them out. They then tied their hands first behind their backs and then to their ankles, haltering them completely. They gagged their mouths and covered their heads with sacks. Each pair carried their guard to the horse barn and left them in a vacant stall.

As Tiburcio, Malverde, and the bandits furtively made their way through the grand hacienda, the luxury of its interior took their breath away. Ornate chandeliers cast a warm, golden glow on intricately carved furnishings. Rich tapestries depicting scenes of exotic lands and legendary heroes adorned the walls. The intense smell of sandalwood and magnolia enhanced to grandeur within. The gang swiftly and carefully maneuvered through the lavish corridors. Their footsteps barely made a sound against the polished marble floors. They had meticulously planned this heist, studying the habits of Don Hernández and his overweight wife to ensure they would remain undisturbed throughout their endeavor. Entering the study, Tiburcio marveled at the shelves lined with leather-bound books, their spines displaying years of wisdom and knowledge. A grand desk dominated the room. It was sprinkled with parchments containing secrets only Don Hernández knew. With careful precision, Malverde led his comrades toward Don Hernández's chamber. The plush carpets on the grand staircase muffled their footsteps. They could hear Don and his wife both snoring as they reached the top floor. The moonlight cascaded through a window left slightly open. It cast elongated shadows across the sizeable four-posted bed where the two portly elites slept.

Don Hernández, hearing strange sounds, stirred from his slumber, groggily nudging Rosalinda awake. Shock and fear set in as they recognized the looming presence of the eight bandits, their faces obscured by rugged, green masks and the sound of blades being unsheathed. One of the bandits, a tall, imposing figure (Malverde) with piercing eyes, stepped forward. His voice carried a low but chilling ferocity as he addressed Don Hernández and Rosalinda.

"Good evening, Don Hernández. You both look so comfortable, and that can remain so if you show us where you hide your jewelry and gold coins. There is no need to scream for your guards; they are all asleep and tied up like pigs."

"I think you are mistaken; I don't keep any of that here. It's all in the bank."

Hernández was feigning authority, but his voice quivered with fear, betraying his false confidence. Malverde smiled and motioned to one of his men, who was carrying a short machete.

"José, take the tip of that blade, and please cut off the nose of this lying fat man."

"As is your wish, Señor."

José walked slowly over to the Don; the moonlight reflecting off the machete's blade was menacing. Hernández shuffled to a sitting position and pulled his pillow before him, falsely hoping it would offer adequate protection. Malverde laughed.

"You are a funny and stupid man, Don Hernández. After José cuts that pillow out of your hand, it will be half a second when your nose joins it on the floor."

"OK, I'll show you where the money is. Please don't hurt us," he whimpered, his voice muffled by the pillow he had pulled tightly to his face.

Tiburcio noted to himself, as an observer, how threatening language from bandits seemed to be the same wherever he went.

The sprawling hacienda seemed to hold its breath as Don Hernández waddled in his silk pajamas and led the bandits down the grand staircase of the main floor. His mind raced, searching for any way to outsmart these thieves who had invaded his home. The atmosphere was tense, every step now echoing through the opulent halls. The glowing candlelight gave way to a haunting dance of shadows against the intricately carved wooden walls, priceless artworks and exquisite tapestries. Don Hernández's breathing was shallow, his chest tense from that, and his heart pounding.

They reached the study, where he hid his most prized possessions. The bandits surveyed their surroundings with giddy anticipation. A beam of moonlight filtered through the ornate windows that shined a divine spotlight on the chest holding Don Hernández's most precious treasures. Standing before the imposing safe, Hernández turned to face the gang's leader, his voice as authoritative as it could be.

"Now see here. I've cooperated thus far, as you requested. You're not going to take it all now, please."

Malverde responded laughingly.

"Not all, just most of it, Señor. I have to share it with the people that you take advantage of. Be thankful you still have a nose."

Hernández now understood the gravity of the situation and why these men were invading the hacienda.

"You are El Generoso bandido," he whispered.

"At your service, Señor," Malverde reciprocated.

"Open it."

The Don's trembling hands were causing him to fumble with the safe's combination. Sweat dotted his brow as he took a deep breath to steady himself. He turned each dial meticulously until finally, with an audible click, the lock released. The heavy door creaked open, revealing the treasures within. A gasp escaped one of the bandits. The sight before them was of large, exquisite necklaces, earrings, rings, and baskets of gold coins.

"Pack it all up, men. Leave a necklace for the Señora," Malverde ordered.

Don Hernández's shoulders sank woefully as he witnessed his treasured possessions being taken away. The gang tied the couple up and left as quickly as they had come. They used the large leaves of the local area tied together behind their horses to erase the tracks as they escaped.

The following day, around eleven, Tiburcio and Tess met at the same cantina for another breakfast. Tess started the conversation.

"So, what were your impressions of last night, my friend?"

"Your crew is well trained, and I was very impressed with how you entered and made your escape covering your tracks. I'll have to use that when I return home."

"When do you expect to return to California, Tibo?"

"If you don't mind, Tess, I would like to spend the rest of the month here and maybe pick up a few more tricks. I am also enjoying my first trip to the homeland. Mainly, it's food and women."

"Tibo, you are welcome to stay as long as you like."

Malverde then handed Tiburcio a medium-sized sack full of gold coins and jewelry.

"I want you to go home with a large enough stake to manage your life, Tibo. You don't have to go right back to robbery. Try leading a normal life and see how that goes for you. Maybe they will get tired of hunting you."

"This gift is something I didn't expect Tess. Thank you. There are many warrants out for my arrest, and although my wish is to own a horse ranch someday, I don't think that will ever come true. I could turn myself in and then lead an honest life, but I have spent half of it in prison already, and I will not go back again. So, I guess I'm doomed to continue the life I'm now leading."

Tess thought for a moment before replying.

"I understand Tibo. I shouldn't have thrown out advice on living a straight life without knowing all the facts about yours. Who am I to advise on living with the life I lead?"

Tiburcio went on three more raids with Malverde and learned more Mexican tricks. He had about two thousand American dollars to bring back to California. He returned to his disguise and booked a ship to San Francisco.

Twenty-One

Tiburcio Vasquez was happy to return to California soil. He purchased a horse and saddle for only three hundred dollars and set out to find a new home. Although he could no longer stay with his closest relatives, Tiburcio had a large family. He rode to the Hollister area to reconnect with his cousin Concepción Espinosa, whom he had known since childhood. Concepción was a respected rancher in the Pine Rock area, owning a massive property that spanned over one hundred acres.

Happily, Concepción welcomed Tiburcio with open arms, knowing of his good reputation among their people. The bandit discovered that Concepción's half-brother, Juan Castro, a few years his junior, lived nearby.

The flickering candlelight danced on the walls of Juan's humble abode as Tiburcio and Juan sat at a small wooden table, their plates filled with steaming dishes of stew and crusty bread. Juan's excitement mingled with the enticing aroma of the hearty meal as the conversation quickly went to wanting to hear about Tiburcio's exploits. Savoring the first mouthfuls of stew, Juan leaned forward, his eyes gleaming.

"Tibo, I've always dreamt of a life filled with adventure and thrill. I've heard tales of your daring exploits as a bandit, and I can't help but feel drawn to that lifestyle. Is there any way that I can ride with you and learn?"

Tiburcio chuckled softly, his weathered face looking noticeably older than it did in his younger years but betraying no less of a hint of admiration for Juan's enthusiasm.

"Juan, my friend, being a bandit is no ordinary endeavor. It requires courage, cunning, and skill with weapons, which only experience can forge. It also means constantly looking over your shoulder for your pursuers. Many nights, you will have to sleep outside and even go hungry. Are you truly prepared for such a life? Do you even own a gun?"

Juan looked down at his bowl, feeling his face flush from embarrassment.

"No, Uncle, I do not," he replied, his voice barely above a whisper.

Tiburcio laughed again and took a large spoonful of stew into his mouth. He leaned back in his chair and stared inquisitively at Juan, who was now uncomfortable. For years, he had embraced the life of a bandit, reveling in the thrill of the chase and the taste of stolen wealth. He had grown accustomed to adrenaline coursing through his veins, with each successful heist only deepening his commitment to this treacherous path. But now, faced with Juan's earnest request, his heart weighed heavy with uncertainty.

His mind wandered back to simpler times, memories of laughter and innocence now distant echoes in the dark expanse of his troubled conscience. He felt an encroaching burden of responsibility, considering the repercussions of Juan's request. It had struck a chord deep within him, stirring up a whirlwind of conflicting emotions. It was an invitation that, he knew, would change this young man's life forever, and he would be culpable should that choice prove unfortunate or fatal. He furrowed his brow, his gaze drifting into the distance as he grappled with the dilemma. A lifetime of banditry he had brought him an existence devoid of stability, where danger lurked at every turn. Did Juan truly understand that? he wondered.

The young man across the table had always looked up to him, but Tiburcio knew his shoes were big to fill. He was a skilled horseman and a renowned sharpshooter, and the young man wanted to prove that he had what it took to follow in his footsteps.

Tiburcio could sense his nephew's nervousness and leaned forward in his chair.

"Listen, Nephew," he said.

"If you want to ride with me, you're going to have to prove yourself first. You should know that there is no turning back, and the negativity in your life will increase drastically. Do you understand?"

Juan took a moment, but only a moment.

"Yes, Tio (uncle), I understand."

Tiburcio continued.

"I want you to find a colt pistol, a good horse, and a saddle and return here. Then we'll ride together for a week and see if you're close to capable."

The young man nodded, feeling a surge of energy.

"Okay, Uncle," he said.

"I'll do it. Where should I start?"

Tiburcio smiled warmly.

"Start by going into town and finding the items I mentioned. Meanwhile, I have to retrieve my horse, Viento. Let's meet in one week and see how you've done. I also want you to use the week to rethink your desire to live this type of life."

Tiburcio got up from his chair and left the room. The young man sat motionless for a moment, flooded with excitement and apprehension. He knew the next week would be the biggest challenge of his life, but he was determined to prove himself worthy of his uncle's respect.

Tiburcio returned with Viento several days later. He put him in Juan's corral and waited for his nephew to leave his cabin. He finally did, and Tiburcio greeted him. Juan smiled back, pointing to a horse running free in the corral, and declared it his own.

"I did as you said, Uncle," he said, beaming with pride.

"That horse is swift, and I have practiced a lot with my colt pistol. I have practiced for hours daily and can also draw very fast."

Tiburcio was impressed with his nephew's progress. He had always believed that the young man had a natural talent for horsemanship and gunfighting and had been working hard to improve his skills. Tiburcio patted his shoulder with pride.

"You've done well, Nephew. Let's go out tomorrow morning and see."

The sun was scorching the following day. Tiburcio was mounted on Viento, and Juan stood at the edge of a dusty trail. They were surrounded by endless plains spotted with tall trees. Tiburcio's expectation and Juan's anticipation were palpable, crackling as electricity would from a live wire. Viento pawed at the ground impatiently, eager to witness Juan's riding prowess, too. Juan adjusted his hat and grinned confidently.

"You'll see, Uncle. I've got the best aim this side of the Rio Grande and the fastest draw you've ever seen!"

Tiburcio chuckled, judging the young man's overconfidence.

"Well, Juan, talk is cheap. Let's see if you can back up those words."

Juan adjusted his holster with a confident smile. He mounted his recently acquired gelding with a sudden and fluid movement. He took a moment to adjust his grip on the reins and glanced back to make sure his uncle was watching. The glint in Juan's eye could only be described as devilish as he spurred his horse forward, and it galloped full out for two hundred yards.

He turned the horse around, spurring it on to return to Tiburcio, who was still seated calmly on his horse. As the gelding approached, Juan quickly pulled it to an abrupt stop, jumped off, and drew his pistol with lightning speed. He fanned six quick shots at a nearby tree limb, severing it from its host and causing it to fall to the dirt.

The sound of the shots echoed through the clearing, and for a moment, there was silence. Then, Juan turned to Tiburcio with a grin, holstering his pistol. It was clear that he had been testing the limits of his new horse and practicing his sharpshooting skills. Tiburcio nodded, clearly impressed, as he addressed his nephew.

"I see that you have indeed worked hard as I had asked. You have acquired basic skills. It will not be enough."

When he paused, Juan looked flummoxed and trodden.

He responded, "I don't understand."

Tiburcio continued.

"You have to learn self-control while maintaining a command presence. I have been in many gunfights, but I have never killed a man. If you ride with me, you must conduct yourself with grace and only shoot if your life or mine is in ultimate danger. I don't rob Californios, only foreigners. Do you understand?"

Juan stared directly into Tiburcio's eyes and humbly replied, "Yes, I do."

He understood that if he wanted to ride with his uncle, he had to be more than just a good shot. He had to be disciplined, controlled, and ethical.

For two grueling weeks, Tiburcio relentlessly drilled Juan on the intricacies of their highway robbery - how to stalk, manipulate, control, and skillfully bind any potential escapees. He instructed him to always give back to the community, for it would protect him. Tiburcio spoke of some things he learned in Mexico on tracking and preventing being tracked, highlighting the importance of avoiding detection and staying one step ahead of the law. Known for his infamous career as a bandit, Tiburcio found himself in a rather unusual situation. He felt responsible for his nephew for the first time and would protect him at any cost. This selflessness put Tiburcio in a vulnerable position as he had to consider the safety of someone other than himself. Weighing the risks and willing to face any consequences that may arise from his action, Tiburcio stood by his decision to protect Juan.

As a final warning, Tiburcio showed his battle scars to his nephew, recounting the agony and near-death experiences that came with this lifestyle. When he exposed the lash marks, then pain engraved into his flesh at San Quentin, it was a stark reminder of the consequences that awaited them if they were ever caught. Tiburcio's past misdeeds and the impending risk of Juan's decision instilled solemn respect in his nephew's mind, one preparing him for a life of crime without mercy or remorse.

They staked out the stagecoach station at San Benito. Tiburcio used the same tactic at Soap Lake: find a turn on a steep incline with nearby copses of trees or boulders to hide behind. About four miles east, he found precisely what he was looking for. They lurked in wait under an ominous, grey sky. Their horses pawed at the ground with restless energy as though anticipating the ambush as well.

A rumble of wheels caught their attention. It was a large wagon pulled by a team of four horses driven by a farmer named Dutch John. Tiburcio appeared to his partner as they rode out to meet the unsuspecting victim. Both men were dressed in black with bandanas pulled tight over their faces. They symbolized a threat that inspired fear. As they rode in front of the struggling wagon, Tiburcio's hand hovered over his gun, ready to strike. Dutch John's eyes widened in terror as he glimpsed the weapons clutched in their hands and the fierce steeds prepared to give chase.

"Hands up!" Tiburcio demanded with authority.

"We don't want trouble, just your valuables."

Shaken though he was, Dutch John quickly obeyed and lifted his arms in surrender.

"Please...don't shoot," he pleaded.

"I'm unarmed and have no wish for any harm. I only have about thirty dollars and a watch."

"That'll do; guide your horse off the road behind those four large boulders yonder."

Dutch did so immediately. His captors guided him to the boulders, one on each side of the four horses pulling and ordered him off the wagon.

Juan immediately slid from his saddle, tied Dutch to a wagon wheel, put a sack over his head, and told him to stay quiet. Tiburcio pulled on the wagon's brake to ensure the horses wouldn't spook if any gunshots went off when the stage came by.

It was another two hours before Tiburcio heard the stagecoach approaching. He nearly missed it because he was giving Dutch water from his canteen. The stage rumbled along the dusty road, its passengers unaware of the danger lurking ahead. As planned, the stage had to slow down at the incline, and the two masked bandits galloped to it with guns drawn. Juan was overly excited but had been told to follow Tiburcio's lead and to keep his mouth shut.

No guard was on the stage, and it was carrying six passengers. As before, Tiburcio told the driver, in this case, George Chick, to pull the stage off the road and park it near the wagon behind the boulders. Chick did as he was told and was astonished, shocked really, to see a man tied to a wagon wheel with a hood over his head. With guns pointed at their heads, Tiburcio ordered everyone off the stage.

"Good afternoon, everyone. We mean you no harm if you do as we ask. I want you all to sit in the dirt except for the lovely lady. I don't want you to foul up your pretty dress."

"Just do as he asks, please, everyone," Chick told the passengers.

Juan and Tiburcio walked around asking everyone to empty their pockets, except for one lady who said she was a newlywed. She was a scared and excited one at that, so Tiburcio laughed and left her alone.

It was slim pickings when the bandits compared what they found, which only added up to about thirty-six dollars and a couple of watches. Tiburcio jumped onto the stage, opened the mailbag and all the trunks, and kicked them to the ground. They had found little of value and now frustrated, Tiburcio told Juan to check the passengers' bindings. He did, and the two mounted their horses and left the chaotic scene. The victims were left shaken and helpless, their meager possessions stolen, and their sense of security shattered.

Feeling unsatisfied, the bandit duo continued two miles back toward Hollister and came upon two men on horseback. They donned their masks again and pulled their guns.

"Dismount your horse," Tiburcio ordered.

Juan was excited more than he had imagined and admired how calm his uncle was every time he wanted something done. He guessed it was to keep the situation clear and minimize escalation. Tiburcio, having witnessed many crimes and knowledgeable of how different bandits robbed victims, found that yelling only slowed things down and excited situations.

"What's your name?" he continued.

"George, and this here's Edmund."

"Well, George and Edmund, empty your pockets for me."

George and Edmund complied immediately, producing two dollars between them.

"Pitiful," Tiburcio said.

Juan tied the victims up to a nearby tree with their horses while Tiburcio maintained a guarded watch. They then continued heading south.

Upton Mathis was a well-known rancher. He was traveling north on the road with his friend Charles Pierce. He had just sold a few cattle in Hollister and was returning home. Tiburcio and Juan repeated their highway robbery action by stopping them and telling them to dismount. Both men did, hesitantly. Tiburcio could tell they were thinking about drawing their guns.

"My friend here is good with his pistol," he said, motioning to Juan.

"I can see that you are thinking of maybe using yours. I would advise you not to. Drop them by your sides, please. Not because he will kill you but because he will shoot you in an elbow or hand or a combination of them. He is so good he might shoot off an ear."

The ranchers thought it wise to heed the advice and dropped their pistols.

Juan dismounted and leaned over to pick them up when his mask dropped from his face.

"Shit!" he said as he picked them up and stuffed them in his belt.

He clumsily repositioned the mask and went through their pockets, netting only eleven dollars.

"I know him. That's Juan Castro," Mathis whispered to Pierce.

Tiburcio spurred Viento over to the victim's two horses and untied the two saddlebags.

"Let's see what's in these bags."

He found over eight hundred dollars in Mathis's bag.

After two failed robberies, this was enough to make Tiburcio smile behind his mask for the first time.

"This will make our day's efforts worthwhile, Señors. Gracias."

Tiburcio had spent time teaching Juan how to tie a proper bandana mask. For some unknown reason, it slipped off, revealing his face, but Tiburcio didn't see it happen and didn't know Juan had been compromised. Mathis and Pierce knew who Tiburcio was, considering his all-black clothing and black stallion. It was imperative to the bandit, however, that no one knew who his nephew was.

The dust-covered passengers from the stagecoach robbery had finally untied themselves and eventually stumbled into the local sheriff's office. As they were being interviewed, Mathis burst in, his face flushed with anger. He quickly informed the sheriff that he recognized one of the robbers as Juan Castro and suspected the other to be the bandit, Tiburcio Vasquez.

After conducting thorough interviews with all the shaken victims of the day's events, the sheriff was able to piece together matching descriptions and clothing to confirm. He wasted no time obtaining a warrant for their immediate arrest.

Back at the house, Tiburcio remained unaware that Juan's bandana had slipped during their previous robbery attempt.
Juan was oblivious that he had been recognized during their heist. Even if he suspected he had been, he was too frightened to confess it to his uncle, considering it was their first robbery together.

The situation spiraled out of control when Tiburcio left the next day to spend some of his money in a bordello outside Hollister. They revered him there and always supplied him with good food, women, and entertaining distractions. Meanwhile, the sheriff had gathered a posse and rode out to Juan's home at dawn.

The posse led by stern-faced Sheriff Carter thundered purposefully toward Juan's modest adobe. The echoes of galloping horses disrupted the quiet town as the men approached and announced their arrival to anyone within earshot. The townsfolk, drawn by curiosity and whispers of the recent stagecoach heist, watched warily behind closed shutters. The young bandit awoke to a yard full of commotion. He crawled out of bed in his long underwear. Panic surged through his veins and flooded his chest. His youthful face went pale with fear. His uncle wasn't there to help.

The sheriff's sharp voice sliced through the formerly silent night air.

"You can't hide forever, Castro!" he yelled out, his tone merciless.

"We've got the house surrounded! It's only a matter of time before we come barging in through that door! Do us all a favor and come out with your hands up!"

Juan peered out from behind the tattered curtains; his entire body was quaking. His mind fought desperately for the resourcefulness he needed to find a way out, but deep down, he knew in his heart there was none. The law had caught up with him, and now he was cornered like a frightened animal. It had happened so fast and after only one outing with his uncle.

"Don't test my patience, Castro! Think again!"

The sheriff's voice was laden with disdain.

"I'm not going to stand and wait on you forever. Come out now!"

His panic turned to horror as he heard the thud of boots on the porch and fists pounding on the front door. The capture and arrest were inevitable.

"I'm coming out! Don't shoot! I am unarmed!"

Juan opened the door slowly, putting both arms out before him. They were quickly grabbed by two deputies who threw him to the porch and handcuffed him. They immediately escorted him to jail while the sheriff searched the cabin. He found Juan's half of the money, two pistols, and four watches seized as evidence. His horse, saddle, black outfit and bandana were also taken.

That night, Juan experienced the confinement of a cell for the first time. It was a dim and claustrophobic space tucked away in the depths of the county jailhouse in the heart of Hollister, located on Fourth Street. Its thick stone walls had been weathered over time by the despair of countless occupants. Every sound seemed amplified within this confined space, each wail and whisper accompanied by the smell of sweat, dirt, and the lingering scent of stale tobacco. The only light source was a small, barred window where faint rays of sunlight fought through layers of grime. The flickering of a solitary candle made the shadows appear larger and darker than they were. Or perhaps it was the misery felt all imprisoned there that did. Juan entertained both possibilities as he lay on the mildewed mattress and recalled the first conversation he had with his uncle. He was warned this might happen. But so soon? He felt restless, beating himself up at his stupidity. I was stupid enough to enter a life of crime, he silently berated, and then foolish enough to get caught after one day.

Two guards were on duty that cold night. They were both hunched over by the stove, trying to stay warm, when the front door was kicked in, and approximately ten masked men entered, waving their firearms. The deputies immediately raised their hands to the vigilante mob. They knew from experience what was happening.

"Stay where you are. Do not alert anyone, and don't follow us. Nod, if you understand," the leader instructed.

Both deputies nodded in the affirmative.

Juan was breathless with terror. He was forcefully thrown around between masked men and was immediately blinded with a hood thrown over his head. It was hard enough to breathe through his panicked state, let alone the hood. He was overcome with a feeling that he would pass out.

The vigilantes lifted him onto a horse. He felt other horses' bodies pushing on his legs as the mob moved him slowly forward to an unknown destiny.

"What are you doing to me? Where are you taking me?" he finally pleaded.

His attempt to get answers was only met with silence. He started shivering uncontrollably. The night was cold, and he wasn't wearing a jacket.

Matt Tarpy was no stranger to violence. He had blood on his hands from previous vigilante hangings and beatings, including the first one he participated in: the brutal murder of young Pedro Rodriguez in a dark barn. Matt was an obese merchant who relished any opportunity to join a posse. He basked in the sense of authority and power it gave him among his peers. Though a coward alone, he puffed up like a peacock when backed by a gang of self-righteous citizens. As he stood amongst the crowd for the sixth time, preparing to take part in yet another lynching, a depraved smile crept across his face, fueled by his need for domination and violence.

Young Juan Castro sat atop his horse. The hood covering his face muffled his cries for mercy, while the tight grip of the ropes further intensified his hopelessness. A chilling wind rustled the leaves of the towering oak tree he could not see but knew was there. It would witness his grim fate as one among many. The ethereal glow of the moonlight added to the impending doom.

The vigilantes, wearing a roughshod combination of unidentical hoods, guided him towards the tree. Every moment passed in the cadence of the horses' hoofbeats. Juan's dread deepened, forcing his quivering voice to break through the silence.

"Have mercy. What are you going to do to me? You can't do this."

"Oh yes, we can, and yes, we will," retorted a hooded figure riding beside him.

Juan couldn't see it, but the stranger's tone of righteousness was as unforgiving as steel. The group stopped abruptly; no one in the mob spoke, leaving Juan anticipating what was next.

Tarpy's voice boomed through the air.

"Juan Castro," he declared.

"You are now sentenced to hang for your heinous crimes of highway robbery."

Juan choked on his breath, realizing his fate was sealed.

"We have multiple witnesses confirming that you and your partner in crime, Tiburcio Vasquez, terrorized innocent travelers, stole their belongings and left them with nothing but fear and anguish. For these despicable actions, you will pay the ultimate price. What are your last words, young man?" Tarpy asked unsympathetically.

Juan's unbridled sobbing could be heard under his hood.

"But you can't do this. I have to have a trial. This isn't right!" he cried woefully.

"Trials take too long, and we know you are guilty. This is how we deal with your kind of Mexican who strikes terror through our community daily. Make your peace with God, Juan. You'll be seeing him soon."

Tarpy motioned to another vigilante holding the rope to complete the deed. The noose fell over Juan's head and tightened around his neck. Fear welled in his throat, cutting off his breath and ability to speak well before the noose did. The next thing he heard was a hand slap on his horse's withers as it lurched forward and left him swinging. The death was slow. He felt every minute of it, and it took a whole fifteen minutes for the strangulation to come to completion. His feet kicked for an invisible purchase, as did his mind, faced with the unfolding reality. The rope compressed his carotid arteries and veins, starving his brain of oxygen. The young man's panic gave way to unconsciousness. His last breath on earth gave way to his first in heaven or hell.

Twenty-Two

News of Juan's lynching reached Tiburcio, sending him into a fit of rage. His blood boiled with hatred and shame. His inability to rid himself of the burden of responsibility for his nephew's death crushed him. He had been the one to lead Juan down the path of crime. It would have been effortless to reject Juan's offer! But Tiburcio's pride blinded him, and now his nephew was gone, a victim of his regretful choices. Guilt and remorse gnawed at his soul. He could have saved the young man if only he had made a different choice. If only he had stayed with him the first night instead of frolicking in a brothel. The torment of these realizations was unbearable.

Tiburcio wanted revenge, but he was now alone. There was no gang to support his effort. He headed for the mountains and valley south of Hollister and wandered them with Viento for a year, again questioning his life choices and pondering how to move forward. He found solace in the untouched beauty of nature. The towering trees whispered ancient tales. Trudging through the rugged terrain for weeks, he critically recounted his successes and failures. He had become a solitary figure, a lone wanderer searching for answers that lay within himself. Besides Viento, the valley's vastness and the wilderness's silence had become his only companions. Days blended into nights as he roamed, each step deepening his contemplation. He reflected upon his past. The life of a bandit had brought him power and riches, but it had also left him empty, devoid of any proper purpose or genuine connection to family and the death of Juan.

For all the bandit's notoriety and infamous reputation among his people, he remained elusive and often sought refuge in humble homes or small hotels. The Mexican population welcomed him, fiercely protecting him from law enforcement, constantly helping him one step ahead of capture. He still had a bit of money that he generously shared with churches and impoverished families in the area. Everyone knew of his presence except for the law, who continued to search for him in vain. He moved through the California landscape like a ghost, leaving behind mere rumors of his whereabouts. To those who knew him and were touched by his generosity, though, he remained a beloved figure, a symbol of resilience and courage in the face of injustice.

Tiburcio resumed isolated robberies by himself in the San Joaquín Valley. He was even spotted dancing in a fandango hall. While riding near a creek bed, he came upon a small adobe home where a beautiful young lady named Susan Shell was throwing hay into her horse's corral. Tiburcio felt an immediate attraction to her and approached.

"Good afternoon, Ma'am. Would you be willing to spare some water for my horse and me? I would be ever grateful for your kindness if you could."

Looking up into the glare of the sunlight, Susan saw a man dressed in black on a black horse. As she shaded her eyes, she realized from the description that Vasquez, the famous bandit, was mounted before her.

"Yes, there is a water pump on the other side of the corral. If you lead your horse there, I will pump some for you."

"Thank you. What's your name?"

"Susan, I know who you are, sir. Your reputation and description precede you."

"Well, I am honored that knowing who I am, you have no fear of me and are willing to provide."

There was an undeniable sexual tension between them as Tiburcio dismounted and walked with Viento and Susan to the pump. Unfortunately, Susan had a brother who also recognized Tiburcio and was watching from one of the windows in the adobe. He was highly protective of his pretty young sister and kept an eye on the goings-on.

Susan offered Tiburcio a cup of water while Viento drank from a trough. After drinking slowly from the cup, Tiburcio grazed Susan's cheek lightly with his index finger in a flirting thank you gesture. Susan leaned in and smiled.

A fired gun unexpectedly interrupted the moment. Susan's brother had fired a warning shot in the air. Tiburcio turned to see Miguel Shell yelling at him.

"Get away from my sister, Vasquez! I am a crack shot, and you have one second to get on your horse and spur out of here!"

Susan backed away immediately and yelled in response.

"It's ok. He only wants water!"

Miguel yelled back, "I know what he wants!"

Tiburcio raised his hand in a gesture to let Miguel know he had nothing to worry about when a second shot went off at his feet. Needing no further incentive, he vaulted onto Viento, and they galloped away. He looked back over his shoulder to see the flirtatious Susan waving goodbye.

Tiburcio eventually moved his operations to the Santa Clara Valley. He had old friends there from childhood, Abdon and Rosario Leiva. The exterior walls of their modest adobe bore signs of age and weathering, the subtle cracks in the clay traces of time's passage. Over the years, Rosario had lovingly adorned the windows with vibrant geraniums, their scarlet blooms adding a touch of life to their humble dwelling. The front door, crafted from weathered oak, creaked gently when opened.

They invited Tiburcio inside, and immediately, he felt a warmth embrace him as he stepped across the threshold. The adobe walls retain heat during cold winter nights and keep the interior cool during scorching summer days. Today, the atmosphere felt perfect. The sunlight streamed in through the windows, adding a feeling of calm. The couple was poor but felt obligated to allow Tiburcio to stay for a while.

Abdon was a practical man who liked to keep things simple. He was below average in height and weight, with a slight pot belly and a long beard. His wife found him to be a bit dull and lacking in excitement. Rosario was plain but had a certain charm and sensuality that made her attractive. She had an unrestrained interest in men and often welcomed them with open arms, Tiburcio included. She greeted him kindly with a kiss on each cheek and an uncomfortably long hug for Tiburcio and her husband both. Abdon looked away from the physical display of affection between his wife and their guest. He had reservations about Tiburcio's visit but remained courteous and hospitable towards him. Rosario coyly handed the bandit a steaming cup of tea, her eyes welcoming of mischief. Abdon tried his best to hide his jealousy, but his grip tightened around the handle of his cup.

"Please, make yourself at home, Tibo," Abdon said, forcing a smile.

"We are honored to have a guest like you under our humble roof."

Tiburcio smiled with gratitude.

"Gracias, amigo. Your hospitality is truly appreciated."

Rosario leaned in closer to Tiburcio, an obvious flirtation.

"Tibo, you truly are a man of mystery. We've heard tales of your daring escapades and your skill with a pistol."

Tiburcio took a small sip of the tea, and a faint smile reappeared on his lips. His pleasant demeanor hinted that he was enjoying the conversation.

Abdon sensed that Tiburcio had something important to discuss. Perhaps he wanted to delve into a more personal matter than the formalities of their discussion. Whatever it was, he was maintaining his composure and engaging with Abdon in a friendly manner.

Tiburcio leaned back against his chair, taking a long moment to stare at Abdon, who uncomfortably squirmed in his seat. Finally, he returned forward and presented his audacious plan to Abdon. Rosario, standing nearby, couldn't help but cast lingering glances at Tiburcio, her provocative nature seemingly unaffected by her husband's presence.

"So, Abdon," Tiburcio began with a sly grin.

"I've heard whispers of Henry Miller's fortune. I am told he'll have a hefty sum at Firebaugh Ferry in a few days."

Abdon crossed his arms tightly across his chest; he knew Tiburcio had something on his mind. He gazed downward as he contemplated the proposal.

"Henry Miller is a mighty powerful man, Tibo. He is the most successful cattle baron in California and holds sway on a lot of influence, owning hundreds of thousands of acres and tens of thousands of cattle and sheep to fill those acres up. I know this because I have worked on his ranchos from time to time. I understand the allure of stealing such wealth, but you know I've always steered clear of such dishonest pursuits."

Rosario's eyes danced excitedly as she interrupted.

"Abdon, don't be such a worrywart! Think of what we could do with that money, like build a proper home, buy beautiful things."

She nodded agreeably toward Tiburcio to further encourage him.

"My friend, this plan is foolproof. If we raid the Firebaugh ferry, we can make off with Henry Miller's hefty payroll. We'll be set for life," he added.

Abdon furrowed his brow, his apprehension perceptible as he scratched at his grizzled beard.

"But is it worth the risk? We have a peaceful life here. I don't want to threaten or jeopardize my or Rosario's safety."

Standing nearby and listening intently, Rosario stepped forward and leaned into her husband, hugging his neck.

"Oh, Abdon, think about it!"

Night settled in as Abdon glanced at Rosario with love and concern etched on his weathered face. He sat on a creaky wooden chair, his face lit only by candlelight.

"Abdon, mi amor," Rosario purred seductively.

"Just imagine the riches we could have. Henry Miller and his payroll, it's an opportunity of a lifetime."

Abdon sighed, his tired eyes searching for answers in the dancing flame.

"Rosario, I've never been one for trouble and deceit. We've managed to lead an honest life so far. Why must we risk it all now?"

Rosario's eyes sparkled devilishly as she brushed her fingers along Abdon's cheek.

"But my love, think about what this could mean for us—no more struggling to make ends meet."

"There's no pressure, my friends. Take time to think about it."

"We will, Tibo," Rosario replied.

"Meanwhile, I will cook you a meal like your mother Doña used to make."

Later that night, Tiburcio was awakened by candlelight entering his guest room. The night was quiet except for crickets and an isolated coyote call. It took him a moment to focus and realize Rosario was holding the candle. She wore thin cotton night clothes, made to appear sheerer by the candlelight. They clung to her stocky but firm body and heightened the sensuality of her careful footsteps. She approached his bed and got on her knees. Her face was close to his as she whispered.

"Let me make you happy, Tibo."

She reached under the bed sheets to find his manhood.

Tiburcio was immediately aroused, making it easy for her to find his erection. She moved to kiss him. He turned his head away, grabbed her hand under the sheets, and stopped it just as it reached him.

"This is very tempting, my love. As you can see, I am aroused, but this is in the home of your husband and my friend, and I cannot in good conscience continue. Please don't be embarrassed; I understand your desires, as I have them, too. This will be only between us as if it never happened. O.K.? Will you forgive me?"

"I should be embarrassed, but you turn me down so eloquently and softly that it only makes me want you more. I will leave you alone tonight, but I won't make promises that I won't try again in the future. Good night, sleep well. You will now think of me and what might have happened under the sheets tonight."

She rose slowly and walked out as silently as she had entered.

For Tiburcio, Henry Miller was a ruthless Anglo shark, invading territories and seizing lands without regard for the original Californios who inhabited them. This thought fueled his determination to go through with the robbery. It was not only an opportunity to score a large sum of money but also a chance to fulfill his lifelong dream of buying a ranch. He knew, of course, that he could not remain in the United States, but if successful in this endeavor, he would take a steamship and start a new life in South America. All he needed was for this one robbery to go smoothly. With rumor circulating that tens of thousands of dollars were stashed away in the payroll satchel, Tiburcio's resolve to claim it for himself had no limits. This money was his future.

He sat high in the saddle atop Viento, looking down on Firebaugh's Ferry. He had been there for a couple of hours, watching the goings on, planning his entrance and an escape route. It was a stagecoach stop near the San Joaquín River used for loading and unloading boats and coaches. There was a two-story hotel nearby with a store attached. George Hoffman was the ferry operator and had been so for a long time.

The temperature dropped from the setting sun, and a gentle breeze picked up. A group of five heavily armed horse riders, Tiburcio, Abdon, August de Bert, Clodoveo Chávez, and Teodoro Moreno approached the hotel. De Bert, a Frenchman, stood out from the others with his noticeable hunchback. Clodoveo, an old friend, had very long hair under his hat and a dark complexion set into a thick neck. Teodoro Moreno had scars all over his face, hidden under his mask, while his muscular physique threatened to break out of his clothing. With his slightness, Abdon looked ridiculous by comparison. Carrying a large rifle and having a noticeably nervous demeanor did not help. The guests eyed the menace of approaching masked men and the firepower they carried. The atmosphere grew tense, and they needed no clarification on the bandits' intentions. Some hotel guests carried firearms, and Teodoro sensed that they would likely draw them on the gang, so he quickly moved forward and pointed his rifle at them.

"I'll take those," he said, efficiently confiscating their arms and tucking them into his belt.

Tiburcio followed with his accustomed statement of intent to rob them.

"Everyone inside. Please don't make me ask twice, as you see that my men here have much less patience than I do. If you remain calm, I will also keep them restrained. They are on short reins, so don't test our patience."

The bandits then tied the hands of all the patrons behind their backs.

Hoffman and his wife had been eating dinner in an adjoining private room next to the lobby and had no idea what was going on. The bandits searched the patron's belongings. They had netted around fifty dollars when an unsuspecting Hoffman walked in on the robbery. As an army veteran, he immediately evaluated the situation and raised his hand, asking everyone to remain calm. Tiburcio approached him and removed his watch. Hoffman's wife walked in behind him and asked him not to take it.

"If you please, sir, please return the watch to my husband, and I will go to our bedroom and give you another to replace it. That one is from our anniversary. Please, if you be so kind, you can escort me."

Tiburcio admired the woman's grit and accepted a suitable replacement watch. Returning to the hotel's ground floor he again addressed Hoffman specifically.

"Take me to the safe."

Hoffman complied, rewarding Tiburcio a few hundred dollars. Meanwhile, his accomplices in the other room were looting the hotel of all its valuables, including clothing, cigars, and whiskey. The robbery of the hotel was a success, though the night's work was far from over. They were waiting for the stagecoaches from Gilroy, carrying something much more rewarding than their recent plunder. They sipped on whiskey to calm their nerves. Chávez was particularly enjoying the moment. Leaning back in the chair with his cigar, he raised his feet to the top of the table. He relished the excitement of their illicit activities and used the opportunity to express his appreciation.

"Thank you, Tibo, for having me along. There is no better way to make money and no better people to take it from than wealthy Anglos."

Chávez couldn't help but feel alive and sated.

As fate would have it, the stagecoach driver was none other than Dennis Conroy, who had previously testified and sent Narciso Rodriguez to San Quentin for his involvement in the Soap Lake robbery. Little did Dennis know that he was again about to cross paths with his former adversary. Walking out of the hotel with menace in their eyes, they aimed their rifles at Conroy. He pulled up on the reins immediately, and Tiburcio demanded that he stop the carriage and hand over the box.

Conroy, clearly intimidated, made his disapproval known.

"Jesus, again? When will this end? Ok, I won't stop you; please don't shoot anyone."

"Good, amigo. Throw down your pistol and the Wells Fargo box."

Conroy complied, and on this occasion, the box broke open, mainly revealing papers but a large sack of coins, which Abdon, of all people, went to retrieve.

The temperature plummeted drastically with the sun now set, sending shivers down the spines of anyone out in the open. The starkness of the winter sky was a sight to behold, thousands of stars twinkling like diamonds. The bandits, however, were in no mood to appreciate the beauty. They made a hasty departure, galloping into the darkness and leaving behind nothing but the sound of echoing hooves as they diminished into the distance.

Tiburcio and his men arrived at Abdon's house late afternoon the following day. Their journey had been long and arduous, and everyone was tired and hungry. Rosario waiting for them with a warm and delicious meal immediately lifted their spirits. She had prepared a feast fit for kings, and the aroma of the food filled the air, making everyone's mouths water. Abdon did not miss the lust in Rosario and Tiburcio's eyes whenever they made eye contact.

Tiburcio instructed the men to place the stolen property on the table as they ate. Dividing the loot charged the room with exhilaration. He kept a double share for himself, as was his right as the group leader. Rosario's eyes widened as the men counted their money and valuables. She was in awe of so much wealth in one place, as well as Tiburcio's sense of command over his men. She fell for him as she watched him in action and welcomed the tingle in her groin as she fantasized about him.

While outwardly confident, however, Tiburcio felt disappointed. The information about Firebaugh Ferry being one of the most lucrative sites to rob had not panned out. While a respectable score, once divided among his men, the leader realized further heists and robberies would be necessary if he were to leave the country and start a new life.

Twenty-Three

The following day, all the men left Abdon's home, heading in different directions. Abdon sensed he was safe and that he would not be easily identified. The humpback Frenchman de Bert escorted Tiburcio, and they headed toward Peach Tree Valley, where they stole several heads of cattle and a few horses. The two split up a hundred miles later after they sold the livestock. Tiburcio headed toward Elizabeth Lake, another hundred miles away and east of Stockton. He stayed there briefly with his brother Chico and his daughter Felicita.

Felicita seemed to always have a smile. Her full lips framed glistening white teeth, immediately forcing Tiburcio to stare constantly when she spoke. He was uncontrollably attracted to her tight, muscular body and breasts, which seemed to be firm and constantly trying to escape her blouse. For the first two days there, he struggled not to force himself on her. The young girl, in turn, was enamored with Tiburcio's reputation and found his good looks breathtaking. Knowing he was her uncle might have dissuaded her feelings toward him, but unaware of their familial relation, her desire for him was more potent than anything she had felt before. Chico did not sense the attraction between them, and Tiburcio being Felicita's uncle, he thought nothing of them spending time together going on horse rides.

The first ride was brief and innocent, but Felicita had become increasingly flirtatious by the end and well into the evening at home. It roused Tiburcio's passion, and he began to think about what it would be like to be with her. He lay awake for much of that night, conflicted by his fantasies for her and the guilt they led to. The following day, their longer, second ride brought them to a sizable copse of trees. Tiburcio could barely contain his lust as he rode through the dense forest with his young, beautiful niece at his side. Felicita's dress revealed hints of her supple breasts, and she had unbuttoned her blouse a little as a further enticement for her uncle to look at. The horses walking close together caused their legs to rub against each other with each rhythmic step. Despite his inner conflict, Tiburcio was overcome with temptation and pulled her off her horse into a hidden clearing among the trees. Their lips met in a passionate embrace. As their bodies entwined, pangs of guilt surged, but the overwhelming desire for the temptress was stronger. They spent the next few hours in each other's arms before returning to the house. The ride back was quiet, and neither acknowledged the intimate encounter. Both tacitly understood it would be the only one. They kept their affair a secret until Chico found out, which was the day Felicita could no longer hide her signs of pregnancy. Tiburcio was long gone by then. Chico pressed Felicita, who gave him up as the father. Chico immediately vowed to kill his brother on sight.

Eventually, Tiburcio returned to Cantua Creek, southwest of Fresno. This was home to George Castro, one of the deadliest men in California. Rumors spread that Vasquez and Castro got into a gunfight, and Vasquez was killed, but it was later proved false. Vazquez was alive and well, but not so for the vigilante Matt Tarpy, who had participated in seven lynchings, including the recent one of the young Juan. He had also murdered a woman over a land dispute and was arrested by Sheriff Watson in Monterey.

As fate would have it, Tarpy was jailed directly across from the adobe that Vasquez lived in as a child. Watson, still a weak and incompetent Sheriff, was no match for the vigilante mob that came for Tarpy. They overpowered him and took Tarpy, to hang him from the first tree they could find. It was a sense of poetic justice, perhaps that a Californio put the noose around his neck. The loudmouth vigilante showed his cowardice as he pleaded incoherently for his life.

"Please. Please! I will do anything. Don't do this!"

Those were his last words as his weight fell to the noose. His face and tongue swelling as he gagged involuntarily... until still.

With his share of the money, Abdon moved to the Cantua Creek area with Rosario and bought himself a small plot of land with a moderate but comfortable adobe. It was not unusual for Tiburcio to visit, and Abdon sensed that something more than friendship was bringing him around. He feared the two were having a relationship, but weak man that he was, even if they were, he would not and could not do anything about it. Deep down, he was a coward.

Under a cloudless morning sky morning sky and stifling humidity Tiburcio rode to Abdon's house. He noticed that his horse was missing, a possible sign of trouble. As he knocked on the door, he couldn't shake the feeling of unease creeping up his spine.

Rosario opened the door with her usual honeyed charm.

"Tibo, what brings you here at this hour?"

"I've come to discuss another mission with your husband," Tiburcio replied, maintaining his composure in Rosario's alluring presence.

"One that could bring you and him even more wealth," he continued.

Her smile widened, and she stepped closer.

"He won't be back until tonight. Why don't you come in and tell me all about it? I'll make us some tea."

Tiburcio entered the dimly lit adobe, his spurs clinking on the wooden floor. He felt a rush of desire as Rosario's ample bosom brushed against his shoulder when she leaned over to serve him tea from behind. Her seductive tone only added fuel to the fire already starting to burn within him.

"So, what mission you have in mind, Tibo?" she purred, leaning closer as she walked to his side. She had unbuttoned some buttons, revealing the lovely light brown skin below her neck.

"This time, I have information about a herd of cattle that graze without supervision," Tiburcio replied, his eyes unable to tear away from Rosario's intoxicating figure.

"We could drive some of them away and sell them for a profit."

Rosario's fingers trailed lightly down his arm as she moved behind him again. Her breath was hot against his neck as she whispered.

"That sounds like quite an adventure. Count me in. I can sense your tension, Tibo. Allow me to ease it for you.

Her hand traced a line down his chest before landing on the button of his pants. His body tensed as she leaned in and pressed her lips to his neck. He quickly unbuttoned her blouse, freeing her large, luscious nipples, which had been straining against the fabric. Their lips met, and their tongues explored each other deeply. With one swift movement, he slid his hand under her dress and was met with the intoxicating wetness of desire. Their breaths grew ragged as she pulled away and sank to her knees, eagerly undoing his pants and releasing his throbbing member.

In the back of his mind, he was considering taking Rosario with him. It would be nice to raise a family in South America. She was a good cook and a lover to boot.

She took him into her mouth, and within moments, he was overcome with pleasure and erupted into her waiting lips. The intensity left them both gasping for air as they collapsed into a tangle of limbs and sweat.

A few days later, Tiburcio returned to Abdon's adobe with Chávez to initiate the plan he had mentioned to Rosario. They scoured the San Juaquin Valley and found a dozen heads of cattle grazing unattended. They moved in with their ropes to haze them away, but as they did, one of the vaqueros, Rafael Ponzo, having lunch in a nearby group of trees saw them. He and mounted his horse to quickly reach them and investigate.

"What do you think you're doing here?" he asked with authority.

Tiburcio noted the brand on the horse's hind quarter when he galloped up as the Brand of Henry Miller's company. Rafael Ponzo had worked for Miller for a decade and recognized Abdon. He was surprised when Tiburcio and the two other bandits pulled their guns. They crowded their horses close to Ponzo's, leaving no room for escape.

"I know this man. His name is Rafael Ponzo, and he works for Miller."

"I know you too, Abdon. So now you are a cattle thief? You think you will get away with this. You don't know who you are fucking with here. My boss will see you all hang."

Tiburcio's eyes narrowed as he glared at the vaquero, his grip tightening on the handle of his Colt revolver. The scorching sun was beating down. The wind blowing through the long grass carried the unspoken threats.

"I admire your backbone and loyalty to your boss, Ponzo; you're coming'with us. No need for any trouble."

Rafael's mind was racing, trying to think of a way out. He glanced at his horse, but the bandits had positioned themselves strategically, cutting off any possibility of a swift getaway. His face hardened with fear and defiance. He knew he was outnumbered and outgunned, but his loyalty to Miller demanded he fight back.

"Why?" he asked contentiously.

"Because you will gallop back to your master and tell him about this. Therefore, you will accompany us until we decide what to do with you," Tiburcio replied.

"We should just kill him now, Tibo," Chávez said.

The leader leaned forward again in his saddle.

"Stay cool, Clodoveo. We have plenty of time to figure out what to do with this insolent vaquero. Understand?"

"Si, Jeffe," Chávez said as he tipped his hat.

They headed southwest toward the coastal ranges, hoping to sell the cattle away from Miller's immediate influence. They found a bushy area to put the cattle in and settled in as it got dark, taking shifts to watch over the herd.

The full moon cast a pale blue light over the cold landscape. Tiburcio felt a chill on his shoulders as he watched the herd while atop Viento. He was preoccupied in thought with what to do with Ponzo, a vaquero he respected but now saw as a threat. Maybe when they neared their destination, Tiburcio thought, he would let Ponzo go on foot, hoping it would buy them enough time to escape his vengeful boss, who would indeed be hot on their trail soon enough. As he tried to fully relax, a coyote spooked the cattle and caused a commotion. Tiburcio sprang into action. Viento, a fine-cutting horse, quickly contained the spooked cattle. That's when Tiburcio heard shouting coming from the campsite.

It was Chávez, barking orders at Ponzo to stop and surrender. Ponzo had slipped free from his bindings and vaulted onto his horse, galloping away into the night. Chávez and Abdon struggled but finally mounted their horses in pursuit, leaving Tiburcio alone with the remaining cattle. He knew he couldn't help in the pursuit; he could only listen helplessly as his men desperately fired shots, attempting to bring down Ponzo. The situation had escalated beyond control, and bloodshed seemed inevitable.

Ponzo's heartbeat matched the rhythmic pounding of his horse's hooves against the rugged terrain. His grip tightened on the reins, urging the steed to push beyond its limits. The wind whipped his face. He glanced over his shoulder, catching sight of the menacing figures chasing on horseback. He was gaining ground with each passing moment. His will to live fueled his desperate escape. He knew that if they caught him, his fate would be sealed. Sensing his fear, his horse snorted and quickened its pace, carrying them both through the dark, treacherous landscape. Dust kicked up beneath its hooves, leaving behind a trail only fate could follow. The world around him blurred as adrenaline coursed through his veins. His mind raced, searching for a plan to outwit his pursuers. The forest loomed ahead, its dense foliage offering a temporary sanctuary. Without hesitation, he steered his horse through a labyrinth of trees, their branches clawing at him in protest. Time distorted with each stride, stretching out into an eternity. His thoughts mixed with his breaths, both ragged and labored. Prayers fell from his trembling lips, promises to an unseen deity. He squeezed his eyes shut, feeling the horse under his legs sensing the danger as well. He deftly evaded his pursuers, knowing they would kill him if he failed to, darting through the dense trees like a fox on the run. Behind him, he could hear the shouts of his pursuers growing fainter.

Ponzo finally emerged into a clearing at daybreak and stumbled upon a small group of vaqueros. They escorted him to some law enforcement officers, and he quickly informed them of the events. He kept his eyes downcast, not wanting to catch anyone's attention or reveal any names for fear of retaliation.

As they escorted him to safety, Ponzo's mind raced with thoughts of hiding out on one of Mr. Miller's sprawling ranches, hoping it would provide a haven from those who sought to harm him. The lush surroundings and comforting scents of nature would offer solace amidst the chaos and danger he had narrowly escaped.

~

Abdon Leiva's self-image improved significantly after the cattle rustling incident. He felt more confident in himself and his abilities, especially now that he was living in a new home. Being an outlaw had given him a sense of power and masculinity that he had never experienced before, and he carried a gun with him wherever he went, feeling safer and more secure. Abdon felt more in control of his destiny. It was a false sense, considering he was still the unconfident skinny farmer who on his own, could not back up his bravado. However, he now had to look over his shoulder since Ponzo knew who he was, and it would only be a matter of time before someone came for him.

Abdon took a day to ride into the nearby mining town of New Idria. The late afternoon sun beat down, casting long shadows over the wooden storefronts and causing beads of sweat on his forehead. Seeking refuge from the scorching heat, he dismounted outside a local saloon, its weathered sign creaking softly in the breeze. He adjusted the gun holster strapped awkwardly around his waist. Its unfamiliar weight pressed against his abdomen. It was a constant reminder of his newfound status as a man with a weapon.

He pushed open the swinging doors, immediately hit by a wave of noise and commotion. The dim interior was abuzz with conversation and random outbursts of raucous laughter and clinking glasses. It was a haven filled with the stench of whiskey and despair. Worn-out miners slumped over their drinks, looking for solace in the bottom of their glasses. A lingering haze of cigarette smoke cast an eerie pallor over the room. A black man was mopping the sticky residue, continually spilling liquor onto the age-ridden floor.

Abdon was an unlikely figure amidst these rough and calloused men. He leaned on the bar with an air of misplaced confidence. His ill-fitting clothes hung loosely on his bony frame, accentuating the strangely protruding anomaly that was his potbelly. His thick mustache twitched nervously above a pair of shifty eyes that darted about, trying to appear tough but failing to hide his innate cowardice.

He ordered a whiskey and then another. He thought about his wife, Rosario, who still refused to engage in sex with him even though he was a different man. He always had suspicions that there were other men, especially Tibo. He had never seen them together, but when Tibo visited, he saw the undeniable attraction they tried to hide from him.

He finally moved to sit in the corner, nursing his third whiskey of the afternoon. Swirling the amber liquid in his glass, he caught the eye of a grizzled miner named Tom, seated a few stools down from him. The two men initiated a conversation, but it quickly became a heated argument about territorial rights in the local mine.

Abdon, encouraged by the alcohol and his inflated sense of self-importance, raised his voice and leaned in closer to Tom. Despite the inconsequential nature of the topic, the argument escalated, now drawing the attention of other patrons in the bar. Abdon immediately launched into a tirade about how farmers like him were being exploited by miners like Tom and how the land resources were being taken away from the people who needed them most. Tom had heard this argument countless times before and was in no mood to engage in another futile debate. He tried to brush Abdon off by suggesting they agree to disagree and go their separate ways.

Abdon, however, felt he was not the man he used to be and refused to back down so quickly. He saw Tom's reluctance to engage as a sign of weakness and a lack of courage. He continued provoking and taunting Tom, making increasingly inflammatory remarks about his character and profession.

"Fuck you Gringo. Can you back up your words with action?"

Abdon's face reddened with fury as he clenched the gun handle and stared at Tom. Save for the occasional clink of glasses and the distant chatter of patrons. The room had fallen into an eerie hush, each man visibly bracing for the impending storm.

Tom scoffed, his broad shoulders square and defiant. He was a proud and self-respecting man and couldn't take it anymore. He pushed back his chair and stepped toward Abdon, with his hostility mounting by the second.

"Fuck me? No, fuck you, little man."

After realizing he had leaned on his luck too far, Abdon panicked and pulled out his gun. He fired wildly, missing Tom, and hit an innocent bystander seated behind. The sound of gunfire had stirred panic and confusion in the bar. Abdon saw it as a chance for escape. He ran out the back door, around the building, and climbed clumsily onto his horse, fleeing into the night.

The following day, a frenzied mob of miners descended upon Abdon's adobe, pounding on the door with clenched fists and shouting for his blood. Rosario bravely answered the door in a state of fear and confusion. Before she could speak, the mob violently stormed into the house, pushing her aside. They ravaged the place, searching for Abdon. Rosario could only watch helplessly as they tore through her home, fueled by their desire for justice. She frantically begged for answers.

"Why are you doing this?!"

The leader of the mob sneered at her and spat out the horrifying truth.

"He shot someone last night, and now he will pay. We'll find him and deliver our form of justice."

They left Rosario alone in the wreckage of her home, shaken and on the edge of what might follow. Abdon, whom she had not seen since, was also wearing on her mind. She knew that if he found out that she was pregnant, he would be shocked and confused, as they'd had no intimate relations in recent memory. She felt a mix of emotions, fear, uncertainty, and a growing sense of responsibility as she prepared for the arrival of the child who undoubtedly was Tiburcio's.

Twenty-Four

Tiburcio, José Moreno, Blas Bicuna, and Clodoveo Chávez had spent around a month camping in the mountains near Gilroy to brainstorm and plan various robberies. None had panned out. Frustrated and determined to make a successful hit, they set their sights on the Twenty One Mile House, a popular stopover for travelers between San José and Gilroy. The establishment was owned by William Tennant and was known for serving the best patrons in the area. With their sights set on the prize, the group set off for their next criminal episode.

The bandits approached the front of the Twenty One House and dismounted, their boots thudding against the crusty ground as they led their horses towards the nearby watering trough. The animals' tongues lolled out in anticipation of the cool, refreshing water. They loosened the reins, allowing their horses to drink their fill before they secured them to a nearby hitching post removing their rifles from their sheaths. The sun beat down on their backs.and their spurs jingled as they strode to the entrance porch. The anticipation grew with every step.

Blas Bicuna was known for his ruthless behavior. He had a long face with a large, white mustache and striking black eyebrows. Bicuna had a distinct preference for wearing traditional round Mexican hats, which he often donned in public. Despite his violent tendencies, Tiburcio was convinced to add him to the gang after Bicuna promised not to harm anyone. On the other hand, Chávez had been a regular member of Vasquez's group for quite some time. He was an experienced rider, and his skills were invaluable to the gang's operations. José Moreno was a former soldier who was tall and thin with short hair. He kept his beard well-trimmed, which added to his rugged appearance. Although he had less experience than Chávez, Moreno was eager to learn and was committed to doing his part for the gang.

The adrenaline rush that awaited them inside, and the thrill of the heist, were both exhilarating and terrifying. They knew the risks of their chosen profession, but the lure of the reward was too great to ignore. They steeled themselves for what was to come, their senses tuned to any signs of danger. Since Moreno was new, he stayed outside and watched the front door. He was charged to act but remain calm, perhaps owing to his previous military experience. He watched as the three men entered the hotel. There were only about a half dozen guests in the lobby. Tiburcio took control with a calm voice.

"Good evening, everyone. You are about to be robbed. Please do not resist and hand over your weapons before sitting on the floor."

The patrons froze in shock, unsure if it was a hoax. But, when the trio brandished their rifles, the chilling realization set in instantly that it wasn't. One of the male patrons recognized Tiburcio from wanted posters and revealed his identity.

"That's Vasquez, the bandit!"

Terror gripped the room. They were at the mercy of ruthless criminals. Only two of the patrons had guns, which they quickly dropped to the ground in surrender, knowing it was futile to fight back against such dangerous odds. Bicuna and Chávez each grabbed a gun and shoved them into their belts. They then searched all six men who produced only twenty dollars and a couple of watches between them.

"Shit, these bastards don't have any money!" Bicuna grumbled.

Tiburcio's frustration boiled over as he interrogated the crowd.

"Where is the cash? Someone, show me the safe!"

Met with silence, he seized a teenage boy and shoved him towards Bicuna. Bicuna's fist connected with the boy's face with a sickening thud, sending him sprawling to the ground. The others recoiled in shock and fear but didn't respond, so he pulled out a knife and started poking little holes in the boy's chest. The young man screamed out with every prick of the blade that left small trickling swaths of blood behind on his white cotton shirt.

It was too much for the clerk, Fredric Finley, who knew where the money was.

"For God's sake. Stop! I will show you where they are!" he yelled.

"Hold up, Bicuna, Tiburcio instructed.

"At least until we see what he is going to show me."

Bicuna let the whimpering teenager slump to the floor.

As Tiburcio followed Finley, he noticed how well the man knew the hotel. They made their way to a trunk tucked away in a corner. The man deftly unlocked it, revealing a stash of cash inside. His eyes widened as he saw stacks of bills totaling around fifteen hundred and eighty dollars. Curiosity got the better of him.

"Is there a hotel safe?"

"There is a safe," Finley replied, "but only Mr. Tennant has the combination, and he is currently out of town."

"Show me."

They went into the basement, where Tiburcio was astonished to see a thick metal safe built into the floor. It's impenetrable, he thought and would take forever to break into. He felt a twinge of disappointment but quickly dismissed it, grateful for the generous amount of money that had just been handed to him.

With a satisfied grin, he strolled back into the lobby with Finley. The wealthy patrons sat on the floor, tied up and helpless. The other bandits followed suit, all taking seats at the bar. Chávez reached for an expensive bottle of whiskey and confidently poured four glasses. The amber liquid sloshed gently over the rims as he passed them out to his compadres with a chuckle.

"I'd say that went pretty well, Tibo."

Bicuna agreed, wiping his mouth with his sleeve.

"Better than I thought, amigos."

"I could get used to this."

He poured some of his liquor on his knife to wash off the boy's blood. Tiburcio's face split into a forced smile.

"Yes, men. Let's hit the road before it gets too dark."

The five raised their glasses in agreement before swiftly downing the whiskey, each grabbing a bottle for the road. They strolled outside and casually mounted their horses. As they rode toward the mountains, the clanking of glass bottles and laughter filled the air, a testament to their victory and camaraderie as outlaws on the run.

After interviewing the patrons Sheriff John Adams identified the thieves as the Vasquez gang and felt it not a stretch to connect the heist to the Firebaugh Ferry robbery. He still was on the lookout for him since the Pellegrini murder. Additional warrants went out for Vasquez, and the Santa Clara newspapers described the robbery as "the coolest and most impudent ever perpetrated in Santa Clara County."

Flush with cash, Tiburcio galloped to Hollister to spend some of his money on his favorite pastime; women. He unsaddled Viento and watered, fed, and brushed him down before strolling into Madame Sunshine's, a new bordello in town. The candle-lit brothel bustled with activity. The scent of incense mingled with the pungent aroma of whiskey, perfume, and cigarette smoke. The walls were adorned with lavish tapestries depicting scenes of Asia. At the entrance, Madame Sunshine sat gracefully behind a carved wooden desk framed from behind on either side with statues of dragons. Her eyes were welcoming. They spoke of her wisdom and experience without her saying a word. Tiburcio approached expectantly and with a grin.

"Ah, a new handsome client graces my establishment. How can I help you, sir?" she inquired, her voice smooth as silk.

"It seems fortune has favored you, and you wish to celebrate, perhaps?"

Tiburcio's grin widened into a charming smile. He tossed some gold coins onto the desk.

"Indeed, my dear Madame Sunshine," he answered with self-satisfaction.

"I have come seeking pleasure tonight, and I desire none other than your most alluring gem."

The madame's facial expression showed her understanding. She waved her arm to three women sitting on couches nearby. She also motioned to the bartender to bring Tiburcio a bottle of sake and a small drinking glass. The three prostitutes approached the madame, each with a different body and attitude, giving her new client a distinct choice according to his taste.

"Do you want only one girl or all three, sir?

"Only one, Madame. But one who experienced the Oriental way of making a man happy. I have heard much talk of this among my friends who have slept with some of your kind from far-off lands."

He had silently already chosen the woman on the left because she aroused his loins just looking at her. Her beautiful brown eyes pierced through him, and he hoped this would be the maiden's choice. Nothing escaped the boss; she sensed the choice.

"This is Jade Lin. Do you like her?"

"Yes, I do, and is this your choice as well?"

"Indeed, it is," she replied.

Jade walked to Tiburcio's side and took his hand. He followed like an obedient puppy. Each step toward the room fueled his anticipation for a night of indulgence.

Jade escorted Tiburcio to a bathtub where another woman poured hot, soapy, scented water. She stopped Tiburcio from removing his clothes, motioning that she would do it. She did so slowly and with erotic patience, which immediately made him hard. He was slightly embarrassed, but she showed no emotion as she helped him into the bathtub. She then removed her clothes with her back to him, revealing the entirety of her sensuality. She turned and approached the tub.

Tiburcio gulped hard as she kneeled behind him outside the tub. She took a bowl of hot, soapy water, and poured it over his head. Then she leaned her modestly sized breasts against the back of his head and massaged his scalp slowly to clean it. He could feel her erect nipples as he closed his eyes in total surrender. After five minutes, she joined him in the tub, facing him, and slowly massaged his feet. He had never experienced such joy. She worked her way up to the top of his thighs. He anticipated her going further, but she stopped and slowly got out. Her wet, glistening body could not have been more enticing.

He opened his eyes, taking in Jade's beauty as she grabbed a towel for him to step into. She dried him off, touching every part of him except his erection and guided him to the bed where she had him lay on his stomach. She then gave him a massage, which he had only hoped to experience someday. The touch of her was healing and, at the same time elicited in him sensual desire and yearning. After fifteen minutes, she had him turn over, starting at his scalp and working throughout his body, finally arriving at his manhood. She took him in her mouth and magically used her tongue. He had to stop himself from finishing, though she knew how to stop at the right moment. She finally straddled him and guided him into her wetness. Moving slowly, she eventually leaned over, kissing him. Their bodies moving slowly and rhythmically, he could feel her controlled thigh muscles, which ultimately guided him to an ecstatic climax. After Tiburcio's body had again relaxed, she left the bed and retrieved a wet hot towel to clean him before lying beside him. He immediately fell into a deep, satisfied sleep.

Tiburcio awoke to an empty bed and instinctively reached for his gun under his pillow, but as he rubbed his tired eyes, Jade appeared with tea and sweet muffins, her movements graceful and silent like a ghost. She walked to the bed, draped a silk robe over his shoulders, took his hand, and led him to a table adorned with a single rose. She sat opposite him after pouring them tea.

Tiburcio started the conversation as they had not yet spoken to this point.

"Jade, do you speak English?"

She poured some milk into her cup and stirred it slowly before answering with a hint of amusement in her accent. She nodded in the negative.

He hesitated for a moment.

"My name is Tiburcio, but everyone calls me Tibo."

Jade's piercing gaze seemed to read his every thought. He sensed she knew precisely who he was and why he was there, though she gave no indication that she did. Jade responded in the soft tones of traditional Mandarin Chinese. Her voice was soothing and set him at ease. She looked deeply into his eyes as though delving into his thoughts. That there would be no conversation added to her mysteriousness, but Tiburcio wanted to know more about the woman he now craved to have again. Unfortunately, he knew that staying for too long in any place meant the law could catch up with him. After the tea, Jade brought him his clothing that had been washed and ironed. He left an extra coin on the table.

"I hope to see you again, Jade," he said as he departed.

She merely bowed in response.

Tiburcio moved freely in the area because the local Californios kept him apprised of law enforcement movements. He also paid for discretion, which kept him ahead of being captured or shot. It had always been this way and would continue. He returned three more times to Madame Sunshine's and asked only for Jade each time. She became even more intimate, showing him secrets of the Orient that turned his addictive nature and overwhelming urges into uncontrolled desire. He knew Jade was ultimately a distraction to satisfy his oversexed needs, which had been with him since adolescence. But the girls in the brothels were Tiburcio's only chance of intimacy with a woman. A criminal on the run, he would never settle down, which made the reality of Jade a whore and he a bandit. A story bereft of a happy ending.

Marshal Orson Lyon had learned that Tiburcio Vasquez had been spending time at Madame Sunshine's. He put a posse together and surrounded the building. Lyon entered the lavish brothel, where Madame Sunshine attempted to engage him.

"Can I help you, Marshal?"

Lyon ignored her and sent men into every room, kicking down doors and pulling blankets off men trying to hide. They found four men lying with women in different exotic positions, but none were Vasquez. He had eluded them yet again.

Word got back to Tiburcio about the raid, and he regrettably realized his visits to Jade would have to be put on hold or ceased for good. He returned to the Cantua Creek area, which the locals still protected for him with information. Later, law enforcement discovered they were often very close to Vasquez but would continue to fail to apprehend him due to his army of informants.

Riding Viento through the region's arid terrain and vastness without his gang invariably led Tiburcio to reflect on his path in life and the choices he had made. This blistering sunny afternoon was no exception. For the first time, the bandit questioned whether his desire to settle down on a ranch and leave a life of banditry would make him happy. Deep down, he knew he was hooked on the thrill of committing crimes, particularly highway robberies and livestock theft. He accepted the fact that he may be a wanderer who wished not to have a family and that he relied on Viento as his best friend and companion. Not robbing banks or trains kept law enforcement less interested in him and more focused on outlaws like Jesse James. Men, on average, made twenty dollars a month, women around eight dollars. The hundreds he had stolen had made for an exceedingly comfortable lifestyle.

Tiburcio's lust for women and the adrenaline rush of the chase were a part of who he was. He struggled with guilt, sure, but hid it behind a mask: a knight of retribution sent to help his people escape the poverty inflicted by foreigners. He had never killed anyone—the most heinous crime imaginable—so God would forgive him. Besides, it was more a matter of "thou shalt not steal unless giving to the poor and oppressed." His deeds were not all bad, after all. His actions championed his people and served to right injustices that had long been committed against them. Injustices, he thought, were and had been far worse than the material objects and monies he had stolen.

In fact, Tiburcio had not seen the truth of who he was. He had reasoned that his actions were righteous and that pursuing a dream of owning a ranch would someday make everything okay, that returning to the happy days of his youth on his uncle's ranch, where hard work was valued, would bring him back to the sunshine and divine grace. Giving his people money gave him a false reputation for being a savior, further fueling and validating the criminal activities and, in the end, ensuring that he would continue the inescapable life of crime he had been living. He would never see the day when his dream of raising cattle and sheep and riding his ranch on Viento would come. How much money would be enough? Could he trade one identity for the other? He'd have to realize that dream. And, forasmuch as Tiburcio wanted that, he felt destined to be what he was: a bandit. It had

been his choice, but for reasons beyond his doing. There ultimately was no easy answer, and unbeknownst to his crew, it weighed heavy on his mind and in his heart. In the end he succumbed to the
realiazation that being a bandit and womanizer was indeed his nature.

Twenty-Five

Abdon Leiva had thought he projected an air of confidence and fearlessness. But now, he found himself running scared. The difficulty of his position had finally caught up with him. He, too, had been living a life of deceit and lies, and now it was time to face the consequences of his actions. That included leaving the state with Rosario, but the thought of facing the wrath of Vasquez, the leader of the gang, all but drowned him with fear. Abdon had yet to separate himself from Tiburcio's crew and lacked the confidence to confront him on his suspicions of the affair.

Tiburcio called a meeting with Clodoveo Chávez, Teodoro Moreno, Joaquín Castro, Romulo Gonzáles and Abdon. He presented his latest plot to the group, and Abdon found himself nodding with the others, even though he secretly despised the idea. If he and Rosario were to leave the state forever for Arizona, he needed to participate again. He was in too deep to back out and had no choice but to go along with whatever Tiburcio said.

Rosario prepared a feast for the gang, which roused a feeling of camaraderie among the group. After gorging themselves on her fine cooking, they enjoyed some tequila and relaxed into Tiburcio's new plan.

"I plan to hold up the stage that passes through Hollister and then go to Snyder's store south in Tres Pinos. We will meet next week at Gonzáles's cousin's house. Then Chávez, Moreno, and I will rob the stage while the rest of you stay nearby at the Tres Pinos store and wait for us. I want everyone to bring their most powerful arms, including Henry repeater rifles, shotguns, and revolvers. Clear?"

Everyone nodded in agreement, and Tiburcio raised his glass in a toast.

"To a successful day on the road to prosperity!"

Tiburcio tossed and turned in his bed, unable to escape the suffocating grip of frustration. The moonlight filtered through the dusty window, casting eerie shadows across his troubled face. It was not just the failed attempts at making large amounts at his robberies that plagued him; it was a more profound discontent that gnawed at his very core. His mind danced with memories of a time when his ambitions soared higher than the peaks of the Sierra Madre. He had once dreamed of escaping this lawless land, leaving behind the life of banditry and embracing a path paved with honor and respect. But now, he was tangled in a web of deceit and violence, surrounded by men who reveled in crime and ignorance.

His education set him apart from his companions, though it was lonely. They admired him for his intelligence and relied on his leadership, but he knew deep down their loyalty was, and would always be, easily swayed by the whims of fortune. Worsening matters, Rosario wouldn't leave him alone and wanted to escape with him and have a baby together. **In the back of his mind, he considered it to an extent.**

Maybe this new round of robberies could be the key to finally hitting it big and getting out of California for good, he thought, hopefully. He'd spent months sharing his profits with ingrates. He felt a surge of determination to end it.

He whispered to himself. I will not let anyone, or anything stand in my way, not the law, my rivals, or my doubts and fears.

Tiburcio, Chávez, and Moreno staked themselves out for the stage robbery while Abdon and González rode to Tres Pinos. The bandits were well-equipped with high-powered repeating rifles and large caliber pistols, ready to attack the next stagecoach that came their way. Waiting on a rocky outcrop overlooking the trail, they spotted a cloud of dust in the distance. A stagecoach was approaching, one apparently loaded with passengers, as several figures could be seen sitting on top.

As the stage drew closer and began to slow, Tiburcio's sharp eyes recognized one of the riders on top. It was Tom Williams, one of the foremen at the New Idria Mine, along with his entire family. Tiburcio and Tom had been friends for a long time, and Tom had always been kind to him. The bandit felt a pang of guilt and indecision on whether to follow through, knowing the harm it would bring to his friend and his family.

"Shit!" muttered Tiburcio under his breath.

"I know these people. I can't bring myself to put them through this... Fuck!"

His demeanor indicated frustration and disappointment. He signaled his fellow bandits to stand down and let the stagecoach pass unharmed. Anger swelled in his throat. He mounted Viento and called back to his men.

"Let's get the fuck out of here. Already, this day is going downhill. Mount your horses. We'll head for Tres Pinos and meet up with the others."

He spurred Viento, leaving the others in the dust.

Tres Pinos was a small place. Less than one hundred people lived in the area surrounding a small collection of buildings consisting of a two-story hotel, stable, blacksmith shop, and store. The settlement was at the crossroads of New Idria Road and Old Hollister. Andrew Snyder ran the general store with his wife. Gonzáles and Abdon cantered into town. It was windy and hot. Dust devils intermingled with an occasional tumbleweed that blew across the road confusedly before settling with others in the corner of a building. They dismounted outside the store, which housed a saloon and telegraph office and catered to stages passing through.

The two bandits sauntered up to the bar and asked the young clerk, who doubled as a bartender, for a drink. Without a preamble, the thinner of the two men, Abdon, spoke up gruffly.

"Two whiskeys."

The clerk shook his head apologetically.

"I'm sorry, sir, we don't serve hard liquor here, but I can get you beers if you like."

Abdon, acting tough, grunted in assent. His eyes scanned the room for trouble.

"Beers are fine."

The room was filled with about a dozen patrons doing different types of business. They paid no attention to the two bandits, who sipped their drinks slowly, waiting for the crowd to thin out. Abdon and Gonzáles exchanged a few words in hushed tones as they plotted their next move. The patrons were engrossed in their business. Some were huddled in groups; others sat alone, nursing their drinks, lost in thought.

Suddenly, Moreno barged into the room without any warning, wearing a bandana on his face. Lacking common sense, he pulled out his pistol, brandishing it wildly about at everyone in the vicinity and yelling aggressively at the top of his lungs.

"Everyone, put your hands up and don't move a fuckin' finger!"

As surprised as the patrons were but without hesitation, Abdon and Gonzáles sprang into action. They walked around the room, approaching each of the bewildered citizens and forcibly removing any weapons they were carrying. Feeling an unwarranted sense of power, Abdon began pushing people to the floor, causing even more chaos and panic. Their cries and whimpering irritated him.

"Shut the fuck up, and you won't be hurt."

Under any other circumstance, the skinny, pot-bellied man would have been overwhelmed and beaten by onlookers, but a gun adds power to a coward.

John Utzerath; the clerk, Lewis Smith, the blacksmith; a young man named Henry Murray; Tom Snyder; Louis Scherer; Tres Pinos's saddler; Leander Davison, his wife Elizabeth, and her brother were among the patrons, having stopped by the store for various reasons. Henry lifted his head to see what was going on when Abdon approached, and the bandit pistol-whipped him across the top of his head. He fell to his face, groaning in a pool of blood with Abdon admonishing him.

"I told you, and now I show you, do what the fuck we tell you!"

John Utzerath unwisely intervened.

"No reason for violence. We'll do as you say."

Moreno was standing next to him and kicked him in the stomach with the point of his boot. Utzerath grunted from the blow rolling to his side. He gasped at the looming figure above.

"I know who you are, Moreno; you're not fooling anyone with that mask."

Moreno kicked him again, even harder.

"Fuck you do. You want more of my boot. Keep yappin'."

Within a couple of minutes, Tiburcio and Chávez arrived outside with a pack mule. They entered the room, taking in the groaning, beaten bodies on the floor.

Disinterested in the spectacle, Tiburcio spoke first.

"What's the hold-up? Are you through getting these people's stuff?"

"Almost," replied Moreno as he put sacks over the victims' heads.

"Gonzáles, go outside by the front door and warn us if anyone is coming in. Especially watch out for anyone armed," ordered Tiburcio.

When Tiburcio had ridden up, he noticed it was an unexpectedly hectic day with citizens rambling around doing business in the streets. The words no sooner entered Gonzáles's ears when a cowboy named Buck, carrying his saddlebags, approached from the side of the hotel. He jumped on the porch to enter to reserve a room for the night. Buck was about six feet tall, two hundred pounds, and wore a new Stetson hat that was all the rage. Gonzáles looked around so as not to be conspicuous and followed the cowboy. Entering the room, the cowboy stopped abruptly. He witnessed the gruesome sight before him and turned to leave, but Gonzáles lifted his rifle to port arms to stop him. The cowboy was too big and too fast. He pushed his saddlebags into the face of a surprised Gonzáles, knocking him down as he leaped over the porch railing and ran around the hotel in retreat. The bandit chased him around the back of the hotel, where Buck had left his horse at the livery stable. He had a pistol but no time to draw it. He looked back and saw Gonzáles kneeling to aim, so he pulled his gun to fire in defense. It was too late. The bullet from the bandits Henry repeater struck Buck in the nose as he was turning to shoot.

Moreno ran out the back of the hotel when he heard the shot and saw Gonzáles rising from his kneeling position. They stalked Buck, who lay on the ground in a pool of blood. He was making ungodly sucking sounds, attempting to breathe through the hole that was once his nose. Without a moment of hesitation, Moreno lifted the gun out of the cowboy's hand and shot him in the head with it. They quickly dragged the body deep into the stable.

The blacksmith's son Lewis was in the livery stable and witnessed the gruesome murder. He tried to hide, but Gonzáles saw him.

"Hey! Stop where you are and get down on your knees."

Lewis was cornered. His eyes widened in fear as the two bandits approached him.

"I said get down on your knees!" Gonzáles repeated.

Lewis was too slow to respond, so González pistol-whipped him across his temple. He fell immediately, with blood seeping from his scalp. Moreno helped lift him, and they carried him through the side door back to the back of the hotel. Tiburcio met them at the door.

"What the fuck happened out there?"

"A cowboy saw what was happening and tried to run. We had to kill him. He was going to shoot us or get the law," Moreno replied.

Tiburcio was furious. His eyes narrowed as he peered over Gonzáles's shoulder, catching a glimpse of a teamster wagon pulling up to the livery with a load of fencing in the back. The driver was a stout man with weathered hands and a patch over one eye. It was George Redford, known to the locals as "Deaf" for his lack of hearing. Tiburcio told the bandits to tie up the boy and sack his head. Neither he nor his father noticed each other, for they could not see each other and weren't talking.

Now standing in the doorway at the back of the hotel, Tiburcio kept an eye on the teamster as the man walked toward him. As he got close, Tiburcio motioned with his shotgun for the man to continue toward him.

"Keep coming, hombre."

Suddenly snapping to attention, Redford froze in his tracks. He couldn't hear Tiburcio's words, but the sight of the gun pointed at him spoke louder than any sound. In a panic, he turned and sprinted back towards the livery where his wagon was parked, reaching under the seat for a rifle. Tiburcio's adrenaline surged, and he took off after him. Redford fumbled for the rifle under his seat.

"Stop! Don't make me shoot you!!" the Tiburcio yelled.

The deaf man, of course, did not hear the threat and found his rifle. He quickly turned toward Tiburcio and started to lift the barrel to aim. Tiburcio yelled again.

"Nooo!"

It fell on the deaf ears. Tiburcio was a crack shot and fired one round at the man with a patch on his eye. The loud report of the shotgun ripped through Redford's body, eviscerating him. The blast disemboweled him, exposing his intestines, internal organs, and spine. His lifeless body slumped forward onto the ground. He never had a chance to fire his weapon and would not take another breath on this earth; the total of his hopes, desires and memories were gone in an instant.

Tiburcio looked down at what was now a slumped-over corpse. He had never seen such gore, and it hit him like a wave crashing against rocks. He had just taken another man's life without hesitation. At that moment, everything changed foTiburcio Vasquez. I am now a killer, he thought. It had taken seconds. Why hadn't the man heeded his warning? He tried to shift the blame to his victim.

"No, no, no," he whispered to himself as he shook his head in denial.

Moving back in time, his mind searched desperately for a way to outsmart the finality of his actions. There wasn't one, and his awareness that he had murdered Redford in cold blood compelled him immediately to race to the hotel.

The citizens in the room had heard the gunfire echoing through the small cluster of buildings. Scherer frantically untied himself and his wife, knowing they had to escape before it was too late. In his mind, killing was already happening, and he needed to protect her and himself. The bandits were occupied at the back of the hotel, which gave the two a chance to make a run for it. Scherer grabbed Elizabeth's trembling hand, and they sprinted towards the front door, crouched low to avoid getting caught.

Scherer cautiously opened the door slowly and peered out, scanning for any sign of danger. He whispered urgently to his wife.

"Stay close and follow me. We have to move now."

Emerging from the porch, their eyes suddenly locked with Tiburcio's. Fear and horror seized them as the bandit in black raised his shotgun towards the couple. They froze in their tracks, unable to move as the extensive gun barrel glinted in the sunlight and found them in its sights. Tiburcio was losing control of the situation, and in a fit of helplessness and rage, he fired his rifle as a warning at the couple as they scrambled back into the safety of the hotel. Splinters flew everywhere. The bullet tore through the wooden door, hitting Scherer square in the face. The spray of blood and splintered wood encompassed his lifeless body as he fell to the ground. His wife's heart shattered. She fell to kneel beside the grotesque form that, less than a minute prior, had been her husband. Tears streamed down her blood-stained face as she cradled his head in her lap, fingers numbly tracing over the wounds on his face.

"No!" she cried out, her voice raw with grief. She gently placed his pock-marked head, covered in his blood, in her lap and whimpered helplessly.

"Please, my darling; wake up...please don't leave me..."

Her anguished murmurs dissolved into hopeless sobs as she clung to her husband's cold body, begging for him to come back to her. There was no response, only the deafening silence and overwhelming despair descending upon her.

This had occurred in minutes, and citizens outside the hotel who witnessed it were scattering. Tiburcio walked back into the hotel lobby, now hit with the reality of his second victim lying on the floor. He stared at the corpse, resigning himself to this cursed day. He sat on a chair, placing his shotgun between his legs. He slowly reloaded it as if in shock. As he closed the chamber, he started rambling to himself.

The leaden weight of his actions fell upon him. The sound of the gunshot was still reverberating in his ears, and the spicy scent of gunpowder lingered in the air. His trembling hands tightened around the grip of the pistol, the cool metal offering no solace to his tormented conscience. Guilt clawed at his heart and tore into his soul. He had never wished harm upon anyone; he had only been driven to this point by desperation and circumstances beyond his control. Yet, as he looked upon the lifeless body held in the woman's lap, he knew he alone was responsible for the day's untimely deaths.

His racing mind desperately sought justification for what he had done. There was none. He had seen death since the first hanging that he witnessed. Now, he was the one who delivered it. He had lost complete control of himself and now could only describe himself as a murderer of innocents. He sat in the chair for another fifteen minutes while his men searched every room.

They emptied a cash drawer and ransacked the building, removing new clothing, cigars, food, and whiskey from the store racks. Chávez grabbed a new black hat for Tiburcio, the kind he knew he favored. The bandits netted almost two thousand five hundred dollars plus the goods. As they exited the hotel, Chávez handed his uncle the hat. Tiburcio, lost in thought, grabbed it without so much of a nod. Everyone except Tiburcio drank whiskey and smoked cigars. They all mounted their horses and went to the body-strewn stable that smelled of spilled blood, putting reins on four other mustangs to take with them. They left the pack mule.

Utzerath struggled madly to untie himself as he heard galloping horses fade into the distance. Finally free, he immediately attended to a pair of his captured companions, and they worked feverishly to release the rest. They stumbled out of their bindings. Utzerath's eyes caught sight of the dead body lying at the front door, his blood freezing in terror. Unable to face the horrific scene, he hastily retreated through the back, only to come face to face with another ghastly sight of Redford's corpse, the deaf man's entrails exposed in a lake of blood. Finding no horses, he raced to the nearest farm. The family's shocked expressions mirrored his own as he explained what had transpired in town. Shocked by the story, they entrusted him with a horse and agreed to spread the word. He rode for Hollister with every ounce of strength left in him. His horrifying tale spread like wildfire, one that later etched in history as the infamous Tres Pinos Tragedy.

Messages were telegraphed throughout the state. Every newspaper ran the story. One writer for the Los Angeles Star described it "as one of the most terrible events that has transpired in our state since the bloody raids of the terrible Joaquín Murrieta." The popular legend of Joaquín Murrieta told of a peace-loving man driven to seek revenge when he and his brother were falsely accused of stealing a mule. His brother was hung, and Joaquín horsewhipped. His young wife was gang raped, and in one version, she died in Joaquín's arms. Joaquín had killed many in his vengeance, and now Tiburcio Vasquez, albeit under different circumstances, was a killer.

If not well known before this, the bandit was now to be recognized statewide. Governor Newton Booth put out a reward and capture notice.

Tiburcio and his band had a price of one thousand dollars on their heads for all or any of them.

Sheriffs from the area teamed up to search for the notorious bandits. Rumors spread that it was a gang of at least fifteen to twenty men. Sheriffs Watson and Adams tried desperately to raise a posse but, after a few days, could only get six persons to join.

The San Francisco Chronicle warned the public through headlines based on testimony from two men at Snyder's store. The two men murdered by Vasquez alone…Fears of further depredation…The course taken by the bandits on their flight…The county aroused a swarm of pursuers… One party close upon the murderer's trail…An inquest upon the bodies of the victims…A sketch of the Red-handed outlaw's career…A drawing of Vasquez's face accompanied the above.

Of course, being a wanted man was not unfamiliar to Tiburcio. Still, he knew his day of unmitigated, nonsensical rage had now put him in the big league of criminals sought by the state. As he pursued an escape route south into the valleys and mountains, his blank stare betrayed a head swirling with conflicted emotions; regret, confusion, and fear.

The gang drove their horses to exhaustion. Even Viento suffered to the point of stopping and refusing to continue. Chávez left his horse lying on the ground, unable to continue, and exchanged his tack, putting it on one of the six stolen horses to carry on. After resting for six hours, they awoke and continued slowly, covering the forty miles to the home of Tiburcio's brother, Lorenzo. His wife prepared food for them, and they cleaned every morsel from their plates, leaving some of the stolen supplies for her. They wasted no time laying down to rest there.

Tiburcio approached Lorenzo and his wife, Paula.

"We have to go. Thank you for your generous hospitality. I fear I may never see you again. Lately, I have made decisions that have many people out hunting me. I am sure you will hear about it soon enough. I love you both."

He hugged his brother and kissed his sister-in-law.

The group, except for Tiburcio, exchanged their weary horses for fresh mounts from Lorenzo's stables and continued their journey south through Bitter Water Valley. That afternoon the sky's dark clouds threatened to burst open. Their first few raindrops escalated nearly instantly into a downpour, drenching everything in sight. The horse's hooves slapped against the muddy ground with every step, and the men's heads hung low under their soaked hats and ponchos. The wind picked up, slowing their progress even more.

Thunder rolled in. Lightning bolts illuminated an abandoned barn in the distance. The group slogged toward it, their clothes and gear laden with water. Finally reaching the barn they dismounted and led their tired horses inside. After removing wet saddles and blankets, the men fed their horses what little feed they had left from Lorenzo's ranch. They closed the front doors to seek shelter from the storm and settled on some stacked hay to rest. Exhaustion quickly took over, and most fell into a deep slumber.

As tired as he was, Abdon couldn't sleep. Rain pelted loudly against the barns roof. He ruminated about Tiburcio and

Rosario. What was he going to do? Their feelings for one another were evident whenever he caught her gazing at her lover. His anger burned, recalling that she had never looked at him during their marriage that way, with such a mix of love and lust. Feelings he now saw that Tiburcio reciprocated.

"Perhaps I should just kill him," he muttered bitterly to himself, "and let the law take pity on me."

Gonzáles, who had been drinking heavily throughout their escape, even managing to steal a bottle of whiskey from Lorenzo's and was now stumbling around drunkenly. It was clear that at this rate, he would not be able to continue much longer on their journey.

The next day as they fled towards Los Angeles into the Tejon Pass, the gang's thoughts focused solely on finding a safe spot to spend time to recuperate. Tiburcio rode ahead of the band of thieves, eager to find refuge. The cold night had left them weak and hungry. They came across a ranch and stole a calf for sustenance. Gonzáles stumbled upon some whiskey in the nearby barn and happily grabbed it.

They camped under oak trees in the pass and slaughtered the calf the next day, all the while gazing at the distant San Joaquín Valley below that they had just traversed.

The unimpeded view of the valley dotted by low-hanging clouds was spectacular, but Abdon was too preoccupied in thought to concern himself with it. He was building up the courage to kill Tiburcio. Finally, the thought of him on top of Rosario was too much, and he rose from the campfire to stand over the gang's leader, who was lying on his back with his head on his saddle and hat over his face. Seeing Abdon's unmistakable boots, he sensed someone standing near and peered from under his hat's brim.

"What is it you want, Abdon?"

"I know about you and Rosario. I think you are a piece of shit."

"So what are you going to do? Stand there and kick me? Shoot me?... Abdon?"

Abdon clenched his fists, his anger bubbling within him. He had rehearsed this confrontation countless times in his mind, but, now standing face to face with Tiburcio, the challenge felt more formidable than he anticipated. His mind failed to find the right words to match the intensity of his emotions.

"You think I'm afraid of you?" Abdon retorted, his voice strained with a mix of fury and vulnerability.

"You underestimate me, Tibo. I won't let you use or hurt Rosario any longer. I know what you have been up to."

Tiburcio's eyes relaxed with surprise and amusement as he sat up, removing his hat and placing it beside him. Abdon noticed in his gaze an unsettling calmness that sent shivers down his spine. He swallowed hard. He had expected Tibo to respond with anger, with a threat perhaps. The man was no longer predictable, as evidenced by his recent killings, yet his face remained impassive, masking any hint of emotion. Abdon took a step back, suddenly unsure of himself.

"You planned this in your head, did you, Abdon?" Tiburcio's biting tone threatened.

"You're playing a dangerous game here, amigo. Is it playing out how you thought it would? How do you want this to go down?"

Abdon's breathing remained shallow as he regained his composure, letting his hand timidly move toward his pistol. He had never stood up to Tiburcio before, had never challenged him like this. The thought of Rosario being used and discarded by the man had no shame or bounds, yet it was true that Abdon lacked the backbone and grit necessary to follow his threats with physical violence, and Tiburcio knew it. Abdon also didn't know Tiburcio had a pistol under his blanketed hand, ready to shoot. The palpable tension between them and his calm confidence paralyzed Abdon's will to act.

"Get out of my face, Abdon. Go sit down before I lose my patience. You can't come up against me or any other man by yourself."

Abdon's bluff was called. He stared hard at Tiburcio for thirty seconds, then turned heel and went back to his bedroll. Tiburcio, seemingly unfazed, laid back down and put his hat over his face. He knew his world was unwinding and felt out of control of his destiny for the first time, but he needed sleep.

Gonzáles and Abdon proceeded to drink every last drop of whiskey left and fell asleep in drunken stupors. The following day, they continued their climb through the El Tejon area. As the gang mounted their horses, Gonzáles, still hungover, fell from his saddle to the ground and passed out. Tiburcio looked back in disgust as he spurred Viento forward.

"Leave him."

He galloped off, once again, with a wake of dust. His cohorts continued tracking along the mountains east toward Tehachapi, finally catching up to their leader the next day at Lake Elizabeth.

Twenty-Six

Sheriff Adams arrived in Tres Pinos and as expected, found the community in disarray, its citizens filled with trepidation. He walked in his knee-length duster among the townspeople with a pistol in his front belt while carrying a shotgun. He projected confidence and power, but his attempts at forming a posse failed even as he insulted citizens. He thought them cowards. He finally found three volunteers and a full day behind the bandits, set off in pursuit. Any longer, and the trail would go cold. As he passed through the Hollister area, he added a few more men to the group, continuing south. One wholeheartedly joining the posse was John Shell, the brother of Susan Shell, who had shot at Tiburcio when he spotted him flirting with her.

The trail led them to Lorenzo Vasquez's property. Sheriff Adams eyed the ranch's vast expanse from one corner to another. The sun beat down relentlessly, mirroring the intensity of his pursuit. He spotted Lorenzo leaning against a weathered porch railing, seeking respite in the shade, his arms crossed defiantly.

Adams rode slowly toward him, followed by his cadre of deputies. He remained mounted on his horse as he looked down on Lorenzo to assert dominance. Lorenzo stepped forward from the porch, wiping his hands on a faded leather apron. His weathered face amplified his suspicion and hostility as he locked eyes with the Sheriff. The tension between them was charged with unspoken words and hidden secrets.

The sheriff spoke first, his voice portraying a man of authority.

"Lorenzo, I reckon you know why I'm here. I've been tracking your brother Tiburcio and his gang for days now. The trail led me straight to your doorstep. Have you seen them?"

Lorenzo felt the posse's eyes focused on him.

"Sheriff, I have not seen my brother in years." He spit to the ground before continuing.

"I did see a group of riders on the horizon riding in that direction. Maybe those are the culprits you are looking for, eh?"

"I see," the sheriff responded.

John Shell spoke up contentiously.

"He's lying, Sheriff. Let's string him up. That will make him talk."

"Easy, John, I'm sure Mr. Vasquez would tell us the truth…Right, Mr. Vasquez?"

He paused to let it sink in. Lorenzo stared back at the group.

"Because if I find out you're lying, I will be back, and we won't be so neighborly. I guarantee it… Let's go, boys."

He turned his horse, and the posse followed him, trekking southeast.

Sheriff Adams was a man with conviction and purpose. He was an expert tracker with an eye for detail and a mind to professionalism that showed also in how he dressed. He always wore a suit, his badge in view and his cross-holstered colt on his belly. Convinced that the bandits were at least thirty to forty miles ahead, he headed to the Fresno area to telegraph his findings to the authorities in Los Angeles County. He planned to separate from the posse and catch a train to Bakersfield to make up time. It was in the valley north and below the Tejon and Tehachapi Mountain areas. He was, indeed, at least on the right track.

Sheriff William Rowland in Los Angeles received Adams's telegram gathered up his posse and met Adams upon his arrival in Bakersfield. Adams also gathered a posse of one dozen and set out for the Lake Elizabeth area. Climbing winding Stagecoach Road into the mountainous region, they confronted a sheepherder leading two mustangs that matched the description of some of the extra horses taken from Tres Pinos's stables. The older man, dressed in torn clothing and a worn-out straw hat, looked up at them questioningly. His face was a deeply wrinkled, dark brown, and unshaven, adorned moreover with very few teeth.

"Where did you get those horses?" Adams asked.

"Up toward the lake, Señor. They were watering without anyone around. I led them to grass to feed and am taking them back to sell if I can't find the owner."

"Did you see anyone in the area?"

"No, Señor, there were many tracks and old campfires, but I never saw anyone."

"Ok, old man, continue on your way." Adams motioned him in the direction of Bakersfield.

The posse headed toward where the horses were found and immediately picked up the gang's trail, which led to Fort Tejon in the pass. They came upon another witness who had seen a group of riders led by a man dressed in black on a black horse. He pointed them toward the Mojave Desert.

Meanwhile, Deputy Ronald Short formed a third posse in the north and, communicating with Adams, planned to come in from that direction of the Tejon Pass while Adams pushed from the mid-pass to trap Tiburcio in a pincer movement with Rowland from the south.

Jim Heffner ran the stage station near Lake Elizabeth. Word had come to Adams that Vasquez had eaten dinner there just two nights before. If true, the posse was gaining ground. The rumor was true.

Heffner had immediately recognized Tiburcio and two of his fellow bandits. They appeared to be hardened men on the run, desperate and hungry. He had spent time in prison himself and recognized his kind. He was a balding man with an overgrown grey goatee, typically dressed in blue overalls and a black shirt. He had approached the lead rider, whom he recognized as the infamous bandit. The black suit and vest and a shotgun held loosely at his side made the identification indisputable.

Tiburcio asked if they could impose for some water and a chance to spend the night in the barn to rest their horses. Heffner had agreed and let the worn-out bandits into his home, preparing some beans and bacon for them. As they sat at the small candlelit table eating, Heffner started the conversation.

"Want to tell me what you guys are running from?"

Tiburcio had nothing to hide any longer and recognized a fellow ex-con.

"My name is Tiburcio Vasquez. We are being hunted by a posse from up north for the last robbery we committed."

"I already knew who you were. The information came to the stagecoach station to be on the lookout for you and your band. I just wanted to see if you would not insult me by being honest."

Tiburcio looked at him for a long moment and replied.

"I understand, and I respect that, Jim. We are in your debt for helping us in our hour of need. We will leave at first light so as not to jeopardize you."

"You can stay for a couple of days to rest up. I see you can use it. Then, of course, you must go. A long time ago, someone helped me when I was on the run; it's my way of doing the same for someone else, even if you are bandits. You do know, Tiburcio, that the governor has put out a reward for you and your gang. People are looking all over here for you."

"I'm sure that's the case, Jim. Again, I thank you for your hospitality. We will stay one extra day, only if we don't see anyone coming up the pass and be out of your hair."

The following day, Abdon was nowhere to be found and had apparently abandoned the group. He was headed for Los Angeles, where he intended to turn himself in and throw himself on the court's leniency. Being entirely downhill from the San Gabriel mountains to the small town of Newhall, it was an easy ride for Abdon, and when he arrived, he turned himself into local law enforcement constable William Jenkins at the Lyons Road station.

Adams's posse continued their journey without rest, traversing over one hundred and twenty miles until they finally reached the San Bernadino area. With a sense of relief and determination, they met with Rowland and his men at Martins Ranch in the El Cajon pass. The ranch was a peaceful oasis amidst the rugged landscape, surrounded by towering mountains and lush greenery. As they sat down to compare notes, George Martin, the owner, welcomed the weary travelers with open arms. To honor their meeting, he slaughtered a cow, and his sisters cooked up a mouthwatering barbeque with all the fixings. The aroma of sizzling meat would have persuaded even the most exhausted of men to eat.

Under the stars and feeling the warmth of a crackling fire, Adams, Rowland, and several deputies enjoyed some well-deserved beer. As they relaxed in their chairs, Adams spoke up about their common enemy. The frustration was evident in his voice.

"This killer Vasquez has humiliated us up north," he began.

"I don't doubt that crime is just as rampant down here as it is for us. But this fucker stands out; he is a mastermind of terror. I recently visited Tres Pinos, where he and his gang mercilessly killed three innocent people. In the past, the Mexicans have protected him, giving him information about the lawmen chasing him as well as food and refuge. They see him as some kind of hero. He is cunning, desperate, and ruthless."

Adams leaned back in his chair as he spoke, letting the firelight dance across his face. It cast an eerie glow from under his chin. It was clear that Vasquez had become a personal vendetta for him and his fellow lawmen. He was determined to take the bandit down by any means necessary.

Rowland responded firmly, leaning forward.

"We are here to end this madness. Together, our group will hunt his sorry ass down."

The force of his words, undaunted by what that would take, could be felt in the cooling night breeze. He was committed to making the bandits pay.

The next morning, the posse awoke to the aroma of chorizo, bacon, and freshly cracked eggs sizzling in pans. They prepared themselves for the days ahead. Their demeanor was one of fatigue mixed with tenacity. As they devoured their hearty breakfast, the hunger they felt ran deep. It was one charged also by apprehension.

Sheriff Adams took a sip of his coffee, relishing its bitter warmth. It was as if each sip fortified his resolve, reminding him why he had taken up the badge in the first place. When he was young, he had witnessed a sheriff handily take down a group of three men intimidating and bullying a woman in an alley. He had never seen such strength while dealing justice to a criminal element. He wanted to grow up to be like that, and here he was now trying to do just that. His thoughts were broken when a Paiute Indian cantered up and hopped off to deliver a message.

"I am looking for Sheriff Adams," he said in broken English.

"I'm the sheriff; what do you have for me," he nodded in acknowledgment as he accepted the message from the rider. He unfolded the paper, studying the words detailing Vasquez's whereabouts. The news jolted him, and mingled with the morning caffeine buzz, charged his determination.

"Sheriff Short isn't one to be wrong about these matters," he said to Rowland, his mouth half-full of bacon.

"We best saddle up and head out before Vasquez slips through our fingers, John."

Rowland nodded.

"Finish your food, boys; we're heading out."

Without wasting another moment, the posse sprang into action. The clinking of spurs and the whinnying of horses entrenched their pursuit. The sun climbing higher in the sky cast long shadows across the mountains as though to welcome the dust cloud that followed the dozens of horses' hooves approaching Little Rock Creek (later known as Palmdale). The area, which sits between the Mojave Desert and the San Gabriel Mountains, was known for its abundant desert brush and sand washes.

The three possies, led by Sheriffs Adams, Rowland, and Short, maintained higher ground in an effort to locate any sign of the bandits in the washes. They spotted an old campfire under a tree, from which the remains of a butchered beef carcass hung. Possibly remnants from the gang. Short climbed up a canyon on his horse and followed the ridgeline. The sun partially blinded his vision, but as he shielded it with his hand, he thought he saw a man on the opposite ridge seventy-five yards away. As his hand allowed a clearer view, he was sure it was a man standing near a horse. It was Clodoveo Chávez. Short called down to Adams, who was below and closer.

"Adams! There, Chávez is above you. Can you see him?"

Adams, hearing the other sheriff's voice echo in the canyon, looked up and saw Chávez. The echo also got Chávez's attention, and he immediately mounted his horse to flee.

Adams dismounted quickly, pulled his Henry repeating rifle out of the sheath, leaned it on the saddle, and aimed at Chávez. It was a fifty-yard shot. Chávez heard the whining bullet as it grazed his cheek. The burning sensation caused him to instinctively lower his head to his horse's neck as he spurred it into a full gallop. The entire posse advanced in pursuit. He urged his horse down the steep canyon to the sandy wash, the veil of dust growing the faster he pushed. Although the posse members repeatedly fired at the panicked bandit, the fresher horse he rode allowed him to gain ground.

Tiburcio was watering Viento and a group of stolen horses in a shallow about a mile and a half away when he heard a large volley of approaching gunfire. He mounted Viento and spurred him into a trot toward the commotion. He saw Chávez galloping toward him with the large cadre of men in pursuit. He turned Viento's head, grabbed the horses aligned in tow, and galloped to higher ground. Chávez followed. Tiburcio picketed the horses among some rocks and brush and took out his rifle, aiming it toward Adams, who was leading the charge. The group slowed when they reached where the wash climbed into a canyon. Tiburcio aimed. He had a clean shot but thought twice about killing another person after Tres Pinos. He struggled with the decision, knowing he didn't need another charge against him, especially a lawman. He fired some warning shots that ricocheted off rocks next to Adams. The sheriff and the other pursuers returned fire, inaccurate at best, given the one-hundred-yard range.

Adams, undeterred, slowly climbed using cover fire from the others and rock outcroppings until he was level opposite Tiburcio. He yelled down the canyon.

"Come up and join me! I have Vasquez in my sights!"

None of the posse answered. They were retreating from the barrage raining down from above.

"Where the fuck are you going?!" Adams shouted, receiving no response.

He was beside himself and, under his breath, upbraided them.

"Five hundred miles, finally, we are close, and you assholes are too tired to finish this. Fuck!"

He climbed back down the canyon, mounted his horse, and rode to where Tiburcio was. The elusive bandit was nowhere to be seen. He yelled loudly.

"Vasquez, where are you? I'll find you fucker!"

He got down with his canteen, removed his hat, and wiped his brow in defeat. Thirty minutes later, the rest of the men joined him, accompanied by three stolen horses Tiburcio had let go of when they failed to keep pace with the speedy Viento.

The rest of the day was spent gathering more another stolen horse and tack taken from Tres Pinos. Adams wanted it preserved as evidence. When he finally returned to his base camp in Newhall, he received a telegram that Sheriff Watson from Monterey had taken Moreno into custody on a ranch where he had been working shearing sheep. Watson then boarded a steamship headed for Los Angeles, where he took Abdon into custody and transported him back to a jail in Salinas.

Adams, incensed by the recent turn of events, made it a point to return to Lorenzo Vasquez and arrest him for lying about his brother. Eventually, Lorenzo was released because they couldn't prove he had harbored his brother. Also, the release came for turning the state's evidence against Moreno, who had put the final bullet into the cowboy, Buck, at Tres Pinos.

Twenty-Seven

The portrait photograph Wilbur Bayley had taken of Tiburcio in San Francisco eight years earlier resurfaced to haunt the bandit. The collodion process provided Bayley with a glass negative that he offered to a constable in search of a likeness of Tiburcio. It was made into a wood engraving usable on a printing press. Actual photographs in newspapers in the 1870s were rare since the halftone process was not commercially viable until later in the century. Images had to be glued or tipped in, which was not an economical or efficient method for distributing them. The engraving, however, gave The San Francisco Chronicle the means to print a clear likeness of Tiburcio's face, which accompanied an article by Eugene Sawyer detailing the Tres Pinos tragedy.

Tiburcio sent Chávez to meet with his old friend, Greek George. George was from the Middle East; Turkey. He worked for Henry Hancock, who had been a Civil War commander and now owned Rancho La Brea, a 650-acre parcel near the Los Angeles tar pits. Hancock had purchased some camels to start a transportation route from Los Angeles to St. Louis. An adobe was built for George to live in with his wife and tend to the camels. It was the first built in the area.

George had faked his death in 1865, assassinating the son of New Mexico Governo Charles Bent in Taos during a card game in a saloon. A few months later, after leaving a suicide note with his horse, which returned to the city without its rider, he reemerged in Los Angeles as George Allen. He eventually met and married Cornelia López. The camel experiment ultimately failed because although they could carry heavy loads over long distances, horses tended to stampede at the sight of them. He eventually set the camels free, and they wandered in the Hollywood hills for some thirty years.

Chávez guided his horse to the adobe, dismounted, and knocked on the door. George answered and greeted Chávez with a warm Middle Eastern hug, kissing him on each cheek. It was a custom unknown to Chávez, from which he tried to pull away while remaining no less courteous. George had middle-length hair, a full beard, high cheekbones, and wrinkled skin from spending most of his life in the ravaging Middle Eastern sun.

"Come in, come in, Clodoveo. Make yourself home."

They entered a modest adobe with sufficient light for Chávez to appreciate the intricate motifs of the Turkish carpets covering the floors. Cornelia brought Chávez some tea and biscuits. When she walked away, George pulled his chair closer.

"So, how can I help you?"

"Tibo sent me to find some men to organize a group to take back up north. He thought you might be able to help."

"Well, I am not into that anymore, but go into Sonora Town and look up Ysidro Padilla at Margaritas. Tell him I sent you, but know he is dangerous. You can take your pistol and leave your rifle and horse here."

"Thank you," Chávez said kindly.

"I surely will do that."

Margaritas was a hole-in-the-wall saloon that Ysidro heavily frequented. He was about five foot eight and made of lean, hard muscle with slicked-back hair. He was what was known at the time as a 'Greaser,' which was a slur for Mexicans. Padilla had been convicted of killing five men in a store robbery in Stockton a year earlier. Along with his partner, Jesus Tejada, they had been sentenced to hang but were acquitted for lack of witnesses.

Padilla took less than a minute to accept Chávez's invitation to join the gang. He was excited to ride with the famous Tiburcio Vasquez. While Chávez was in the saloon, he heard talk about Tiburcio and that Rowland had been hunting him. He also heard he had recently given up the search. Valuable information to bring back to his boss. The two men agreed to meet up at Greek's adobe. Chávez, unable to help himself on the ride back, stopped a man, dragged him into an alley, and pistol whipped him until he was unconscious. There was two hundred dollars in coins on him. Chavez was becoming a sociopath and became more violent with every illegal encounter he had.

When Padilla met up with Chávez a couple of days later, they paid the Greek well for his hospitality and headed toward the Tejon pass to meet with Tiburcio and start their trek north.

Reaching the outskirts of Cantua, Tiburcio got word that Rosario had experienced a miscarriage in his absence. His heart ached at the thought of her distress. He needed to find her and make things right between them. When he spotted her in the distance, he quickened Viento's pace until he dismounted and was standing before her. Her face was drawn and pale, her eyes filled with sorrow upon seeing him. Her hand instinctively went to her stomach, where their child should have been growing. There was now only emptiness.

"I'm so sorry, Rosario," Tiburcio whispered, taking her hand in his.

"It was not meant to be, Tibo," she replied softly.

"Where is Abdon?" she inquired.

"The coward turned himself in and will testify against us all. Does he know?"

"No, I kept it from him, and he left when I was not showing very much. I am not surprised, Tibo. I am sad that our child did not come into the world," she said, her voice breaking with emotion.

"But we can try again."

"We will, my love," Tiburcio promised, his eyes conveying his strength of mind.

"I will return when I am done in the North, and we will start a new life in South America."

Rosario's lips trembled as she shuffled closer to him. She started to drop her dress and lead him to the bed, but Tiburcio stopped her. While a loving gesture to ease his torment, it was not the kind of sext that could abate the hurt. He only sought comfort and solace in their shared embrace. They had faced pain and hardship, but their love remained strong and unwavering, and they together would face more of both yet known on their journey towards a better life.

While Tiburcio found refuge in Rosario's embrace, Chávez and Padilla found a way to kill time. They stumbled upon a dilapidated hut near the main street of Cantua Creek and eagerly sought shelter within its decaying walls. As they rested, they overheard a drunken rancher boasting to a friend outside their door about a large sum of money he had recently acquired. He mounted his horse and said goodnight to his friend. Greed ignited within the two bandits, and they followed the drunk man into the Cholame Valley. Finally catching up to him, Chávez hailed him like an old friend. As the man turned, he smiled and was surprised to see Chávez pulling out his gun and immediately firing three loud shots from his hip. The man fell to the ground, blood gushing from his wounds. Padilla wasted no time dismounting and rifled through the victim's pockets. He was rewarded with over two hundred dollars.

Chávez slowly slid from his saddle. He had other plans. Pulling out his knife, he began hacking away at the man's neck in an attempt to sever the head from the body. He tried slicing and prying but to no avail. Blood smeared his sleeve and face, turning Padilla aghast.

"What the hell are you doing?"

"I'm going to bury his head somewhere so no one can identify it," Chávez snarled, his eyes as lifeless as the corpses.

"You know what they say, no body, no crime."

"Stop it, God damnit, Clodoveo. You're an animal. Stop it!" Padilla insisted.

Chávez stopped and looked at Padilla incredulously.

"Fine, you're right," he replied.

"Stripping him of his face will be easier."

He sliced off the man's face from his forehead down to his chin, leaving behind a gruesome sight. The sound of Chávez's gunshots echoed through the area, drawing the attention of a local man who rode toward the sound. He stumbled upon the bloody scene and quickly returned to town, rallying a posse of vigilantes to hunt down the perpetrators. A group of angry men set off in pursuit of the murderous pair.

They caught up with the bandits the next day. A violent confrontation of gunfire unfolded. Padilla, whose horse had bucked him off out of fear, made a futile attempt to hide in some shrub brush. He was immediately surrounded and tied onto his horse. Chávez, meanwhile, managed to evade capture and flee into the hills. As the vengeful mob dragged Padilla away, he could only sob and plead for mercy while desperately trying to shift blame onto his accomplice.

The vigilantes wasted no time and held a trial for Padilla the following day. Despite his protests of innocence, they sentenced him to death by hanging with no semblance of justice or ceremony whatsoever. Without remorse or hesitation, they led him to the nearest sturdy oak tree and strung him up, a lifeless puppet on display for all to see. The end was brutal end for someone who had willingly followed the wayward lead of an ever-increasingly sadistic Clodoveo Chávez.

The San Joaquín Valley, one of the most fertile regions in the world, was hot in the summer and cool and foggy in the winter months. With mountains on either side running the length of central California, from Bakersfield to San Francisco, hundreds of different crops grew in soil fed by the San Joaquín and Sacramento rivers.

Tiburcio traveled north to the town of Panama on the Kern River south of Bakersfield. The Kern River flows southwest with dangerous rapids from Kernville that drained from Lake Isabella. He was flush with money and spent a week with various women dancing in the Fandango houses and brothels. His fame and popularity kept him safe from outsiders while he lived a life of debauchery.

It was there while lying beside a beautiful young woman in the quiet morning hours, that exhaustion finally overcame him. Even in his drowsiness, memories of his recent murders haunted him. Alcohol reliably numbed his pain and assuaged his guilt, but it no less willingly betrayed his need for a more permanent solution. As an introspective man living on society's fringes, he had always taken risks and felt powerful doing so. Women were drawn to his recklessness, and he used their admiration as a crutch. He believed he was seeking revenge for the wrongs done to his people by the Anglos, but awakening each day with blood on his hands, he couldn't deny that he was lying to himself about his true motivations.

During the middle to late 1800s, the stagecoach was a common target for robbers, with over four hundred and fifty recorded incidents. Out of those, Wells Fargo fell victim to three hundred and forty-seven heists. Being part of this criminal enterprise did not make Tiburcio feel alone or out of place.

Although he had always wished to escape eventually to South America with Rosario, the promise to go grew out of reach with every day and crime that passed. A dark feeling of foreboding began following him. The certainty of capture and being hanged was constantly on his mind.

He decided to put together his largest gang yet. He went to the town of Libertad and recruited a band of twelve, which included Chávez, Bicuna, Francisco Gómez, Procella Anamantoria, Ignacio Rangel, Manuel López, Márquez, and a sheepherder named Ramón. Domínguez, Agustín Hernández and Juan Flores would be joining soon. The entire crew except Ramón Molina were hardened criminals loyal to Tiburcio. The crazed Chávez was the primary enforcer.

The stagecoaches of the time were adorned with bright colors and intricate murals, making them stand out on the dusty roads. The wheels were even painted yellow to hide the dirt covering them. They were often filled to the brim with as many as fifteen passengers crammed inside and sitting above with valuable cargo. Their flashiness and promise of wealth made them prime targets for robbers, the color being particularly helpful to spot by outlaws planning ambushes. In response, Wells Fargo employed armed guards to protect their coaches and ensure the safety of both passengers and precious metals on board.

Tiburcio Vasquez's first target would be the town of Kinston on the Kings River. It was remote, with some homes, a couple of stores named The Pioneer and Sweet's, a few saloons, Reichert's Hotel, and some other small businesses. With Domínguez in charge, the bandits picketed their horses across the river and pulled up their masks. Tiburcio decided not to wear a bandana. His bravissimo, he felt, was vital for him to display to his men. They had armed themselves with pistols and a variety of rifles, though Tiburcio conspicuously displayed two pistols and carried a third in a shoulder holster. The moonless, December sky allowed them to stealthily cross the bridge into town. They straight away went for the bridge operator, throwing him down and binding his hands and feet. Gómez removed the coins from his pocket.

Tiburcio split up the groups to control the town better than in his last foray. One, led by Anamantoria and López, walked to the stable where locals Bozeman, Potts, and Woods were working.

"All of you get on your bellies and turn your heads away!"

Bozeman and Potts dropped immediately, but Woods protested.

"These are my Christmas clothes, and I won't ruin them! Um, I mean if it's okay with you, sir. My wife would be upset with me."

Wood's insistence took them aback. Anamantoria didn't know what to do with him, so he let him stand while López hog-tied the other two victims' hands behind their backs and then tied all four legs together. They rifled through their pockets, accumulating one hundred and eighty dollars. The three robbers marched Woods toward the hotel in his Christmas clothes while the gang members split between the hotel and the Pioneer store.

Tiburcio led his men into the hotel's saloon and was surprised to find twelve occupants drinking and playing cards.

"Drop your cards and your drinks, men. I'm Tiburcio Vasquez, and I am here to rob you. None of your valuables are worth your life, so don't put up a fight. My men have short fuses. Don't test them. Now, all of you get on your knees and put your hands behind your backs."

A black cook named Henry in the adjoining kitchen overheard Tiburcio and ran out the side door to seek safety from a powerful local rancher named John Sutherland. The citizens grumbled as they went down to their knees.

"Put your fucking heads down!" Chávez yelled.

Using ropes from their belts, the bandits restrained the victims and rummaged through their pockets for valuables. Any guns were tucked away in their waistbands. Some men implored them not to take their watches as they were mainly keepsakes. The bandits sometimes heard the sentimental stories and chose not to.

With the others ransacking the room and patrons, Tiburcio, Bicuna, and Chávez moved to the next one and found a man named Ed Douglas trying to hide behind a large plant in the corner.

"Seriously?" Tiburcio said laughingly.

"I think I see you, Señor. Drop down to the floor."

Douglas didn't respond, so Chávez walked up and punched him in the head, sending him to the floor.

"Fucker. Are you ignorant?"

Tiburcio relieved his pockets of coins while Bicuna moved on to the dining room.

Lance Gilroy, who worked at the Pioneer store across the street, was eating dinner there. He had just been served by a young waitress who screamed and ran as soon as she saw the masked bandit enter the room waving a gun. Gilroy had no knowledge that others had accompanied the drunken masked man, and when the screaming girl distracted the robber, he got up, grabbed a chair, and threw it at the intruder. It caught Bicuna by surprise, at the same time knocking him out. Chávez heard the commotion in the next room and rushed in. He got there just as Bicuna hit the ground.

"Dumb shit!" he grumbled, referring to Bicuna. He ran to Gilroy and struck him on the side of his head with his large .44 pistol.

Meanwhile, others in the gang barged into The Pioneer store, sending the clerk fleeing out the side door and into Mr. Sweet's store beside it.

"There are bandits next door robbing us!" he yelled.

Mr. Sweet was in the next room resting, and when he overheard the flustered clerk, he jumped up.

"What's going on, Fred?"

"It's Vasquez and his gang, Mr. Sweet, here to rob the town," he explained, fighting to catch his breath.

"I don't give a shit about that Mexican thug. I'm not afraid of him," Sweet challenged.

He grabbed his gun, stepped out the front door of the store, and was immediately seized by his hair and the nape of his neck by two bandits who, at the same time, yanked his gun out of his hand and threw him to the ground.

"Where do you think you are going, Señor?" said Gómez.

Tiburcio was walking out of the Hotel and witnessed Gómez kicking Sweet repeatedly in his ass in front of his store. He approached and grabbed Sweet by his long hair, pulling his face within inches of his own.

"Take me back to the store and open the safe," he demanded through gritted teeth.

Sweet still had some fight in him.

"I don't fear you, Vasquez. You and your friends can go to hell."

"Really, gringo prick? I think you will be the one going there."

He head-butted Sweet. Gómez heard the snap of the store owner's nose breaking. Tiburcio added a knee to the groin, and Sweet groaned, falling to the ground, writhing in pain. He then lifted Sweet and dragged him to the store's main room, where eight people were drinking at the bar, unaware of the heinous events unfolding nearby. He pushed Sweet into the room, followed by Gómez brandishing his rifle.

"Everyone put your hands up and drop to the floor," Tiburcio demanded.

The patrons gasped at the sight of three masked bandits behind their friend Sweet, who was bleeding profusely from his broken nose. Tiburcio escorted Sweet to his office to open the safe, leaving his two compatriots to subdue everyone else and empty their pockets. Much to the victims' chagrin, Lucky, a very friendly bloodhound known to many, annoyingly took advantage of the circumstances and further aggravated the torture by licking everyone's faces. Sweet, barely conscious, opened the safe, which, fortunately for him, had only five hundred dollars in it. Two days earlier, it held three thousand. The losses would have been far worse. Tiburcio tied and gagged him and retreated to join Chávez and the others across the street.

The black cook Henry, who had narrowly escaped, panted heavily from the long run to John Sutherland's porch. He jumped onto it and pounded on the door while bent over, trying to catch his breath. Sutherland came to the door with a cup of coffee in his hand.

"Henry, what's the problem, boy?"

"There's a bunch of bandits robbing the town, sir."

"Stay right there, son; let me get my guns, and we'll gather some of my men."

Sutherland was able to grab three of his cow hands, and, making sure they were armed, they rode to the walk bridge across from the buildings being robbed. They lay down about fifty yards from the bridge with a clear view of Sweet's Store, where Ramón was leaning against the front door, his face still covered with a bandana. Sutherland lay down with his rifle and carefully aimed center mass at Ramón, who was standing under a gas light. He let out a slow breath, slowly squeezed the trigger, and hit the bandit in the chest. His body immediately went limp, falling face-first into the dirt. Tiburcio heard the shot and went to the front door where Ramón had been standing. He was bleeding out quickly into the dirt.

"Let's go compadres! Let's get the fuck out of here!" he yelled loud enough for all his men to hear.

He quickly pulled the bandana from Ramón's face and shoved it into the bullet wound to try to stop the bleeding. Chávez joined him, and they lifted him onto a local horse as splinters of wood from whining bullet hits resounded around them.

As soon as the gang members exited their buildings, Sutherland and his three cowboys opened fire, raining down bullets as fast as they could. Tiburcio grabbed the horse's reins and pulled it as he ran to the bridge with the rest of the bandits, who were firing toward the sound of the incoming rounds. Their aim was wildly inaccurate, as they couldn't see their assailants. They continued across the bridge under the intermittent staccato of gas lights overhead mixed with flashes from their gun barrels. Tiburcio shouted over the overwhelming cacophony gunfire.

"Keep moving, stay low, and get to the horses! Domínguez, bring them!"

Domínguez mounted his horse and, grabbing the reins of the bandits' horses, cantered up to meet the fleeing gang. As they reached the end of the bridge, they saw Sutherland's position and returned fire while mounting. Gómez screamed in pain as a round glanced at his neck. Chávez was hit in the leg and needed help getting up into his saddle. Losing sight of the retreating bandits and running out of ammunition, Sutherland's posse ceased firing.

Galloping when they could, Tiburcio led his men twenty miles to Libertad, where they barged into the local doctors' home to get Ramón, Gómez, and Chávez stitched up. The bleary-eyed physician had opened the door to an obvious menace. Out of fear and duty, he invited the men into his home and had his wife make coffee for the unwounded of the group. He quickly performed triage, tending first to Ramón, who was unconscious. Whiskey and opium were passed to Chávez while the doctor removed a large slug from his thigh. Gómez's wound finally stopped bleeding. Three hours later, all in need had been treated, and Ramón was still unconscious and pale from the loss of blood.

While the wounded were being treated, Tiburcio had distributed each of the men's shares from the twenty-five hundred they had scored, knowing they would break up. The adrenaline that kept them going finally expired, and the bandits fell asleep where they sat or lay. Tiburcio thanked the exhausted doctor and his wife and gave them three hundred dollars as they retired to their bedroom.

Twenty-Eight

The sun timidly peeked over the horizon, casting a soft golden glow upon the earth. The bandits rose from their uneasy slumber. Rubbing the sleep from their eyes, they stumbled out of the cabin in which they had sought refuge. A biting cold wind greeted them, nipping at their exposed skin and causing their breath to form crystalline puffs. With a mixture of weariness and awe, Tiburcio gazed up at the sky, where hues of orange and pink painted a breathtaking canvas. The sight seemed to defy any lingering darkness, filling his ever-hardening heart with newfound hope. The magnificent display reminded him that, even after a night filled with chaos and uncertainty, beauty persisted in the world.

He roused each bandit but found no response from Ramón, who had expired while they slept. Gómez volunteered to take Chávez to the town of Poso Chane, where he had friends, and they both could heal. One by one, they stepped into the crisp morning air, finding solace in the tranquil stillness surrounding them. A profound silence settled, broken only by the crunch of frost-covered grass beneath their boots.

While the gang had sought medical treatment and rest at the doctor's cabin, the posse crossed the bridge only to discover more than thirty citizens still tied up. Lucky, the bloodhound had tired of licking faces and was snoring in the corner of the room.

Sutherland went to the telegraph office and spread the robbery news throughout San Joaquín Valley, Fresno, Bakersfield, and Visalia. The local newspapers told the harrowing story with witness statements, causing panic throughout the valley. Each town formed a posse, and vigilante groups heavily armed themselves in expectation of the impending thievery from the bandit known as Tiburcio Vasquez and his ever-growing gang.

Tiburcio, accompanied by Bicuna, Domínguez, and three more, rode back to the Kern River Valley to recuperate, returning to the town of

Panama, where he was becoming known as the 'Captain of Bandits' and 'Chief of the Mexicans.'

Women lined themselves up to spend time with Tiburcio while the other bandits whored, danced, and drank themselves into stupors.

Satisfied with a successful night of dancing and lovemaking with a pretty girl, Tiburcio made his way to the bustling cantina. His eye caught notice of the mix of admiration, reverence, and fear in the faces of the townspeople passing him on the street. He sat down for breakfast at his usual restaurant, and the waitress handed him a newspaper. His name was splashed across the front page, and not in a positive light. His mood shifted to one of internal rage. The article described him as a heartless criminal who refused to hold himself accountable for his actions, instead using excuses to justify his crimes. Tiburcio felt anger and resentment towards those who judged him without knowing his story. His earlier feelings of contentment gave way to rage and self-condemnation. He desperately tried to push away the guilt that again started to gnaw at him. Damn, those, he thought, who wanted to analyze the reasons for his actions seeing him as a monster! He read further into the incriminating analysis of his character. "Bloodthirsty killer and common thief protected by local Mexican communities" stood out as particularly damaging. He threw the paper to the floor and whispered to himself, "Fuck you. Fuck you all."

Coyote Holes, later known as Robbers Roost, was an outcropping that overlooked a vast expanse of sagebrush-covered desert. One can see for miles in all directions, which is why
Tiburcio and a now healed Chávez were climbing. They had dismounted and were making plans for their next robbery as they ascended.

"See, Clodoveo, you can view the roads to Los Angeles and Bakersfield Intersection, where the Coyote Holes Stagecoach Station is."

"Yes, I can see, Jeffe. But my shot-up leg is not enjoying this fucking climb.

Tiburcio continued, "I am told that the stage from the Cerro Gordo Mine makes regular trips along that road below. We'll be able to see it coming from way off."

They retreated slowly as Chávez limped to an overhang of rock to start a fire and spend the night comfortably for the next day's antics. In the morning, they restoked the fire to cook coffee and bacon. They climbed the monolithic rock, a silent guardian of the desert's vastness with a weathered face carved by time. The sun peeking over the horizon awakened the barren endlessness with its rays. Before them lay breathtaking splendor.

The sagebrush and occasional Joshua tree shimmered from the kiss of dawn's light, the sand and brush a sea of speckled gold.

Perched upon the cold rock they surveyed the scene before them with calculating eyes. Their faces were concealed beneath wide-brimmed hats, and their every breath was visible in the frigid morning air. Rugged appearances to the contrary, they both were captivated by the sublime beauty surrounding them.

Tiburcio leaned against the stone, and his eyes narrowed in the cold morning breeze.

"Look at this place, Clodoveo," he murmured, his voice unburdened.

"There is no law out here, my friend. Just us, the desert, and all the fortunes a stagecoach will hopefully bring. After the stage passes, we'll go to the station and take all we can."

Chávez adjusted his bandana around his neck for warmth and fixed his gaze on a distant stagecoach that lumbered along the snaking trail below.

"Maybe we will hit it big this time," he said with a quiet, hopeful chuckle.

The coach passed. The duo climbed down and mounted their horses, heading to where Freeman Mason and his wife ran the stage station. They approached within a mile. A cowboy cantering in their direction closed distance to Tiburcio and Chávez.

"Good morning, gents," he said.

"Good morning. Are you coming from the station?" Tiburcio greeted.

"Yup, I have some stray cattle I have to find today. Have you seen any on your way here?"

"No, we haven't." Tiburcio paused for a moment and continued.

"My name is Tiburcio Vazquez, and this is my associate, Clodoveo Chávez. Whether you have heard of us, we are here to rob the station. Clodoveo will come over and take your gun if you please."

The cowboy's eyes searched the uncovered bandits' faces in dismay.

"Ok, no need for any violence here."

"Clodoveo, tie him up. We'll take him back to the rocks. When is the next stage due?"

"They told me late afternoon," the cowboy divulged.

"Gracias, my friend. Now follow us."

It was just their luck to cross paths with Freeman Mason, returning from an overnight trip. He had no time to react to seeing the cowboy tied up on his horse. Tiburcio pulled his gun, pointing it at him.

"Stop, Señor. I am Tiburcio Vasquez. Drop your pistol. Who are you?"

"I am Freeman Mason. I run the station."

"Do you hear that, Clodoveo? Fate has granted us good fortune. Tie him up. Instead of returning to the rocks, let's take them both to that small hill overlooking the station."

Chávez responded by nudging his horse next to Mason's and tied the new victim's hands behind his back. The group of four made their way to the small hill overlooking the station. They tied the horses to some large sage and put their prisoners on the ground. The bandits dismounted and took up prone positions with their rifles pointed at the station building, not knowing who was inside.

"Let's put a bunch of rounds into the building as a warning before we go in," Tiburcio suggested to Chávez.

They both opened fire, emptying as many as twenty rounds into the station. Splinters exploded outwards.

"Stop firing, Clodoveo. I am going to ride in close."

He mounted Viento, rode within fifteen feet and yelled to the building's occupants.

"We are here to rob you. All of you come out now. If not, I will burn down the building."

There was no response, so Tiburcio rode back, helped Mason mount his horse, and led him back to the station.

"Tell them who I am and that I am serious. If they do as I ask, no one will get hurt. I am not here to rob them; I just want to rob the coach when it gets here."

Mason called out to his wife, who came to the door and peeked through.

"Ma'am I am Tiburcio Vasquez. Allow us to come inside, and no one will be harmed. We are here to rob the stage. I don't want to burn you out. It's up to you."

She went inside, finding herself in the company of six unarmed men.

"We only have the one shotgun here, and a gang of bandits is out there. Freeman is being held hostage. I think we should surrender."

All agreed and filed out the front door. Tiburcio directed them to sit along the side of the building. Chávez rode down with the cowboy in tow and guarded the hostages. Tiburcio went to survey the barn, where he found an intoxicated man named Old Tex.

"What the fuck you want Mexican?" he slurred.

"What I want is for you to put your hands up so I can see them."

It only took a second for Old Tex to draw his pistol, but due to his intoxication, it was too slow, and Tiburcio drew his .44 and shot Tex in the leg.

"Owww!" he screamed.

"Next time I ask you to do something, do it, or I will shoot you in the head, you old drunk."

He grabbed the wounded Texan and helped him to the other prisoners, and the bandits took everyone to a small hill about three hundred yards behind the station. They had them lie down, threatening that they would be killed if they moved. Seeing Tex bleeding from his leg convinced the hostages of their seriousness.

Tiburcio and Chávez tied their horses behind the station and waited inside for the stage. It arrived two hours later; as soon as the driver brought the stagecoach to a halt, the duo came out of the front door, guns drawn, firing warning shots in the air.

Mr. Belshaw, the owner of a mine, was sitting on top by the driver.

"No need for that, men. What is it you want?"

"Tell your passengers to get out," Tiburcio ordered.

Belshaw shouted down.

"Craig, Fessenden, get out!"

The two passengers who worked for Belshaw exited the stage with their hands up. Tiburcio went through Craig's pockets and relieved him of several dollars.

"That's a nice pair of gloves you are wearing. I want them too," he demanded.

"Please don't take them. They're brand new, and I need them to keep my hands warm, sir."

"Ok, amigo. I tell you what, I'll buy them from you because they will keep me warm. Here you go," handing him back two dollars.

Fessenden had significantly more money on him, fifty or so dollars, as well as a telescope. He watched the transaction between Tiburcio and Craig and asked to keep the latter.

"No, my friend, I think I like this thing, and it will come in handy."

Belshaw had twenty dollars and a shiny silver watch. Tiburcio went through his carpet bag and found a brand-new pair of boots, which happened to be his size.

Belshaw saw the restrained victims standing watching from the small hill where Tiburcio had left them, mistaking them as part of the bandit's gang. Tiburcio ordered the driver to throw down the Wells Fargo Express box, unhitch his team, and put them in the barn. Chávez pried open the box and found $10,000 in mining stock with other books and papers.

"Fuck, there's nothing here, Tibo."

"Take these men to the hill with the others," Tiburcio said.

"Then come back, and we'll take the horses in the barn with us. This has been a shitty day, amigo."

They headed toward the Mojave Desert knowing they would have to traverse it to get to Los Angeles County.

Crossing the one-hundred-mile medley of mountains and sand washes, took only two days at their brisk pace. Dunes and old lava cones stood by now-old corpses of volcanoes. The evening light brought with it brilliant vistas of mesas and rocky croppings. Fortunately, it was February, so it was cooler. Tiburcio unsaddled Viento and rode the stolen horses, changing them regularly as they maintained a reasonably rapid gait. They ended up in Soledad Canyon, just northwest of Los Angeles.

Word got out about the robbery to Sheriff Morse. The witnesses, save the drunken Tex, explained that although threatened, Vasquez had been a gentleman. This held absolutely no sway with Sheriff Morse, however, who was about to make it his sole mission to capture Vasquez.

The Little Rock Republican referred to Vasquez as the "Dick Turpin of California." Turpin had been popularized during the preceding century; a legendary English highway robber romanticized as a gentleman.

The Chicago Inter Ocean printed, "This desperate robber has for years been the terror of the Pacific Coast. His exploits and career rival those of the bandits of any age."

The New York Times described the bandit's elusiveness and "characteristically bold and daring outrages."

These accounts stoked false rumors and reports of Vasquez sightings from all over California, all, of course, proving useless for law enforcement. What they did offer, however, was further notoriety, bolstering his fame and popularity in the eyes of Californians, which the The San Francisco Chronicle authenticated.

It wrote, "outlaw that he is, among the native Californians, he is considered a veritable hero, whose lawless deeds are worthy subjects for emulation."

Tiburcio reveled in the attention. It helped him absolve himself of guilt as a killer. The state of California, however, had had enough. Lawmakers convening in the San Juaquin Valley drafted demands to Governor Newton Booth to act aggressively to capture the "The Vazquez Banditti." The Governor responded by assembling a team to hunt Vasquez and funds totaling $15,000 for the manhunt including $5,000 for a posse, $3,000 for the capture of Vasquez alive, and $2,000 for bringing him in dead.

Sheriff Harry Morse's reputation preceded him. Lauded for being a skilled horseman and a master shot and for hunting down and capturing robbers and horse thieves; when he set his mind to a task, it got completed. He had a fair complexion, light blue eyes, a thin mustache, and a trim body, and was rarely seen in attire other than his recognizable uniform. The suit of the time was a jacket, vest, and tie over a white shirt, with the chain from his vest attached to a silver watch in its pocket.

The first piece of business was to pick an eight-man posse that wouldn't mind being on the road for extended periods. He chose Sheriff Tom Cunningham and former Sheriff Ambrose Calderwood. Calderwood was blind in one eye after being stabbed by Faustino Lorenzana in a fight. He had reason to hunt Tiburcio just for being Faustino's cousin. Ramón Romero would be the possies scout. Boyd Henderson was a correspondent from The San Francisco Chronicle who was allowed to follow the posse in its adventure.

He reported, "Rumors of the movements, daring deeds, and whereabouts of the red-handed outlaw have, almost daily of late, been telegraphed from the lower counties of this State.
Every stage robbery and lawless deed committed within a range of a hundred miles was credited to Vasquez."

Such accounts and the public's perception of Vasquez incited the posse. They set out for Firebaugh's Ferry with a herd of support horses and a wagon with a four-up to pull it. None in the group realized they were embarking on what would prove the longest manhunt of the 1800s, one covering almost three thousand miles over two months and running the length of California. Faltering was not an option, and they knew it. Aware that Vasquez spent much time in Cantua, Morse contacted a source in the area who could spy for him.

The posse reached Cantua Canyon, where they had intended to meet up with their Mexican guide. It didn't surprise them that he never showed. Knowing the locals would warn the Vasquez bandits of their presence and communication, Morse and his posse posed as surveyors and buyers of livestock.

Morse's initial search efforts were flawed. The strategy was to park their supply wagon at a given location, take a week's provisions, and head out in a particular search direction. It proved futile even when Morse offered one thousand dollars for any information leading to Vasquez's location. Although unsuccessful, the posse came up against the bandit's reputed elusiveness; rather than be deterred, they became emboldened. They would find him, no matter the cost. Sheriff Cunningham, a semi-balding man with blue eyes who sported the famous mustache and overgrown goatee of the time, had long been Morse's confidant, and he shared with him an intense desire to bring Vasquez to justice.

While searching the Poncho Chane area, Cunningham happened upon Johnny Robb, an Anglo thief he had once arrested in Monterey, whom he knew to be a friend of Vasquez. He stopped Robb and Ruiz Romero and held them for a few days of questioning, hoping they would break. Not even the reward tempted the two desperados to snitch on their fellow outlaw. Since they were not facing charges themselves, they had no need, incentive, or reason to cooperate.

After releasing them, the sheriffs knew word would get out to Vasquez that they were hunting him nearby, so they decided to seek out the widow of the infamous bandit, Joaquín Murrieta. Mariana as she was called, was a woman of medium height and eye-pleasing proportions living in a sheep herder's tent at Kittleman's Plains. She was recognized partly by a scar on her face running between her ear and nose. Her captivating beauty was complemented by dresses made with vividly colored fabric and rich textures, her beauty so much so that it was thought to be the reason why Joachim remained loyal to her even after discovering she had committed adultery. Her animated storytelling that she had been in the company of cattle thieves, murderers, and highway robbers for much of her adult life was astounding. Her reputation as a prophet led many to call her Mariana Loca or Crazy Mariana. She knew Tiburcio and often drew comparisons between Joaquín and him, seeing the latter's exploits as petty thefts.

Morse had found out that she was witness to the bandits passing by with their wounded after the Kingston raid. Morse had correctly assumed that Vasquez was in the Southern California area but had also made a terrible mistake. It didn't help that most of the Mexican population in the area sympathized with Vasquez. The only thing positive in the manhunt by this point was the retrieval of stolen horses left behind by the bandits to outrun the posse.

Women continued to see Tiburcio as a handsome hero and would have married him on the spot had he proposed to them, and many Anglo men who dealt with him in various business transactions described his manner as gentle. He presented himself as a man of integrity, always paying his bills, and on matters of theft, he did not harm his victims if they cooperated as he asked.

Boyd Henderson's portrait of Tiburcio, drawn from various sources, added integrity to the positive light in which many saw Tiburcio. Considering the bandit's dealings with the Mexican families he visited, he portrayed the bandit helping the poor with the gold he gave them in exchange for their hospitality, ensuring a network of loyal supporters. Henderson's account also put to rest a persistent myth about Tiburcio, that he had a constant gang of bandits assisting him. The truth was, he assembled his gangs as needed, and given the extent to which his people would lie for him, they could be considered an extension of them.

While on the run, Tiburcio and Chávez were becoming more daring in their robberies, stopping everyone in their path to relieve them of their valuables. They had been heading to a picturesque area (known today as Acton) of beautiful rolling hills dotted with large rock outcroppings. An ideal place for the duo to continue eluding and robbing. They stopped a Stagecoach heading to Los Angeles. After tying up the passengers and driver, they broke open the express box, rewarding themselves with three hundred dollars. An elderly passenger started shivering on the cold ground.

"I am freezing on this here ground."

"Fine," Tiburcio replied.

"If you have the money, you can buy my cape to stay warm. It will cost you ten dollars."

"OK, there is some coin in my pocket."

Tiburcio went through the man's pockets and found more than ten dollars but only took the ten agreed upon. The man thanked him when he stuffed the rest of the coin back in the old man's pocket. Henderson's account was fast becoming truth. He recognized another passenger, a Mexican blacksmith, whom he favored.

"I know who you are. I have seen you pounding metal for a living, and I am only taking from them so that I won't take any of your money."

Tiburcio and Chávez mounted their horses and headed toward Soledad Canyon. Happening upon a wagoneer, they relieved him of twenty dollars. It wasn't long after that the sun dropped below the horizon, and the two entered the silhouetted town of Soledad. The wind howled through the narrow streets, carrying with it the scent of desert dust. The moon stayed hidden behind a thick blanket of clouds, casting an eerie darkness over the deserted town.

Tiburcio and Chávez, their figures barely distinguishable in the dim light, cautiously rode towards the outskirts. They passed the open doors to Sam Harper's Stable and then turned back, seeing no one in them.

As they dismounted near the open door, they saw a wagon and six horses.

"We best move quickly," Tiburcio whispered to Chávez.

"The longer we stay in this cursed place, the greater our chances are of getting caught."

Chávez nodded, eyes scanning the deserted streets for signs of life.

"Agreed. Let's load up this wagon and horses and make our way out of here. We don't want any unwelcome surprises."

They loaded some bags of provisions stored on a nearby table onto the wagon, all the while remaining vigilant of their surroundings. The town seemed to hold its breath as though it knew of their illicit activities. Leading the six horses rigged to Soledad Canyon.

Tiburcio joined up with others of his gang; at times up to a dozen men, and hid in the Elizabeth Lake area high in the mountains for the next few weeks. When they wanted to go to town, Sonora town in Los Angeles was preferred. Mid-way, there was an area of large sandstone outcroppings over twenty-five million years old that covered almost one thousand acres. The rocks rose to easily two hundred feet. Within these outcroppings, there were many caves and other places to hide. One day, this area would come to be frequented by tourists and known as Vasquez Rocks.

Tiburcio was known to enjoy cock fights and had a favorite prostitute named La Coneja, slang for the bunny. He had spent a week with her when word got out to Sheriff Rowland of his whereabouts. But as before, by the time the sheriff investigated the address, the bandit was gone. The silver mines in the area provided a further means of eluding the posse. It was also true that Los Angeles' population was expanding quickly, around fifteen thousand, large enough for Tiburcio to get lost in when he visited. He became an avid reader of the local newspapers, which fed his ego as more and more stories described his escapades.

It was during this time that he discovered details of Felicita's birth of his son, Alfredo, whom his brother and his wife were raising. Tiburcio wanted to ask for forgiveness from his brother for the illicit affair with his daughter. With the sun stifling the air with heat, he rode to Chico's ranch, dismounted Viento and called out loudly.

"Chico, it's your brother. Come outside."

Chico came out, pulling up the suspenders on his pants. He looked at Chico, and his eyes filled with desperation and guilt.

"I know I've done you wrong, Hermano," he said, barely above a whisper.

"I can't take back what I did to your daughter, but I can at least offer you this."

He drew his pistol and tossed it to his brother, who barely caught it. Tears welled in his eyes.

"There is eight thousand dollars in reward money for me dead. You can kill me now for revenge and honor and, at the same time, make yourself rich from my sin. Just pull the trigger."

Chico stared at the revolver in his hands, its weight heavier from the gravity of the situation. He could feel the cold metal pressing against his palm. Standing before his brother was a stark reminder of the betrayal that had torn their family apart.

"I don't want your blood money, Tiburcio," Chico said firmly, his jaw clenched in anger.

"No amount of gold can wash away the shame you've brought upon us."

Tiburcio lowered his gaze, a silent acknowledgment of his brother's words. The truth denied his anguished conscience the sense of comfort it fiercely desired—that it needed. The darkness suppressed by his ego's recent reveling in notoriety once again filled his mind. He realized for the first time that forgiveness could not be bought with silver or gold. Their eyes met for a fleeting moment, a silent understanding passing as Chico tossed the gun back, landing in the dirt.

"Now go, Tibo. We never want to see you again."

He stared hard at Tiburcio for ten seconds, turned his back and returned to the house, quietly closing the door. The click of the lock, a hundred times louder for Tiburcio than it truly was, was jarring. He picked up the gun and left.

Twenty-Nine

Tiburcio brazenly rode through the Los Angeles Mountain area, picking and choosing whom and when to rob. He came across the county tax collector, Irish Mike Madigan. They rode side by side through the Tujunga Canyon area for a few miles. Madigan had immediately recognized him but felt no fear of the man. Instead, they carried on a friendly conversation.

"Mr. Madigan, let no one say I don't pay my taxes. How much would the toll tax be?"

"Two dollars, Mr. Vasquez."

"Two dollars it is." Tiburcio put two dollars worth of coins into Madigan's palm, who stopped his horse long enough to write the receipt he handed to the bandit.

The sun beat down as they rode deeper into the canyon, casting long shadows across the dusty trail. He squinted as he scanned the rugged terrain, his hand never straying far from the hilt of his trusty revolver. Madigan rode beside him, a slight smirk playing on his lips as he glanced at the coins in his hand.

"You know, Tiburcio," Madigan started, "I never took you for a man keen on following the law. Paying your taxes is a step in the right direction; I'll give you that."

Tiburcio chuckled lowly, his eyes flickering with amusement.

"A man's got to keep some reputation, don't you think? Besides, it's not like I will outrun the law forever. Might as well make nice while I can."

Their horses' hooves echoed off the canyon walls, creating a rhythmic beat that matched the steady pulse thrumming through the uneasy, though friendly ride.

"Be safe, Mr. Vasquez. Many people are searching far and wide for you," Madigan said, reaching the bottom of the canyon.

"I know, Mr. Madigan. I am enjoying the chase and evasion. Have a good day, Señor."

If there were a word to describe Tiburcio's next move, brave, daring, audacious, bold, or fearless would not be the most robust of choices. He decided to move his base of operations into the very midst of Los Angeles' population, the Greek's adobe.

Greek George welcomed him, Chávez, Francisco Gómez, Renaldo Ortiz, an alumnus from the early days in San Quentin, and a want-to-be bandit sheepherder named Librado Corona, who looked up to Tiburcio as a god. The new hideout was perfect as high bushes surrounded it north, west, and east. The view facing south was wide open into the valley. Though growing rather quickly, Los Angeles still had a lot of empty space dotted by occassional taller buildings.

Tiburcio nodded in appreciation at the invitation, his eyes scanning the modest adobe and taking in the rustic charm of his surroundings. George and his sister-in-law, Modesta, who lived with him and his wife, engaged him in conversation as he settled in, their voices mingling with the sounds of the bustling city outside. The sun dipping below the horizon cast a warm glow over the nearby willow grove where Tiburcio's men had set up camp. While Modesta's appearance was plain, not quite homely, there was a kindness in her eyes that Tiburcio found comforting. He knew that genuine kindness was a rare treasure worth holding onto in the world of bandits and outlaws. It took him no time to be invited to her bed while his men camped outside.

Tiburcio decided to pick the brain of his new intern, Librado. He leaned into his recruit with a sly grin, his sharp eyes remaining vigilant of his surroundings and taking note that George was not nearby.

"Tell me, my dear Librado," he began, his voice low and gravelly.

"What do you know of this area? Are there any wealthy men we could target for a big score? If you provide me with valuable information, I will reward you generously and welcome you into my fold."

Librado pondered for a moment before speaking up.

"There is one man who comes to mind," he said cautiously.

"I used to work for him as a sheep shearer. His name is Alessandro Repetto. He's a massive man, easily three hundred pounds, and sold an enormous herd of sheep for ten thousand dollars recently."

Tiburcio's eyes sparkled as he considered this information. It was clear that Alessandro might make for his first lucrative target in the area.

A blanket of fog greeted Tiburcio and his gang, muffling the sounds of their horses' hooves on the rocky ground. The sun struggled to pierce through the dense mist, casting a pale, uncanny light over the landscape.

Shapes loomed in and out of view, distorted and ghostly. The air grew colder and damper as they rode on, seeping into their bones and sending shivers down their spines. The ominous atmosphere had little impact on Tiburcio's resolve; it remained unshaken as he guided his horse toward the silhouette of the sandstone monolith Fat Rock. This would be their base camp for the robbery of Repetto's immense ranch.

Tiburcio planned to get into Repetto's house by disguising himself as a provider of sheep shearing services. His men stayed near the corral while he knocked on the front door. It took a few minutes, and he was about to leave when the door opened, revealing a pasty-faced, extremely obese man. It was Repetto, exactly as Librado had described him. Repetto inquired in a falsetto voice high enough to be mistaken for a female.

"Yes? Can I help you?"

"Yes, Señor, I am looking for work for my crew. We do any work with sheep, and I understand you have many that need attention."

"You're too late as I sold most of them a week ago. Maybe come back next season."

He went to slam the door but was stopped by Tiburcio's boot.

"Not so fast. I lied. My name is Tiburcio Vasquez, and I am here to get the cash I know you have inside."

Tiburcio pulled out his pistol and put it under the nose of the flaccid-faced man whose eyes opened widely in disbelief.

"Now, Señor, let's return to the house to find that cash."

Repetto backed up, almost tripping over his own feet. It took very little to push him off balance onto a couch.

Seeing that the two had entered the house, Chávez told the men to follow him as they, too entered, closing the door behind them. He was unaware, however, that one of Repetto's vaqueros witnessed Tiburcio putting his gun in the portly man's face.

Tiburcio leaned in close to Repetto, whose panicked eyes kept shifting from Tiburcio to the other bandits who had just entered.

"Now let's save a lot of time, fat man; tell me where all the cash is from that big sale you just made."

"It's in the bank already! I wouldn't keep it here because of fear of being robbed. Believe me, please. If you let me up, I can show you the deposit receipt."

"Help this pig up, Chávez, and follow him to get the receipt," Tiburcio ordered.

Chávez walked over and strained to help the man off the soft couch in which he had sunk. They walked to his office. Repetto's hands were shaking so severely that he struggled to isolate the lone receipt among his other papers. Finally, he found it and handed it to Chávez. They walked back to the living room, and Chávez, who could not read, passed it to Tiburcio. He was incensed.

"The fat man was right," he said to Chávez. He motioned to the rest of his men.

"Go through the house and take anything of value. How much cash or coin do you have here, fat man?"

"I only have about eighty dollars." He went into his pocket and handed it to Tiburcio.

Meanwhile, the vaquero who had witnessed the robbery was galloping to the nearest sheriff's office. He barged into Sheriff Rowland's office.

"Sheriff, my patron is being robbed right now. I think it's Vasquez and his gang!"

Rowland stood immediately, grabbing his hat and a rifle.

"How many men does he have, and how long ago?"

"About thirty minutes ago. When I left there, Sheriff, I saw only four."

Rowland went out the door and mounted his horse to raise a posse. It took twenty minutes to get all the deputies and constables organized. A dozen strong set out for Repetto's ranch.

Tiburcio, Chávez and Gómez raided the food and liquor while Ortiz looked out for anyone approaching the ranch.

"Lucky we are here to eat all this food, amigo. It will save you from gaining any more weight on your obscene body," Tiburcio said, insulting Repetto.

Suddenly, Ortiz yelled out.

"A posse is coming! A whole bunch of them!"

Tiburcio threw down the chicken leg he was gnawing on.

"Get to the horses!"

Tiburcio vault mounted Viento and raced off in seconds. Their distance increased as the outlaws were all on mustangs that outran the older and more weary horses in pursuit. Tiburcio was smart enough to keep about three-quarters of a mile distance and no more so as not to tire out their steeds. This also kept them out of accurate rifle fire. As they were retreating into the Arroyo Seco area, they came upon a teamster on a wagon with a passenger. Out of habit, unable to control their thieving minds, they all pulled their guns.

"Give us your money!" Tiburcio yelled.

John Osborne raised his hands submissively.

"I don't have any money. I am just delivering these pipes to town."

The bandit saw his gold watch and spotted an expensive gold lever English repeating rifle below the seat.

"Hand over the watch and rifle. I don't have time to haggle with you. You see those men back there? I am Tiburcio Vasquez, and they are after me. Have a nice day!"

Rowland helplessly saw the robbery take place in the distance.

"The audacity of this fucker is endless," he whispered to his deputy, then spurred his horse to continue the chase.

Tiburcio and his men started the climb into the Big Tujunga mountains. They raced through the treacherous terrain, their horses pounding against the rocky ground as they desperately tried to outrun the posse. The path grew steeper and sharper, forcing the horses to hoist themselves up with all their might. Their muscles quivered with exhaustion, and their nostrils flared with hot breath as they struggled against the unforgiving incline. Blood dripped from their hooves as they fought for every inch of purchase, knowing any misstep could mean disaster. Tiburcio urged them on. His heart raced as he pushed them further and harder, determined to reach the top before it was too late.

The struggle intensified with every stride against loose rocks and slick patches of mud, the bandits' horses faltering in Viento's wake. Their breaths came in labored gasps as their hooves sought stability. Chávez reined in his horse.

"Tibo, let's stop and set up an ambush. They will be helpless as they climb. We have the high ground."

Tiburcio looked down the slope at the struggling posse. Their horses were slipping and falling from the same exhaustion.

"No, Clodoveo, if we kill any of them, they will call in more and more men, maybe even the army."

The sun was disappearing behind the jagged peaks. Deep shadows obscured the precarious ground, and Tiburcio knew one misstep could mean a deadly fall to the rocky canyon below.

"Whoa, Viento. Let's stop here, men. This flat area is a good place to camp for the night and gives us a good view of them below. I see they are stopping to camp as well. We are about a mile ahead of them, and the horses desperately need rest."

The following day, the outlaws and the posse broke out what little water they had in their canteens and stared at each other. As soon as Tiburcio mounted Viento, Rowland mounted, and the pursuit continued. With each mile gained, their hearts pounded faster.

As the sun peaked at noon, Viento led them to Grizzly Flat, a large mesa overlooking the unforgiving landscape. Panic set in as they cantered to the edge. They had reached a dead end.

Below them lay gaping chasms with thousand-foot drops on all sides, choking in on them like a deadly trap. Time was running out as the posse slowly closed in, leaving them nowhere to go but down into the abyss.

Viento pranced around the edges as Tiburcio's eyes sought any type of escape. Time was running out, leaving them nowhere to go but down. Rowland was relentless, moving slowly higher but with caution to his prey. Desperate for an escape route, Tiburcio signaled Chávez to join him.

"Ride your horse towards that dense manzanita thicket," he commanded.

"See if you can force your way through and find a path down."

Chávez's determined response was grim.

"I'll do it, or we'll die trying."

With no other options, he led his horse afoot into the thorny maze, pushing through the sharp branches with sheer willpower, with blood increasingly trickling down his arms and the horse's shoulders. Every step brought them closer, either to freedom or certain death. The trail down was only eighteen inches wide, and Chávez's horse kept slipping into the gravel-strewn earth. He eventually mounted about fifty feet down as the rest of the gang led their horses on foot. Chávez's horse reached a point where it would go no further.

Any effort at purchase on the slope became impossible. He kicked his horse fiercely, digging his spurs into its side, urging it forward on the loose rocks. Its hooves gave way and sent both man and beast tumbling down the steep incline. Tiburcio looked on in horror as Chávez fell off the horse's back. His screams were lost in the deafening roar of stones and dirt as he slid a hundred feet before grabbing onto a stout bush. The horse's cries echoed in the canyon as it plummeted hundreds of feet more, finally coming to a bone-crushing halt at the bottom. Blood and gore, mixed with shards of broken bones, created a gruesome tableau that no one who witnessed it could unsee.

Tiburcio desperately clawed his way down the unforgiving path, his hands and knees bloodied from the jagged rocks and branches. Every step was a struggle as he fought to keep Viento from tumbling down to the same fate as Chávez and his horse. The men's curses echoed through the canyon as they pushed downward, enduring cuts and bruises to protect their faithful steeds.

It took most of the day to descend the jagged slope. Tiburcio looked up as he helped Chávez to his feet and saw Rowland peeking over the manzanita. He and his gang were hidden well. Their pursuers could no longer see them.

Rowland turned to the posse.

"I'm sorry, men. He got away again. I will not risk our lives and animals to descend into that treacherous canyon. Let's turn back, and we'll catch him on another day." They turned their horses and cantered for home.

Tiburcio and his men's parched throats silently screamed for water, and their empty stomachs gnawed with hunger. They napped for a couple of hours and headed back to the Greek's adobe.

Following the raid on Repetto's ranch, the Los Angeles newspapers were up in arms that Vasquez was laying siege on their city. The Los Angeles Express wrote articles that claimed that the Mexican community was harboring the outlaw. La Cronica, the local Mexican newspaper, responded that only a few were aiding Vasquez. They appealed to their readers to help participate in his capture. The paper was concerned that there would be violence between the Mexican and Anglo communities if Tiburcio and his fellow bandits were not soon caught.

To push the point, they fabricated a story that Vasquez was planning to raid the city with two dozen heavily armed men. Owners of banks and high-end stores panicked, and guns not usually worn were brought out of closets for protection against the impending invasion.

Judge John Nichols owned a ranch a few miles into the hills from Greek George's adobe. Every year, he would host the ranchers in the area to a dance. Greek George warned Tiburcio against impulsivity and recklessness, but the audacious bandit decided to go. He felt invulnerable. He had always evaded capture. Moving to Los Angeles and attending a socially elite party was the height of bravado and self-assurance. Eugenio Rafael Plummer, a local interpreter for Anglos and Mexicans, was sipping from a glass of expensive red wine when a well-dressed Mexican confidently approached him after finishing a dance with a lovely lady.

"I was just talking to my dance partner, who said you are a well-read man."

"That would be a true statement, Sir. My name is Rafael Plummer. I own a ranch a few miles from here."

"I assume you read all of the newspapers then."

"Indeed," Rafael replied.

"I am curious then. What have you read about the bandit Tiburcio Vasquez?"

"Only what everyone else is reading. His exploits are well known, and law enforcement is busy in every part of California looking to bring him to justice. The Anglos want him captured or dead, and the Mexicans idolize him. However, that is starting to change as they fear being stigmatized by the Anglos owing to his actions. I believe that even though he is a bandit, he is for his people, so I respect him while abhorring his ruthless behavior."

"I see," said Tiburcio.

"Since we are confidently discussing such a subject, may I ask your name?"

"You can, and in confidence, I will tell you if you will not be shocked in such an atmosphere of this mixed ethnicity gala."

"You have my assurance, Sir," Rafael replied.

"I am Tiburcio Vasquez. The very one in our conversation."

After an astonished pause, Rafael whispered nervously, "It is my honor to meet you, Mr. Vasquez. Why don't we step outside to continue this conversation,"

As they walked to the patio, Tiburcio added, "Call me Tibo."

"So, Tibo, why are you in Los Angeles? Aren't you uncomfortable here in the lion's den?"

"This is where the action is for me at the moment. It is too hot, and too many people know me up north. I eventually would like to make enough to leave the country and settle down with my family."

"I see; I have admired your exploits for some time now. Listen, Tibo, I understand how some of you, bandits that is, have had it as tough as the earlier settlers, our people, had their land stolen by the Anglos. Even now, they try to cheat me out of mine. How can I be of service to you?"

"If I give you sixty dollars, would you buy a dozen pairs of boots and some food supplies and bring them to Greek George's for me?"

Rafael measured Tiburcio with his eyes to get a measure of the man.

After a slight pause he said, "Yes, I will."

A couple of days later, a dozen boots were outside the Greek's adobe. Tiburcio had given Rafael the location of their camp in Big Tujunga, where a few saddlebags full of food provisions were delivered. He watched from a safe position as Rafael approached and, once convinced that no one was following, rode Viento down to show him the cave.

"Thank you, Rafael, this helps us a lot."

"Good. May I ask a favor of you? Two of my horses have been missing from the ranch. One is a dapple grey and the other black. They bear my brand. Maybe in your travels, if you come across them, you can arrange to have them returned to me?"

"I might have seen such horses, Rafael. Let me see what I can do."

Two days later, the two horses were in Rafael's corral.

Sheriff Morse and Billy Rowland were still searching for the gang in different locations. Morse found where the dead horse lay at the bottom of the ridge, and Rowland found a campsite in San Fernando where he believed the bandits had spent a night. Both Rowland and Morse wanted the bragging rights for the capture of Vasquez, so they sometimes kept important information to themselves, which only benefited the notorious outlaw. However, Morse had reason to think that Vasquez had headed back north to his old haunts. His posse had to return to their responsibilities, so he combed the local Mexican community alone for leads.

María Villa, Felicita Vasquez's mother, harbored a deep hatred for Tiburcio for impregnating her daughter. She had been born into a big family with ties to the famous pioneer Claudio López. Her grandson José López was in love with Felicita and despised Tiburcio. Interestingly, José's father's cousin was Cornelia López, the wife of Greek George. The hatred ran deep, and Cornelia did not like Tiburcio using her home as a base for his gang. On top of that, Modesta, who was occasionally sleeping with Tiburcio in the Greek's home, found out about the Felicita story, and she became furious when she read in the Mexican newspaper that Vasquez was known to be spending time with La Coneja, the prostitute.

The drama among the women was too much to bear, and Modesta decided to go to Sheriff Morse and reveal that Tiburcio was spending a lot of time at Greek George's. Morse decided to bring Sheriff Rowland in on the information and rode to his office. Rowland was sitting behind his desk reading the newspaper, a cup of coffee in his hand. He looked up to see Morse step into his view.

"Sheriff, what can I do for you?"

"I have it on good information that Vasquez is hiding out at Greek George's. I thought I would come by, and we and a couple of deputies could go out and see if it's true."

Rowland mulled it over briefly before answering.

"I have a pulse on the Mexican community and many informants, Sheriff. This information is probably erroneous. Let me check it out, and I will get back to you, ok?"

Morse trusted Rowland's judgment and, having a lot of respect for him, agreed.

"Well, if you think that's best, I will wait to hear from you. Thanks."

Rowland sent one of his deputies, D.K. Smith, to keep surveillance on the Greek's adobe from a bee farm nearby. As the adobe had a clear view to the south for a long distance into Los Angeles proper, the farm provided a good view and cover for Smith to keep an eye on the property. Meanwhile, Governor Booth increased the reward for capturing Vasquez to $6,000 alive and $8,000 dead.

Tiburcio read the news in the paper and felt compelled to make an emotional decision. The article evoked in him a feeling of dread lately, and he sensed his time was running out. The hefty bounty on his head would surely lead to his capture before long. He mounted Viento, grabbed one of the stolen horses, and rode out from the cave hideout to the rolling hills of Acton, where the orange California poppies were spread in every direction. He dismounted Viento with the fiery sun slowly sinking in the distance. The orange glow of sunset mixed with the poppies felt surreal. With a heavy heart, he decided to set his loyal friend free.

Tiburcio's emotions were a storm of regret and sorrow. He shed bitter tears as he put his arms around the stallion's neck, hugging and kissing him as he removed the reins from its shiny black head. Then he pulled off the blanket and saddle as he rubbed his beautiful black coat.

"I love you, my friend. You have been wonderful and have saved my life many times. It's your time now to run free again. Find a girlfriend of your own and make a family."

He slapped Viento, who refused to leave.

"Go, go, please, Viento!" He slapped his hindquarters again.

Viento trotted ten feet and looked back. Tiburcio stared at the beautiful stallion and then walked to him. His beloved horse deserved freedom and a life outside of their dangerous exploits. Viento looked tired from the years on the run and the countless adventures they had shared, nowwore down upon Tiburcio's conscience. With one final gentle pat on the horse's neck, he knew it was for the best.

Viento sensed it as only a soul mate could. He flicked his mane and started his gallop away. Tiburcio knew that they would never again see each other. There would be no reunion down the road, a feeling that contrarily gave him a sense of relief. At least one pure soul would be spared the consequences of his actions, and as Viento galloped off into the distance, Tiburcio knew a good part of himself went with him. He saddled up the Mustang that was in tow and returned to Greek George's.

Thirty

Sheriff Rowland decided to heed Morse's information but did not include him in his plan to make a move on Vasquez. He hand-selected his posse, which consisted of the Chief of Police, a detective, some deputies, and a newspaper reporter. He wanted to make a move on Greek George's home, but leaning on experience, he knew if he did it in daylight, word would get to Vasquez, and he would escape again before they arrived. He decided to wait until two a.m. They met at the corral at Spring and Fifth Streets. They even made sure to have the guns boxed in to avoid arousing suspicion and came as individuals to form up for the posse.

They quietly left the corral, their horses' hooves barely making a sound. The sense of foreboding was inescapable as they moved through the fog, blanketing the sleeping town. The men rode in silence, their eyes penetrating the darkness for any sign of misadventure that would give them away. The only sound was the soft rustle of leaves as they passed, blending seamlessly with the whisper of the wind through the occasional trees. They were apparitions moving through the night, hunting their prey with a deadly determination.

They finally arrived at the bee ranch where D.K. Smith had been spying since daybreak. Deputy Mitchell and D.K. took up a position with a spyglass to observe the comings and goings of Greek George's. Only a grey horse was outside George's, thought to belong to Chávez. After an hour or so, a wagon pulled up near the observation point with two men sitting aboard. D.K. made the two Mexicans get down, and he searched the canvas-covered back end of the wagon. It was empty. Fearing that the men might give them away, they detained them and had them sit under the wagon.

They observed a man get on the grey horse and leave Gethe shotgun blast from the chief hit the escaper with a glancing blow to his head and arm. The shot amazingly didn't drop him. He turned and threw up his hands.

The man yelled, "I give up! Don't shoot! You caught me!"

The Chief approached the man, who he still couldn't identify because of the blood all over his face and body.

"What's your name?"

"My name is Alejandro Martinez."

The chief pulled out an old photograph of Vasquez and held it next to his bloody face. The man had aged and gained weight, but it was Tiburcio Vasquez. Chief Hartley called out Tiburcio's feint.

"Yes, Alejandro Martinez sometimes, and sometimes something else."

The heavily armed posse came in to surround the wounded prisoner.

"Search the house for evidence," Hartley said.

"Anything you find, we will put in the wagon and take back to the jail."

He then turned to Tiburcio.

"You are bleeding badly. We'll take you to the doctor immediately. Do you think you can make it?"

"I feel I am about to die," he groaned in agony.

A crimson puddle had begun to form on the dusty ground at his feet.

Vasquez fell to his knees.

"Looks like we finally caught you, Tiburcio."

"Please, call me Tibo." He laughed weakly, blood seeping out of his mouth and filling his beard.

"You may have caught me, but I'll always be a free man," he finished defiantly.

"You're no longer free, Vasquez," Hartley replied coldly.

"You're a walking dead man. Many people want you to hang out, and in my estimation, you will. I, for one, plan on attending."

He pulled out a flask and offered the bandit a drink. Word was sent ahead to Sheriff Rowland of the capture while the posse escorted the wounded outlaw lying weakly in the wagon.

A hushed silence fell over the large crowd when the wagon trundled through the town square. The posse on horseback had to push aside the crowd of onlookers to clear a path. Some faces were twisted in anger at the sight of Tiburcio, who was pale with pain, while others watched with fear and admiration for the notorious bandit.

"Thief!" someone shouted, their voice cutting through the tension like a knife.

"He robbed us blind!" another voice added, the anger palpable in his tone.

But amidst the accusations and cries of anger, there were whispers of awe from some spectators. Mothers clutched their children close, warning them of the dangers of straying from the path of righteousness. Young men whispered tales of Tiburcio's daring escapades under the cover of darkness, their eyes alight with a mixture of fear and admiration.

"He's not so tough now, is he?" sneered one man contemptuously as he glared at the wounded bandit in the back of the wagon.

"He may be a criminal, but you can't deny he's got guts," retorted another with grudging respect.

A woman pushed her way to the front of the crowd, her eyes filled with anger and something else, perhaps a hint of longing.

"Tiburcio may have broken the law, but he's always stood up for what he believed in and our people!"

She reached into the wagon and kissed his hand.

As the posse dismounted in front of the jail, they forced an opening through the crush of bodies and helped Tiburcio off the wagon to enter. Sheriff Rowland was waiting with a doctor who set to work immediately on cleaning out the buckshot lodged in his body.

"Please be careful and not tear my shirt, Doctor," the wounded bandit asked.

"A friend of mine embroidered it."

The doctor heeded the wishes of his patient and carefully pulled it off the blood-stained body. It didn't take long to clean and dress the wounds, and Tiburcio was locked in his cell.

"Is it really him?" a young boy asked, his eyes wide with wonder as he stood on tippy toes spying into the jail window.

"He's a legend," a grizzled old man muttered to his companion, shaking his head in disbelief.

The cell grew dark with the sun now set, lit only by a few candles. Tiburcio looked up from his cot as Sheriff Rowland entered the cell, his gaze steady and unwavering. The palpable tension between them thickened the surrounding atmosphere. He could see triumph in the sheriff's eyes, a smug satisfaction that grated against his sense of righteousness.

"You have caught me, Sheriff," Tiburcio began, his voice low and steady.

"Congratulations are in order, but no amount of boasting about your tracking skills will convince me that you found me independently. Tell me who it was that gave me up."

Sheriff Rowland chuckled a deep rumble that echoed off the cell's stone walls.

"Thank you, Tiburcio, but even the most cunning of bandits must fall eventually. You are not the exception, and you weren't going to evade us forever. You are just another full of shit common thief who has an over-inflated ego and a sense about you that is unwarranted. Just look at how many years you have been locked up in your lifetime and how many nights you slept in the cold, afraid that we would find you again. You have even failed at your chosen craft with nothing to show for yourself in life, and now, my friend, have fallen to be judged by twelve and sent to the gallows."

Tiburcio tried to return the sheriff's glaring stare, but he was too weak. The lawman's description of his life of crime was a truth that he, at that moment, had no strength to argue against.

"Sleep well Tiburcio. There are long days ahead of you. Be prepared to be looked on as the caged animal you are."

The notorious bandit stared at the key, turning in the lock, realizing there was no escape as Rowland walked away.

Tiburcio awakened, not knowing where he was, a common occurrence for someone who never sleeps in the same place consistently. He was greeted by the residual pain from the doctor's probing to clean out the buckshot and other wounds. A deputy unlocked the cell door and approached the ashen-faced prisoner with a metal plate covered with eggs, bacon, and biscuits. Tiburcio slowly arose to a sitting position on the cot and was greeted by firm hands on his legs. He looked down, his eyes narrowing to see the deputy attaching heavy leg irons to his ankles that connected to a long chain from the cell bars. The cold metal and clinking of chains settling onto the floor starkly contrasted with the aroma of the hearty breakfast.

The deputy stood there, his expression guarded, clearly ready for any sign of resistance from Tiburcio. But Tiburcio remained eerily calm, his gaze fixed on the plate of food. With deliberate movements, he picked up a piece of bacon and took a bite, settling into the moment's reality. He looked at the deputy.

"Really? Is this chain necessary?"

"Sheriff Rowland's orders."

Tiburcio was taking his last bite of breakfast and sipping coffee when the sheriff approached the cell door.

"I gather you slept well, bandit. The chains are to keep your image true to the nature of your breed. The mayor and city council have told me to open the door to visitors. Your capture is plastered all over the nation's newspapers; everyone wants to see you. My job is to keep the jail secure and your image to be kept for what you are. A prisoner. No more, no less."

Thirty-One

Over the next week, the jail was inundated with visitors to the bandit's cell. Many were women bringing flowers, so many so the cell had become a garden full of them. Newspaper reporters wanted interviews. A veritable circus, Sheriff Adams thought.

Tiburcio sat calmly in his cell, surrounded by the sea of colorful flowers that filled the small space with a medley of scents. The constant stream of visitors brought a sense of life to the otherwise dreary jail. His charm and wit entertained the curious onlookers.

"Thank you for the flowers, my dear ladies. They bring a touch of beauty to this cold cell of mine," he said with a smile, his eyes dark and mischievous as ever.

Reporters were also clamoring for his attention, eager to capture every word that fell from his lips. Tiburcio obliged, spinning tales of his daring escapades with eloquence and flair.

"Ah, the life of a bandit is not for the faint of heart," he would say, his ego injured with bravado and nostalgia.

As many anticipated, Tiburcio's demeanor remained unaltered despite his circumstances. He carried himself with a confidence that drew all eyes. He didn't know who and how he was betrayed, but he would.

One of California's leading photography companies put out an offer to take a photograph of the celebrity bandit to make cabinet card images to sell to the public. They offered to pay Tiburcio twenty-five cents per card. The bandit agreed, and Valentin Wolfenstein planned for Tiburcio's temporary release to sit for it behind the jail.

Sheriff Rowland was incensed by the attention Tiburcio was receiving. The bandit had recovered well enough from his wounds, so it was time to send him to trial. Loaded with handcuffs and leg irons, authorities transported him by carriage to the port to board the steamer *Senator* headed to San Francisco. Rowland and three deputies accompanied Tiburcio. From there, they would go to Salinas to stand trial for the Tres Pinos murders.

After three seasick days on the steamer, Vasquez was content to step onto dry land. Crowds at the pier struggled to catch a glimpse of him, but he was hurried off to a covered wagon and transported with a large guard contingent to the Salinas Jail. Once ensconced in Chief Cockrill's custody, the crowds formed around the building, still trying to view the 'Captain of Bandits.' In Adam's eyes, the sideshow continued.

A cacophony of cheers and jeers echoed off the stone walls of the jail, reverberating through Tiburcio's very being. His heart raced with a heady mix of exhilaration and terror as he stood at the window, looking at the many people below. Each face in the crowd seemed to hold a different emotion—admiration, fear, fascination. In their eyes, he was both a hero and a villain, a mysterious figure they couldn't comprehend.

His newfound celebrity soon began to feel like a heavy cloak tightly wrapping around him. Crowds chanting his name and clamoring for a glimpse of him brought him an intoxicating comfort. It was not enough to escape the deep dread threatening to swallow him whole, deep down, in his soul. The people who now cheered for him would just as quickly turn against him, their adoration fickle, easily succumbing to anger and condemnation. Would a vigilante group steal him in the night to hang him from the nearest tree, he wondered. He was under no illusion that he would be able to escape jail this time, and the cloud of the trial and eventual hanging hung in the air.

Early the second morning, Chief Cockrill walked to Tiburcio's cell.

"Ninety percent of the Californios out there support you, Vasquez. Are you opposed to them coming by your cell to look?"

"No, I'm not."

"I'll tell you what I'll do. I will charge them each fifty cents to walk by. I will keep half the money you make and the other half you can pay your lawyer with."

Tiburcio nodded.

Cockrill had his deputies march citizens, half a dozen at a time, in and out of the jail, forbidding them from speaking to the prisoner. Tiburcio had earned sixty dollars toward his legal fund by the day's end, and Ben Darwin from San Francisco was set to represent him. Darwin was a former judge and now a prominent attorney. He met with Tiburcio, finding the outlaw's education impressive. He brought him three books to pass the time: Don Quixote de la Mancha, Guzmán de Alfarache, and Amalia.

Meanwhile, Abdon Leiva had been making enemies during his stint in the San José Jail. He was nearly murdered by a fellow convict over a card game. The convict took offense to accusations of cheating in a game of cards, hitting Abdon over the head multiple times with a two-by-four.

Rumors spread that Vasquez had put a hit out on his old compadre, but the truth was never revealed.

Word also got back to Tiburcio that Chávez had been tracked and ambushed by a posse of vigilantes who fired so many bullets at him that they tore one arm off and shattered his entire body into an unrecognizable bundle of flesh and bone. His corpse, what was left of it at any rate, had been thrown into an unmarked hole.

Lawyers again changed the venue due to vigilante rumors in San José. Tiburcio, by fate's hand, was going to be tried in the same town his family had helped settle, the very same loved ones who had warned him not to pursue the life of banditry. He knew they were right and that his dismissal of their pleadings had led to this predictable outcome. The venue change did not eliminate the attraction of the bandit's celebrity, however. Some seventeen hundred more visitors came to ogle him over the next week, more than a hundred and twenty of which were women. Sheriff Adams was forced to limit visiting days to two per week. Flowers, still being delivered in overabundance, were thinned out daily.

Finally, a jury was chosen from one hundred people. More than two hundred spectators filled the small room; of them, fifty finely dressed women wrestled for the front rows. Additional seats were placed close to the witness stand for reporters to hear the proceedings better due to poor acoustics. Tiburcio made his appearance, pleading not guilty. His two lawyers, Ben Darwin and Bob Tully could not agree on the best action plan. Tully threatened to quit continually.

Abdon made his appearance as the star witness for the prosecution. When he passed Tiburcio, they shook hands, but no love was lost between them. His testimony stated, along with all the eyewitnesses from the town, that Tiburcio Vasquez had killed Redford and Scherer. The latter's widow, Elizabeth, attended the trial. It later came out that it was Moreno who put the final bullet in the fallen cowboy that Gonzalez had shot, putting their dual trial and final death by hanging into motion.

Subpoenaed but failing to appear as requested, Rosario was finally arrested on a warrant and forced to show up. She testified against her former lover, stating that she witnessed the Tres Pinos planning led entirely by Tiburcio. Her testimony led him to the realization that his world was crumbling around him with no hope or help in sight.

His heartbeat thundered in his ears. Every breath felt like a struggle, bringing with it the harsh truth that he was being condemned to die a criminal's death. The judgment continued echoing in his mind. His hands clenched into fists, nails digging into flesh as he fought to keep his composure. He refused to let them see him break, to witness his fear and desperation.

His first cousin, Augustina Vasquez, visited with her young daughters during the trial's completion and the day of reckoning. Tiburcio appreciated their visits to no end and wrote the following poem.

With truest love I worshiped you
When you, so lovely, were at my side
My soul with true devotion adores
You, most beloved idol.
Separated now from you, lost and alone
Sadly, my lamentations become my pastime.
My only memory is the beloved idol
The only object of my lonely contemplations.
I cry out and beg you to stand by me,
Sharing my burdens and bitterness.
I deeply believe that you hear me
During my moments of madness.
Even though we are far apart
Constant beats my loving heart,
And I embrace with these humble hands,
You, the angel, my love, the very reason for my existence.

He was convinced after the trial that Modesta was the informant who led to his downfall. Reflecting on his life, he was not surprised that his uncontrolled affairs with women eventually led to jealousy, which would lead to his ruin. Wanting to leave something behind about himself, Tiburcio also wrote a ballad known as a Corrido. He titled it The Vasquez Romance.

It is in the year 1875, today, the Americans say,
That Tiburcio Vasquez is the leader of all the Mexicans.
The tyrants are saying that he will have to be hanged,
For crimes committed in several counties.

In Los Angeles, it is true, Vasquez lost his head, and the police took him.
No longer will he roam the desert.
For he was ruined by confidence he misplaced,
For the great tyranny a woman betrayed him…
The robberies and damage he has caused to many, he himself has confessed.
But he has never killed anyone, for Vasquez is not and assassin.

Father Lorenzo Serda received Tiburcio's final confession for the last rites and told him he would be buried in Mission Santa Clara's cemetery. The bandit asked Sheriff Adams if he could make a speech at the hanging. Adams, under the influence of the priest, said it would be better to write something, so he did.

To the Fathers and Mothers of Children throughout the world who may read the incidents of my life to take warning in a time of the example before them of me and realize the force of the saying, 'The way of the transgressor is to bring yourselves in the end to my own fate. Take warning then, by my fate, and change your course of life while you may.

Tiburcio spent the night before his final day on earth with Sheriff Adams. They talked about their first meeting when Tiburcio acted as a translator. Tiburcio had nothing to lose, so he confessed to his involvement in the Pellegrini theft and murder by Chavez.

The sheriff wanted to understand the mentality of the prisoners as they traded their versions of the shootout in the wash and the damage Adams found when he entered Tres Pinos. He held no respect for this bandit, but his desire to grasp Tiburcio's motives was in earnest, those of his fellow bandits, too.   When their versions of the hunt finally ended, they sat in the dimly lit cell, both staring at the floor.

"Can I ask a favor, Sheriff? Tiburcio inquired, breaking the silence.

 "Yes, of course."

"When I set foot onto the gallows, would you offer me a glass of wine and a fine cigar?"

"I think I can arrange that, Tibo."

"I would also like to see my coffin, please, since I will be there for eternity."

"I will arrange that as well."

The coffin was brought to the cell area by the undertaker, who opened it for Tiburcio to inspect.

"The plush white satin and cushions seem comfortable enough, but it seems too small for me."

"I measured it to just over five foot eight, Sir. It will fit," the undertaker replied.

"Ah, I see."

Tiburcio closed the lid, seeing on it a silver placard.

"Tiburcio Vasquez died March 19th, 1875. Aged 39 years."

He stared at it for a full minute as the finality of the future event slammed him in the face. After a long pause, he ran his hand over the wood.

"It's very nice. I shall sleep long and well here."

He looked at Adams's unemotional face.

"I have been a bad man, but I am not a murderer. It was not my intent. It would have been better that I had been killed when captured than to suffer death in the disgraceful manner that I must. For myself, I do not care, but my family and friends are disgraced through my death. If I had been guilty of murder, I would not have been fool enough to have returned to this country after having made my escape into Mexico. But death advances and I must meet him boldly. I will show you how a brave man can die. I am not afraid. You will see that I am a brave man."

In the meantime, some three hundred printed invitations were being published for lawmen and other prominent citizens to attend the hanging along with many newspaper reporters. The hotels were filling up fast, booking solid in no time as thousands from all over came to bear witness to the famous bandit's end.

The hanging was set for 1:30 P.M. Tiburcio ate his last meal, consisting of roast beef, claret, pudding, and pound cake, that morning. He shook his head, pushing away all the food except for the pound cake that he ate slowly while sipping the wine.

After an hour, Sheriff Adams and Father Serda walked to Tiburcio's cell.

"It's time," Adams stated.

Tiburcio nodded with a polite smile. Walking toward the hangman's gallows, he felt a calm sense of resignation. The weight of his crimes had been pressing heavily on his conscience for some time, the memories flashing through his mind in a cruel montage. He had thought of all the people he had wronged, the lives he had shattered with his ruthless deeds. Yet, amidst that storm of guilt and regret, one looking into his eyes could see an unextinguishable glimmer of defiance. I am not going to beg for mercy or forgiveness, he thought, I will face my fate stoically, with the decorum befitting of my reputation.

He climbed the steps to the constructed gallows stage slowly and steadily. As he reached the top, he turned and faced the large crowd of witnesses. He thought back to the first hanging he had attended as a young man, watching Domingo Hernández look firmly into the face of death. The rope had broken that day, sparing his life, but Tiburcio was under no fantasy that the same fate would save him.

The crowd was deathly quiet. A dozen sheriffs stood on the stage next to him, along with Father Serda and the hangman, Theodore Winchell. Father Serda led the crowd in The Lord's Prayer, after which Sheriff Adams read the death warrant. A glass of wine and a cigar were on a table as promised, and Tiburcio took a sip, leaving the cigar. He felt it too audacious to smoke it, instead finding it more dignified to speak on his own behalf.

"I am Tiburcio Vasquez. I am prepared today to die, and I ask that God have mercy on my soul."

The hangman guided him to step onto the trapdoor below the forbidding noose. He took a deep breath. The thick rope loomed ominously above him, swaying gently in the wind. Memories flooded his mind with a bittersweet intensity—daring escapades, narrow escapes, whispered promises made under starlit skies. He looked down at the trapdoor, knowing it would fall away, and tried to make himself light as he stepped onto it. His knees suddenly weakened as Winchell put the noose over his neck. The knot was uncomfortably tight and was placed near his left ear so the drop would snap his neck and not strangle him slowly to death.

"Can you loosen it a little, please?" Tiburcio asked. Winchell complied. "Thank you."

Winchell gently draped his shoulders with a white cloth and slowly placed a dark hood over his head. Tiburcio's eyes saw the last light of day. He heard his breathing intensify in the enclosed hooded space as he screamed out his last word.

"Pronto! (Ready!)"

The trapdoor opened, and his body fell to the end of the rope, snapping his neck instantly with a cracking sound that echoed throughout the courtyard. It took eight full minutes for Vasquez the Bandit to take his last breath on earth.

Epilogue

A Mexican father held his small daughter's hand as they walked through the Mission Santa Clara Cemetery to deliver flowers to her grandmother's grave. As they walked past a large granite stone with a small four-by-four-inch photograph leaning against it, the little girl paused. She pulled on her father's hand to walk closer to look at the picture. It was a portrait of Tiburcio Vasquez. The light grey headstone said only Vasquez and the years 1835-1875. There were fresh flowers at the base of the stone.

"Papa, who is that?"

"That, mija (daughter), is Tiburcio Vasquez."

The father pointed to the weathered tombstone, the name "Tiburcio Vasquez," clearly visible under a layer of dust and time.

"You see, this man was both a hero and a bandit." he began, his voice soft but solemn.

"To some, he was a ruthless outlaw, feared by many. But to others, he was a defender of the people, a symbol of resistance against injustice."
The little girl looking up listened intently, her eyes wide with curiosity.

"Did he do good things or bad things, Papa?"

Her father sighed deeply, his gaze distant as he recalled the tales of Tiburcio Vasquez.

"He did both, mija. He stole from the rich and gave to the poor, much like the legendary bandits of old like Zorro. But he also caused harm and brought sorrow to many."

"It was true that Tiburcio Vasquez was a man of contradictions. To some, he was a hero, fighting for the rights of the oppressed against corrupt authorities. To others, he was a bandit, stealing from the wealthy and causing chaos."

"But Papa," the little girl frowned, "how can he be both?"

Her father sighed again, still looking into the distance as if searching for an answer in the swirling grass.

"Sometimes, mi amor, it is not easy to separate the two. History is written by those who win, but the truth often lies in shades of gray. Vasquez was a man who lived by his own code, for better or for worse."

The little girl nodded thoughtfully, her small hand reaching out to touch the cold stone marker. As they stood by the grave in quiet contemplation, she took a small flower from her bouquet and added it to the others at the base of the stone. Just then, a gust of Viento (wind) swept through the cemetery, stirring the leaves and carrying the whispers of legends into the desert...to live on.

~

Places named for Vásquez

Geographical features

Vásquez Rocks, an area of distinctive rock formations in the Sierra Pelona Mountains, popular as a filming location for movies and television.

Vásquez Canyon in Saugus, California

Vásquez Tree, outside of the 21-Mile House, in Morgan Hill, California

Vásquez day use area in the Angeles National Forest

Tiburcio's X and (Vasquez's) Monolith, two rock faces popular with climbers in Pinnacles National Park, were named for the legend that Vásquez hid out in a cave below the Monolith.[31]

Robbers Roost, also known as "Bandit Rock", in Kern County, is named for Vásquez and his gang, who used it as a hideout.[32]

Buildings and facilities

Tiburcio Vásquez Health Center, Hayward, California and Union City[33]

Vásquez High School in Acton, California

The Alisal Union School District near Salinas, California named a new school Tiburcio Vásquez Elementary School in 2012. The choice of name attracted much criticism and the school was renamed to Monte Bella Elementary in 2016.[34]

Vásquez House in Monterey, California. Vásquez built it for his sister; it is now California Historical Landmark #351.[35]

https://en.wikipedia.org/wiki/Tiburcio_Vásquez#Places_named_for_Vásquez

*Carte de visite portrait of Tiburcio Vasquez taken in San Francisco in
1865 by Wilbur F. Bayley. © John Boessenecker*

Acknowledgments

My express gratitude goes out to Heather Parsons. Previously, my college teacher who spent hours upon hours to help edit and enhance portions of this novel. Without her professional eye, the novel's descriptions and important passages would not have been so well reasoned and comprehensive. She is a rare breed of an educator who goes beyond the basic expectations of an instructor to develop her student's talents with resolve and untiring dedication.

A sea of faces, nameless and forgettable, blur together in my mind as I think back on the countless teachers who have crossed my path from grade school to college. Only one name stands out, etched in bold letters across the pages of my memories. For she was not just a teacher, but a guiding light, propelling me forward towards success with her unwavering support and encouragement. From the moment I first handed in an assignment to this very moment of publishing this book, her words have spurred me on. And for that...I am eternally grateful.

~

Note

This novel is a work of fiction. I have used many actual names and locations as much as the storyline would allow. It could not have been written without the exceptional non-fictional work of historian and author John Boessenecker, published as Bandido: The Life and Times of Tiburcio Vasquez (University of Oklahoma Press, 2010).

Readers wanting to know the full biographical details of Vasquez's life and the complexity of his story will find Mr. Boessenecker's biography the most comprehensive account published on the famous bandit to date.

The novel's story draws from the historical factual content and interpreted narrative reconstructed as Bandido. The extensive bibliography compiled for that, including archived material, unpublished accounts, original newspapers, books and articles that Mr. Boessenecker consulted, must also be acknowledged for contributing to this novel.

In appreciation and with due credit, the content sourced from Bandido: The Life and Times of Tiburcio Vasquez (and other sources and notes) reads as follows in the bibliography:

Bibliography

Bandido, Chapter One, "Sons of the Conquistadores," pages 6, 9 and 13; and Chapter Two, "In Old Monterey," pages 23 and 27-31. The name of Tiburcio's father, Hermenegildo Vasquez, was changed to Juan Vasquez.

Chapter 1
Bandido, Chapter Two, "In Old Monterey," pages 26 and 32-33; Chapter Three, "A Boyhood among Bandits," pages 38-39 and 50. The name of Tiburcio's uncle, Felipe, was changed to Fernando, and his sister, Manuela, to Graciela.

Chapter 2
Bandido, Chapter Three, "A Boyhood among Bandits," pages 38-39, especially the events surrounding Solomon Pico and Domingo Hernández.

Chapter 3
Bandido, Chapter Three, "A Boyhood among Bandits," page 50; and Chapter Four, "The Roach-Belcher Feud," page 68. The last name of Sheriff Andrew Watson was changed to Watson.

Chapter 6
Bandido, Chapter Five, "He Never Showed the White Feather," pages 73-75 and 78-79.

Chapter 7
Bandido, Chapter Five, "He Never Showed the White Feather," pages 85 and 87.

Chapter 8
Bandido, Chapter Five, "He Never Showed the White Feather," page 88; and Chapter Six, "The Big Break," pages 90-93.

Chapter 9
Bandido, Chapter Six, "The Big Break," pages 96, 98 and 100.

Chapter 10
Bandido, Chapter Seven, "Bandido," pages 104 and 107-08.

Chapter 12
Bandido, Chapter Seven, "Bandido," page 110. Rosalía de Castro, "I Know Not What I See Eternally," the ink brain: literary and other thoughts, "Rosalía de Castro: Selected Poems," 2 February 2012, translation by Muriel Kittel: https://theinkbrain.wordpress.com/2012/02/02/rosalia-de-castro-selected-poems/.

Chapter 13
Bandido, Chapter Seven, "Bandido," pages 113-16 and 118-19. Rosalía de Castro's poem "Hour After Hour, Day After Day" is noted above.

Chapter 15
Bandido, Chapter Eight, "In the Saddle with Juan Soto," page 127.

Chapter 16
Bandido, Chapter Eight, "In the Saddle with Juan Soto," page 143. Sheriff Wasson's name was changed to Watson.

Chapter 17
Bandido, Chapter Nine, "Stagecoach Robber," pages 154-57.

Chapter 19
Bandido, Chapter Ten, "Shootouts and Lynchings," pages 166-67 and 169-71.

Chapter 20
P. Price, "Of bandits and saints: Jesús Malverde and the struggle for a place in Sinaloa, Mexico." Cultural Geographies, 2005, https://doi.org/10.1191/1474474005eu325oa.

Chapter 21
Bandido, Chapter Ten, "Shootouts and Lynchings," page 175.

Chapter 22
Bandido, Chapter Twelve "I'm a Ranger, By God," pages 202-04.

Chapter 23
Bandido, Chapter Twelve "I'm a Ranger, By God," pages 205-07.

Chapter 24
Bandido, Chapter Twelve, "I'm a Ranger, By God," pages 208-11.

Chapter 25
Bandido, Chapter Thirteen, "The Tres Pinos Tragedy," pages 213-19 and 221-24; page 222, reprint-reproduction of the San Francisco Chronicle from original in John Boessenecker's private collection.

Chapter 27
Bandido, Chapter Thirteen, "The Tres Pinos Tragedy," page 222; Chapter Fourteen, "Pursuit and Betrayal," page 246; and Chapter Fifteen, "Raiders of the San Joaquin," page 262. Noel-Marie Fletcher, 'Greek George': a wanted man, a slippery escape," Taos News, 22 September 2019, https://www.taos-news.com/magazines/leyendas-tradiciones/greek-george-a-wanted-man-a-slippery-escape/article_635f1c63-9392-5864-b167-631d004d1019.html.

Chapter 28
Bandido, Chapter Fifteen, "Raiders of the San Joaquin," pages 262, 272-76; and Chapter Sixteen, "Harry Morse Tries His Hand," pages 277-83 and 285.

Chapter 29
Bandido, Chapter Seventeen, "Manhunt in Los Angeles," pages 292-93 and 303-06; and Chapter Eighteen, "Dead or Alive," pages 309-14.

Chapter 30
Bandido, Chapter Eighteen, "Dead or Alive," pages 309-15.

Chapter 31
Bandido, Chapter Eighteen, "Dead or Alive," pages 321-23 and 325; Chapter Nineteen, "The Murder Trial," pages 330-32; and Chapter Twenty, "To Die Game," pages 345-50 and 353-58.

For individual biographies of the Vasquez bandits, please Bandido, Appendix, "They Rode with Tiburcio Vasquez," pages 383-411.

References

Boessenecker 2010, pages 31-35

~

About the Author

This is the sixth book by Rick Avery. His first was an autobiography co-authored with Tom Bleecker, *A Life at Risk*. Followed by a photography book about the homeless in Los Angeles, *Sidewalks*. Next was a historical adventure about two pilots flying from Sydney to London in the 1963 air race, *The Challenge, of the Spirit of Sydney*. His career as one of the top stuntmen in Hollywood was published as *Too Old to Tell Lies*. *Hardened Warriors* was a book about the Master Boxers who compete into their seventies. *Vasquez the Bandit* is his first work of fiction.

~